# Gods & Proxies

# By M.R. Kayser

Cover Art by Alex Gavrilas
Book Design by Logotecture

# GODS &

PROXIES

# Virtual

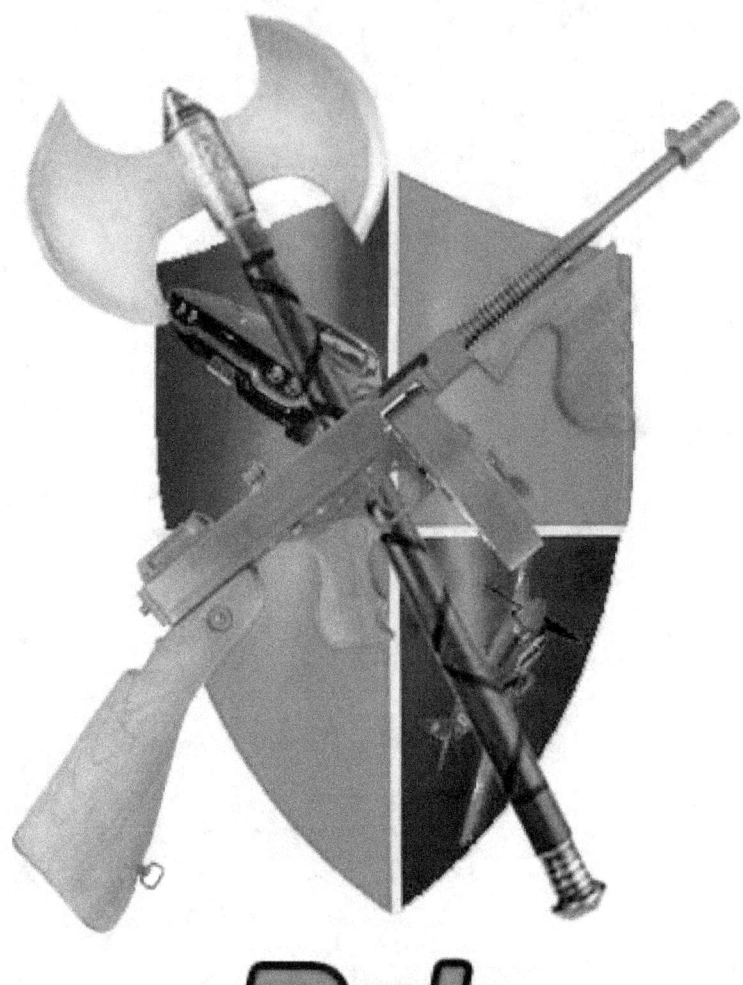

# Pulp

# Prologue

Call me Rachivel.

I've been around from the beginning, and I've never abandoned my post.

I'll begin this story simply by mentioning the asteroid. I noticed when it passed the planet named after Tarshish and streaked for the orbit of the planet called Orone.

Again, I hadn't abandoned my post. I'm a Watcher, so I notice everything.

If you're limited to the five human senses it may be difficult for you to fathom how I can perceive things in all directions and at once, and at any range. Nevertheless, I noticed this huge asteroid cracking as it continued along its trajectory, even while faithfully watching my assigned places.

Why did I take notice of the asteroid? It was a by-product of another story—a momentous one. However, that story should be reserved for another time.

When I calculated the trajectory of the asteroid, I had a pretty good idea where it would wind up. That will prove relevant later.

My primary assignment...which I'll remind you again I never faltered from...was to observe the creatures on one specific planet. The inhabitants had different names for their own planet, depending on their language. The people I watched closest called it Kadur Ha'aretz.

There is a region on Kadur Ha'aretz, once called the Kenaan Land

Bridge, in a region where three continents join. Kings and generals have longed to control this area for ages, since aspiring conquerors must march their armies through Kenaan on their way from one continent to another.

However, the land bridge wasn't just contested by kings and generals, but by the gods as well. El Elyon, the god I serve, had designs on Kenaan. He had promised it to a specific nation; but a pantheon of other gods disputed his right to bequeath it. In fact, some of them abandoned their posts, mated with mortal women, and bred a master race to populate it. These Titans–a hybrid of men and gods–were called Gibborites, or Gibborim, which, roughly translated, means "mighty heroes." Their purpose, in this particular incursion, was to possess Kenaan and enforce the will of their ancestor-gods. In about four centuries, the Gibborim had reproduced to the point that all of Kenaan was under the tight control of the Titan god kings–vice regents appointed to rule in the human world on behalf of their immortal progenitors in the Hidden Realms.

This was the situation when El Elyon determined it was time to enforce his claim on the land.

His choice of enforcing agents? A young nation of desert nomads–the children of slaves–with nothing but a rag-tag militia for an army. The average man from Yacov was less than half the size of the Titans they would face, and they had no cavalry, chariots, or even enough swords with which to arm more than one of their tribes.

Called "The Invisible God," and "The God-of-Many-Names," El Elyon ordained a priestly class to intercede with him on behalf of the other Yacovim. From the same tribe, he had also ordained a humble, unassuming outsider as their leader and his liaison

Moshe was not a soldier, yet under his leadership, the nation of vagabonds had gained some battle experience in wars against the eastern kingdoms. But Moshe had grown old shepherding the Yacovim, and would not live to set foot on the land Yacov hoped to take from the god kings and their mighty heroes.

At the same time the asteroid was streaking past Tarshish, Planet Ma'adim was drawing very near to Kadur Ha'aretz.

Yes: the two planets...or "wanderers"...had intersecting orbits in those days, and passed nearby about every 108 years—or a multiple thereof. As you can imagine, this caused many disturbances on the surface of both wanderers. Lebanah (the moon of Kadur Ha'aretz) normally regulated the tides, but by this time was losing its gravitational influence to the enormous Ma'adim. The waves in the Western Sea were already towering in height.

But this story begins far inland, east of the Yarden River, along the Aborim mountain range, near the base of Mount N'vo.

# Between the Mountain and the River

At the base of the mountain a nation was encamped. Their tents were pitched in straight ranks and columns extending for leagues through the lush valley.

Yacov was an enigma to the inhabitants of the nearby cities and surrounding countryside. The very fact of their survival was a substantial unlikelihood by itself—they should have been scattered, shattered, slaughtered, starved or dehydrated out of existence dozens of times. A historian could write a long list of their peculiarities; yet even if one knew nothing of their history, the very shape of their camp was itself bizarre. Impressive, but impractical by any man's estimation.

It was remarkable how tightly human beings could be packed. Fitting all the soldiers, women, and children of the 13 tribes inside the combined camp was crowded enough. Today they were all gathered within the square sub-camp of the L'vim, which was significantly smaller. They crowded in a semicircle, facing their portable Temple.

The Radiant Mist hovered over the Temple—the same nebulous mystery that had guided them for decades. The buzzing murmur of the multitudes hushed when Moshe emerged from the Temple entrance. In his hand was the luminous sapphire staff which he'd been using since before he returned to Mizraim. Rumor had it that he found the staff stuck in the earth at the home of his father-in-law, where nobody had been able to pluck it from the ground. Nobody until Moshe. Those who had been in close proximity to Moshe knew that the Unspeakable Name of their god was engraved on the head of the staff.

Moshe was no young sprout when he began his tenure. Now he was a tired old man. He moved slow, lost his balance easily, and everything but his voice had grown weak. There was no shortage of extravagant apparel in the war treasury; yet the one-time prince of Mizraim still wore the simple clothes of a shepherd.

Eleazar emerged from the tent on Moshe's heel. The high priest had assumed his position only after the recent death of his hapless father, but he seemed to be comfortable in his role. He was a bit pudgy, but unlike Moshe was otherwise fastidious about his appearance. His turban and other priestly garments were spotless, and more ornate than any other fabrics visible in the camps of the Yacovlm.

Last to emerge from the tent was Y'hoshua (whose birth name had been Yeshua; but Moshe had instagated use of the other name). Unlike Moshe and Eleazar he was not L'vim, but from the tribe of Efrayim. A young buck when he first became Moshe's lieutenant, and a seasoned veteran when he took command of the army, he was now one of the three oldest men in Yacov, with the hard countenance of a field marshal. As Moshe stood facing the center of the huddled masses, Y'hoshua automatically took a position behind and to his right.

With a gesture of one withered old hand, Moshe urged Y'hoshua to step forward. The old field marshal did so, and now the two faced the tribes of Yacov abreast.

Moshe turned to his loyal subordinate and asked, in a subdued tone, "Did you understand everything he told you?"

Y'hoshua nodded with a solemn expression.

"You've got to be strong," Moshe said. "And bold. Hashem is with you. He won't forget you, or abandon you...He'll actually be going in ahead of you, so don't get scared."

Moshe gestured toward the people. "Don't let what you or they see discourage you. El Elyon is greater than the usurpers and all the Gibborim in their armies."

Y'hoshua nodded again. He was well aware of how easily spooked his countrymen were.

"Hashem" was one of the many names for their mysterious god. Nobody fully understood how or why it was that Hashem and El Elyon were one and the same...but also two distinct persons. When their god chose to manifest in the presence of men, for instance, it was always Hashem who took on human form to do it.

Toward the front of the crowd was a group of young men from Y'huda, Yissakhar, Z'vulun (all three tribes shared the same camp), plus one from the L'vim. Playmates as young boys, they had grown up together and usually shared the same campfire to this day. Most of them were soldiers in the army now, though a couple were not yet old enough. Pinchas, one of the oldest, and renown as zealous and learned, was from the priestly clan and exempt from military service.

It was Pinchas who saw it: a bird-like shape descending from the Radiant Mist to light upon Y'hoshua's nape.

He turned first to Achan, then to Othniel. "Did you see that?"

"What?" Achan replied.

"Did we see what?" Othniel asked.

Pinchas pointed to the cloud and began choosing words to describe what he saw, but second-guessed himself. Had it been just his imagination? Some trick of the light? He studied the faces of all his companions, but found none as agape as he.

"Never mind," he said.

Moshe raised his voice to say, "You've all seen how El Elyon protected and provided for us in the desert. Remember that! Remember it when our enemies come at you from all sides, and remember it after he's given you victory, and you're relaxing, enjoying the largess he gives you."

"We'll remember!" Othniel shouted back.

"Our god is great!" Paltiel, commander of Yissakhar, declared from the center of the semicircle, where the tribal chiefs were gathered. "There's none like him!"

Sentiments like these were echoed by zealous men throughout the masses.

"Relaxing," Achan said, with that infectious grin of his. "I'm looking forward to that."

Yebdod, the young rookie soldier from Yissakhar, smiled and grunted agreement. Like so many of the younger men in the camp of Y'huda, Yebdod looked up to Achan. Achan had a quick wit and charisma that transcended clan and tribal loyalties.

When the noise died down, Moshe continued. "I'm at the end of my journey. But Y'hoshua will lead you across the river. Follow him like you followed me..."

Under his breath, so that only Y'hoshua and Eleazar heard it, Moshe added, "Or how you *should* have followed me, anyway."

Once again in his full voice, he said, "...And Hashem will guard you. He'll march in front of you, and cut down your enemies!"

Othniel and Achan slapped spearheads repeatedly against their shields while howling and barking their agreement. Warriors on either side of them followed suit, and the enthusiasm spread through the ranks of the army. Even Kalev, Paltiel and some of the other tribal generals beat weapons against shields. The young boys cheered and the women ululated

Quite a different nation than it was a generation ago, Y'hoshua thought. And he had witnessed Moshe himself change a lot, too. Once was the time when Moshe could barely utter a sentence without stuttering or getting tongue-tied.

Moshe nodded to Eleazar, and the priest handed him a scroll. When the people quieted down, Moshe cleared his throat and said, "Obey the Law of El Elyon, and don't deviate from it, in any direction."

Y'hoshua closed his eyes and, under his breath, recited, "Meditate on it day and night."

"Hold up your end of the Covenant, and Hashem will give you rest from our enemies on every side," Moshe continued.

"Thank-you, Hashem!" Kalev shouted. Others expressed the same sentiments, though not as loud, and their voices blended into a collective murmur.

Moshe opened the scroll and read, "This is what our god says: 'I, El Elyon, am your god, who brought you from the land of Mizraim—from the place of slavery. You must not have any other gods besides me'!"

The Radiant Mist throbbed as Moshe read El ELyon's law. Pinchas dropped to his knees, as did most of the L'vim. As Moshe read on, nearly all the Yacovim either kneeled or prostrated themselves.

"How many times do we have to listen to the same thing?" complained Yebdod.

Othniel and Pinchas glared at him.

"Repetition is an effective teaching technique," Achan said, amiably. "He wants to make sure we don't forget."

"All because of the *Sh'mot* Generation," Yebdod grumbled.

Achan shrugged. "It took them how long after Moshe turned his back to start worshiping a different god—a day? An hour? Half a heartbeat?"

Yebdod, young Zuar and several others grumbled under their breath.

Eliab, another Yissakharim close in age to Yebdod, was about to throw out an irreverent quip, when something smacked him on the side of the head. Eliab looked up to see Salmon standing over him, with an irritated scowl on his face.

"You muttonheads need to shut your bread-holes right now," he declared, humorless. "You may be too stupid to show a little respect and wisdom, but there's smarter people all around you trying to listen."

Grins disappeared and the young men became still as rock.

Salmon was revered among Y'huda's rank-and-file, and his reputation was beginning to spread to the other tribes, too. His ferocity as a warrior was surpassed only by his sternness as a disciplinarian. A veteran of the battles against Arad, Sichon and Og, he was now a lieutenant, and drilled his fifty rigorously in tactics. No doubt he would be promoted to lead a hundred soon, and possibly his entire clan before the coming war was over. He let his men relax or horse around when possible, but there was a time for silence and Salmon was nobody to trifle with. Unfortunately, he didn't easily forgive mistakes, nor forget them quickly.

The young men suddenly paid sober attention to what Moshe was saying.

Salmon himself had heard the words Moshe read aloud several times. There were many regulations to remember, and powerful motivation to do so. El Elyon gave them an ultimatum: follow his law faithfully and he would guide them to victory, peace, and prosperity; be unfaithful and disaster would fall upon them from every angle.

Salmon was a stout, solemn warrior with thick black beard covering the lower half of his face—except where the long scar, that began at his temple, interrupted it. The scar was a reminder that he was the youngest veteran of the war against the Emorim kings.

Salmon had no trouble obeying rules and following orders, himself—for the incentive offered by their god; and he also believed wholeheartedly in Y'hoshua's leadership. A good leader at the top tended to enrich the entire chain-of-command under him. And Y'hoshua could be seen, and heard, and touched. None of that could be done with the Invisible God Moshe preached, who was ready to smite Yacov any time they fell short of his requirements.

Moshe, sometimes called the Great Liaison, had talked with The God-of-Many-Names face-to-face. His late brother, Yaharon, and Eleazar, and even Y'hoshua claimed to have heard the voice of the great El Elyon. Salmon was satisfied to not see or hear him—the prospect was terrifying.

El Elyon only appeared to certain men, at certain times. Centuries could, and often did, pass between such instances. The gods of other nations, however, weren't bashful about making themselves known. They displayed their power, and authorized their followers to craft representations of themselves out of wood, or stone, or metal. That way their followers at least had a crude image of their god at all times, even when the deity chose not to show him or herself.

In fact, some gods were represented not just by man-made statues, but by the very objects in space.

As Moshe droned on and the shadows grew long, Salmon's eyes turned skyward. Lately Ma'adim was so close as to be visible long before the dark of night when the stars appeared. As Salmon understood it, the Mizraimim believed the red wanderer belonged to their god, Horus. People from the heathen nations all considered the planet the property of *their* war god—called Nergal by most.

Maybe Nergal took the red wanderer from Horus. Salmon didn't know much about the foreign gods.

Leaving the gods out of the matter, Salmon respected Moshe. The young men owed respect to Moshe as well, and nobody was going to accuse Salmon of failing to instill discipline.

Othniel had no trouble paying attention to Moshe...until he caught sight of Aksah, who sat just behind and to the left of her father, Kalev.

Othniel looked even younger than his 17 years. His baby face inspired aggression from many a peer his own age, and kept certain elders from taking him seriously.

Elders like Kalev—the tough old commander of his tribe—for instance.

A bride had yet to be arranged for Othniel, and he suffered mixed emotions about that. He felt slighted because his older brothers had all been assigned a mate by 17. Yet it also gave him hope, because Aksah had not yet been assigned a mate, either. She was Kalev's only daughter, and born to him in his later years, so he treasured her highly, and guarded her accordingly.

Othniel had been attracted to Aksah since before his voice changed. At times like this he could just stare at her for hours on end, drinking in the sight of her. Sometimes he assumed himself to be in love with her, because the emotions she provoked were so strong.

She must have felt him staring at her. Her aquiline countenance changed, and her head turned on that graceful neck, searching the crowd for the source of her unease. Her dark eyes found Othniel quickly, and her eyebrows furled ever-so-slightly. Her lips pursed for a moment, then her eyelids lowered.

Othniel felt shivers sometimes just from how her long, black eyelashes fell and rose.

When her eyes opened, she looked away, but only momentarily. When their eyes met again, Othniel flashed her a smile. Down went those long lashes. She tossed her head and, even partially hidden by her head covering, her silky black hair was glorious as she reached up with one hand to pull it behind her ear. It was subtle, but a smile took over her mouth. Some may have missed it, but Othniel had studied that face enough to know a smile, subtle or not.

Unfortunately, Kalev also knew, and didn't approve. He shot Othniel a stern glare, then took his daughter by the arm and pulled her into a lean where his lips came close to her ear.

Her face now abashed from some sort of reprimand, Aksah scooted around until Othniel's view of her was blocked by her father, who scowled at the young man until he looked away.

Night fell, and the Radiant Mist glowed like fire. Ma'adim hung among the stars like a sphere of blood. Hours had passed, and Moshe's voice was hoarse by the time he said, "Today I invoke god and man as a witness against you that I've set life and death, blessing and curse, in front of you. Choose life so that you and your children will live!"

Moshe cleared his throat, rolled up the scroll and handed it back to Eleazar.

"I also implore you to love El Elyon your god; to obey Him, for He gives you life and enables you to live continually in the land he promised to give you."

The crowds muttered affirmation of all he said. Then, straining to get the sound out, Moshe taught them a song that would help them memorize their history. It set to verse how El Elyon, The God of Gods, gave the nations of the world as an inheritance to the divine beings of his Council, but kept Yacov for himself, to govern directly. The song went on to reprise the record of El ELyon's faithfulness, despite Yacov's unfaithfulness.

When the words of the song had been spoken, Eleazar and the L'vim led the singing of it. So many voices united in song made an impressive sound wafting across the Yarden Valley and off the sides of the Aborim When the song ended, the Yacovim shared a resolve to serve their god diligently and avoid the mistakes of their fathers.

Pretty well spent by that time, Moshe turned and, supported by two L'vim, trudged off toward his own tent.

"That's it," Y'hoshua declared. "You're dismissed for the night."

The enormous gathering got to its feet and dispersed, each to his own camp, raising clouds of dust with the movement.

"How many times will we have to go through this?" grumbled Yebdod, under his breath, as he sauntered away with the others in his clique, waving at the dust in front of his face.

"This one sounded like his farewell address," opined Achan.

"Just because he said Y'hoshua is taking over..." Othniel said, but trailed off before concluding his thought.

"The two of them are climbing the Aborim tomorrow," Achan said, pointing to the silhouette of the mountain range beyond the camp. "To the top of N'vo, if I heard right." He pointed to the highest peak on the Aborim

"That's where El Elyon speaks to him," Othniel said. "Atop mountains."

"It's also the place," Achan added, "where you can see across the Yarden into all the territory that will be ours. Moshe can't cross over with us, so he wants to at least look at it before he dies."

Even the young men were silent, as all of them wondered what life would be like without Moshe leading them.

# A Prophecy of War

The "god-king" of Urshalayim, and his entourage, stood near the edge of a rocky outcropping, watching the towering waves crash below, a few leagues in from the beach.

"Those breakers are enormous," observed one of the king's advisers "The locals say they are growing every day."

If it weren't for the coral reefs breaking up the waves prematurely, the gigantic breakers would have been even more frightening. The broken bodies of sea creatures, great and small, were strewn about the land, along with torn sails, broken oars, and the splintered remains of ship hulls.

"Sailors are too terrified to come near the sea," another adviser said. "So many of them have been swallowed by it. Every fishing village along the coast has been demolished and swept away."

"These people along the Western Sea worship a fish god, do they not?" asked the king.

"Yes Sir," the adviser answered. "He is a god of the sea itself."

"Find a priest of this god," Adonaizidek said. "We'll add them to my court and take them back with us. You never know—if the sea keeps moving inland like this, we may have a beach near Urshalayim soon."

Some of the king's entourage chuckled at this, but most didn't find it a laughing matter.

The king's name, Adonaizidek, meant "lord of righteousness" in some tongues, and his attire was as gaudy and grandiose as that title. His expensive purple robe was embroidered with white piping. All six fingers on each hand glinted with gold, and gold bracelets adorned his arms and ankles as well. The 17 members of his court were only a little less lavishly dressed for this visit to the coast.

The priest of Hapy, from Mizraim, bowed before voicing his protest. "Lord of Righteousness, live forever. But it is not the fish-god you must appease,"

"It is not appeasement that is required," the priest of Enki declared, with a distasteful glance at his rival.

"Explain," said Adonaizidek.

"It is not that the god of the sea is angry," the priest of Enki replied. "All the gods are vexed. They strike bargains and form alliances with each other, because a war looms and they all have a stake in it. Nergal, Moloch, Chemosh, Dagon, Al Illah..." He pointed upward, where the red planet was visible in a patch of blue sky beyond the roiling storm clouds. "Nergal's concern in this war is plain for all to see."

"A war of the gods?" asked the king.

"By proxy," the priest replied. "Blood will flow like the water below."

"The wise rulers will begin feeding the gods an extra ration of blood before the first battle is joined," added the priest of Hay, anxious to prove his counsel was just as important as that of his rival.

Adonaizidek frowned. A war would reduce the population of his kingdom, and increased sacrifices beforehand would further strain his manpower. "A proxy war, you say. Who are the players?"

"Just as the gods are joining together," Enki's priest replied, "so must we ally with other cities in Kenaan."

"Who do the gods war against?" asked the king.

"The One-God-of-Many-Names," said the priest.

"The Invisible God? The one stingy with knowledge?"

The priest nodded. "The Great Tyrant. He fights for the Yacovites."

The king sneered. "Those jackals? I know all about that churlish mob of whining cowards. Their ancestor was a conniving mollycoddle and their leader is an old stuttering lunatic with one foot in the grave. Their 'army' is a militia at best."

The king's youngest adviser bowed. "It is true that Moshe is old and feeble. He might indeed die any day. But his successor has been chosen already. The one called Y'hoshua, by all accounts, is a warrior of some distinction."

"A warrior?" Adonaizidek pronounced the word as if it were the punchline of a joke. "We're talking about an 'army' of undisciplined rabble, armed with farming tools. They have no chariots. They don't even have horses! And there's not a Gibborite among them."

The king held his hand out, palm down, at about hip-high—or where the head of an average-sized Yacovite might reach, were one standing beside him.

"I've heard the same reports, o King," the adviser said. "And yet the Emorites fell to that churlish militia, before their cities were put to the sword."

"It is neither the warriors nor their weapons that should concern us," Enki's priest said. "It is their One-God-of-Many-Names." He pointed to the priest of Hapy "The god of Yacov challenged all the gods of Mizraim, and humiliated them in the sight of everyone. They were powerless to stop him."

Though most cities had temples and idols and high places built for multiple gods, each nation was under the dominion of one specific god. The exception was Mizraim, which was ruled by a council of several deities.

"Tell me you don't really believe all those tall tales," the king said.

"Eye witnesses still tell the stories, your Majesty," the young adviser said. "It wasn't just the sea god that was humbled. Their river god; their frog god, their sun god..."

The king turned away from the cliff and inhaled audibly, and, addressing the priest of Enki, said, "Well, it's more than just the gods of Mizraim this time. You said they're all banding together. Maybe the sons of the gods should band together as well. We've all had our differences, but the time may be upon us soon when we need to put those behind us."

He glanced up at the convulsing storm clouds that had closed to block the view of the red planet, then added, "We'll see how the Yacovites fare against our combined nations; and their god against our combined gods."

# A Carnal Bargain

Rachav turned her face upwards so the guards would recognize her as she shuffled through the enormous gateway into Bet-Yariq, a bundle of flax slung over her back and one tucked under her left arm. Her brothers were loaded down with four bundles apiece. Surely they'd both be able to carry twice as much when they grew to manhood, but they were already a big help.

She shuddered as one of the guards, nearly three times her height, ogled her blatantly. Two of the others exchanged whispers and wry grins. One said, "Greetings Rachav. When are you going to be ready for a full-sized man?"

She kept her mouth clamped shut and kept moving.

"I just love those fat little lips," another one called. "They look designed for pleasure."

Her brothers also knew better than to speak. Anwar's face burned with shame, twisting into repressed fury, when the guards turned their attention to him. Their innuendos grew increasingly provocative, and Rachav hurried her pace. She glanced at their brothers, afraid one might protest or lash out with an insult, but with tight-lipped scowls seemingly carved from marble, they hurried along abreast of her.

What if one day the Gibborites did more than just taunt and verbally humiliate? Imagining that dreadful day made it very difficult to sleep well.

Once around the corner from the gate, Rachav pulled her veil into place again. There was no need for anyone else to see her face now that she'd been recognized and admitted. Leaving her face exposed only invited more lecherous men (and some women) to notice and comment about her lips.

She wore baggy clothing when going to the fields for the same reason, lest more Gibborites notice her figure and be inspired.

After the changes first came on her, a few years before, she had initially enjoyed all the sudden attention from men. Her parents noted the attention as well, and her mother was the one with the savvy to know they could capitalize on it for the betterment of the family.

Rachav's mother taught her how to handle men, and arranged the first several encounters. It was much more exciting than braiding rope, at first, but as she grew more experienced and learned more about the nature of men, Rachav decided she would rather just work at the family business.

Her mother wouldn't hear of it—men paid much more for one night with Rachav than they would for an entire week's worth of flax oil, rope or linen products.

Rachav had tearfully petitioned her father, to little avail. Her father never contradicted his wife, and seemed to live in fear of provoking one of her tongue-lashings.

Rachav eventually learned to cope with her situation, though it felt like she lost another piece of herself with every man she took to bed. Once all the seductive play-acting and bartering was done, while in the act of servicing her various customers, she pretended that each time she was giving herself to the same man.

A man very different from anyone she had known.

She took some solace in that she had never been with a Gibborite. It wasn't just their size and deformities that bothered her—there was something else; some unnameable quality which led her to believe that the stories about their ancestors were true.

Only once Rachav and her brothers were past the city square did she begin to breathe easier. They also avoided the bazaar, since they had no shopping to do and Rachav would prefer her brothers not witness any of the abominable rituals practiced there—or be solicited by the temple prostitutes. With Anwar now leading the way, they wove through the narrow streets between houses until they reached the South Stairway.

Nadir ran his fingers over the darker-colored mortar in between the stones of the city wall. For whatever reason, during the construction of the walls, a different compound was used for mortar here, than in every other part of the city. The change in color served as a subtle landmark, confirming that they had reached the section of the wall they called home. They began to climb.

The city walls were enormous, even from a perspective inside of them. Outside they were even taller. It would require three Gibborites standing on each others' shoulders to even reach a hand to the top of the parapet.

A deep trench had been dug for the wall's foundation, and the dirt from the trench heaped inside where the walls would go. The excess dirt was then graded into a level plane upon which Bet Yariq's conventional housing was erected. The stone blocks of the impressive outer wall were so massive that only Gibborites could lift or move them. Against that thick outer wall, an inner superstructure was affixed, and finished off with an inner wall which made the fortification seem to be one enormous monolith. Engineers claimed that it was even stronger built this way than if the entire structure were solid. In any case, Rachav's family and other non-Gibborites in Bet Yariq were relegated to the apartments inside the city wall.

Rachav's family lived in a top-floor apartment and her mother found the climb exhausting. It was no problem for her children, however.

Anwar reached the top of the staircase, strode quickly along the balcony with little brother Nadir trotting to keep up, reached their doorway and stepped right in. Because the weather was warming up, Mother kept all the windows and doors open.

Following her brothers inside, Rachav first went to the store room and took stock of the work space. It was pretty crowded, so she had Anwar and Nadir take most of the new flax upstairs.

From two different rooms there were ladders up to wooden trapdoors atop the city wall. Their family had been storing flax there for years now, and nobody seemed to mind.

Rachav greeted her parents. Her thin, rawboned father, busy

separating seeds, grinned with relief and said, "No trouble with the gate guards, then."

She removed her veil, loosened her head covering, and thought about how to convey her worries regarding the guards' increasingly lascivious behavior.

"What took so long?" inquired Rachav's plump mother, who sat at a small table working the seed press over a bowl.

"Nothing, Mother," Rachav replied. "We went straight there, gathered the flax and came straight back. But when we came through the gate..."

"Don't cover for your brothers," Mother interrupted. "I know Nadir likes to dawdle around all the time. Anwar indulges him, and you coddle them both."

"Not at all, Mother. In fact, Anwar..."

"Don't argue with me. Go check on your sisters, then get busy in the kitchen."

"Yes, Mother."

As Rachav prepared the meal, Anwar and Nadir returned from the top of the wall, talking excitedly back and forth. Nadir came up alongside his big sister and embraced her from the side. She took a moment to squeeze him back.

"Guess what, Rachav? We saw an army camped across the river. They're right below Abor. I bet it's the Yacovites!"

"You can see all the way to Abor, hmm? My, what strong eyes you have."

"It's true," Anwar said, leaning in the doorway. "On a day like this you can see for leagues and leagues, from the top of the wall. There's some kind of camp over there, laid out in a strange shape."

"Why would you think it's Yacov?" Rachav asked, turning back to slicing vegetables.

Nadir shrugged. "They're coming, right? Everyone knows they're coming. And that camp is gigantic—like it's an entire nation all living in tents."

"They don't have chariots or even horses," Anwar said, "and yet the Emorites on the East Bank haven't been able to stop them."

"Their general's name is Y'hoshua," Nadir announced, proud of having this news to share.

"I thought it was Moshe," Rachav said, carefully watching what she was doing, but trying to visualize what the boys had seen at the same time.

"He was their chief or something," Anwar said. "But this new leader has taken over. Nobody seems to know that much about him."

"It's not their chief or general that has the king worried," Rachav mused, aloud. "It's the god of the Yacovites."

"The god?" Nadir scoffed. "Who knows if they even have one! Nobody's ever seen him. Nobody is even sure what his name is."

"That doesn't mean he's not powerful," Anwar said.

Nadir held his hands parallel, to about the size of a tomato. "You saw how big Nergal is in the sky. Let's see Yacov's god try bringing a planet so close."

"First of all," Anwar said, "It's not that big yet, though if it keeps getting closer... Anyway, secondly: how do you know it's not the god of Yacov doing it?"

"The red wanderer belongs to Nergal," Nadir said.

"Boys," Rachav said, reaching up to tuck a stray wisp of her hair back under her head covering, "go somewhere else to play or bicker. I've got work to do."

"No time for playing," Anwar sighed as he herded his younger brother out of the kitchen. "We have to help Papa with the seeds."

Once the boys were gone, Rachav shook her head to herself. Nadir's young mind couldn't accept that an invisible god could defeat a god whose image was commemorated by statues, and who appeared sometimes to priests and priestesses.

Rachav had her own sources of news. The Gibborites hated one particular rumor, and she wondered if it wasn't true: that the god of Yacov was the Supreme God over all, who had created the lesser gods and everything else. Indeed, she hoped it *was* true–the god of

Yacov seemed to be just. He didn't require children to be passed through the fire. In fact, he forbid human sacrifice of any kind, along with the mingling of the lesser gods with mankind and animals. He also punished the wicked—even his own people when they did wrong; yet he sought excuses to show mercy at the slightest glimmer of repentance.

But if all that was true, and he was leading Yacov into the land promised their ancestors, then what would happen to her and her family? Would they be slaughtered in the invasion? Certainly the evil debauchery in and around Bet-Yariq was enough to bring down a judgment on them, if the Invisible God was indeed in the punishing business.

Halfway through supper, someone called a greeting from outside the doorway. Mother nodded at Nadir. He shot up from his seat and rushed to go see who it was.

Nadir returned in a moment to say, "It's that man who was here last month. The king's messenger."

By the way Nadir's gaze bounced between Mother and Rachav , it was clear that the messenger wasn't here to deliver a message.

Mother finished chewing the food in her mouth, swallowed, then gestured toward Rachav. "Go wash and perfume. Hessa, go invite him in and make him comfortable."

"Why do I have to let *my* food get cold?" Hessa protested. "It's not my customer."

"Because your mother told you to," Father said. "Now go."

The apartment was separated into two sections. The large one included the great room, a kitchen and a private room for the mother and father. The small section was closed off from the rest, except for a single doorway with curtains. It included a closet, a room for the bath, and a room for a bed.

The small section served as an inn for travelers. It was also where Rachav entertained customers.

Supper grew cold for all the children. Hessa ushered the king's messenger inside, brought him wine and a plate. The boys began hauling water inside from the South Spring, then heating it for a bath. Faryel, the youngest daughter, removed the man's sandals and washed his feet.

Once the envoy had eaten, drank, and bathed, Rachav entered the guest chamber. Her attire had changed—no longer meant to conceal, but to display. She wore form-fitting silk; her black hair was uncovered and hung down to her lower back; her eyelids were painted purple, and she smelled of roses. She added a smile to her costume when she saw him reclining on the couch. She sat at his feet.

Some customers preferred her to be bashful or aloof. Some even liked her to be skittish, and resist their advances. This one was pleased to have her be friendly, forward, and engage him with lively chatter for a while. Rachav didn't mind the small talk—it was a chance to learn news, since the messenger traveled extensively as part of his duties.

"Hello again," she said. "Some time has passed since your last visit."

He patted her on the arm with some affection, and sighed. "This is the first chance I've had to rest in the last few weeks. The king has had me on the go, without ceasing."

Rachav raised her eyebrows. "Is something special amiss?"

The customer had no obvious Gibborite lineage. In fact, he was barely taller than Rachav. He wasn't physically repulsive, either. The long treks he regularly undertook kept him from growing fat, and he cleaned up well.

"Possibly," he replied, his gaze crawling down from her eyes to her prominently presented bosom.

She scooted closer and leaned forward slightly to give him a better look, while resting one hand lightly on his leg. "Oh? Pray tell."

He licked his lips, but then frowned as if reminded of something bothersome. "It's the Yacovites. They're getting closer and closer. They're camped below the Abor Mountains right now, and there are rumors they may try to ford the Yarden right across from us."

"Wouldn't that be dangerous at this time of year?" Rachav asked.

The Yarden was running at flood stage. It was hazardous to cross, even in a boat.

The customer nodded. "Not just dangerous–foolhardy. The king believes, if they attempt it, that they'll bog down in the mud and be easy pickings for our army. What's more, Bet-Yariq is the strongest city in Kenaan, and they have no siege equipment. They should want to cross over anywhere but here."

Rachav cocked her head, slightly. "I guess that would be foolhardy. But it seems as though *something* has you worried."

"Well," he said, gaze shifting briefly to the window, "what if the rumors are true? Their god supposedly opened the sea for them to cross, then closed it back to drown their enemies. What if their god really is Most High, the Creator, over all the other gods?"

Rachav was able to make many of her customers comfortable enough to confide in her. Generally speaking, she could speak freely with them as well. Yet she was careful to adjust her tone of voice so that what she said next sounded purely hypothetical. "If he truly was supreme over all the gods, then wouldn't it make sense to follow him instead of some lesser being?"

The customer's expression soured. "If it was anyone but him, certainly. But he's a tyrant. Intolerant. He allows no worship of any god but himself. And he's selfish–he withheld knowledge from humankind. When Enki shared knowledge anyway, he responded with curses and eternal hostility."

"What makes you think it's all true?" Rachav asked. "About their god's power, that is?"

"There are just too many eye-witnesses," he replied. "The things that happened to Mizraim. Moshe kept the Yacovites in the desert since that day, and they didn't starve or die of thirst. He gave them water from dry, solid rock. He fed them with bread that appeared on the ground each morning. None of them got sick. Their sandals never wore out–in 40 years! And then Sichon of the Emorites, and Og of Bashan...the Yacovites vanquished them both. No Gibborites among them. No chariots. No horses. No iron weapons. And yet that dusty rabble–the spawn of slaves, yet–conquered the two most powerful armies on the East Bank, full of Gibborites who were seasoned warriors. Modern, powerful armies, defeated by goat-herding runaway slaves."

"It does seem rather impossible," Rachav mused, "doesn't it?"

The envoy lowered his voice, speaking in confidence. "The king of Urshalayim is calling for a formal alliance against the Yacovites, composed of all the cities west and south. Frankly, I hope we agree to it."

"Do you think our king will join?" she asked.

The customer pressed thumbs against temples for a moment, eyes closed, then shook his head back and forth. "I came here to forget about all this for a night, not to worry even more."

Rachav scooted closer still, so that her hip was near his waist. She gave him a reassuring caress to his forehead. He captured her hand and kissed it. "Ahh, I've missed you."

He squirmed briefly, produced his purse and opened it to count out her fee for the night.

Before he handed over any silver, an idea struck Rachav. "You know, I've been thinking. Perhaps we could work out an alternate form of payment."

Confusion twisted his features and he froze in place.

"Maybe you could find someone to do some work for us," Rachav suggested. "I need someone to go gather our flax and bring it here. In fact, someone who would handle all our outside work, so that my brothers and I don't have to suffer accosting from the men in town anymore."

"You're...you're saying I should take the money I pay you and use it to hire such a person?"

She nodded, and stroked his arm. "You're well-connected. Surely you know of people who could do it, and make such an arrangement."

He pondered this silently for a moment. "I can probably make it happen." He leaned up and grabbed her arm with one hand, while the other extracted silver from the purse. "It would mean I come to see you on a regular basis. But for now, take this. Come to bed with me and let's forget about gods and goat-herders."

Rachav accepted the payment and blew out the candle.

# The Death Of a Chieftain

It was a testament to his inner strength that, as feeble as he was, Moshe could still climb a mountain...and talking all along the way, no less.

Y'hoshua and Pinchas each took one of his bony old elbows to help Moshe negotiate a steep rise in the rocky trail. Without missing a beat, he continued his story.

"...His father said, 'don't mock me! This idol didn't take the hatchet and smash all the other gods. It's made of stone, formed by human hands. You must assume I'm a half-wit.'"

Y'hoshua chuckled and said, "If the sandal fits, eh?"

Moshe nodded his gray head. "So Avram told his father, 'If it was formed by human hands, why did you tell me it was him who created the world? And if the other gods were incapable of defending themselves from a puny hatchet, why do you worship them?'"

Moshe and Y'hoshua both laughed. Pinchas nodded, grinning. This was the first time he'd heard Moshe tell the story.

Moshe and Y'hoshua sobered quickly when a rumbling tremor shook the mountain. Y'hoshua grabbed a small tree growing up through the rocky soil with one hand, and clutched Moshe's arm tightly with the other, bracing to keep the old man upright should the tremor grow worse.

Pinchas took a short step backwards on the steep incline, waving his arms for balance.

The tremor subsided and all three men looked up at Ma'adim hanging over them in the sky, even closer than yesterday.

"El Elyon prepares for battle," Y'hoshua muttered, with a faraway look and a grim set to his jaw.

They continued climbing until Moshe stopped for a brief pause to catch his breath–which was his habit. When he resumed the climb, he had enough breath for both the effort and for words. "I can't help remembering another time we climbed a mountain, Y'hoshua. When we heard the noise of insanity from the camp, you said it sounded like our countrymen were making war."

Still glancing warily up toward Ma'adim every few seconds, Y'hoshua said, "I was fairly naive, wasn't I?"

Moshe smiled fondly remembering Y'hoshua's assumption more than the behavior of their countrymen–who had resorted to idolatry shortly after El Elyon had freed them from the chains of Mizraim.

Then a frown took hold of his face. "I'm not coming back down this time, Y'hoshua."

Sadly, Y'hoshua nodded.

No more words were spoken until they reached the crest of Har N'vo–the dominant peak of the Aborim Even the young Pinchas stood panting for a few moments to catch his breath.

There was something different about this time and place– Y'hoshua could feel it. He noticed Pinchas looking round about, and upward, expectantly.

*So he feels it, too.*

No anticipatory feeling could have prepared them for the voice that thundered out of nowhere...and everywhere. Both Pinchas and Y'hoshua jumped back at the sudden, booming sound.

"Look across the Yarden, Moshe. There is the land I promised to your ancestors. You won't set foot on it, but you may look at it before you leave your body."

Moshe, more familiar but no less awed by the voice, took feeble steps until he stood upon the very peak of the mountain, then turned to face the west.

Across the river lay the land promised to them by the voice so long ago.

The land he would never tread on.

His gaze swept over the mountains with their harsh rock features and sporadic, prickly vegetation that littered the dry soil; the valleys with their mosaic pattern of farms, vineyards, and orchards; the forests to the north; the desert to the south. It was rough country, but beautiful in a rugged way. The land was fraught with dangers, but also great potential. His people had waited centuries to return and claim it.

His gaze rested on a pasture between a brook and some grassy foothills. He imagined building a house on the slope of those hills. It was easy to picture his grandchildren grazing the flocks in that pasture...

Pinchas noticed the tears rolling silently down the old man's cheeks, and turned away, feeling a lump in his own throat.

Y'hoshua had already shrugged out of his haversack and turned away, granting what privacy and dignity he could to his longtime mentor. He didn't want Moshe to be embarrassed, or feel any more sad than he did already.

Y'hoshua examined the land first as a whole, then in detail. Being a land bridge between three continents guaranteed not only profitable trade routes, but that it would be an avenue for the armies of ambitious warlords for as long as nations marched to war.

The central mountain range would be formidable to navigate, much less attack. But it could be easily defended, once taken.

The lowlands made good chariot country...but he had no chariots.

Here and there he could see movement in the closer regions. The little specks were people, and animal-drawn vehicles. The people. He remembered from his reconnaissance decades ago that a good number of the inhabitants were Gibborim. He shivered, involuntarily. He had once witnessed one of those giants lift an enormous boulder over its head, preparing to hurl it at a crowd of Yacovim. Had El Elyon not struck him dead, many would have been slain with that one throw. Without El Elyon, it would have been impossible to win even one single battle against armies of such creatures.

Y'hoshua also noted the cities that were close enough to discern. Each one had forbidding walls, and most were located atop mountains or hills—veritable fortresses, with the mightiest warriors in the world to defend them.

In the foreground was Bet-Yariq, close enough to study it in some detail. So far as Y'hoshua could tell, it was the strongest city in Kenaan, which was saying a lot. Even from atop this mountain, those walls looked insurmountable. The stone blocks composing the city wall must be massive. Observing the height and depth of the walls, he could only conclude that they were impregnable—even if his army had siege engines.

Which it didn't.

A cough and rasping cry yanked Y'hoshua out of his thoughts. He whirled to see Moshe lose his grip on the sapphire staff, and teeter. Y'hoshua ran toward him as Moshe began to fall. Pinchas did the same from the other side. But Moshe crumpled to the ground before either reached him.

Pinchas examined him frantically, but Moshe was gone—only his tired, expired body remained. Pinchas met Y'hoshua's gaze and nodded. "He's dead."

"I'm so sorry you don't get to go with us, my friend," Y'hoshua whispered. "You stood in the gap for us too many times to count. You were the most humble man who ever lived, and yet no man has ever done greater things. I have tremendous shoes to fill. I pray I can finish what you started."

Dusk settled in as both men improvised a eulogy for their chief.

Pinchas softly muttered a song through his tears.


"In a desert land he found him,

In a barren and howling waste.

He shielded him and cared for him;

He guarded him as the apple of his eye,

Like an eagle that stirs up its nest

And hovers over its young,

That spreads its wings to catch them

And carries them aloft.

Hashem alone led him;

No foreign god was with him."

Night had fallen when they were jarred out of their mourning by movement in the air above. They opened their eyes and tilted their heads upward.

There, silhouetted against the red orb of Ma'adim, descended a breathtaking winged woman, garbed in golden armor, with long, flowing hair just as golden. She swooped down until both Ma'adim and Lebanah, were blocked from sight. Y'hoshua shot to his feet, ignoring the painful protest of his aging joints, and pulled Pinchas back with him out of her way.

The two men stood transfixed as the valkyrie landed gracefully on the mountain peak. Her head turned, and eyes found them. She paused to flash a dazzling smile, then turned away, squatting to lift the body of Moshe.

So bewitched were they by the vision before them that they couldn't have stopped her even if they knew they should.

The environment had changed. Though it was dark, their surroundings were clearly perceptible in stark relief. But everything seemed different—painted in a palette of colors they had never seen before. Moshe's body didn't even resemble Moshe, but was nothing other than a strangely empty shell. The mountain underneath them was still there, yet every plant and moving creature was ethereal. Above them was not just the blackness of space, but overlapping layers of some super-reality, swarming with living beings. Nearly every star in the sky shone through the essence of a being that abided in the star—the realms in which both the stars and the beings existed overlapping. Other beings flew about, and still others remained still, watching closely what happened on the apex of Har N'vo.

Before Y'hoshua or Pinchas could wrap their minds around what was taking place, an enormous creature, resembling a great eagle, dropped to the ground on the opposite side of the lifeless flesh

Moshe had once animated.

The valkyrie appeared as startled as the two men as she froze in mid-reach for Moshe's body. "You!" she hissed.

But it wasn't a winged woman anymore. It was a giant, coiling snake.

For that matter, the great eagle was no longer an eagle, either, but now a gargantuan ox facing the serpent over the tiny human body, horns poised to ram.

"What is all this?" Y'hoshua asked.

Or did he? He wasn't sure that his physical mouth actually opened and the words came out, but Pinchas reacted as if they had.

"We must have entered the realm of the gods!" Pinchas replied.

Again, Y'hoshua wasn't sure Pinchas had spoken via his tongue and vocal cords, but his words came to Y'hoshua somehow.

"You're early," the snake told the bull-like creature. "Our appointment is for another time. Move out of my way and quit interfering." As it spoke, the snake grew legs; its head changed shape; it became a terrible horned dragon.

During the transformation, the ox also changed. Now a lion stood guard over the human body, crouched to leap at the dragon. Its eyes narrowed and it bellowed a terrifying roar.

Sure they must be hallucinating, both Y'hoshua and Pinchas blinked. When their eyes reopened, a luminescent satyr stood where the dragon had been. It faced a fantastic armored warrior with a flaming sword—taller than any Gibborim.

"Oh, we *are* going to encounter each other again," the warrior vowed. "And that's an appointment you can be sure I'll keep."

"Is that supposed to frighten me?" retorted the satyr. "I was higher than you!"

"*Was*," emphasized the warrior, eyes blazing like his sword. "How you have fallen."

"Not quite yet I haven't," spat the satyr.

It seemed the ambiance was changing again. His surroundings faded back to normal, but Y'hoshua couldn't tear his attention away from the two fantastic figures squared off on Har N'vo's zenith.

The satyr lunged for the empty body, but the warrior's sword flicked out. A wisp of smoke rose from the wrist the sword had nicked and the satyr jumped back, nostrils flared, hissing.

"It's settled," the warrior said. "In eternity it's already happened."

"You're going to lecture me on interdimensionality?" the satyr scoffed, clutching at his wrist. "He's got you so enthralled." He summoned down chain lightning from the sky, that crackled, sparked and boomed, illuminating him from behind. A gale-force wind came out of nowhere of a sudden, blowing against the warrior. It was no normal wind, but had a strong musical quality. Minor chords blended into an ominous melody that seemed to say nature itself was on the satyr's side. "Now stand aside. The body is mine."

The warrior blinked his eyes against the supernatural wind but stood his ground, shaking his head. "You're not going to so much as touch it."

"You always were an obedient little pet," the satyr said with a scornful sneer. "You're content to be his mindless slave. 'Come here; go there; do this; fetch that; speak these words; worship me.' You fool! You could have been with us, ruling this planet! You could be doing anything and everything you want to do, while these pathetic beings..." the satyr now pointed at Y'hoshua and Pinchas, "...worship *you*!"

The satyr sidled one direction, then the other, as if estimating what it would take to snatch the body before his opponent could react. "I once thought you were smarter than this," he said. "Which is the better life: to exist as gods like us, or to maybe get a pat on the head occasionally like some stupid, obedient beast?"

With repressed outrage, the warrior replied, "May El Elyon rebuke you!"

The windstorm ceased and the lightning disappeared. The same voice that had spoken to Moshe earlier now boomed out from nowhere, and everywhere, "Adversary!"

The satyr winced and cowered a bit. Grudgingly, it answered, "Yes, Sire?"

"What are you up to?" demanded the voice.

Y'hoshua was astonished at how the satyr—so full of pride and blustering power a moment before—was now rather sheepish as he muttered in reply, "Roaming through Kadur Ha'aretz, wandering here and there."

"Report to me, immediately," the voice commanded.

Looking one last time at Moshe's body on the ground, then throwing a contemptuous glance at the warrior, the satyr bellowed a scream of rage as it leapt into the sky, vanishing even as it resumed the image of the horned dragon on the way.

The quiet serenity that settled over the mountain was startling after the atmosphere of a moment ago. Both Y'hoshua and Pinchas were dumbstruck. They didn't notice that the warrior was still present until the movement of him sheathing his sword caught their attention.

Both men put their faces against the ground, arms outstretched toward the awesome being.

The warrior shook his head. "Don't do that! Don't bow to me—I'm a fellow servant of El Elyon, The God of Gods."

Y'hoshua and Pinchas slowly lifted their heads, and rose from their prostrate positions.

"Worship El Elyon, and no other," warned the gigantic warrior. "That was Him you just heard—and who the Adversary obeyed." The two men cringed, because every forceful word from this creature struck them almost like a physical blow. He could smash them dead as easily as a man could swat at a fly. Both Y'hoshua and Pinchas were acutely aware of their own weaknesses and frailties in the presence of this being.

The warrior pointed at Y'hoshua. "Don't be afraid."

Y'hoshua nodded, eyes wide and face pale.

"Be strong and bold," the warrior said. "After you've finished mourning, take three days to prepare your people, then move them down to the river."

Y'hoshua nodded again.

The warrior swept one enormous hand toward Bet-Yariq in the distance, "Once everyone is across, attack there, first."

With a parched tongue, Y'hoshua licked dry lips and finally found his voice. "Before I even take the highlands? Bet-Yariq is the strongest city in the region. How do we breach those walls?"

"Hashem will be going in front of you," the great warrior replied. "His power is the spearhead of your army. Everywhere you set your foot, He's giving that ground to you. Trust in Him—not in your own battle plans."

The warrior scooped up the body of Moshe, and the sapphire staff, then fixed his fiery gaze on Y'hoshua for a moment. "Be strong and bold. Hashem is with you, just like He was with Moshe."

In the blink of an eye, the warrior was gone, along with the sapphire staff and the puny dead body.

Y'hoshua and Pinchas stared at the location where the warrior had been an instant before, then exchanged a look with each other.

"What just happened?" Y'hoshua asked. "You saw and heard it too, right? It wasn't just my imagination—Moshe's body and his staff are both gone."

"It wasn't your imagination," Pinchas replied, shaking his head. "We just saw into the realm of the gods. That was Halal who wanted Moshe's body. I think the other one was our Guardian Prince."

Y'hoshua wiped his face, circling the spot where the incredible scene had taken place. "Mikhayel? And the Adversary. What was that all about?"

Pinchas shrugged, grimacing. "Why does Halal want Moshe's body?"

After much circling, shaking of the head, and futile attempts to puzzle out what they had witnessed, Y'hoshua finally exhaled heavily and retrieved his haversack. "Well, the part I do understand is that I'm supposed to take Bet-Yariq first."

The mountain trembled again, and both men struggled to keep their balance.

"We better find a place to set up camp," Y'hoshua said, "and spend the night up here."

Pinchas nodded and looked around for his own haversack. Descending the Aborim in the dark with all these tremors was too dangerous. "Pardon my asking, Sir," he said, "but you seem kind of dismayed by Mikhayel's instructions."

Y'hoshua slung on his haversack and began retracing his steps down from the peak to an area he remembered that would provide some shelter from wind and rain, should such come in the night. "I had thought to bypass Bet-Yariq and take one of the small mountain fortresses first. That would give us a foothold in the highlands. It just makes sense, militarily. We could come back to take Bet-Yariq when our troops are well-seasoned, and when we've acquired some siege equipment."

They arrived at the area Y'hoshua remembered—a notch-like cut in the mountain with a level surface to bed down on but a steep rock wall to block the prevailing wind. Both men dropped their haversacks again and began unpacking the makings of camp.

"Hashem must have a reason he wants you to attack there first," Pinchas said. "Maybe it's a test of your faith, and ingenuity."

Y'hoshua frowned, as he unrolled his bedding. "Perhaps." He hated tests of faith. His record was pretty good; but still, he hated them.

# A Glimpse Into the Hidden Realms

## (Rachivel)

The asteroid was closer, now, I saw a chunk crack off as it hurled through space.

The red and blue planets were swinging ever nearer each other in their respective orbits, as well. The little tremors on Kadur Ha'aretz were only a shadow of what was to come.

Old Y'hoshua and young Pinchas had, indeed, seen into "the realm of the gods." For "gods" is what they call beings like me, who can travel between realms...dimensions. Or see through all of them, in my case. (Because I follow my assignment faithfully, which doesn't include travel.)

Of course, it is possible for me to travel through, and appear in, any plane of what some might call the "super-reality" (the word "universe" connotes limitation to four dimensions, for some reason, so I avoid using it). But just because one has the ability to do something doesn't mean one *should* do it.

By the way, I'm not boasting when I emphasize that I've never left my post. I just want to make a distinction, because so many of my peers have deserted their assignments. Not only that, but they've appeared to man, demonstrated their power to him, taught him secret knowledge, and demanded his worship. These are the "gods" that men in those days were familiar with.

I am not one of them.

These beings are free moral agents, of course, but they informally recognize Halal...the Adversary...as their chieftain. He is known by many names in many languages. One of them is Enki.

It's hard to describe his relationship to El Elyon without causing confusion. On the one hand, he is the Chief Adversary. On the other, he is still accountable to El Elyon and only does what he is permitted to do.

Yes, they are on a collision course for a war that transcends all dimensions—but for now he operates within the boundaries set for him.

The matter of Moshe's body was almost an exception. Pinchas was right to wonder why he wanted it so badly. The reason concerns future matters I am not at liberty to divulge.

I can tell you that, after Halal left the mountain, he presented himself before El ELyon's Court, in the Secret Realm.

Warriors were present, facing the throne, in addition to the seven Messengers normally posted there. The 70 Princes were also in attendance. Upon the throne, El Elyon's image was composed of such blinding, colorful light, that Halal could not look upon him without combusting on the spot. So the ancient rebel bowed—not out of respect, but for self-preservation.

To the right of the throne sat Hashem, the projection of El Elyon whom lesser creatures could gaze upon without perishing. As spectacular as Mikhayel was to behold, Hashem was far more so.

"You will not have Moshe's body," declared El Elyon, in a voice like thunder.

"Am I not free to do as I please on Kadur Ha'aretz?" Halal asked. "After all, the planet is under my jurisdiction."

"It doesn't belong to you!" a Warrior snarled, hand moving to the hilt of his sword. "You didn't create it, or anything that lives on it."

Halal turned to the Warrior with a condescending smile. "Ah, but El Elyon left the planet under the stewardship of someone who forfeited his dominion to me. That gives me legal title, does it not?"

The Warrior glared, opening his mouth to retort, but was silenced by a gesture from Hashem.

"Remember," Hashem told his servants, "The Adversary is a liar, a thief, and a murderer."

Halal winced with all three accusations, despite himself.

"He is lawless," Hashem continued. "But The God of Gods faithfully follows the established rules, even though there is no authority above Him, and nobody who can compel Him to do anything." He gestured back to Halal. "We will defeat this lawless, lying thief, while obeying the law, and fulfilling everything according to the appointed times."

We'll just see about that, Halal thought.

Hashem then turned toward Halal. "Understand this, Adversary: you may not touch what belongs to me. And Moshe belongs to me."

"Moshe's soul, of course," Halal said. "But his body as well?"

"That's right," Hashem said, eyes blazing like fire.

"Very well, Lord," Halal said. "Only...why do you go to such lengths to preserve these stubborn, ungrateful people? After every time you bless them, they forget you and offer their worship to others. They have not a shred of loyalty or faithfulness toward you."

Halal did not always lie. In fact, he had mastered the formula for deception—it involved mixing just enough truth in with his lies to make his deceptions appear valid. His accusations against Yacov happened to be true.

El Elyon's matrix of colors changed as the grief of Yacov's repeated infidelities swept through him.

"We will continue to watch over my people," Hashem said, with a sad frown. "Not because they deserve it. Not because they are faithful. Because of the covenant made with their forefathers."

"They are nothing like their forefathers," Halal pointed out. "They have contempt for your altruism. They take your favor for granted. They spit on your blessings and dare you to curse them. You already know, if you grant them victory in this war, they'll forget you inside one generation. They'll grow comfortable in the luxuries you give them, and assume it was their own wisdom and might that caused them to prevail. In fact, they'll attribute their fortunes to me and my Princes."

El Elyon's colors deepened further. The loyal attendees of his court hung their heads, sharing his anguish. Showering love on someone who repays you with scorn and disloyalty breaks the heart of anyone–even The God of Gods.

"Pull your shield off them," Halal implored. "Let me destroy them. It's what they deserve, and you know it. Put an end to the grief they cause you. You can find amusement in some other nation or creature."

"Stop!" boomed the voice of El Elyon.

The blast of this command hit Halal like a hot cosmic wind, flipping him backwards to land on his face again, in a most undignified position.

"You will not tempt El Elyon, the Most High," Hashem stated, tersely. "He will have mercy on who he so chooses. He will heal and restore even your victims, when he so determines. And your reign of horror won't last forever. You will be dealt with at the appointed time, just as you were told."

Halal choked back further argument. Everyone in the Council– even those who couldn't look upon El Elyon directly–noticed the pain he suffered just now. He could be hurt.

El Elyon was wounded by injustice, by the spilling of innocent blood, and by the cold, fickle infidelities of the humans.

Especially the Yacovites.

I witnessed this scene in El Elyon's court without leaving my assigned post, of course.

I can perceive beyond the five human senses. I can also "read" what is inside a self-aware being (in fact, part of my job is keeping record of not just actions and speech, but thoughts). Halal is not just clever and crafty, but also ingenious. Too many humans make the mistake of underestimating him. He has fearsome power, and exceeding intelligence. But as with any creature, pride can cause blindness, and negate wisdom.

Anyway, where Mikhayel spirited the body off to has been kept secret from all living humans.

As I said, I have no authorization to clearly reveal the future; but

I'll make just two points, and leave it at that for now.

Point One: Truly great men are often not appreciated during their living years—it is only after their death that they are recognized as great. During his life, his people rarely heeded the words Moshe spoke. That will change drastically now that his soul and body have parted ways.

Human beings, for various stated reasons, are inclined to worship nearly anything except their Creator. Surrounded by cultures caught up in ancestor worship, it is possible that having their great leader's remains kept in some tomb that they can see and touch would be a snare to succeeding generations because of their idolatrous nature.

Point Two: Though his methods are clever and often quite sophisticated, Halal's aspirations and motivation can be summarized simply: to thwart El Elyon's plans at any and every opportunity—in part, or in whole if possible.

Knowing that, I infer that even though Moshe is now dead, El Elyon still has some purpose in mind for him. The Great Liaison still has some part to play in the unfolding agenda of the god he served.

Though this topic is fascinating to me, at least, I've let it pull me away from the story I am telling. I will continue, now.

# Love and Military Discipline

While the women of Yacov went out to gather frost bread in the morning, the army drilled a league past the outer edge of camp.

This morning Salmon paced in front of his men, still perturbed by their breakdown in discipline the other night. "You might think I'm wrong, in how I run this fifty," he said, hand on the pommel of his officer's sword. "You might think I'm too strict, that my training is too difficult, or my punishments are too severe. Some of you may entertain the idea that you know better than me, that you're smarter than me, or have better ideas. In fact, you may be more convinced of that than in anything else you believe in."

As he paced, he studied the face of each man he passed in front of. Most of them stared at the ground, and dared not lift their eyes. Achan and some of the older troops met his gaze, though not defiantly.

"Well, you need to understand something," he continued. "And the sooner you accept this, the sooner you'll be able to make peace with your life." He paused and scanned faces again for a moment.

"It doesn't matter what you believe about how fair I am or what I should do differently. I am in charge; you are not. I'm the officer; you are my soldiers. Your job is to help me accomplish the mission. You don't have to agree with me. You don't have to like the orders I give you. It doesn't matter at all, in the grand scheme of things, whether you do or not."

He paused again, to let his hard words sink in. He concentrated more on Achan than any other soldier in particular.

"I try to be fair, but sometimes, in war, it's not possible. If one of you has more capability than the man standing next to you, I'm probably going to expect more from you. I may work you harder. I may assign you the more difficult task. In such case, you should feel flattered, not oppressed. Is this fair? Probably not. But who determines what is fair, anyway? Who decides? Is every man in the world in perfect agreement about what is fair and what is not?"

"No Sir," muttered one of his soldiers. Salmon thought it might be Othniel.

"What makes you think you have the right to judge whether I am fair or not? You think *I'm* supposed to conform to *your* standards? Or are *you* supposed to conform to *my* standards?"

His men murmured, but he clearly heard Othniel say, "We conform to your standards, Sir."

"You embarrassed me," Salmon said. "Moshe, who led this nation out of Mizraim, was giving us his farewell address. *His farewell address!* It was the last time we got to hear him before he died. But instead of listening respectfully to the leader of our nation during his last address, you were jabbering and joking around with each other like unsupervised children."

He raised his spear. "Nothing like that had better happen ever again. Now, it's time to work."

His men raised their spears and shields, grateful that the reprimand was over so quickly.

Salmon drilled his fifty in individual *katas* and techniques first, and would move on to group tactics a little later. Other fifties conducted their own training, while Kalev strolled from hundred to hundred, overseeing the training.

For all of their tribe, the drills were in the use of shield and spear. Officers all carried the sickle sword. Some soldiers had acquired swords or hatchets, but they were officially secondary weapons. Stone-headed spears were much easier to find and craft than swords were. The only tribe fully equipped with swords were the Gadim, hence they were trained in its use.

Salmon's fifty used staffs for close-order drill, to avoid stabbing or slashing each other while sparring.

One particular match caught Salmon's eye. Othniel was matched up against Avnur, and clouting him repeatedly on the side of the head. As Salmon approached, he noticed ugly welts rising all across the side of Avnur's face.

"Hold fast," Salmon ordered, and the two young soldiers relaxed, straightening.

Salmon addressed Othniel first. "There are no rules in love or war," he said. "I'm glad you grasp that. A spear is designed for thrusting, mainly. But the spearhead can cause damage with a slashing motion, too. Exploit whatever opening your enemy gives you. However, I think that point has been proven, and Avnur has suffered enough damage to that part of his body for one day. Stop hitting him there."

"Yes Sir," Othniel replied.

Salmon turned to Avnur, who should have been a perfect match for Othniel, physically speaking. "Do you understand why he's hitting you there so often?"

Avnur, a picture of frustration and fatigue, appeared afraid to answer.

"Get in your combat stance," Salmon said. "Face me, and try to poke me with your training staff."

Avnur frowned, but complied.

"Freeze!" Salmon commanded, in mid-thrust. "Don't move a muscle."

Avnur froze in place, resembling a statue of a warrior in battle. Salmon slowly swept his arm over the top edge of Avnur's shield, toward his face. Avnur flinched from the expected blow, but Salmon stopped before touching the young man.

"Every time you thrust," Salmon explained, "you drop your shield and push it back. Your opponent noticed this and used it against you."

Avnur slumped, shooting a dirty look at Othniel before letting his head hang down in exhausted failure.

"If Othniel had a real spear, that first swipe could have taken out your eye, and you'd be blind on that side. Helpless."

"Yes Sir," Avnur muttered.

"It's natural for your shield arm to counteract the motion of your spear arm. But you have to discipline all the parts of your body to work together, presenting the smallest target to your enemy, even on the attack."

Avnur nodded.

Salmon clapped Othniel on the shoulder. "Come have a word with me, soldier."

Othniel allowed his lieutenant to guide him to a spot out of earshot from Avnur.

"Am I in trouble?" Othniel asked.

Salmon released his shoulder and turned to face him. "Relax. Trouble? No. As a spear man, you're doing what I expect of you."

Othniel let his breath out and visibly relaxed.

"But I need to say something to the potential leader up there," Salmon added, using his knuckles to rap on what passed for a helmet with most Yacovim—the bronze bowl atop a sweat-soaked turban. "I see leadership ability in you," Salmon said. "And with your family connections, chances are you'll be in a leadership position one day."

Othniel wiped sweat from his eyebrows before it dripped into his eyes.

"There's no advantage in maiming your sparring partner," Salmon continued. "He's not your enemy, and you're only frustrating him. It could grow into resentment. Do you want somebody who resents you, because you injured and humiliated him, guarding your flank when you're facing the swords and spears of a real enemy?"

"No Sir."

"The wise thing to do is teach him. After you've bashed him a couple times, he'll probably be willing to listen to you. Then your comrade will grow into a better fighter because of it. Somebody you can depend on that much more. And he'll trust you."

"I understand, Sir," Othniel said, nodding soberly.

"Good. Now help him. No contact for the rest of the drill—have him practice on an imaginary opponent, and you watch his form.

Coach him into good offensive and defensive techniques."

"Yes Sir."

Salmon lightly slapped him on the back as Othniel marched back to his partner.

As Salmon turned back toward his fifty, ready to resume supervision, he saw Kalev had wandered into his area.

Salmon felt a little spike of fear that every soldier experiences when someone of much higher rank shows up unexpected. The general had chosen to inspect Salmon's fifty at the exact moment Salmon pulled Othniel aside. Salmon hadn't done anything wrong, and, in fact, his guidance had been too congenial to even be considered a reprimand. Nonetheless, Othniel was a closer relation to Kalev than Salmon was, and people in authority could let the pride of their position blunt their rationality.

Kalev's ever-present runner gave Salmon a curt nod. Kalev's hard black eyes stared straight at Salmon. The lieutenant ignored the runner and locked eyes with his general, saluting him by a backward half-twirl of the sword so that the blade pointed behind at the ground and the pommel was shown to the superior officer.

Kalev casually returned the gesture. "Is he giving you trouble, Lieutenant?" He nodded toward Othniel, whose back was to them as he returned to the drill grounds.

A bit relieved by the question, Salmon replied, "Not at all, Sir. He's a good soldier, and quite adroit with the spear."

"Hmmp," grunted the general, as if skeptical of the answer.

"He's a natural, in fact," Salmon added. "But there's always room for improvement."

Kalev's frown softened. He seemed to like this answer. "Your men seem to be doing well, from what I can see."

The old general inhaled deeply, staring out across his tribe. "Everyone's still mourning Moshe; but we're soldiers. We have to mourn and drill at the same time, don't we?"

It was a rhetorical question, but one always should answer a general's question, rhetorical or not, just in case. "Yes Sir," Salmon replied.

"What's your name, soldier?"

"Salmon, son of Nachshon, Sir."

"Oh, yes. Of course. Forgive me. The clan grows faster than I can remember the names."

"It's fine, Sir. You haven't had much interaction with me."

Kalev noted the black spear symbol embroidered into one of the dangling ends of Salmon's turban. "You're a veteran of the campaign against the Eastern Kings."

"Yes Sir."

Kalev dipped his old chin slightly–a gesture between two blooded soldiers. Salmon returned the gesture.

"Do you need anything, son?"

Salmon puffed his cheeks. "We could always use more spears, Sir. Extra water gourds. Bronze bosses for our shields. A sword for every soldier would be nice."

Kalev chuckled, winking at his runner. "So the same thing everyone else needs, and then some."

The runner grinned knowingly back at his general.

"I'm working on the water gourds," Kalev said. "And shield bosses are being issued, though we'll have to wait for the smiths to finish Naftali's shields before they get to ours. Spears...probably not going to happen except replacements for broken ones. All the shafts and heads are being made for javelins. Javelineers use up a lot more weapons than spear men, of course. And I'd like the entire tribe to have swords, son, but we just don't have the bronze yet. The only swords and extra spears we're going to get will have to be taken from the enemy."

"We'll make do as best we can, Sir," Salmon said.

Kalev pursed his lips. "I value the feedback of my experienced officers, Salmon. It's unfortunate that I don't have the time for more interaction with all of you. But don't be afraid to come to me with suggestions, or questions that your chain-of-command can't answer. Is there anything you'd like to resolve while I'm here?"

Salmon cleared his throat. "Actually, Sir, there is something I've been thinking about lately."

"Go ahead."

"Close order drill: it's vital, of course. But would it be possible to make it inter-tribal? Maybe on a rotation, so that each sparring session, a man squares off against a different partner? I think there would be more than one benefit. It would expose each soldier to several different fighting styles, size and strength of opponent, even different weapons. It would promote competition between the tribes while maybe increasing esprit *de corps* within tribes. And we'd reduce silly feuds within clans and families that sometimes get started simply because of blows traded during sparring."

Kalev was silent for a long moment, which made Salmon worry that the old general considered it a stupid idea, and was framing a professional-sounding rejection.

"I like it," Kalev finally said. "I like that a lot. I'm meeting with Y'hoshua later, and will suggest it to him. The other tribes would have to be willing, of course. And we'd have to figure out how to do it without killing each other. But it's definitely worth consideration."

As the general and his runner turned to continue their roving inspection of the training, Kalev gave Salmon the same sort of slap on the back Salmon had given his own subordinate.

Once the frost bread was gathered and baked, training was paused and the army released back into camp so the men could break fast.

Othniel took his usual place in the circle of his chums. Almost nobody besides Achan spoke. They were tired, and the death of Moshe still weighed heavier on all Yacovim than most would have guessed. Many considered him a nuisance and a killjoy while he lived. Only now that they would never benefit from his leadership again did they truly begin to appreciate him as a leader, or as a man.

Aksah walked up to the group, carrying a large basket.

"Hmm. I wonder what's on the menu today?" Achan intoned with mock sincerity. Aksah lowered the basket, he reached in, took a cake, and stared at it as if surprised while Aksah moved on to the next soldier. "Oh, frost bread! I never would have guessed."

Most ignored Achan's facetious humor. A few smiled. Yebdod and young Zuar laughed out loud.

Othniel felt a strange heat in his skin as Aksah drew near him. When she reached him and lowered the basket he tilted his head up to meet her gaze. He intended to drink in the sight of her at close range, and maybe get a smile or some kind of friendly word from her.

She simply gazed back at him with a blank expression. Or was it blank? Perhaps it bordered on expectant curiosity.

Othniel could smell her fragrance this close. Her scent reminded him of wind-dried laundry, mixed with wildflowers. He was suddenly aware of his own sweaty musk. Pulse racing, he muttered, "Thank-you," and quickly looked away.

She moved on to feed the next soldier. He felt the pang of missed opportunity. He should have held her gaze, smiled at her, said something clever...or at least thanked her without mumbling.

His eyes locked onto her feminine form as she continued lowering the basket for other men. As if she could feel the heat of his gaze, she turned to catch him staring. Othniel steeled his will and refused to look away.

*Smile, you idiot! Smile!*

He couldn't do it. Many people could smile on demand, but Othniel couldn't force it if he didn't feel it.

Aksah's brow furrowed, then she turned away and moved on.

When her basket was empty, she made her way out of the area, back toward her father's tent. Othniel sat mesmerized by her graceful locomotion. When she disappeared behind a tent, and he again became aware of the world around him, his comrades exploded into raucous laughter.

The noise startled him, and he tore his eyes away from where Aksah had disappeared. Soldiers stared at him as they laughed.

"What's the matter, Othniel?" Abidan asked, with a condescending grin.

Zuar pointed at Othniel. "He's as red as Ma'adim...look!"

More laughter. Othniel hoped it didn't draw Aksah's curiosity.

Too many disparaging comments were directed at him for Othniel to discern more than the teasing intonation of their sing-song accusations.

Even Achan joined in. "Looks to me like she scares him more than her father does." The young men snickered some more. Achan's joke hurt a little, coming from somebody all of them, including Othniel, looked up to.

But once the amusement died down, Achan gave Othniel's arm a no-hard-feelings *thump*. "Have you talked to your father about her?"

"I've mentioned her. Hinted. Suggested. Even asked if the arrangement wasn't a great idea. But I can't say we've 'talked' about it."

Achan's mirth faded, to be replaced with sympathetic sobriety. "What does that mean—he's non-committal in his answers?"

"He doesn't answer at all," Othniel replied. "He just ignores it. So one time I asked him who he was planning to get for my wife. Know what he told me? I'm too young to be worried about it!"

"Interesting," Achan said.

"Never-mind that everyone else has had a wife picked out for them since they were 12 or younger."

"It's probably that baby face of yours," Achan said. "Appearance means a lot to people. I know we're not supposed to judge people based on how they look...but it's the natural thing to do."

"That's great. It's not like there's much I can do about how I look."

"Grow a beard!" one of the older soldiers suggested, laughing.

Othniel had been trying to grow a beard, without much luck. He had little more than peach fuzz on his jaw.

"Smear charcoal on your chin," Abidan said, smirking. "At least from a distance you'll resemble a man."

The others laughed some more, and Othniel wished they'd go back to mourning Moshe, already.

Achan shrugged. "I could beat you about the face with a sparring staff. Break your nose. Knock some teeth out. That might make you look more mature and experienced."

"Very funny," Othniel said. "Guess what? Salmon knows I'm a good soldier. He doesn't think I'm too young or innocent."

"Salmon is rare," Achan replied, suddenly sober. "He doesn't judge by looks. He examines everybody based on behavior. Attitude. Performance. Trouble with him is, he's a perfectionist. You make mistakes too big, or too many times, and he writes you off permanently. Doesn't matter how well you do after that–when he looks at you, all he sees is that mistake you once made."

Othniel had been staring off into the space Aksah had occupied moments before. Now he turned to focus his eyes on his older friend.

"I made some big mistakes when I first came into the army," Achan said, sadly. "I'll probably never be promoted because of that. Not under Salmon, anyway."

"What kind of mistakes?"

"My family never had much," Achan explained. "Most everyone came into a lot of wealth right before they left Mizraim. I don't know if my parents got shortchanged, or maybe they lost it or spent it all somewhere. Anyway, I've always wanted nice things. I'd like my wife to have nice things. I wish my kids could have what I never had. So I took some items...not knowing others had rightful claims to them. I gave it all back when I found out. So nobody can say I'm a thief, but Salmon sees me as...covetous. As far as he's concerned, I have an integrity problem. Pay attention sometime, how he talks to most soldiers...and then how he talks to me. You can tell by his demeanor, his tone of voice, even, that he thinks I'm untrustworthy."

"I don't follow you," Othniel admitted.

"He thinks I'm too materialistic," Achan said. "He thinks I might be a thief, who might steal something at first opportunity."

This shocked Othniel. He considered Achan the most likable soul in the tribe. He had assumed everyone loved Achan.

"Scuttlebutt has it that his perfectionism led Salmon to divorce his betrothed before they ever consummated. She didn't have enough lamp oil, or sewed him a tunic that didn't fit, or something."

Othniel chuckled, having been pulled out of obsession with his own worries. "I'm sure that's an exaggeration."

Achan shrugged and waved his hand. "Anyway, as far as anyone knows, Kalev hasn't pledged Aksah to anyone else yet. So you've still got a chance."

Othniel snorted. "He's got her locked down so tight, he may just keep her in his tent until she's old and gray."

Achan leaned back and chewed his bread. Othniel took the first bite of his own.

"Well," Achan said, "you appeal to your parents, and she'll have to appeal to hers."

"Why would she? She doesn't seem to be half as interested in me as I am in her."

"Then that's what you have to change first," Achan said. "And if you can't, forget her."

Two impossible tasks, Othniel thought. How was he supposed to make her want him? And how could he ever forget about her?

# A Clandestine Mission

The official mourning period for Moshe was 30 days. Shortly before it was over, Salmon was summoned to Y'hoshua's command post one night.

The runner who brought the message instructed Salmon to say nothing about where he was going, or why. Salmon had no inkling of the purpose, so that part was easy.

Salmon couldn't help but be intimidated, as he entered the Command Post. Inside the tent was one of only two survivors out of all the grown men who left Mizraim many years ago. Not only that, but he was the commander of the entire army. It was only natural for Salmon to fear he was in some sort of trouble...but he couldn't remember doing anything bad enough to warrant a meeting with the General of the Army and Judge of the Nation.

The runner escorted Salmon to the tent door. There he nodded to the guards and gestured for Salmon to enter.

Salmon gritted his teeth and stepped inside.

The tent was sparsely furnished. Y'hoshua sat on a cushion of burlap, facing a low, wide table cluttered with stacks of parchment. Many of the parchments appeared to be maps, while others looked like rosters.

Standing, facing Y'hoshua across the table, was a man in priest's garments. He looked familiar. Salmon had seen this L'vim sitting around the fire with soldiers from Yissakhar, Z'vulun, and Y'huda— including a handful from Salmon's own fifty.

Y'hoshua looked up as Salmon entered, and he briefly forced his mouth into the form of a grin. "Ah, there he is."

Salmon stood at attention and saluted. Y'hoshua acknowledged the salute with a nod. He was an old soldier not concerned much with formality. But his cool expertise in battle, from the time of his youth, was legendary throughout Yacov.

"Thanks for coming by," Y'hoshua said, as if a soldier had any choice when summoned by his commanding general. He gestured to the floor. "Relax, men. You can take seats."

The priest, seemingly not as intimidated as Salmon, turned to grab a cushion from along the wall, and sat on it, facing the general. Salmon followed suit.

"Salmon, I've heard good things about you," Y'hoshua said. "I understand you're the one who thought up the idea for training, that Kalev has been suggesting to me."

Salmon nodded. "Inter-tribal sparring? Yes Sir."

"Have you two met each other?" Y'hoshua asked gesturing between Salmon and the L'vim.

Salmon had heard that the other man was also son of the High Priest. "I've seen him around, Sir. But I'm not exactly sure of his name."

The priest turned his head to face Salmon and gave him a smile of greeting. "Pinchas," he said. "Son of Eleazar. Nice to meet you."

"Nice to meet you," he replied. "Salmon, son of Nachshon."

"I called you both here for a special assignment," Y'hoshua said. "I know we're not quite done mourning yet, but I've got an army to command, as well as a nation to lead. We're close to starting the last campaign in this war, and some military considerations have to take precedence."

Salmon nodded. Pinchas raised his eyebrows.

"Everything I'm about to tell you is classified. You are not to discuss it with anyone, at any time, until I declassify it. Understood?"

"Yes Sir," Salmon said.

"Understood," Pinchas said.

Y'hoshua pulled one of the maps from a stack, set it in its own space on the table, and motioned both of them to lean in for a closer look. "I need the two of you to scout the west side of the Yarden. I need detailed intelligence on Bet-Yariq in particular. Defenses; troop strength; dimensions and composition of the walls; guard shift schedules–if you can get it; how many Gibborim are there; what is their morale; and what do they know?"

Salmon puffed his cheeks. This was a lot to dump on him out of the cold.

Of course Y'hoshua knew it was a dangerous assignment–he himself had been sent on a similar mission long ago. He and Kalev were the only surviving scouts from that reconnaissance.

"Both of you are quick on your feet," Y'hoshua continued, pointing to his temple with one index finger. "And I've been told you're both good at memorizing things. You're going to need that. Can't risk being caught with drawings or any sort of notes you take along the way."

Salmon said nothing, but wondered how their chief decided he was fast on his feet and had a good memory. Somebody must have sung his praises up the chain of command.

He felt a pang of guilt about his reputation from the battle against Arad. He had been green, impetuous, and more than a little lucky. Others were not so lucky; yet it was Salmon who was treated like some sort of mighty man.

"When do you want us to go?" Pinchas asked.

Y'hoshua leaned back, locking eyes with both of them, in turn. "When I dismiss you, return to your tents and get ready. You'll be leaving tonight during Third Watch. You'll need to pack light. Take a sword, a sling, a gourd, and some simple bedding. You'll have to forage for food. Plan on returning in a week." The old general rocked forward and pointed to a spot on the map. "We'll have moved camp by the time you return. Close to the river–right about there."

Both men took a close look at the spot indicated.

"Do you have any questions?" Y'hoshua asked.

Salmon knew there must be several important questions to be asked, but he could think of only one at the moment. He nodded toward Pinchas. "No offense meant to him, or any of the priests, Sir, but shouldn't I be going with another soldier?"

Y'hoshua frowned, but Pinchas' face betrayed no emotion.

"I have reasons for my choice, Lieutenant," was Y'hoshua's stern reply.

After entertaining all the questions each man could bring to mind on such short notice, Y'hoshua dismissed them with a warning not to tell anyone they would be leaving, and to pack in secret.

As they left the command post, Pinchas walked beside Salmon a ways. "Don't worry, Salmon: I know how to handle a weapon."

"Again: no offense, friend," Salmon replied. "But you wouldn't want me trying to do the job of a priest. And I'd feel better going by myself than being yoked to a priest trying to do the job of a soldier. Handling a weapon is fine, but it's not the same as being trained for battle."

"This is a mission for spies," Pinchas said. "Not soldiers. If we find ourselves in a battle, we've probably done our jobs poorly. Besides, L'vim are trained. Who do you think guards the camp when the army is away?"

Salmon didn't see the point in debating. The decision was made. He had to do his duty whether he agreed with it or not. He pointed northwest. "There's a tall cedar in the middle of a grove about half a league past the edge of camp. Think you can find it in the dark?"

Pinchas tilted his head back, glancing at the two orbs—one white, one red—dominating the night sky. "There should be plenty of light by that time."

"Right. I'll meet you there in the Third Watch."

"See you then," Pinchas said, and veered away, toward his tribe's camp.

# The Scouts Set Forth

They met at the tall cedar during Third Watch, and from there made their way toward the river in the reddish glow of the ever-larger Ma'adim. When clouds blocked the nocturnal light, they made camp for the night.

Out of habit, Salmon awoke in the hour just before sunrise, when the sky is darkest, people normally sleep heaviest, and when savvy enemy soldiers choose to surprise attack. He was pleased that Pinchas, though not a soldier, stirred at first light.

They packed up their bedding, gathered some frost bread, baked it directly on the rocks of a small, hastily assembled fire pit, and ate silently before either of their stomachs were awake enough to spark their appetites. They didn't wait around to digest, either.

They reached the river while shadows were still long and the air was cool. The Yarden was swollen, her muddy brown water well over the banks, turning the ground into marshland for half a league on either side.

Salmon grumbled and cursed. "She's at flood stage. Even worse, thanks to all the storms lately. The army will be sitting ducks when we try to ford. Crossing in the spring is a really bad idea." The moment those last words left his mouth, he regretted them. They sounded like a criticism of Y'hoshua, which he preferred not to voice. He believed in the old field marshal, even if the man did make a mistake like this. Criticism might cause others to lose confidence in their leader, and Salmon didn't want to see that happen..

"Well, the army doesn't have to cross this morning," Pinchas said. "We do. Any ideas?"

Salmon scanned their surroundings, then nodded. "Let's wade out and grab a couple of those logs floating by. They'll keep us afloat, and we can use our hands and feet to paddle toward the far bank."

The recent storms had torn limbs off trees. Lightning sheared some trunks in two. Such objects, plus debris of every size, littered the muddy, swollen river. The two men waded out, bracing against the current, picked out floating wood that was neither too large nor too small, and hitched a ride along with those natural boueys.

They floated downriver rapidly, but moving across the current was not nearly as fast or easy. They kicked and paddled furiously, barely able to make even minute progress toward the west bank. Bet-Yariq came up in their water-blurred vision until it dominated the landscape. Then they passed it. The impressive fortress city shrank from sight, and nothing but lush countryside flowed by. Still they fought to slip sideways across the current, and still the river carried them along at a steady, alarming pace.

The crossing took hours. It separated Pinchas from Salmon by such distance that they almost lost sight of each other. By the time they got enough of a foothold to resist the current on the opposite side, they were both exhausted.

Salmon hardly had enough strength left to stagger through the marshland away from the river's pull. Fear of being dragged away by the current to his death gave him just enough energy to stay upright and keep moving.

He trudged toward Pinchas, who wrapped an arm around a tree and let his log go. The log floated away. Pinchas sagged, clutching onto the tree with all his remaining strength, gulping air in pained, ragged breaths.

It seemed to take an eternity for Salmon to reach him. When he finally did, he held onto the tree for a while himself, to rest.

Salmon decided that the longer they stayed there, the harder it would be to summon the energy to get moving again. Also, now that they were still, the cold spring air made itself known through their soaked clothing to their waterlogged skin. They needed to get warm and dry as soon as possible, or they might die of exposure instead of drowning.

He leaned away from the tree, with a hold on Pinchas' arm. He didn't have strength to hoist his partner up, so he simply leaned away, using his weight to tug. Pinchas added his own effort to the maneuver, and lurched to a standing position. Together they teetered along toward dry ground.

Not long after they got out of the marsh, Pinchas bent over, stooped, then collapsed to his knees, emptying his stomach.

Salmon waited, but averted his eyes until his comrade finished throwing up.

"Sorry," Pinchas panted, afterwards. "I swallowed too much of that water, I guess."

The sun was high by the time they reached an area of high brush with a relatively soft patch of ground for the rocky area. They unpacked their bedding and other meager gear, spreading it on the bushes to dry. Soon they did the same with their clothes. Both of them were bruised all over, with multiple small wounds where various debris in the river had gashed open their wrinkled, softened skin.

All Salmon wanted to do was lay in a sunny spot and rest, but the soldier instead gathered dry wood, tinder and kindling. He used his flint to start a fire, and they both huddled around it until the violent shivering stopped.

When their clothes were mostly dry, they dressed again. Their muscles were sore and they were still tired, and now hunger was setting in. All their bread had been ruined in the river. They dumped it out of their satchels onto the ground.

Salmon knew they should get moving, and Pinchas was game mentally, if not physically. When his bedding dried and he stood to pack it away, he lost his balance and his muscles were too taxed to right himself before falling. Salmon decided they needed something to eat so they could regain enough strength to resume the journey.

As Salmon began to pull his own dry bedding off the shrubs, he noticed what his tired eyes had missed when they arrived. There was a banana tree a short walk away with a ripe bunch ready for picking. A lemon tree bore its own ripe fruit in another direction. Closer still were melons, clementines and avocados. Then, before he was done taking visual inventory, two birds landed nearby to peck up the soggy frost bread he had discarded.

He was too sore to move all that quickly, but he tossed a blanket in their direction. He expected it to flutter harmlessly past, scaring them away, yet it dropped over them perfectly, covering both birds. Urging his muscles to respond with haste, he dove to the ground, his arms pinning the blanket down around the birds. The trap was completed when he pinched the blanket together like a purse, around what would be the meat of their meal.

Later, as they finished their roasted poultry and began on their fruit dessert, Salmon wiped his mouth and said, "That must be the easiest bit of foraging anyone's ever done. Looks like Moshe was right about how good the soil is over here. Food grows everywhere, even in the wild."

Pinchas nodded, swallowed his last mouthful of meat and said, "El Elyon fed us. Have you ever caught a bird so easily before? Our god is looking out for us on this assignment."

Indeed, it had been so easy, it was like their god was preparing the way for them. They had better watch themselves, lest they fall out of favor.

"I think we better camp here for the night," Salmon decided. "Most of the day is gone anyway; and I don't know about you, but I'm too worn out to go very far."

Pinchas nodded. "I'm willing to go on if you say so, but I think that's a good idea."

"We'll stay, then," Salmon said.

"If we have the same trouble getting back across," Pinchas said, "that gives us no more than five days to scout the area. And I'd guess we're far to the south of Bet-Yariq."

"Many, many leagues," Salmon agreed. "But we'll make good time, after resting tonight. And we have to come up with an idea for a better way back across."

Pinchas nodded. "I don't disagree. By the way: thanks for coming to get me. I'd probably still be hugging that tree if you hadn't."

Salmon shook his head. "No. You'd have gotten cold and sick, or been swept away by the current by now."

The environment suddenly became strangely silent.

"The animals," Pinchas said, craning his neck to one side, then the other. "What happened to them? It's like all the birds and insects just disappeared."

Salmon didn't have an answer, but the ground did. A low rumbling noise built up to replace the normal ambient sounds. The ground underneath them vibrated. The vibration grew stronger. Their firewood structure collapsed, throwing up a small shower of sparks.

The ground shook more threateningly as the rumble grew louder. Both men climbed to their feet, not sure what to do...if, in fact, there was anything that could be done.

This tremor was more severe than any they'd experienced before. They staggered and stumbled to maintain their balance.

Gradually, the shaking stopped. The birds and insects soon resumed their respective songs and calls.

Salmon's pulse raced. He quivered in fear. He'd been sure something horrific was going to happen, thinking they must have violated some statute inadvertently and angered El Elyon.

"Thank Hashem," Pinchas said, wiping his brow. He took tentative steps toward the fire, and used his staff to poke the burning wood back into a better configuration.

Salmon looked up, for some reason. Dark clouds were moving in from the west. Ma'adim was a little larger in the sky than the last time he noticed. Thunder crackled in the distance. It was like the whole world was getting ready to go crazy.

# A Secret Prayer

Mother got very upset when Rachav first told her about the arrangement she'd made with the king's messenger. Father seemed to be sympathetic, but didn't defend her with the enthusiasm she'd hoped for.

At one point, when Rachav refused to break the deal and go back to cash transactions, Mother slapped her. Father did step in, and put himself between the two women, before Mother could slap her again. Gradually, Rachav and Father were able to convince Mother that the risk of molestation by the Gibborites could both render Rachav unattractive to future customers, and result in the maiming or death of the boys.

Mother finally agreed that the arrangement to have someone else bring the flax in was not a foolish expenditure.

Later during the day of that row, Hessa came to her older sister, her jaw set in stubborn lines, eyes burning with accusatory intensity. Rachav sat on a stool. Hessa stood behind her, beginning to comb and fashion Rachav's hair.

"Why do you let her treat you like that?" Hessa asked. "We're her daughters—not slaves."

Rachav frowned. Mother considered Rachav a rebellious child, and evidently Hessa considered her a spineless fool. Some days it seemed she couldn't please anyone.

"Do you have suggestions, Hessa? She's our mother. Should I have slapped her back?"

Instead of answering the question, Hessa declared, "She'll never do this to me. I won't work as a whore for anyone."

The words stung Rachav as hard as a whip. She felt an urge to jump up from the stool and throttle her sister. Maybe break something over her head. Instead, she took a deep breath and said, "I see you're still an expert in finding fault in others. It will be interesting to see what happens if men begin to find you attractive one day, and Mother notices. I wonder if your tongue will be so bold to her face, then."

"What do you mean:'if'?" Hessa demanded, intentionally jerking at Rachav's hair to cause pain. "I'll be at least as pretty as you—probably more. In fact, I probably already am."

"If you pull my hair again, Hessa, I'll show you what that slap felt like."

Hessa worked silently for a while, then said, "I think it's time Faryel took over these hair-styling duties. She's old enough, now."

"I agree," Rachav said. "I'm sure she'd be glad to trade one of her chores for this one. And Mother shouldn't care, so long as everything gets done."

Later, while Rachav wove a new length of rope, Hessa's caustic words echoed in her mind. One word in particular: "whore."

*Whore! Whore! Whore!*

Every time the word echoed, it felt like Rachav was being stabbed in the heart. What made it worse, of course, was that it was true.

Nadir burst into the room, crying, "Rachav! Rachav! The Yacovites have moved down to the river!"

Her hands went still and she looked into her little brother's excited face. "You're sure it's them?"

"It's them," he said. "They're close enough now, anybody can see them. Come up and see for yourself."

She dropped her work and stood to follow Nadir to the closest ladder.

Rachav saw Anwar perched on the parapet when she climbed through the trapdoor to the top of the city wall. Nadir led their sister over to Anwar's vantage point.

The parapets were not manned. No soldiers were atop the wall. Once in a while a lookout came up here for a perfunctory circuit around the top, but soldiers didn't regularly guard the walls except when the city was at war. Bet-Yariq was so impregnable, it didn't need a regular guard detail, except at the gates.

Standing behind her brothers, she saw across the river to where a huge dark mass swarmed.

"I see tents going up," Anwar said. "But I don't think they would come so close to the river unless they intend to cross it."

"And crossing so close to Bet-Yariq," Rachav mused, "they must not be afraid of us at all."

"It means war," Nadir said. "They're going to attack us."

Rachav couldn't distinguish facial features at this distance, but individual movement was easy to make out, as was body language. Anwar seemed to be fascinated, watching a camp get built up from scratch.

"It has to be the Yacovites," Anwar said. "What other nation travels like a clan of vagabonds; the women and children right along with the army? And there's not a single Gibborite among them."

Rachav nodded. It was them—she was sure of it.

"There's no chariots," Nadir observed. "Or even horses."

"You two need to go back down and get to work, before Mother begins to wonder where you are," Rachav said.

Anwar sighed and rose to his feet. Nadir followed him to the trapdoor, looking back over his shoulder at the distant scene once more before he descended out of sight.

Rachav took note of her rapid heart rate, and trembling. She knew the Yacovites were going to cross over and attack Bet-Yariq. She just felt it in her bones. And walls or no walls, she had a feeling they would conquer everyone in their path, just as they'd been doing east of the Yarden.

She turned about to ensure she was completely alone atop the walls, then licked dry lips and spoke aloud.

"God of Yacov, I have never seen you. And forgive me that I don't know your name. I only know your reputation, and that you are higher than all the other gods. You destroy entire nations when they stir your anger, and I live in a wicked place, full of wicked people. Who am I, to even pray to you? A whore. But I pray anyway, in case you will listen. I beg your mercy. Please spare me and my family. Save us, and I will serve you. I'll learn your ways, and will abandon all other gods."

Nothing answered her but a breeze whistling through the parapets. She sighed, and watched the camp being built for a while.

The camp took on a most perplexing shape.

# On the Bank of Destiny

The Radiant Mist led Yacov to a location close to the river, then stopped. Y'hoshua ordered the priests to set up the portable Temple underneath where it hovered. The L'vim pitched camp in a perfect square around the Temple.

Zuar was still too young to fight in the army, but his father had lately been giving him more and more responsibilities as Zuar approached manhood. Today he assisted his father in setting up the family tent.

"What are you doing over there?" his father asked, noting his son was a stone toss from where the tent should go up. "Pull that stake out and bring it over here."

"Why?" Zuar asked. "We have all the room in the world over here. Nobody ever uses this space between the camps of Y'huda and Ruven. It just gets wasted. We won't be as crowded if our tent is over here."

Zuar's father shook his head. "We camp east of the L'vim. You are southeast." He stood at a spot on an imaginary line extending out from the southern border of the L'vim camp, then stretched out one arm parallel with the imaginary line. "East of the L'vim means our camp can't be any wider than their camp. Where you are is southeast." He then pointed north. "Over there would be northeast."

"Why do we do it this way?" Zuar asked.

"Because that's how we were instructed to do it."

"It wastes so much space."

"Watch your attitude, boy."

While the men and boys pitched tents, women and girls ventured out to forage, and guard details from the army watched over them.

Othniel had volunteered for the guard. It was cushy duty. He could rest and think while keeping watch. Today he strolled out well past where the women foraged, and, his back to where the camp was being set up, sat down under an olive tree, leaning against the trunk.

He lazily scanned the countryside. No threats materialized. If something did, he would shout the warning, and other soldiers guarding sectors to his right and left would be alerted.

As he looked over the scenery, he wondered what it would be like to have a permanent home. He loved the idea of living in one fixed location for the rest of his life, in a house with a bed and hearth, instead of a tent–and moving to a new camp every few months.

"Aren't you on guard duty?" asked a voice from behind him.. "No sleeping on the job."

He craned his neck around the tree trunk to see Aksah stooping over a patch of frost bread, putting flakes in her basket. She wasn't looking in his direction, but there was nobody else nearby, so her words must have been directed at him.

This was an unexpected opportunity, but again Othniel didn't know what to say. So he simply muttered, "Hi."

She did not reply.

Othniel had been thinking a lot about Achan's advice. Maybe trying too hard was worse than not trying at all. He turned back to face the landscape again, trying to forget that she was behind him.

He assumed she would move on and that would be the end of their encounter. Then she moved into his field of vision from behind, set down her basket, pulled her dress tight against the backs of her knees, and took a seat on the grass abreast of him. She was farther than arm's length away, and still didn't look in his direction, but she spoke to him again. "So, I'm curious: have I done something in particular to catch your attention?"

This caught him off guard. "Huh?"

"I can't figure out whether I've impressed you or offended you. And I can't imagine what I might have done to cause either one."

"Why would you think I'm offended?" he asked, cagily, then quickly added, "Or impressed?"

Now she turned to lock eyes with him. "It seems to me that you don't scowl at others nearly as much as you scowl in my direction."

"Scowl?" He didn't remember scowling at her. But then he wasn't always cognizant of his facial expression.

Before either of them could speak again, the ground began to quiver.

The shaking intensified, and Aksah cried out something indecipherable. Othniel jumped to his feet and moved quickly away, telling her, "You should probably get away from the tree. No telling what..."

Even as he was making the suggestion, she began climbing to her feet. But the ground suddenly pitched violently underfoot, sending her sprawling.

Othniel almost fell, too, but used his legs to absorb the shock and remained upright. He stepped close, took her hand and pulled her up, away from the tree. She followed his lead, returning his firm grip, and clutching his wrist with her other hand.

Just as the quaking seemed to subside, the ground bucked violently underneath, and sent them both tumbling. Othniel tried to maneuver under her, to cushion her fall, and they both wound up hopelessly tangled with each other. Putting his palms against the quaking ground, Othniel lifted himself up off Aksah, and stared dumbly at the gaping crack in the ground where they had previously sat. The olive tree was now sideways, hanging over inside the crack.

The quaking subsided and Aksah twisted around to see what Othniel was staring at. "Oh my..." she cried, weakly.

Now the tremors were quite mild. Othniel untangled himself from her and gained his feet, then reached down to give her a hand up. She took it, and he pulled her to an upright position.

Aksah brushed the dirt off her dress, staring at the sideways tree. "You were right. If I had stayed under the tree..."

Miraculously, her basket didn't fall into the crevice, but was sitting safely on level ground right next to it. He retrieved it for her.

"Thank-you. This quaking is getting worse and worse," she said. "If this goes on, it will shake the whole world apart one of these times."

"No," Othniel said. "It is El Elyon, preparing for battle. He is god over the land, the sea, and the sky. We have to be strong and bold. Little demonstrations like this are to remind us of the power he will use against his enemies."

"You really believe that?" she asked, taking the basket from him.

He nodded. She examined him for a moment, then smiled. It was a wonderful smile, that made the quake worthwhile all by itself.

Othniel would have enjoyed spending time like this with her, and all the physical contact, under different circumstances. But right then he suddenly remembered his family. What if the quake was not an assurance, but a judgment? What if his family had been swallowed up by a suddenly appearing chasm like the one they stared at now? Such things had happened before.

"We'd better get back and make sure everyone's all right," he said.

She nodded, but asked, "Would you mind walking me back to camp? I'm a big coward. I don't want to go by myself after that."

"Sure," he said, and silently pondered how a display of nature's power could erase her normal standoffish attitude so completely. He wished they had more time for a prolonged, leisurely stroll. But as soon as he verified that his family was safe, he would need to hurry back to his post and resume looking out. "Let's go."

Aksah a couple steps behind and to his left, they made their way toward camp.

Othniel glanced skyward and she followed his gaze toward the swarming, red-tinted clouds.

"Isn't it strange how the clouds are colored right there?" she asked.

He nodded. "Ma'adim is behind them. We're seeing the light

reflected off it, and filtered through the clouds."

"I remember when Ma'adim looked like just a really bright star," Aksah said. "A pink one. Then it grew to the size of a grape. Then an acorn. Last time the skies were clear, it was the size of a tangerine."

Othniel assumed she would next repeat one of the various theories about Nergal's connection to the red planet. She surprised him by asking, "If I haven't offended you, or impressed you somehow, why do you stare at me all the time?"

For a few moments he was silent—indecisive about how to answer. "I apologize. I didn't mean to stare, or scowl. I'll stop."

"That's not what I asked," she said, with a prolonged, disconcerting study of his eyes and face.

Feeling there was no safe way to answer the question, Othniel evaded it. "Your father is the one who scowls a lot. I don't know what I've done to make him so suspicious—or hostile."

After a moment, she swung her gaze forward, away from Othniel's face. "Do we have to walk so fast? I'm getting short of breath."

Othniel slowed his pace, but worried that Salmon would discover he had abandoned his post.

"Father is just very protective," Aksah said. "I'm a child of his old age, his only daughter, and such children are usually doted on, so I hear."

"But they're usually unaware of it," he said, with a challenging rise of the eyebrow.

"Oh, I'm painfully aware," Aksah replied. "All my brothers have been telling me how spoiled I am since I was old enough to understand them."

He snickered.

"Don't laugh," she said. "It's not funny, or true. Being treated like a prisoner doesn't make me spoiled."

"A prisoner?"

"Father doesn't let me out of his sight," she explained. "I'm surprised he lets me come out and forage like this. Something could happen and I might wind up enjoying myself."

He chuckled. Apparently it was contagious.

"Don't laugh!" she said, laughing. "It's not funny."

"I can tell," he said, amused by her denial. "It's just the way you said it."

They reached the edge of camp. Tents were still being pitched. People were talking about the quake, picking up spilt and fallen items, but nobody seemed to be hurt.

"Have your parents found a wife for you, yet?" Aksah asked, suddenly.

He froze in his tracks and stared at her. "What?"

She stopped, looked him in the eye, and repeated the question.

"No. Why?"

"Just curious," she said, lightly, and walked on.

He hurried to catch up, then asked, "What about you?"

"You'll have to ask my father," she said. "He hasn't had that conversation with me."

They arrived at Kalev's tent—one of the largest in the tribe—still being erected. "Well, here you are," he said, and turned to go find his family. He did not want Kalev to appear and notice him. For one reason, Kalev obviously disapproved of Othniel's interest in his daughter. For another, he might somehow find out Othniel was on guard duty right then...but not at his assigned post.

"Thanks for walking me home," Aksah said to his back. He replied with a grunt. Later, he would remember her gratitude and appreciate it, as well as the opportunity to spend some time with her. For the moment he didn't have time to exploit whatever opportunities existed.

He found that his family was fine...in fact, nobody in Yacov had been killed or hurt in the quake, from what he gathered. Once that good news was learned, Othniel ran back to his post.

Across the river and atop Bet-Yariq's city wall, Rachav took one last look at the Yacovite camp before returning to her work.

"What do you even call a shape like that?" Anwar asked, pointing at the huge camp in the distance.

"It's like a symbol of crossed swords," Nadir suggested. "Or crossed spears."

"It's got to be symbolic of something," Anwar said. "It can't possibly be practical–especially for so many people."

Symbolic of what, Rachav wondered. The only thing the shape reminded her of was what some women hung their laundry on– basically a pole planted vertically, with a wide crossbeam. Cords were tied between two such crosses so that laundry could be hung, two cords wide apart, and one in the center, but higher. The crossbeam was higher than midway up the pole. Similarly, the camp's "crossbeam" bisected the other "beam" of the cross shape off-center, though the sections of camp were at perfect right angles to each other.

The Yacovites certainly had some strange customs.

# The Reconnaissance

Salmon set a brisk pace as the two men marched north. They scouted several cities and villages along the way, but tried to avoid contact with the local population most of the time.

The land was crawling with Gibborim. When interaction with locals was necessary, they always sought out normal-sized men.

Foraging was much easier than Salmon could have imagined. Birds and wild game regularly came within sling range. Sheep, goats and cattle were fat from the plentiful graze. Fruit was easy to find growing in the wild—especially pomegranates and enormous clusters of grapes. The only staple missing on this side of the river was frost-bread.

Who would have thought rugged, mountainous country like this would have such fertile soil? Pinchas observed that normally, plants only thrived like this in valleys, or right beside rivers. It was the good soil and periodic gentle rains, he decided. Local farmers told them that most mornings a light, drizzling rain watered their crops, and the wild vegetation, before the sun rose high. Then the clouds parted and everything dried out before evening. Recently the daily routine had given way to overcast skies and powerful, violent storms which flooded rivers and streams.

Salmon observed everything he saw from a military perspective. What impressed him the most was the town of Ahyee, up in the central highlands. It had a small garrison, and he spotted no Gibborim. Y'hoshua should be able to take it easily, with the right planning. Then once taken, it could be fortified and easily defended, serving as a base to launch offensives down at the surrounding cities.

They logged all they observed along their journey. The last item on their agenda was a reconnaissance of Bet-Yariq.

The city intimidated Salmon, even from a far distance. It was built upon a mounded plateau, which would have provided a formidable defense all by itself. But a moat now surrounded the huge mound, and the city wall was so high, any ladder tall enough to scale it would crack of its own weight. There were windows cut into the wall, but so high up that they couldn't be reached, either.

As with most cities, Bet Yariq was surrounded by farmland. Here the cultivated fields extended out for a radius of few leagues around the circumference of the walls. As Salmon and Pinchas reached a path leading between fields to the city, they noticed other people on similar paths, ultimately merging into a sporadic stream of pedestrian traffic in and out of the city's main gate. The traffic was pedestrian because all the travelers entering the city left their horses, donkeys, or camels in a large, compartmented coral. As they approached closely to this foul-smelling area, Pinchas noticed a man leaving the city handing something to a man attending the coral. That man turned to a young boy, who ran through the coral and soon returned leading a camel. The traveler mounted his camel and rode away.

The man on camel-back passed them on the path, and Pinchas addressed him. "Excuse me, Sir..."

The man reined in his camel and gave Pinchas his attention.

"...I'm just curious," Pinchas said. "Are no animals allowed in the city?"

"Oh, they're allowed," the man replied. "It's just most people don't want to risk their animals in there."

"They'll be stolen?" Salmon wondered aloud.

"Defiled," the man said, with a deliberate stare into Pinchas' eyes, as if waiting for a drastic reaction. "There are a lot of people in the city who lust after beasts, and would molest them."

Salmon and Pinchas both struggled to hide their horror.

"Not that there's anything wrong with that," the man quickly added. "I just would rather not have my livestock used that way."

"I see," Pinchas said, flatly.

"Where are you two coming from?" the man asked.

"We are desert-dwellers from across the Yarden," Salmon replied. Technically, the answer was completely true."And you?"

"Beeroth," he said, then pointed toward the city gates. "If you've never been in the city, take care. The men in there don't just have lustful impulses toward women. Or humans. Not that there's anything wrong with that, of course. It's just that, often, the Gibborites take what they want without asking."

"Thanks," Salmon said, keeping his expression blank. "Safe travels."

"Safe travels," the man replied, and spurred his camel on.

"Not that there's anything wrong with that," mocked Pinchas, once out of earshot. His voice dripped with disgust.

"Be careful," Salmon advised. "We're going to have to keep a neutral demeanor if we see anything that disturbs us. We can't risk drawing attention to ourselves."

Pinchas said nothing, and they walked on. Their path joined others converging at the gate, and they gave the local hand gestures for greeting to other travelers on the way.

As they got close enough that the city wall loomed over them, Salmon estimated that, from the top of the circular wall down to the artificial plateau it sat on, they measured almost 40 cubits high. Encompassing the mound was a moat. Water, perhaps from one of the nearby springs, filled the moat, which was wide and deep enough to delay any army that might want to attack. The city entrance was open now, but could be blocked with three layers of obstacle: heavy wooden gates that swung closed from the inside; the iron-barred portcullis; and a tall outer drawbridge, which now rested in the down position, providing passage over the moat.

Salmon and Pinchas mixed themselves in with a cluster of people moving in the same direction, including merchants of spice, pottery and rugs. The merchants chattered amongst themselves, barely acknowledging the gigantic guards as they passed through the gate. The two Yacovim did their best to appear as if they belonged with the group, imitating their nods and gestures. Pinchas had not seen Gibborim up close before, and forced himself not to stare. His blood ran cold, being in the presence of these abominable freaks. Even discounting their enormity and oblong heads, there was something just downright unnatural about the Gibborim.

No guards accosted them as they went, but Pinchas could sense their suspicious leers, as surely as if each pair of eyes were twin icicles raking over his body.

Inside the wall, a path led to the city square. A bazaar lined both sides of the path, with thousands of voices all talking or yelling over each other. Beyond the bazaar were houses, taverns, temples and other structures so closely-spaced that the Gibborim didn't fit on the narrow paths between some of them. Surrounding the city square were taller structures—more ornate than the average dwelling—including what must be a palace.

Salmon looked over the variety of items for sale—items of silver, gold, ivory, jewel stones and exotic wood.

"Don't touch anything," Pinchas warned in a lowered voice.

Salmon glanced at his traveling companion. Pinchas was hunched with arms crossed, as if wracked by a chill.

"Can't you feel it?" Pinchas asked, shivering.

"Feel what?"

"The charge," Pinchas replied, simply, thrusting his chin in the direction of the wares on display. "They're radiating evil energy. Touch one and who knows what curses you'll be infected with."

Salmon didn't share in this perception, but he deferred to the priest's expertise and touched nothing.

Mixed in with humans and Gibborim throughout the bazaar were creatures Salmon had heard rumors about, but hadn't believed existed: centaurs; fauns; gryphons; minotaurs; and at least one mermaid in a pool.

"Welcome to the House of the Moon God!" a female voice called out every minute or so. Pinchas searched for the source of the voice and finally found it—a sphinx in the robe and headdress of what must be a priestess. She stood behind a table loaded with molded statues. "Each of these household gods are skillfully crafted, blessed, and have been approved for lawful worship." Some passers-by stopped to peruse the idols. Behind the priestess...if that's what she was...an attractive woman with painted eyes and scanty clothing paced as if a queen reviewing her attendants. She searched the faces of bypassers like a wolf watching rabbits. Pinchas was passing close by when she picked out a young man with a sack slung over one shoulder and spoke to him. "You there. Have you completed the spring rituals?"

She had his undivided attention. He took in the shape of her body, then seemed to be locked into a trance by her smile.

"Have you given your offerings?" she asked, in a voice smooth as velvet.

The young man just stared dumbly at her. She slunk toward him, spearing him in place with an intense gaze. Pinchas was nearly mesmerized by the motion of her hips as she moved, but Salmon grabbed him and pulled him away.

They passed several food vendors, statues, and miniature pyramids.

"I'm glad we didn't go to the other side," Salmon muttered half under his breath, nodding across the path.

Pinchas swept his gaze over to follow the gesture, and was revolted. There was a sort of open stable facing one of the wooden pyramids, filled with various animals. The crowds gathered there were thicker than in any other part of the bazaar. One crowd watched a man who had somehow got a jackal and camel to attempt breeding with each other.

Pinchas glanced at Salmon, to determine if his companion saw the same thing he was seeing, but by now Salmon's attention was elsewhere. He blanched, his eyes wide, and mouth agape. Pinchas found his focal point—and that of another fascinated crowd of onlookers. Atop one of the pyramids was an ape and a human being.

Pinchas averted his eyes as soon as the abomination registered. He and Salmon hurried to get as far as they could from the sight.

Atop another pyramid stood a satyr, who had been entertaining another crowd. Whatever he had been saying and doing, he stopped when he noticed the two strangers hurrying past. His eyes narrowed and his lip curled as he studied them. Pinchas felt a dark, cold, sickening force lock onto him, even more disturbing than the stares of the Gibborim guards.

Pinchas ducked behind the tent of a temple prostitute just to escape the skin-crawling sensation of the satyr's scrutiny. With the tent in between himself and the assorted horrors, he sank to his knees and doubled over, fighting the urge to vomit again.

Salmon turned the corner around the tent, saw Pinchas, and stood beside him, one hand on the back of his neck. "I was afraid I lost you. Hey...are you all right?"

Pinchas' face was ghastly pale, and twisted with revulsion. "What sort of place have we come to? What sort of people are these? I can't bear to look on any more."

Rhythmic grunting sounded from inside the tent. Neither man wanted to know who or what was making the noise. Salmon patted Pinchas on the back in an attempt to be comforting. "Let's head into the city proper. It doesn't seem to be all that populated right now."

Rachav did her best to avoid the bazaar as much as possible, but some shopping simply had to be done there. Her mother's kitchen was almost out of salt, and she had a longstanding relationship with a spice vendor who was more-or-less trustworthy. Besides, mother had tasked her with finding more new customers to make up for the lost revenue from the king's messenger. There were more potential customers at the bazaar than any other place she knew of, and usually just showing her face there would attract a few.

She noticed the two strangers as soon as they came within visual range. There was nothing unusual about their style of clothing. There were plenty of non-Gibborites in and around Bet-Yariq, so their size was not unusual. Their complexion and style of beard was not out of the ordinary, either. And yet they stood out like cactus among bean stalks.

It was because she didn't understand what was so different about the strangers that Rachav followed them. The more she observed their reactions to what went on around them, the more intrigued she was.

The aliens were drawing the attention of others, too. Two Gibborites had followed them to the edge of the bazaar and exchanged comments while staring after them. A temple prostitute noticed them, and a minstrel, then the satyr.

The satyr had been appearing in the bazaar every other day for about a month. His ominous warnings seemed to be effective at stirring passions, and people lined up to offer sacrifices each time he was done. When he spotted the visitors, he completely lost focus on his oratory. His anger transformed into...fear?

The two visitors were in more danger than they might understand. Without considering her motives, Rachav decided she should help them.

When the one with the facial scar and the measured, stealthy gait stopped to comfort the one with the weak stomach behind the tent, Rachav approached them and bowed.

"Excuse me, Sirs," she greeted, keeping her eyes respectfully down. "It looks like you could use some water, and to get out of the hot sun. There's a room in my family's house you may stay in for the night. I'll be cooking the evening meal soon. You may wash your feet, and even take a bath if you like."

The stealthy one examined her with hard eyes. "You don't know us," he said.

"Nevertheless," she said, "I offer you hospitality."

The other foreigner stood erect and wiped his brow. He was slightly taller, but compared to the other man he seemed sheltered and innocent–hence his overwhelming emotions after a short stroll through the bazaar. "We accept," he said. "And you have our thanks."

"My name is Rachav."

"I am Pinchas," the innocent one said, then waved toward his hawk-like companion with the scar, "and this is Salmon."

She bowed again.

Salmon looked wary. "I'm not so sure. Maybe we should just turn around and go back the way we came."

"I'm not sure if you've noticed, Sir," Rachav said, "but you've attracted some attention already. If you try going back through the city gate so soon after entering, you'll provoke the suspicion of the guards. Especially given that your faces are completely unknown here, yet you are traveling too light to have come from very far."

Salmon looked her over, tongue pushing against the inside of his cheek, making his beard ripple back and forth.

"She's right," Pinchas said, exchanging a meaningful look with his friend. A whole lot more was communicated silently than with those two words, evidently, because Salmon nodded and blinked.

They followed Rachav to the inside of the city wall, where they climbed a steep, zig-zagging staircase cut out of stone. On the way up, both men noticed the apartments within the upper walls. Salmon glanced down and, even here inside the city, with the higher ground, the height of the walls made an impression on him.

Following her up the steps, it was also impossible not to notice that the woman was shaped exquisitely. She was dressed and painted like a harlot, but by her willingness to help, it seemed she at least had some modicum of decency.

When they reached the top, Rachav led them through an open doorway, calling out to someone that she had company. She ushered her guests into an unoccupied room and bade them wait for her there, while she exited to an adjoining room, pulling silk drapes closed behind her.

They heard Rachav exchanging whispered words with others. Salmon strode to the room's window and placed his arm on the sill. The thickness of the outer wall measured from the tips of his fingers to his armpit.

Pinchas sat on the couch and squeezed his temples. "There is incredible wickedness in this city," he whispered.

"No jest, that," Salmon replied, looking out the window to the ground, far below.

"It's not as bad in here," Pinchas added, now pinching the bridge of his nose.

Salmon's gaze rose from the ground and swept eastward. Our camp has moved, he thought to himself. *You can see it from here— just beyond the far bank of the Yarden.*

Salmon turned from the window when the silk drapes parted and Rachav entered, followed by two girls. The young, small one bore a basin of water, a towel, and a sponge, while the older one brought a pitcher and two cups. The latter poured water with a perturbed expression, avoiding eye contact with everyone.

Rachav had by now scrubbed the cosmetics from her face. Salmon had to admit to himself, she had a striking appearance when painted up like a whore. But she was even more attractive now.

Pinchas and Salmon accepted the cups, but sniffed at the contents. Water was not often safe to drink, but this smelled fresh, like it came from a spring and not the river. They both took cautionary sips, then Pinchas gulped greedily, glad to wash the dry, dusty taste from his parched mouth.

The young girl knelt before Salmon and removed his sandals.

"The two of you have familiar accents," Rachav said. "Where are you from?"

"Our people are from Mizraim," Salmon replied.

It was a truthful statement, though evasive. Yacov had lived in Mizraim for over 400 years, and only left there less than a half-century ago.

Rachav looked thoughtful, as though pondering the careful phrasing of his answer.

The youngest girl placed one of Salmon's now bare feet over the basin. She soaked the sponge in the water, then squeezed water onto his foot and wiped at it.

"How about you?" Salmon asked. "Native of Bet-Yariq?"

"My sisters and younger brothers are," Rachav replied, then excused herself and left the room again.

More muted conversation took place in another room, mostly between Rachav and someone with a mature female voice. Words weren't distinguishable, but the angry tone was.

Pinchas studied the two girls for a moment before smiling and introducing himself. The older girl identified herself as Hessa, and the younger one as Faryel.

"What about you?" Hessa asked, looking at Salmon. "Do you have a name?"

Salmon was taken aback by the impudence of the girl. She spoke to adults as if an equal or superior. Her tone and body language radiated disrespect. Children like this needed correction, if it wasn't too late for them already. Still, it wouldn't be wise to criticize Rachav's family while a guest in her father's house, or while trying not to draw attention to himself in this foreign city. "My name is Salmon. Thanks for the water." He shifted his attention to the sweet girl. "And thank-you, little one."

"You're welcome," Faryel said, smiling while keeping at her chore.

Once the grime of travel was wiped from their feet, they were left alone for a while. Then two boys entered, carrying pails of water, which they dumped into the bath.

It took the boys a few trips to fill the tub. The older one was Anwar, and the younger one Nadir. The water was from a hot spring in the city, and was still warm. Salmon deferred to the priest, and let Pinchas go first. After both men were bathed and their undergarments washed and returned to them (still a bit damp, but much more comfortable than before), they dressed and still had a bit of a wait before the evening meal was brought in.

Rachav's parents ducked in briefly to introduce themselves, make polite small talk, and go through the rituals of hospitality which were customary. The mother said all the right things, but Pinchas could tell she was feeling anything but hospitable.

After the evening meal, Rachav returned with both sisters, who began to collect cups, plates and other eating ware.

The daughters in this house were all strikingly beautiful. Salmon tried not to stare too much at Rachav, lest his thoughts turn lustful. He shifted his focus by seeking information. "You said your siblings are natives of Bet-Yariq, but you're not?"

"The Gibborites relocated my family inside the city when I was young," Rachav said, sitting across from him. "We used to live down close to the river. We raised livestock and had crops—not just flax. My older siblings were already married, and lived in their own houses. But they moved inside the city from their village when news came that the Yacovites were coming."

She watched them for a reaction, but Salmon was careful not to show one.

"They relocated you?" Pinchas asked, with a lowering of one eyebrow and a confused grimace.

Rachav nodded. "The city needed our fields."

"So they just took them?" Pinchas inquired, disbelieving. "Just like that?

Rachav shrugged, and gestured with her index finger in a circular pattern. "Yes. They assigned us a home inside the city, and a portion of the collective produce from the fields. It's only flax, now. We have to buy food in the market, and water from the springs, with what money we can make. And, to be honest, we all do much prefer the clean water, from the springs, to river water."

Certainly the Yarden was a very muddy river.

"You make enough from flax to support your family?" Salmon asked, glancing at Rachav's sisters, then toward the doorway, through which the rest of her family was.

Rachav's head tilted downward, and she blushed. "Not quite," she replied, quietly.

The haughty girl, Hessa, had been doing her part of the cleanup slowly, observing the guests and the conversation. Now she snorted, whirled, and plunged through the doorway out of sight.

Salmon and Pinchas locked eyes, briefly. The reaction of the sisters confirmed that their hostess dressed like a prostitute for a reason. Rachav rented out her body to help her family eat.

The awkward scene was interrupted by a commotion at the outer door. Loud voices echoed in, and the timid voice of Rachav's father replied.

"Your daughter brought two men up here," accused one booming voice.

"Bring them out here!" demanded a second.

"Are y-you certain?" the father asked, then his tone changed. "Nadir, go fetch your sister!"

"You had better turn over your visitors right now," the first voice threatened. "Need I remind you the punishment for disloyalty?"

"R-right away, Sir," Rachav's father said.

# A Pact Only a God Could Keep

Feet still bare, Salmon grabbed his sandals and pulled them back on. Pinchas followed suit.

Salmon smiled at Faryel and mouthed "thank-you". He patted her on the head before standing and groping for the sword concealed under his tunic. The smile was gone now, and his eyes were cold and hard.

Rachav watched with a look of panic, speechless. But she noticed how Salmon took the time to show kindness and gratitude to little Faryel before going for his sword.

"We're here on orders of the king," the loud voice said. "You had better not try to stall us!"

Nadir slipped into the room, eyes bulging, gaze bouncing between Rachav and the two strangers. "It's soldiers from the garrison," he said, in a hushed tone. "Father says you must come to the door."

Rachavpressed her hand against her heart. Her eyes closed for a brief moment. When they opened again, her countenance changed. There was a different set to her jaw, and the fear had been replaced by resolve. She locked eyes with Nadir, gestured towards the visitors, then pointed to the alcove at the back of the room.

At first Nadir was confused. Rachav repeated the silent instructions, punctuating them with a jerk of the head that meant "get going!" and a look of reprimand that only mothers and big sisters could master.

Nadir marched toward the alcove. Rachav waved for the visitors to follow.

Salmon kept his hand under the tunic, where it gripped the hilt of the sword, but he followed the boy, nodding for Pinchas to come along.

They quietly darted around the wall of the alcove, where they found the young boy already halfway up a ladder to a trapdoor in the ceiling. Salmon nudged Pinchas, who grabbed the ladder and climbed after the boy. When he was far enough up to make room, Salmon got on the ladder, too.

Rachav joined her father in the doorway, facing the two enormous soldiers on the stone balcony.

"Turn over the men who came to you," demanded the Gibborite who was obviously in charge. "They are spies!"

Rachav tried to maintain a calm, even voice, as she said, "I did entertain two clients earlier—though I didn't know where they were from. I certainly didn't know they were spies."

"Turn them over!" the huge soldier commanded.

Rachav tried to ignore the irrational fears racing through her mind—like the Gibborites being able to hear how hard her heart was pounding, and figuring out her duplicity. "They left just before the city gates were shut. I don't know which direction they went, but if you hurry, you may catch them."

Both soldiers fixed hard stares down at her, without speaking, for a long, uncomfortable moment.

It was a bit strange, really, how inconsistent were the customs in Bet-Yariq. Obviously the king had little regard for private property, or he wouldn't confiscate the farms of those surrounding the city. Yet violating a family's privacy and entering a home uninvited was still taboo. Not that a Gibborite could fit inside a normal dwelling standing up, or even get through a normal doorway without creative contortion.

Rachav imagined them seeing right through her facade of calm honesty; seeing through the walls; seeing everything, and striking her and her father dead on the spot. But after an agonizing period of scrutiny, the one Gibborite turned to the other.

"Get back to the Court. Report on this, and tell them I'm getting a patrol together to find the spies.."

The other Gibborite nodded and they both turned away, trudging off with heavy footfalls.

The two Yacovim lay atop the city wall, hidden under bundles of flax.

Salmon couldn't see Pinchas, though he knew his companion had also been hidden by the young boy Nadir, under a stack of flax bundles. In fact, Salmon couldn't see much at all. He expected a stealthy enemy soldier to arrive at any moment, yank away his cover and thrust a spear right through him. Salmon's hand remained on his sword hilt. If discovered, he would go down fighting.

Lying still, breathing quietly, and listening intently to every sound, Salmon heard the creaking of wood from below—someone's weight on the ladder in the apartment. Then the trapdoor opened. Through a narrow gap in the flax, he saw movement—someone's clothes blurring past his narrow view. He tensed and prepared to roll away and draw his sword. But he smelled something that didn't signal a threat. In brief moments he heard Rachav's voice.

"It's safe to come out, now," Rachav said, quietly. "Let's get you back down inside before a guard or someone decides to take a stroll up here."

Salmon pushed the flax off and rose to one knee. Pinchas threw his flax off and stood, scratching itches all over himself. "What did you tell them?"

"She can explain downstairs," Salmon said. "Let's get out of here."

Rachav met Salmon's gaze and nodded. Light from Ma'adim and Lebanah lit her face in a way that accentuated her natural beauty. Salmon realized the familiar smell was her perfume.

She led them back down the ladder into the small annex.

Salmon was the first to break the awkward silence as they stood there together. "You have our gratitude, Rachav."

She nodded. For a brief instant her gaze met Salmon's. She peered into his eyes as if searching for something, looking quite vulnerable. Then she looked away and crossed her arms, face fading into an inscrutable mask.

"Why did you take such a risk for us?" Pinchas asked, studying her closely. "You and your whole family could be executed for not turning us over."

She motioned for them to sit, then did so herself, leaning forward with a grave expression. After hesitating, Salmon and Pinchas sat, too.

"I know you're not Mizraimites," she said. "Oh, you came from Mizraim...or at least your parents did. Your accents are similar. But you are Yacovites."

Nobody spoke at first. Then Salmon said, "If that were true, then your behavior is even more confusing."

"It's true," she said. "You can let go of the mysterious pretenses with me. The soldiers were right—you've come to look at the city's defenses."

She paused, and when her guests remained silent, she continued. "Tell me about the god of Yacov. Your invisible god."

"His name is El Elyon," Pinchas replied, "And Hashem, and...he has many names. And it is not that he is invisible; it's just that we exist in a place and a state where we can't see him."

Salmon hadn't heard this summary before. Pinchas had his undivided attention now.

"Is he stronger than other gods?" Rachav asked.

Pinchas nodded. "Not just stronger. He is their father. Creator. They were originally his servants, but there was a rebellion... Mankind rebelled, too. Long ago, El Elyon divided up the nations of the world. He put them under the authority of the 70 Princes in his Council...who later rebelled. Our nation he kept for himself."

Salmon imagined this all sounded pretty egotistical to the woman, but she listened attentively. Besides: what did it matter how it sounded to her?

"The rebellious Princes presented themselves as gods to the people entrusted to them. People worshiped them as gods...still do."

Rachav chewed on a lower lip that Salmon might describe as succulent. "And they interbred with human beings. That's where the Gibborites came from, true?"

"True," Pinchas agreed, face twisting slightly with disgust.

"Why do they all have such misshapen heads?" Salmon blurted.

"The mothers are human women," Rachav said, with a perfunctory glance toward Salmon. "The Gibborim babies are very large. They get trapped in the birth canal and their skulls are squeezed out of shape. That's how the midwives explain it. Anyway, the baby usually has to be cut out. The mother almost never survives."

Salmon studied her silently. An image sprang to his mind of Rachav being cut open and a bloody monster being pulled from her womb. That triggered other images, which he also didn't want to see. He looked away hastily.

"These abominations we see in your city and elsewhere are results of their other breeding programs," Pinchas said, lip still curled into a sickened sneer. "They mix different species of animals. And animals with men. Hashem destroyed all those hideous freaks once already, back in history. But it didn't take long for the evil ones to start all over again. They won't stop until everything and everyone is corrupted—physically and spiritually."

"There's a war coming." Rachav moved her arm in a circular motion. "Your army against the armies of all the cities in Kenaan. Your god against their gods." She spoke this as a statement; not a question.

Salmon shrugged. Pinchas nodded.

"You've got a better grasp of the situation than we could have imagined," Pinchas said. "How do you know all this?"

Rachav shrugged. "I've been contemplating all this every day for some time. And the fear of you is everywhere. Even the Gibborites are scared. I could see it in their eyes a little while ago...though they would never admit fear to a human."

"Fear of us?" Salmon replied, surprised by her revelation.

"Fear of you. Your god. Your general...Yeshua, right?"

Salmon nodded, but said, "Most of us call him Y'hoshua."

Rachav closed her eyes for a moment. When she opened them again, she nodded to herself and said, "Your god is the strongest. He's the father of gods. I know he's going to give you victory over this city. Over all the cities. I know it. Everybody has heard about what your god did to Mizraim, and to the kings across the river. No god can stand against that kind of power. People are right to fear him. To fear you."

"All the more reason for you to turn us over to the Gibborim when you had the chance," Salmon said.

Rachav licked dry lips. "I've saved your lives, by hiding you, and sending your enemies off on a futile chase. Promise me you'll return the favor. When your army attacks Bet-Yariq, spare me and my family."

It sounded fair enough to Salmon, but with all the things that could happen in war, death could, and did, find unintended targets. It was indiscriminate.

"Done," Pinchas said, before Salmon could even form his caveats into words. "We'll remember what you did for us. We'll make sure you, your parents and siblings are spared when the time comes."

"Hold on, now," Salmon protested. "War isn't always cooperative with the plans of men. We have no idea what all will happen and it's impossible to guarantee that anyone's life can be spared."

Without missing a beat, Rachav replied, "It's impossible to guarantee you won't be caught or killed before you make it safely back to your camp, but I did everything within my power to keep it from happening. I ask at least that much. Surely your god has authority over all that happens in battle."

"He does," Pinchas replied, with finality. "You have spared our lives; we will spare yours."

"And my family?" she pressed.

"And your family," Pinchas agreed.

Salmon scowled, but bit his tongue.

She studied each of them intensely, in turn. Salmon stared out the window and wondered if El Elyon might have a cruel sense of humor, with such beautiful eyes set in the face of a prostitute. The face...sure. The face was part of what must get customers interested.

But the eyes supposedly were a portal one could see through to the inner person.

"Why is it he is so confident," Rachav asked, indicating Pinchas, "while you are so skeptical about the same matter?"

Because our god doesn't honor deals with whores, Salmon thought. *And he wouldn't bother protecting one.*

"He's a soldier," Pinchas said, nodding toward his fellow Yacovim. "He's a practical man. Spiritual matters are intangible to him. He can't see or touch them."

Someone else might have sounded condescending giving this explanation, but Pinchas seemed to have meant it as a compliment. In fact, Salmon admitted, it was a rather gracious judgment from somebody whose life centered around spiritual matters.

Rachav studied Salmon for an extra time, then gave her head a shake as if ridding it of unneeded thoughts. "I wouldn't try to escape right now, when the guards are on the alert and everyone has their eye out for you. You should leave an hour or two before dawn. You should go to sleep early, so you'll be rested when it's time to get up. I'll wake you then."

Pinchas thanked her for her hospitality and consideration. Rachav left them to bed down.

Salmon, even more wary than usual, kept his clothes on and his sword close. He sat on the floor, his back against the wall, while Pinchas took advantage of the chance to sleep comfortably on the bed.

"You're not going to take the other side of the mattress?" Pinchas asked as he stretched out under the covers.

Salmon shook his head. "You know she services customers in that bed, right?"

Pinchas had no response, and was soon snoring.

While prostitution was an institution accepted in every culture Salmon knew of (and, in fact, men of his tribe had visited prostitutes right back to their common ancestor); the practitioners of the profession were still scorned by everyone who wasn't enjoying their services at the moment.

Salmon intended to stay awake through the night and keep watch. Maybe it was exhaustion catching up with him from the journey, but whatever it was, he went unconscious in very short order.

He had a strange dream that he was with Yacov, the ancestor of his people, tending a flock near a watering hole. Some of the sheep were solid in color, and some were spotted. The unspotted ones belonged to his father-in-law, and Salmon was disappointed that Yacov had to settle for the blemished ones. Strange things were said and took place, as always happens in dreams. Then one particularly ugly, spotted sheep was given to Salmon as a gift.

Salmon groused about not wanting such an ugly animal, and threw rocks at it to make it go away. But Yacov, sitting by the water and peeling bark off sticks, said, "You know our god can make pure what is blemished."

The blemishes on the sheep all blended together and its wool was transformed until it was all one solid color.

While Salmon marveled at this, the sheep came over and nuzzled against him. He found the warmth of its head against his arm rather pleasant. But in time the pleasant warmth gave way to insistent jerking. He petted the sheep to calm it down, but the shaking only got worse.

When Salmon's eyes cracked open, he saw the source of the warmth was Rachav's grip on his arm as she shook him awake. His hand covered hers, having thought he was petting an affectionate ewe.

He came fully conscious with a start and yanked his hand away.

"Well," she said, letting go of his arm, straightening from her stooped position and meeting his groggy glare. "For a soldier, you sure sleep heavy."

At some point during the night, Salmon had slumped over and curled up on the floor. Now he swung up to a sitting position and looked around, blinking.

The sky outside the window was dark. A small candle dimly lit the interior of the room. Pinchas sat on the couch, fully dressed, tying his sandals.

"You have a couple hours before sunrise," Rachav said.

Salmon grunted acknowledgment, rubbing his eyes as he climbed to his feet. "We have to get out. But answer a few questions first."

Rachav met his gaze and waited patiently.

Salmon asked her about the strength of the garrison, and how many of the troops were Gibborim. She gave him her best estimate. He frowned. Bet-Yariq was a strong fortress, by any measurement.

"Weapons?" Salmon asked.

She shrugged. Her brothers obsessed about such things but she'd never had much of an interest. "Spears; shields; javelins. That's what I mainly see. I don't know if you noticed the boulders atop the walls–they're for dropping on top of besiegers. And of course there would be archers and javelineers up there, as well."

"Are there provisions for a siege?" Salmon asked.

Rachav nodded. "We have the springs, so there would never be a lack of water. And the king's store rooms are full of food that is rotated regularly. Normally a tenth of all crops and livestock are taxed from the farmers. Ever since news of your approach reached us, the tax has gone up to a third."

"How about the guard?"

"The walls are not fully manned in peacetime. Guards rotate shifts walking the wall, as a lookout. My brothers saw your army setting up camp beyond the Yarden, so the lookouts certainly have reported it. The gate is always manned. During daylight, details guard the fields outside the city."

"Besides the gate, is there any other way in or out?"

"Not that I know of," Rachav said. "And speaking of that, the gate is closed. You wouldn't want to try getting out that way, though, even if it were open. I'm sure every soldier is on the alert for you." She picked up the candle and gracefully slipped out of the room, plunging them in darkness.

Salmon dug in his haversack, extracted a bundle of rope, and brought it to the window. He frowned. Very likely, it would not be long enough to reach the ground.

Rachav returned a moment later with a heavy coil of rope.

Noticing how she strained with the weight, Pinchas took it from her.

"Thank-you," she said, then pointed at Salmon's rope. "You might as well put that away. It's not going to be enough."

Both men examined her rope. It was a very great length, and red in color.

"This is the longest, and strongest, rope we have," she said. "We died it red so we could tell it from the lengths that are not as stout. It should be able to support your combined weight."

Pinchas looked from her to the window, then back to her. She nodded. "It's the only safe way out of here," she said.

"Safe?" Pinchas replied, skeptically.

Salmon clapped him on the shoulder. "She's right. Besides, El Elyon will keep you from falling, true?"

Pinchas gulped. "True."

Salmon scooted the couch over to the wall. It was well-built, and wider than the window, so should prove an adequate anchor. Working together, he and Pinchas tied one end of the red rope to the couch; then Salmon heaved the rest out the window, where it uncoiled on the way down.

Salmon checked to make sure his sword was secure, and climbed onto the thick windowsill. Rachav clutched at his arm, almost in the same spot she had touched when waking him.

Their eyes met under the red glow from Ma'adim through the window. She looked so vulnerable at that moment, he forgot she was a harlot as his instincts overwhelmed him with the urge to protect her.

"Give me a sign you'll show mercy to my family when your army attacks," she implored him.

Salmon grabbed the rope and gave it a tug, forcing himself to concentrate on immediate, practical matters. "When our army marches on this city, keep your father, mother and whole family up here in your home. Don't let them leave. Hang this same rope in your window so we can climb back up and we'll know to spare everyone in this apartment."

She nodded.

"If we don't see a red rope in the window," Salmon warned, "then our agreement is void. If you betray us, and tell the king or his soldiers which way we went, our agreement is void. And if any member of your family doesn't stay up here with you when we attack, then their blood is on their own heads."

Rachav nodded her acceptance to these terms.

"I'll go first," Salmon told Pinchas. Grabbing the rope in both hands, he slithered backwards over the edge of the windowsill into the dark.

Pinchas took a deep breath. He was a bit uneasy about executing this maneuver But he climbed onto the sill, took hold of the rope, gave Rachav a nod, and followed his companion out the window.

# The Last Three Days

The soldier and priest found a place to hide in a small canyon, until patrols from Bet-Yariq quit searching for them.

Salmon developed an idea for a faster, less dangerous method for crossing the river. He tied Pinchas' rope to his own for extra length, then they fastened one end to a tree on the west side of the Yarden. They tied the other end to a log, which they carried upstream until the rope was taut. Then they waded out toward the middle of the river with the log, and when their feet lost purchase, they clung to the log for flotation With both of them kicking and one-arm paddling as best they could, they influenced the drift of the anchored log toward the far bank. It moved in a huge arc, at the apex of which, their feet could touch bottom. They let go of the log and strained against the current to wade ashore.

The crossing had required a lot of energy, but they weren't utterly exhausted like after the first time. After a short rest, they made off for the camp of Yacov, letting their clothes dry on the march.

Y'hoshua made the rounds from tribe to tribe, overseeing the training supervised by his field commanders. Most of it was the same battle drills they'd been rehearsing for years.

His shock troops were three of the biggest tribes, armed with spear and shield. They fought primarily in formation. The Gadim were the only tribe completely armed with swords, and they specialized in close-in fighting. Shimon and Menashe were composed entirely of archers, who trained extensively in the use of camouflage. They practiced lying still on the ground, blending in with the scenery, then rising on command to loose showers of arrows from long range. Y'hoshua had three tribes apiece of slingers and javelineers, who maintained spread formations and engaged the enemy from medium range, but he had given one of the javelin-wielding tribes a special assignment. The Z'vulunim, armed with hatchets and other secondary weapons, were busy gathering lumber to build ladders.

Y'hoshua's concept of the operation would be to have Z'vulun use the ladders to scale the walls by night, seize control of the city gate and open it so the shock troops could pour through and swarm the defenses.

When Y'hoshua entered Y'huda's training area, Kalev called the tribe to attention. His marshals, captains and lieutenants relayed the command, and the warriors disengaged from their sparring or marching drills to stand straight, facing their field marshal.

"As you were," Y'hoshua said. "Carry on."

The bizarre weather had given them alternating days of thunderstorms and scorching heat. Today was one of the latter. Kalev glanced at the sun and summoned his marshals. He instructed them to give the men a rest and make sure everyone drank water. This done, he approached Y'hoshua.

Y'hoshua gave him a grin. "How are you, my old friend?"

"As strong as the day you and I left for our reconnaissance," Kalev replied.

The laugh blew out of Y'hoshua in an explosive snort.

"You don't believe me?" Kalev asked, hardening a bicep muscle and slapping it with his opposite hand.

"You've developed a sense of humor in 40 years," Y'hoshua said, chuckling.

"No I haven't. I'm going to keep telling you that until you take it seriously."

Y'hoshua laughed some more, and Kalev chuckled along with him. Once the moment had passed, Y'hoshua said,"After today, I'm going to suspend training. Make sure your men get some rest, eat well, and get a chance for a little merrymaking...within reason. We're crossing over in about three days."

"Three days?"

Y'hoshua gestured somewhere between a nod and a shrug. "Give or take. I'll let you know when to start counting down. But when those three days are over, we're moving out."

"We'll be ready," Kalev said. "But...permission to speak, Sir?"

"Of course."

"I don't understand why you want to attack Bet-Yariq first."

"I know," Y'hoshua replied, with a sigh of his own. "I know. El Elyon sent me a message. There is no doubt who it came from. We attack there, first."

Kalev glanced over his hordes of spear men, then into the sky where Ma'adim was even larger than the day before. "Well, he said Hashem would be our spearhead in this war. It's not us who have to take the city, but him. We just have to obey."

"You're a rock, comrade. A rock." Y'hoshua slapped him on the back. "I've got a special assignment. I need one man from each tribe detached and under my personal command on the day we ford the river. Think over who it is that should represent you."

Kalev nodded, thoughtfully. "Very well."

At the same moment, they both noticed two figures on foot, approaching from a distance. The figures gestured to each other, then at Y'hoshua, who watched with interested silence.

Both the field marshal and his general had lost their near vision years ago, but their eyes could still see sharp at far ranges. As the two figures drew within a couple bow shots, they grew recognizable.

"That's Salmon," Kalev said. "One of my junior officers. The other one looks familiar, too."

"He's one of the priests," Y'hoshua said. "You can start counting down now. We cross in three days."

# The Price of Allegiance to a King

The king's entourage spent the early afternoon touring the architect's estate. Binaizek's house was built better than Adonaizidek's palace.

A miniature aqueduct brought fresh water from a stream to inside the house where it could be diverted into a bath and heated, or into the kitchen for cooking, drinking, and cleaning..

The stables Binaizek designed and built, despite the smell, were magnificent. They would make for a splendid barracks, with little modification.

The same admiration for nature which inspired Binaizek to design the garden led him to build a high tower in his vineyard from which to gaze at nature's scenery. The garden was far too spectacular to use for a parade field, but the tower outside the garden wall could definitely serve military purposes. The entire estate was on high ground, which not only gave it some military value as a potential garrison, but provided safety from all but the most epic of floods.

Binaizek prattled on about the cutting of such-and-such stones, the many years it had taken to build the place into what it now was, and the difficulty involved in building structures of the various shapes on display. Adonaizidek uttered not one single compliment. Taking his cue, his advisers and attendants did their best to hide how impressed they were with the property. This discouraged Binaizek to the point that he spoke less and less as he showed each area of his property. The priest of Enki chanted louder as they went.

When the tour was done and they all sat for a meal, Binaizek finally asked the king, "You don't like my estate, Your Majesty?"

Adonaizidek tipped a goblet of wine to his lips, then said, "Oh no. I do like it, very much."

Binaizek's furrowed brow slackened with relief. He smiled and took a sip of wine for himself.

"...As a site with much military potential," the king continued, watching Binaizek with amusement.

"I..., um... don't understand, Sire," Binaizek said, brow furrowed once again.

Adonaizidek bit off a hunk of bread and spoke as he chewed. "Let me tell you a story."

Binaizek blinked rapidly, put down his spoon, wiped his mouth and gave the king his undivided attention.

"Once there was a sculptor," Adonaizidek began. "He chiseled out statues and busts and other artwork that were prized and renown throughout the land. After many years of selling his sculpture, he amassed a fortune, and used that fortune to buy himself many fine things. But the most prized of all his possessions was a magnificent horse."

Adonaizidek told the tale in an almost-bored tone, with lazy, careless gestures, but when he glanced at his host, he noted Binaizek hanging on every word. "Now the sculptor lived under the protection of a great king. The king was both wise and powerful. One day the king paid a visit to the sculptor. When the king saw the horse, he asked his host if he was loyal to king and city.

"'Of course I am,' the sculptor said. So the king asked that the horse be made a gift to him. Because of the sculptor's loyalty, he presented his horse to the king as a gift."

Binaizek bit his lip, eyes darting around nervously.

"The king hitched the horse to his chariot and went for a ride," Adonaizidek continued. "Then he gave the horse back to the sculptor. Not only that, but he made a gift of an entire chariot team of horses, reserved a place for the sculptor at the king's table for life, and increased the sculptor's lands and riches fourfold. The sculptor had proven he was loyal, and the king was exceedingly generous to those he could trust."

Once finished speaking, Adonaizidek gazed intensely at the architect.

Binaizek was afraid to speak. He had no idea why his loyalty would be in question. Still, the king had the authority to have people thrown in prison or put to death, merely on his command, whether someone was guilty or not of disloyalty...or any other crime. Binaizek wanted to assure the king of his loyalty, but to make a gift of his home...the place he had worked so hard and so long to build into what it now was? Granted, the implication of the story was that everything would be given back, with interest...

"Well?" Asked the king.

Binaizek played dumb. "Well what, your Majesty? I own no horses as glorious as the one you describe."

The king's eyes narrowed, but a sly smile stretched his lips. He spread his arms out, expansively. "But you own this house, and the land it sits on."

Binaizek's mouth was parched. He tried to lick his lips, but his dry tongue stuck to them, and he had to forcefully yank it back in his mouth. He could not afford to be counted as an enemy of the king. He'd seen what happened to others who were considered disloyal.

"By all means, my king," Binaizek said, in a quavering voice, "p-please consider my estates a gift to you, as a token of my loyalty."

"You're making a gift of all your lands, to me?" Adonaizidek asked, with mock surprise.

"Yes, Sire."

"Your lands, and all that are on them?"

Binaizek gulped. "Yes, Sire."

The king wiped his mouth and stood from the table. "A most generous gift. Thank-you." He turned to an assistant. "Have General Puadir move the Royal Guards here immediately, and begin converting the stables into their barracks. Instruct the palace servants to come look this place over. I want this house ready within a week to hold court here if necessary."

"But, Sire," protested Binaizek, "those sound like permanent changes."

Adonaizidek raised his eyebrows. "Well, they are permanent. Not that it's any concern of yours what I do with my own property."

Red in the face, Binaizek stuttered, "B-but...the story..."

"Oh yes. Quite a story, wasn't it? Nice, happy ending. Children would enjoy it, I think."

As the king turned to leave, his entourage abandoned their meal and rose to follow him.

The king turned to another attendant, pointing to Binaizek. "Oh, this man and his family belong to me, now. They all need slave collars as quickly as the smiths can forge them."

"Slaves!" Binaizek cried, outraged.

"These lands and all that are on them belong to me, now," Adonaizidek said, with a smirk. "And I'll not warn you again that a slave must mind his tone when speaking to the king."

Binaizek felt dizzy and short of breath. His face changed color from normal, to red, to pale white, to almost blue. Then he fainted.

Adonaizidek stepped outside, and began dictating to his attendants the changes he wanted made to the house and garden. He was interrupted almost immediately by the arrival of a messenger in a chariot.

"O King, live forever," the messenger said, after dismounting and bowing before the king. "King Addar has arrived from Bet-Yariq with a small party and awaits you at the palace.

Adonaizidek pursed his lips, pondering this for a moment. "it must be important, for Addar to make the trip unannounced. Well, I did want to meet with him, anyway."

He nodded at his equestrian slaves, who hurried to ready his chariot.

King Addar was physically as big as Adonaizidek—perhaps even a bit larger. And his city was much more heavily fortified—easily the strongest in the region. But stature and military might notwithstanding, Addar had called on Adonaizidek. He needed something, which put him squarely in the subservient position.

Adonaizidek made him wait even longer than necessary, just to remind him who had the upper hand. And, Adonaizidek being last to enter the throne room, Addar was obliged by custom to rise upon his entrance.

Addar, his bodyguards, and Adonaizidek's court, resumed their seats once the king of Urshalayim was comfortably reposed.

He noticed right away that Addar looked out-of-sorts. His face was haggard, and pale. He fidgeted with his clothes and jewelry with unsteady hands.

"It was my intention to hold council with all the western courts," Adonaizidek said. "But I had not yet sent the invitations. Nevertheless, here is the king of Bet-Yariq waiting for me. To what do I owe the pleasure?"

"It's the Yacovites," Addar said. "They've moved down to the Yarden, right across from me. It's obvious they intend to cross there."

"That's just silly," Adonaizidek said, with a dismissive wave. "They'd be fools to attack you. They'd be bigger fools to cross near you and leave their supply lines so vulnerable to interdiction from your army."

"Their spies have been inside my walls, looking over the defenses. I'm telling you: they intend to attack me soon!"

"Calm down, Addar." He pointed, first to the other king, then to himself. "One Gibborite is more than a match for the ten largest, strongest humans. A dozen nations of slave-spawn couldn't breach your walls."

Addar's voice rose and his face flushed. "It's not the Yacovites I'm worried about...it's their god! You've heard about the things he's already done, surely. If not, I can tell you!"

Adonaizidek chewed on his lip and kept silent for a moment. Finally, he said, "I've heard all about this God-Of-Many-Names they worship. But he has bitten off more than he can chew this time. All our gods are banding together to fight him. Have you noticed Nergal's red planet drawing closer every day? Have you felt the tremors? If you haven't visited the western sea for a while, you should go behold it now. Our gods are angry with the Yacovites and their Great Tyrant. With them all joined together in solidarity, there's nothing they can't accomplish. That goes for our cities, as well."

Addar bit at his fingernails as he thought this over.

"Our nations should band together just as our gods are doing, Addar. That is why we need to meet will the other kings in southern Kenaan."

"It had better take place very soon," Addar said, "because the Yacovites might be knocking at my door any day, now."

Adonaizidek leaned forward on his throne. "Look, the Yarden is at flood stage from all the rains. They have to wait for the monsoon to subside, if nothing else. And if they're foolish enough to attempt a crossing before that, you can attack them while they flounder in the muck. The Yarden will kill more of them than all your soldiers can."

"I suspect you'd take this threat a lot more seriously if their camp was visible from your palace."

Adonaizidek leaned back and steepled his fingers. "An alliance is in order, so you know you won't have to fight this war alone."

# A Holiday in Kenaan

Rachav didn't really want to be there, but attendance was unofficially mandatory for all citizens of Bet-Yariq. Disinterest would be considered disloyalty, which was a serious infraction in a city on the verge of war.

The courtyard outside the palace had been completely renovated for the wedding of King Addar to the sister of Adonaizidek. Brightly colored decorations adorned the entire city. All the priests and priestesses were in attendance—most of them participants in the elaborate rituals that had taken up the entire week. Soldiers in dress uniforms were posted throughout the crowd to ensure order and respect during the proceedings.

The first two days had been dedicated to sacrifice. Animals and babies were slaughtered upon the High Places throughout the city. Some of the blood was saved for Addar and his young bride to drink. The next two days were consumed by a sexual orgy on the brink of outright anarchy. The animals and children who had survived the first and second days were fair game on the third and fourth. Some women dressed as men, and vice-versa, consummated their charade with whoever consented...and some who didn't. Rachav had no customers during that period, because the men who were satisfied with traditional carnal relations with the opposite sex found plenty of it available from priestesses and their attending maidens. Next came the two days of the great feast. On the seventh day was the expedition...a huge procession, led by soldiers, with buglers behind them...marched to a spot east of the city where Addar was ceremonially "raised from the dead." The procession then escorted him back to the city and when it reached the gate, the entire army began to shout. It was a terrifying noise. As the din of bugles and shouting voices continued, King Addar was carried to the courtyard and placed on his throne.

The whole experience was unnerving to Rachav, but what made it more so was the silence. Right up until the return of the expedition, no words were spoken in the city...not even during the orgies, or the feast. Everyone kept silence in solidarity with their king, who mourned because he had no heir.

For most of the final day's events, Rachav's family couldn't see much at all, due to the Gibborites between themselves and the courtyard. They relied on the word passed back through the crowd from those closer to the front who could see. But at one point, enough gigantic soldiers shifted locations that there was a clear line-of-sight over the heads of normally-sized people to the ceremony.

Taking advantage of the movement of the crowd, Rachav's father climbed atop one of the ceremonial High Places (a brazen stepped pyramid used for daily sacrifices) for a better view. Nadir climbed up to sit on Anwar's shoulders, which gave him the elevation to see over the heads of the human adults.

"Why are they doing that?" Nadir asked, squinting at the ornate ballet taking place in the courtyard.

"The king is circling the bride and her father," Papa explained, "in order to consummate the marriage. Each time he comes around, the king asks for her hand. But the father doesn't give his permission."

"How long does that happen?" Anwar asked.

"Six times he compasses her, and six times he is denied," Papa answered. "But on the seventh...ah, this is it."

"Wow," Nadir said, whistling. "He didn't waste any time. He tore her clothes right off."

Rachav cringed. Her baby brother had already seen too much this week. She could tell by his tone of voice he was fascinated with what he was seeing now. So was everyone else, as the crowd shifted again and the view was blocked.

Anwar cursed. "What? I can't see. Too many people in front of me."

Rachav couldn't see, either. Not that she really wanted to.

"He sure is rough with her," Nadir observed. "And he's so much bigger. Isn't he afraid he'll hurt her?"

"He's ravaging her," their father said, with an amused expression that sickened Rachav. "He's not worried about anything else right now except..."

"That's it!" Anwar said, and, little brother still piggy-back, climbed the High Place to see for himself.

"Get down from there!" Mother commanded.

All around them, other citizens stared in fascination. One boy about Anwar's age decided he, too, should seek higher ground for a better view. But as he began to climb the High Place, two men grabbed him by the wrists. Rachav recognized them as Abdul, the merchant, and Muamar, the jeweler.

"Where are you going, boy?" Abdul asked.

Before the boy could answer, Muamar said, "Are you excited by what's happening?"

Both of them had lascivious grins as they restrained the boy.

"You're a handsome one," Abdul said, gaze roaming over the boy's body. "And nicely slender."

The boy, obviously uncomfortable by their leering attention, forgot about climbing the High Place and tried to break away, eyes desperately searching the crowd, presumably for his parents.

"No, no no," Abdul reprimanded in a sing-song fashion. "You're not escaping us, you tasty little morsel!"

"You're going to enjoy this," Muamar said, soothingly. "I did, when I was your age. It opened my eyes, and a whole world I had never even considered."

The boy cried out his protest, but was dragged away. He shouted louder and made greater efforts to jerk free of their grip as they went, but nobody intervened on his behalf. Some were oblivious, transfixed by the ritual taking place in the courtyard. Others smirked knowingly. Others looked lustfully at the boy themselves, making crude comments. A few were busy capturing children for their own amusement.

"Disgusting!" Mother cried out.

Rachav felt a little consolation that Mother disapproved of the pederasty that took place in the city...especially during festivals. Maybe she would prod Papa into taking action, and rescuing the boy.

Papa was staring at the performance in the courtyard, unaware of anything else going on.

Rachav was horrified to find that Mother's gaze was also locked onto the conjugal scene before them. She bent slightly to watch it through the space between the legs of a Gibborite in front of her, equally oblivious to the abduction and impending molestation of the boy.

"This only encourages the subjugation of women!" Mother continued. "You'd think we had put these barbaric attitudes behind us long ago!"

So much for consolation.

Reminiscent of the previous day, a chorus of bugles sounded and the citizens of Bet-Yariq began shouting at the top of their lungs while the naked bodies of the king and his bride coupled before their subjects.

"The king will have an heir!" declared a thousand voices.

"We have found favor with the gods!"

"Our city is protected!"

"Who is like King Addar? Who can make war against him?"

Mother continued to stare, like everyone around her, but her verbal condemnation of the act was drowned out by the cheers from the crowd.

With everyone's attention focused on the coital display in the courtyard, Rachav found it easy to slip away unnoticed and return to the apartment.

On her way, she glanced upwards. As dusk fell, the thin cloud cover glowed red from the light reflected off Nergal.

"O Yacovite God," she whispered, "I hope with all my heart that you are different from these other gods. That you don't mandate this kind of insanity. That your people are different from this."

Lightning flashed just outside the city wall, and thunder cracked the sky instantly. She jumped back at the startling boom.

"I will trust you," she said, aloud. "I will trust you."

The heavens rumbled ominously, but spit no more lightning that night.

# Seeking Knowledge, Finding Mysteries

The group of soldiers stood around the remains of the breakfast fire at their customary location inside camp, all paying rapt attention to their L'vim guest, Pinchas son of Eleazar.

"I don't get it," Zuar protested. "Why were they arguing over Moshe's body?"

Pinchas shrugged. "I don't know the answer to that. But it happened."

"And you say the Warrior who opposed Halal was Mikhayel?"

"I think so. Legend has it he's the Prince assigned to Yacov. He could have led us to worship him as a god, like the other Princes have done. But he remains faithful to El Elyon."

Othniel shook his head as if to jar cobwebs loose. "Wait, wait, wait!" He held up his hands, as if signaling an army column to halt. "That's...let's just forget about that for right now. You're saying Mikhayel...or whoever this gigantic being was...changed shape right in front of you up in the Aborim Mountains? He turned into animals?"

"No, that's not what I think happened," Pinchas said, shaking his head and biting his lip. "I think that, for whatever reason, I got a glimpse into different...worlds. Worlds we can't normally see with our eyes. Somehow, though, I perceived them that night, in that place."

Pinchas glanced about the circle of men who faced him. They were all either confused or skeptical. Mostly both. He cleared his throat and tried again. "I think there are many realms...worlds. And what we normally perceive is just one of them." Palms inward, his hands hovered over his shoulders, then swept down and back up his body. "And maybe our...image, I guess...is different in each world."

"Our appearance, you mean," Achan said, nodding as if he understood. "Like in one of the other worlds, the color we think of as blue is actually yellow. Or looks that way to somebody else."

"Yes," Pinchas said, remembering how the surroundings had seemingly changed around him up on the mountain. "But it's much deeper than that. Though if you're implying that the worlds overlap, I think you're right. They all overlap, but we can only perceive into this one. We can only interact with this one, normally. But the Messengers, the Watchers, the Guardians, the Warriors, the Princes...they have access to multiple overlapping worlds. And of course El Elyon sees into all of them."

"Why would you see into the different worlds up in the Abor Mountains, but not down here?" Abidan asked.

Pinchas shrugged again. "There must be something special about that location. That must be why Moshe chose to die up there. But I think this whole experience begs some more important questions."

"Like what? Zuar asked.

Pinchas pointed at Zuar. "You had questions about the way we pitch camp, right?"

Zuar nodded.

Pinchas pulled a stick toward him, which had escaped consumption in the fire. He used the stick to draw a square in the dirt.

"This square is where my tribe camps." He now drew lines extending straight from two parallel sides of the square, then closed it off, completing a long rectangle. "Here is the camp of Y'huda." He drew shorter rectangles extending out from the other sides of the square. "Here's the camp of Dan, Ruven, and Efrayim" The drawing now took the shape of a cross.

Zuar pointed to a triangular shape between two of the camps. "That's how we always camp...with all this wasted space, every time."

Ignoring Zuar's comment, Pinchas said, "So right at the center of the camp is my tribe, and in the center of my tribe's camp is the Temple. The Temple is where man meets with El Elyon. Now, the camp of Ruven includes Ruven, Gad and Shimon, but whose banner do they all rally to?"

"Ruven's," Yebdod answered.

"And what image is on the guidon?" Pinchas asked.

"A man," Daghai replied.

"The warrior who came for Moshe's body," Pinchas said, "in appearance, he resembled a man." He drew a man's face at the base of the southern rectangle representing Ruven's camp, then pointed to the northern rectangle. "In appearance his form was human. But both he and Halal had four different...*aspects*. What image is on the guidon for the camp of Dan?"

"An eagle," Achan said.

Pinchas nodded. "And in one of the worlds I glimpsed, the warrior's image was that of an eagle." He drew an eagle in the northern rectangle, then glanced around the circle of men. "Our god dwells in the heavens. An eagle soars in the heavens."

"What's your point?" Abidan asked.

"I think the eagle is a symbol for The God of Gods," Pinchas replied, then pointed to the western rectangle. "What image is on the guidon that the camp of Efrayim rallies to?"

"An ox," Othniel said.

"In one world, the warrior had the image of an ox." Pinchas drew an ox, then pointed to the eastern rectangle. "And the camp of Y'huda?"

"A lion!" everyone replied.

"In one realm, the warrior had the image of a lion." Pinchas drew a lion.

"I'm not sure I understand what you're trying to say," Daghai admitted. A few others nodded. "So each...*aspect*...of the warrior corresponds to the four outer camps."

"Intriguing," Othniel said, "but what does it mean?"

"Is the warrior really a monster with four heads?" asked young

Zuar.

"No, that's not it at all," Pinchas replied, shaking his head. "I mean, what my eyes saw looked like a man. But what I was able to perceive with more than just my two eyes...he was like an eagle. But he was also like an ox. And a lion."

"The beings you saw sound like some of the bizarre gods other nations worship," Daghai said.

"Yes. But *they* are not truly gods," Pinchas replied. "Living creatures. But the Fallen Ones allow themselves to be worshiped like gods. They were once Princes in good standing with El Elyon, before they rebelled. Obviously, they reveal themselves to the other nations, which is why the descriptions of those 'gods' sometimes sound similar to what I'm telling you."

"So what?" Avnur asked, with arms outstretched.

"So what?" Pinchas echoed, incredulous. "There's a meaning in this! The same exact four aspects of the Warrior who protected Moshe's body are the images surrounding the Temple...on the guidons of the four combined camps. More specifically: around the L'vim camp, which is the human shell around the Temple."

"Well, it's nothing for you to lose sleep over," Achan said.

"I'm telling you," Pinchas insisted, "there's something we can learn about our Creator in this. El Elyon made something like this visible for a reason. It's not a coincidence: the same god who created the other 'gods' also told Moshe to have us set up our camp the way we do."

Zuar rolled his eyes and deepened his voice, imitating his father. "'Don't camp over there...that's northeast of the L'vim. Don't camp over there...that's southeast.' Blah blah blah."

"It's not arbitrary that Hashem had Moshe direct us to camp this way," Pinchas said.

"Fine," Avnur said. "I'll bite. What's the reason?"

Pinchas sighed. "I don't know yet. I'm working on it. These four different aspects of the Warrior—even the ones we usually can't see—are the same ones he told us, through Moshe, to surround his Temple with."

Silence fell over the group as they pondered this information.

"Is there any more?" Othniel asked.

"What is the ox a symbol of?" Pinchas asked.

"Servitude," Achan answered. "The faithful servant."

Pinchas nodded. "Just like Y'hoshua, the chief of Efrayim" He used the stick to point between the eagle and man. "So you have god, and man. God, and man."

"And in the midst of the...cross...is where god meets man," Zuar remembered, aloud, pointing to where the Temple would be in the representation of the L'vim camp.

Pinchas changed directions of his waving stick. "God, man; and here you got faithful servant, and the lion of Y'huda. god and man; faithful servant and lion of Y'huda."

The blast of bugles echoed over the plains. Everyone's attention was drawn toward the direction of the L'vim camp. Thousands of arms lifted, fingers pointing at the Radiant Mist, which had begun to move.

Shouts of alarm and instruction from a multitude of voices blended together into a dull roar. All over the vast city of tents, people dropped what they were doing and hurried to strike camp. With well-rehearsed precision, the L'vim had already begun dismantling the portable temple before most of the Yacovim even knew it was time to move.

"This is it!" Achan said, slapping his comrades on the arms on the way to his tent. "We're crossing over. We're crossing today!"

# The Crossing

Across the Yarden and a considerable distance upstream from Bet Yariq lay a small village where nothing extraordinary ever happened.

Until today.

It was the boys who sounded the alarm. "Look! Look!" they cried, pointing toward the river.

Had they described what was happening, fathers and mothers would have scoffed and shooed them away. Instead, their simple warning piqued adult curiosity. Some villagers walked to where houses didn't obscure their vision. Others could see it right where they were.

The river, which had been flowing at flood stage from the recent heavy rains, had come to a stop abreast of the village. In one direction was churning brown water, and in the other was dry riverbed. Where the two met, a towering wedge of water grew skyward.

The entire village stumbled, trance-like, toward the river, agape watching the awesome, gravity-defying display.

Some began to cry out in fear, and stopped moving forward for a closer look. Many shrank from the sight, and reversed direction, instinctively acting as if distance might protect them from the tremendous power piling the river up in a heap.

In Bet-Yariq it was also the boys who sounded the alarm. Anwar remained atop the wall, while Nadir ran down into the apartment to fetch the family. Not only did Rachav's family ascend to the top of the wall, but so did swarms of other wall-dwellers.

Neighbors opined that the Yacovites were committing the ultimate blunder trying to ford the river that time of year, and where their enemies could see them. They'd be easy prey for weeks, and Bet Yariq's garrison would make short work of them.

Such speculation died in peoples' throats as they got their first glimpse eastward over the parapets. The Yacovite camp was gone. Like a churning carpet of ants, hordes of the desert nomads were crossing a dry riverbed where the Yarden had once flowed. Women fainted and men cried out in stark terror.

"What happened to the water?" Papa asked, to nobody specific. His face was pale and his pupils dilated. "Where is the river?"

Anwar, standing at the edge of the parapet, pointed upriver into the distance. "Do you see that?"

Everyone close enough to hear Anwar over the murmur of the crowd turned their gaze in the direction indicated.

"What, by all the gods, is that?" asked one of their neighbors, observing the rising tower of muddy, churning liquid toward the horizon.

"That's the water of the river," replied another neighbor, scarcely believing his own statement.

The skies were unusually clear today. Several people pointed at the red planet, now hanging as large as a grapefruit in the sky.

"Nergal has dried up the river!" Someone cried.

That made no sense at all, Rachav thought. It is The God-of-Many-Names who stood the water up in a heap so that his people could cross over.

The noise level rose as files of Gibborite soldiers began rushing up onto the top of the wall. With expressions of rage, panic, and everything in between, they bellowed at the civilians to clear the walls and return to their homes. Orders passed down from leaders to their subordinates, and the giants took positions at the parapets brandishing spears, bows, and even boulders.

"I thought they were going to get bogged down if they were stupid enough to cross this time of year," complained one giant to his fellows. "We were going to attack and they would be helpless."

"Shut up and man your position!" barked his commanding officer.

"We're doomed!" another giant exclaimed, oblivious to military discipline, pointing at the tower of water climbing into the sky. "We can't fight against a god who can do that! We can't fight against his army!"

The commanding officer began to scream at the soldier, but Rachav didn't hear all of it, as by that time she was herded onto the staircase leading down from the wall, packed in between the other civilians.

On the bank of the dry riverbed, Y'hoshua watched as the last tribe marched across.

He couldn't stop looking at the ground. It was bone-dry. One would expect it to be at least mud that sucked at the sandal with every step, as recently as it had been submerged under so much water. But it wasn't even moist.

He also couldn't help glancing upriver, expecting the towering mass of water to come crashing down at any moment and sweep his nation away. El Elyon had proven himself a faithful and trustworthy god beyond any doubt...and yet Y'hoshua couldn't help being nervous. Only part of his paranoia was due to the capricious nature of other gods. Mostly, it was because he knew his fellow Yacovim were not deserving of a trustworthy god. Y'hoshua doubted his own worthiness, in fact. Every day was a struggle to conduct himself in a manner that would not disappoint El Elyon

When the entire nation stood safely in formation on the west bank, Y'hoshua sent a squad of soldiers back to the middle of the riverbed. They were hand-picked men, representing all of the war-going tribes. Once near where the priests stood, they erected a pile of stones taken from the valley. Then each man found a large stone in the riverbed and hoisted it onto his shoulder. They hauled the stones back to the west bank and stood awaiting orders.

Y'hoshua signaled to the priests who stood in the riverbed.

Each priest held one end of a wooden pole, and the poles suspended the Arown, which was normally kept in an inner chamber of the Temple. The shrouded, golden chest was not to be worshiped; it was not purported to be a god, or a representation of a god. But it was a sacred object, instrumental for congress between Yacov's high priest and Hashem. Nobody was allowed to touch it, and the only time anyone besides the high priest even saw the shape of it under its tarpaulin was during transit between camps.

At Y'hoshua's signal, the priests bearing the shrouded chest left their spot and marched over. They climbed the bank and when the last one's feet left the riverbed, a loud crashing noise sounded in the distance.

The tribes lining the bank looked upriver and saw the towering mass of water falling into the dry bed. As if invisible walls stood on both sides, no water fell outside the banks on either side, but tumbled forward down the wadi. Within moments the churning brown water had reached the spot of the crossing, flowing at flood stage just like it had been before. A few moments more, and there was no evidence that the miracle had ever taken place, save in the memory of those who had witnessed it.

The priests bearing the Arown followed the Radiant Mist as it drifted westward, and at Y'hoshua's command, the enormous tribal formations marched inland, followed by hordes of women, children and livestock.

The Radiant Mist stopped to hover over a large flat, grassy plain, and the priests came to a halt directly under it. The rest of the L'vim swarmed around the priestly detail, setting up the Portable Temple and their own dwelling tents with methodical efficiency. The other tribes grouped together according to camps and began to form the four rectangles extending like arrow-straight spokes from the square hub of the L'vim camp.

Due east of the Temple's outer courtyard, the men from the fighting tribes stacked the stones gathered from the riverbed. The name of the the campsite would become "Stone Circle" because of this round stack.

While the practiced routine of setting up camp took place, Y'hoshua pointed to the pile of large rocks and proclaimed it to be a memorial of how they crossed the river that day. Years later, when new generations asked their parents about the simple monument, the parents should tell them the story of how El Elyon stood the waters up in a heap, and the nation crossed over on dry land.

Inside their apartment, Rachav and her family crowded around the window. By looking out at an angle, they saw the procession from the Yarden to the plain opposite Bet-Yariq. Mother was strangely silent, but her children speculated aloud about what all this meant.

The Gibborites above Rachav's family's apartment, on the roof of the wall, watched the crossing with fascination, confusion, and horror. Some focused on the strange procedures their enemy followed. Some obsessed about their mean fate, faced with an enemy army which was demonstrably unstoppable. Others gave assurance (without much conviction) that no army could breach the massive walls of Bet-Yariq (especially not the puny little militia men on the plain below them, with their makeshift weapons and lack of chariots or horses).

# Exercising Faith

# (Rachivel)

The asteroid hurtled past Shab-tai in two pieces, Then the halves broke into chunks.

Those who dwelt on Kadur Ha'aretz, though, had no idea this was happening so far away from their own planet. But they were aware of the approach of Ma'adim, even when the storm clouds blocked or obscured their view of the red planet.

Fishermen and those who lived on islands or along the coastlands were vexed by the roaring and tossing of the sea. Diverse locations around the globe were plagued by quakes of increasing intensity. Few people understood that the proximity of the red planet was causing the disturbances they suffered. Most of them assumed that the war god (called Nergal in some languages) was steering "his" planet closer as a sign or warning. Some blamed the anger of him or some other god for the quakes, storms and tidal waves.

El Elyon had done incredible works for his people before, but the Yacovim still tended to doubt him...or at least forget. But it took them a while to forget how he halted the river for their crossing.

The frost bread stopped appearing the next day after they had stacked stones and pitched camp. Fruit was plentiful, growing in the wild. Moreover, farmers and villagers from the surrounding countryside escaped to hide behind the safety of Bet-Yariq's walls, leaving their crops free for the foraging.

With the river crossing still fresh in their memory, the tribes of Yacov remembered how the frost bread had fed them for so many years in the desert, when there was nothing to forage. That, and the sudden variety in their diet, reassured all of them that El Elyon had, and would, provide for them. That's why, when Y'hoshua informed them that they would remain in the camp in the sight of Bet-Yariq's defenders for several days...without besieging Bet-Yariq...they were confident their god would also protect them from any attack from the city.

The Yacovim men younger than Kalev and Y'hoshua, in all the years of their wanderings, had never undergone the Traditional Cutting which all the males were supposed to receive as infants. In reviewing numerous details in his mind, Y'hoshua decided it was time to resolve this issue before the first significant engagement with the enemy west of the Yarden. He didn't want to leave any room for offense against El Elyon, either in doing something they should not, or failing to do something they should.

The wisdom of having the entire army undergo this procedure just outside a powerful enemy city was, of course, questioned–by every soldier from the tribal commanders to the men in the ranks. Nevertheless, Y'hoshua insisted, and the order was carried out.

# Folly or Ruse?

The soldiers of Bet-Yariq crowded to the edge of the wall overlooking the Yacovite camp. For the first few days they had manned their posts and maintained unit integrity, but by now discipline was breaking down.

"There's no soldiers...no men at all...in their camp," one young Gibborite said, waving one huge arm in exasperation. "We should attack now!"

"They could be inside their tents," another soldier suggested.

"Why would they spend days on end inside tents?" Someone else asked.

"We weren't going to need worry about them until summer, because the river was at flood stage. Remember?" the first Gibborite said, with a mocking, high pitched tone. "And when they tried ... however high the banks...they would be easy prey. Well, their god dried up the Yarden and they crossed in one cursed day! What now? This may be the last opportunity we get!"

A commotion spread through the mob of soldiers, and they split apart as if an invisible wedge were driven into them. Words died on lips as Gibborites noticed that their king had strolled in amongst them.

"It's a trap," Addar declared. A circle formed around him and he slowly pivoted as he addressed his soldiers. "They want us to attack, men. This is classic trickery on their part—make themselves look vulnerable, or even helpless, hoping to draw us in." He swept one hand over the plain where the cross-shaped camp of Yacov stretched. His soldiers followed the gesture, and took another look at the camp. "Yes, some of them are inside their tents, waiting with weapons drawn. Others have assumed other well-camouflaged ambush positions. They did this under cover of darkness." He fixed his gaze on one soldier, then another, as he continued. "Why do you suppose they haven't even sealed off the routes to and from our city? They're feigning weakness. Deception, from a nation of deceivers! Don't fall for it, men. They're desperate to draw us out because they know they can't breach our walls!"

Some of the officers voiced agreement with this last statement, and the seed of confidence began to spread through the ranks.

"They think they can dupe us," Addar said. "But our god, and the gods of our neighbors, will smash them to putty against our walls!"

Morale improving by the moment, some grunted or muttered their agreement.

"I'll remind you that that rabble down there has only one god," Addar said, holding up one index finger. "But there are many gods!" He wiggled all 12 bejeweled fingers, then, palms up, pantomimed a lifting motion up toward the sky. His soldiers murmured approval. Addar pointed at the red planet—as big as a coconut above them. "Nergal is ready to teach them a lesson in war. Moloch is ready to feast on their children. Chemosh, and Al Illah, and even Enki, are banding together to fight on our behalf. Gods of fire, of the sea, of storms, and the winds, and of the sun, are joining forces against the Great Tyrant—the one god who would place everyone and everything under his feet, demanding he alone be worshiped. But the many gods will overwhelm the one! And when they've led us to victory in this war, we will all be free from the chains of the Great Tyrant! Our fathers the gods; we, their children; the humans; and all creatures!"

Addar paused after each point he made, making room for a collective response from his soldiers. By the time his speech ended, they were cheering, screaming for the blood of the Yacovites and making gruesome, boastful oaths about what they would do when the puny little fools finally dared to approach their walls.

Rachav heard the noise from above and set down her broom on the way to the window in the hopes of seeing what it was the wall guards were yelling about. She saw no unusual activity in the Yacovite camp–other than the absence of soldiers. She sat near the window and listened, soon realizing that King Addar himself was addressing the wall guards.

He made a forceful, convincing argument, she thought. How could Yacov's one god withstand the combined forces of all other gods? How could the exclusively human army of Yacov hope to make war against the many armies of Gibborites arrayed against them?

She didn't know how; she just knew that the God of Yacov would prevail. He was the father of all gods. Their creator. Of course he would prevail.

She swept her gaze over the camp. What were they doing down there? God or no god, their behavior sure was peculiar.

# A Visit From the Beyond

Women bustled hither and yon with water, wine, poultices and other comforts, but only two men had moved about the camp for the last few days. One of them, Kalev, sighed and tore his gaze away from the red orb emerging ever-larger from the stars speckling the blackness of space. He strolled to the westward boundary of Y'huda's camp.

As usual, the three tents of the tribal commanders were pitched perfectly abreast, near the border with the L'vim. Also per usual, Paltiel and Elizaphan had pitched their tents with the entryways facing each other. Both lay recovering inside their own tent, but with their beds near the open entryways so they could converse across the gap.

Both of them were good soldiers, and capable commanders. But in no small amount of discomfort, confused and frustrated by orders, they murmured against their field marshal, questioning his judgment.

"We could have just as easily had the procedure before crossing the river," Elizaphan grumbled, for the umpteenth time.

"Certainly Hashem can protect us," Paltiel said, groaning from the pain. "Certainly. Nobody questions that. But are we not forbidden to put him to the test? It's like we're inviting attack, with the entire army flat on its back."

Kalev strolled up and squatted right between the two tent entrances, so both men could see him. This quenched the conversation momentarily. Into the awkward silence, Kalev yawned.

"You know," Kalev mused aloud, doodling absently in the dirt with a twig, "if our fathers had listened to Yeshua the first time, our people would already have found our rest. Many years of strife could have been avoided."

Neither general had any response to that.

What Kalev referred to was a reconnaissance mission back when they first came to the border of Kenaan. Most of the scouts had been terrified of the Gibborim in the land, and their terror was contagious. The Yacovim couldn't think beyond the fact they would have to fight the armies of giants—and the tangible gods who fathered them. Kalev and Y'hoshua did their best to remind them of El Elyon's power, and that their god had never failed them. But it was futile. Hence, El Elyon delayed the invasion of Kenaan until every man old enough to serve in the army, at the time of that cowardice, died. An entire generation passed away without claiming their inheritance, knowing their children would get the opportunity they threw away.

With that failure of courage staining the national consciousness, the wise Yacovim were usually careful not to murmur against their leadership, lest it lead to another curse.

"Point taken, Kalev," Paltiel muttered. Elizaphan nodded and sighed.

Y'hoshua's mind was not on that long-ago incident, as he walked the perimeter of Stone Circle. He was preoccupied entirely with the task ahead of him: taking Bet-Yariq.

Intellectually, he still remembered the awesome power El Elyon had brought to bear on Yacov's behalf time and time again. Just days ago, in fact, the way he stopped a river at flood stage, piling it in a heap, so they could cross on dry ground...that should have been enough to smooth over any doubt as to the outcome of the coming war, regardless of the odds. But El Elyon's messenger had told him to attack Bet-Yariq first, without telling him how he was supposed to accomplish that formidable task.

Y'hoshua's stomach was in knots. No plan he could fathom

seemed less than desperate. He felt overwhelmed.

He'd had his soldiers building ladders; training with ropes and grappling hooks. The woman his scouts met inside the city had promised to hang a red rope from a window in the city wall and, in fact, he could see the rope and window during daylight hours. Could he get enough of his men through that window (and other windows, hopefully) and inside the walls to surprise the guards? And if they achieved surprise, could they overcome the guards and get the city gate open? And if they got the gate open, could he get enough of his army through the gate fast enough to catch the garrison unawares? And if...?

*If, if, if.*

It was the best plan he could conceive. But was it good enough? Was it worthy of all the responsibility El Elyon was trusting him with? How could he know? Maybe there was a better plan and he just hadn't thought of it.

The imposing wall surrounding Bet-Yariq loomed up from the mound the city sat on, bathed in a crimson glow from the light bouncing off Ma'adim. Y'hoshua silently calculated the size of those walls for the umpteenth time that night. So intent was he on the challenge of that wall, and what lay inside it, that he didn't notice the figure standing in his path until he was only a few paces away.

The figure resembled a man, facing Y'hoshua with a drawn sword.

The old field marshal stopped in his tracks and slapped for his pommel. The blade cleared his scabbard as the sword leapt into his hand. "Who goes there?" he demanded. "Are you with us, or our enemies?"

It was a natural question. Even though the stranger was about Y'hoshua's size, with Yacovim features, he was unlike any man Y'hoshua had ever seen. He appeared young, but his hair was stark white. His face glowed brighter than Ma'adim or Lebanah. His legs flickered as if composed of flame. In fact, a multicolored aura surrounded him. Y'hoshua was certain this was a god in human form. And that was frightening, because it was the fallen gods who were in the habit of appearing to men.

"I fight for neither you, nor the king of Bet-Yariq," the awesome being replied. "I am the Commander of El Elyon's army."

The instant the words struck him, Y'hoshua knew they were true. He instinctively saluted before sheathing his sword and dropping to his knees, then pitching forward, prostrate.

"What message do you have for your servant?" Y'hoshua inquired, voice quavering, face in the ground.

"Take off your sandals," the Commander said. "You're on holy ground."

Y'hoshua nearly tore his thongs, removing his sandals so fast.

"Be strong and bold, Y'hoshua," the Commander said. "Scrap your current plans for infiltrating Bet Yariq and opening the gate from inside."

"Yes Sir," Y'hoshua replied. "I was afraid it wasn't the best plan."

"The plan was fine. But El Elyon is going to do something great in the sight of everyone. We've already delivered the city into your hands. There will be no way to doubt that El Elyon is fighting for Yacov. Pay close attention: I have specific instructions."

# A Perplexing Battle Plan

The tribal generals had been sitting in the command post tent facing Y'hoshua for some time that morning. Most of them were recovered enough from the Traditional Cutting that they could move around fine, and generally felt healthy. However, after listening to Y'hoshua's battle plan, most were dumbstruck and the rest looked panicked.

Pedahel, general over the Naftalim spear men, cleared his throat. "Um, no disrespect Sir, of course...but I'm curious why you've settled on this...*plan*."

Not just his cheeks, but Y'hoshua's whole face darkened with color. "Because our god so commands it."

Pedahel thought about this, nodded, then leaned back in his seat, resigned to say no more about it. Other chiefs exchanged glances with each other, fidgeted, or simply raised brows over wide eyes.

"Any other questions?" Y'hoshua asked, in a tone that forbid further questions. "Good. I need to meet with the priests. Meanwhile, go brief your troops, so that everybody understands what's expected of them. We're going to celebrate the feast of Pesach just like every year. The morning after Pesach everyone should be healthy enough to march. After breakfast on that day, all tribes fall in parade formation, and we'll proceed under my direct command from there."

Pesach was a holiday to commemorate what happened just before their parents escaped Mizraim.

The generals replied with a chorus of "yes sirs" and prepared to rise and exit. But Y'hoshua gave them one more reminder.

"Again, emphasize to your men that nobody can take any plunder for themselves. No loot of any kind. You are dismissed."

The tribal chiefs filed out of the tent, remaining silent until some 40 paces away. Then some began to talk among themselves.

Bukki strode in between, and abreast of Pedahel and Ahihud. He tugged on Pedahel's sleeve.

"Plunder? Plunder?!? Why is he even worrying about loot?"

"We need to worry about those walls," Ahihud said. "And the Gibborim on top and behind them. I thought we had some elite troops training to infiltrate at night and open the gates."

Pedahel shrugged. "You heard him. El Elyon told him to follow a different plan."

"Plan?" Bukki echoed, incredulous. "You mean what he just told us? That doesn't sound like a plan. It sounds like..." His voice drifted off before finishing the thought.

"It sounds like some kind of ritual," Ahihud finished for him. "Don't we have enough of those already?"

"And priests are marching with us?" Bukki demanded. "They don't go to war. That right there should tell you Y'hoshua is not truly hearing from El Elyon."

Pedahel nodded, but with a pained expression, said, "Look, this whole thing has me befuddled, too. But when Moshe died, all of us pledged that we would faithfully follow Y'hoshua. Whatever he orders us to do, no matter how crazy it sounds...we have to do it."

Grumbling, the other two men conceded the point.

Walking in a different direction, Kalev had a similar conversation with Paltiel and Elizaphan. "Hashem named Y'hoshua as Moshe's successor," he said. "And Hashem has never failed us, even once."

"I know," Elizaphan replied, "but..."

"Consider it a test of our faith. A test our fathers failed, by the way."

That silenced them. Nobody wanted to repeat the tragic mistake of the previous generation.

Similar discussions took place within the other tribal groupings, as well. Nobody liked the part of the plan Y'hoshua shared with them. Nobody understood it. But they all grudgingly agreed to carry it out as best they could.

# A Bizarre Parade

King Addar and his new bride reclined in the palace, sharing wine and figs, when the Palace Guards raised a commotion. The king looked up, toward the doorway of his Day Chamber, in time for a Palace Guard to step inside and bow.

"Your Majesty, the Watch Commander is here from the walls, and requests your audience. Urgently, Sire."

Addar sat up straight. "Send him in."

The commander of the watch rushed into the room, locating his king quickly and sliding to a halt on the marble floor six paces away. His eyes were large and round. He snapped to attention. "O King, live forever! The Yacovites have mustered their army. They're marching toward us, now."

Addar handed the bowl of figs to his wife, but they fumbled the transaction and spilled them. He tried to set his wine cup down on the nearby stand, but missed and it went tumbling as he strode out of the Day Chamber.

The Watch Commander escorted his King up atop the wall, where they stopped at the parapets, facing north.

A massed formation of troops marched toward them from the Yacovite camp, armed for battle. The ranks were 50 men wide, and the columns snaked back toward the far horizon.

Pale as a cloud, Addar turned to his watchmen. "Sound General Quarters!"

The buglers began to blow, and the drummers pounded out the

order. The frantic calls echoed throughout the city while soldiers swarmed to their posts.

It was Nadir who sounded the alarm for Rachav's family. They crowded to the window and gasped collectively when they saw the army of Yacov approaching.

This is it, Rachav thought. She stooped and locked eyes with her baby brother. "Nadir: find Anwar, Faryel and Hessa. Tell them to come here at once."

"Faryel and Hessa are just in the next room," Nadir said.

"Very well. But find Anwar and bring him here quickly." She stood again and called to her sisters.

Mother turned from the window long enough to throw her a scrutinizing glance.

"Mama, Papa," Rachav said, "those two men who came here the other night? They were Yacovites."

Mother covered her mouth. Papa's jaw went slack.

Faryel had just entered the room, ahead of Hessa, and heard the confession. "I thought they were Mizraimites."

"Listen carefully," Rachav said. "They were scouting the city, just as the Gibborites suspected. But I made a deal with them."

"You did what!" Mother cried, with that glare in her eyes that usually preceded an outburst of violence.

"They agreed to spare our family," Rachav explained. "But we all have to stay inside our home. If anybody is outside when they attack, then the blood will be on our heads—not theirs."

Papa thought about this, and gradually brightened. "That's good. You have acted wisely, my daughter. We will all be spared."

Mother took longer to think this through, then asked, "Why should we trust them? They probably lied!"

Rachav shook her head. "Their god hates lies. Lying is the only thing he cannot do. When his people give their word, he expects them to keep it."

"You mean the god who won't even show himself?" Mother

retorted. "The god who can't even settle on what name to be called?"

"Please be careful, Mama," Rachav pleaded.

"Yes, dear," Papa said. "The gods don't tolerate being mocked."

"It's imperative that we contact Shondonah and Dariv," Rachav said. "If they bring their families in, they'll be spared, too."

"Your brother and sister have their own homes," Mother said. They're no longer my responsibility. And it would be much too crowded in here with them."

"Do you want them put to the sword, Mama?" asked Rachav. "Because that's what will happen if they aren't in our apartment when the Yacovites come."

Anwar and Nadir burst in through the front door, flushed with excitement. "They've come!" Anwar announced. "They're forming up around the city now."

"Anwar," Papa said, "go quickly to Dariv and to the house where Shondonah lives. Tell them to come quickly if they want to live."

Addar ordered his archers to stand ready. A few of them even drew their bows, wanting to be the first to loose an arrow. But before the Yacovites came into bow range, they turned.

Curiosity mixed with the fear atop the wall as the garrison watched the Yacovite column march parallel with the city wall, just out of bowshot. They continued to stare, perplexed, as the army circled the city.

Not one enemy soldier so much as spoke while they marched, and none of them broke ranks to charge the wall. In between the main column and the rear guard was a small contingent of buglers. Multitudes of feet tramping provided the rhythm for the ominous sounding of the bugles echoing over the plains.

No siege equipment was in evidence, though four ornately garbed men behind the buglers bore, on poles, some sort of object under a pleated tarpaulin. Whatever it was, it certainly wasn't large enough to be a siege engine.

To the astonishment of Addar and all his men who saw it, once the army had marched completely around the city, it performed a column-right and marched away back toward their strangely-shaped camp.

The king and his soldiers were dumbstruck. What had just happened?

# A Baffling Ritual

The alarm sounded again the next day. Soldiers hurried to their posts, and the king joined the guard atop the wall.

Here came the army of Yacov, in one massed column, 50 men wide and leagues long, silent except for the tramping feet and the dirge of the bugles.

The soldiers were still worried, but not as panicked as the day before, as they took their posts. Some of the same commands and warnings were given as the day before, but with not quite as much enthusiasm. Only one archer drew his bow, but would relax the draw without nocking an arrow.

In the apartment below, Rachav's entire family gathered around the window. Rachav's young nephew, the son of her brother Dariv, whistled. "How many soldiers is that?"

"Maybe a million," Anwar replied. "Maybe more."

"I'm sure you exaggerate," his aunt Shondonah said; but watched the dark, menacing formation creep toward them with a worried frown.

"You said yesterday they just marched over, then marched right back to their camp?" Dariv asked.

"They circled the city once, then went back," Papa replied.

"So perhaps they had a close look at the walls, then thought better of it?"

"Well, they're coming again today, so I suppose not," Papa said.

"What's their leader's name again?" Dariv asked.

"Y'hoshua."

"Perhaps Y'hoshua forgot the siege equipment, and so delayed the attack for a day," Dariv mused, waving toward the Yacovite army. "Rather embarrassing for a king, I'd wager."

"They have no king but their god," Rachav said.

"They don't have siege equipment today, either!" Nadir announced, chin resting on the windowsill.

Papa turned to Rachav and said, "You did right, daughter, by making a deal with those Yacovites. With a god on their side who can do what we saw him do to the river, there is nothing that can stop them. They will conquer this city. I feel sorry for our neighbors, but at least we will be spared."

As the day before, before the army drew within bowshot, they turned, and circled the city.

Both Addar and his soldiers were dumbfound by the strange behavior. After completing another trip around Bet-Yariq, the column turned and marched away back toward their camp again. Soldiers atop the wall cried out and cursed from their confusion.

When Yacov marched out from Stone Circle the third day, the city was absolutely silent. Having heard what Yacov had done to other enemies, and what their god had done for Yacov, Bet-Yariq remained fearful. But at the same time, many were anxious for the attack to begin, just to be spared the gnawing suspense.

The city waited to see if today the war began, or if just another anticlimactic marching display would take place. When the formation turned to circle the moat, a buzz of a thousand mutterings broke the oppressive silence. When their enemy turned back toward their camp, cries of outrage burst forth from nearly everyone.

That night, rumors circulated through Bet-Yariq that the Yacovites were working some sort of magic against the city with their marching, circling ritual. King Addar heard some theories repeated by members of his court, but had a theory of his own that he kept to himself for the time being.

On Day Four, the city was even more terrified than it had been on Day One, imagining what devastation the Great Tyrant would inflict upon them after his followers completed their marching ritual. Day Five was similar to Day Three—observers numb or catatonic, watching to see if anything different would happen, but subconsciously assuming it wouldn't.

On Day Six, the bravest of the Gibborites began to taunt the enemy below the walls.

"I see you're going for a walk again—wouldn't you like a change of scenery?"

"Are you hoping to put us to sleep up here?"

"Maybe they think we'll surrender one of these days!"

The Yacovites were speechless as usual, which encouraged their antagonists to taunt them all the more boldly.

"What's the matter—you forgot your siege equipment?"

"Hey you: third soldier back in the 482nd rank—your sandal is untied!"

"What is that down there—a colony of ants?"

"They must know we're having a picnic up here!"

The comments became louder and bolder, and more Gibborites joined in. The spirit spread and strengthened through the garrison. The fear drained away, as they fed on each others' truculence. They accused the Yacovites of cowardice, as if the Gibborites' own panic had transferred to their enemies. After this, Addar's soldiers worked themselves into a frenzy.

"Enough of this waiting around!" one of them said. "Let's go down and attack!"

Hundreds voiced their agreement.

"Obviously they don't want to fight! If they did, they would have done more than march here and back!"

Had Addar waited any longer to interrupt, the ensuing mob insanity might never have been broken.

"You fools!" bellowed the king. "That's exactly what they want! It's just another ploy to entice you down there outside our walls! Can't you see? They've been trying this for weeks—one trick after another. Well, I'm not going to let them use your gullibility to their advantage!"

His men reluctantly fell silent. Addar turned to the commander of the guard. "Keep the normal guard on watch. Everyone else can stand down. Dismiss for the night. We'll see if they want to try this ruse again tomorrow."

# Day Seven

Westward, black storm clouds spit lightning and torrents of rain. The ground rumbled and vibrated underfoot. In the clear section of sky over the plains of Bet-Yariq, the red planet hung, looking the size of a melon.

Predictable as sunrise, the army of Yacov marched out and circled Bet-Yariq the next day. The Gibborites were obliged to refrain from undisciplined uproar like the day before, remembering the admonition from their king, but many still grumbled.

In Rachav's apartment, the children had grown bored and didn't even bother going to the window. Rather than discuss the Yacovites and the possibility of a siege, the adults bickered about the cramped conditions in the apartment, and when the extended family would return to their own homes.

Then, rather than turn back toward Stone Circle, the Yacovites continued marching around the moat after their first circuit.

An excited buzz grew among all those watching the procession. After six days of the same exact ritual, here was something a little different. Observers speculated as to what this variation could mean. Perhaps the Yacovites were growing desperate, hoping to speed up the spell they were casting. Or perhaps their sinister magic required them to now circle the city twice a day for some length of time.

The priests of Al Illah noted that this was occurring on the day of the new moon—Al Illah's holy day. They couldn't see the new moon, since Nergal dominated the sky. Would the Yacovite God-of-Many-

Names also dominate Al Illah somehow?

The observers were even more perplexed when the Yacovites continued compassing Bet-Yariq for a third time.

The army of Yacov made three more orbits before King Addar exploded in rage, "They're making a mockery of my wedding ceremony!"

Everyone who heard the king thought back to the festival. Not only was the elaborate ritual meant to memorialize the marriage of the king; it was also supposed to weave a net of supernatural protection over his kingdom, like many rites designed to appease the gods.

If Yacov's bizarre behavior was indeed intended to be a mockery, that meant the arrogant Invisible God was taunting Addar's god.

Salmon marched in approximately the middle of his tribe's formation. Beside him were the men he commanded; in front of him were other fifties, their commanders, and those who commanded them. For the thirteenth time in a week, he saw Rachav's window in the city wall coming into view. It was easy to spot because of the red rope hanging from it.

Unable to speak during these daily parades, he pondered that rope often. Had the city not been shut up tight in preparation for a siege, someone who ventured outside the wall would doubtless notice the rope and wonder as to it's purpose—probably causing Rachav's family no small amount of trouble. As the ground under his feet rumbled with tremors, and Nergal loomed so huge in the sky as to threaten a collision of planets, Salmon also wondered how it would be possible to protect her family when the battle was joined. Salmon gave his word—something he almost never did—and was concerned by the prospect that an entire family might die because they trusted his word.

Beyond that, Salmon found himself thinking about Rachav a lot in general. There was a kindness and feminine warmth in her that shined through the stigma of her profession. He pondered the contradictions she embodied.

There wasn't much else to do during the daily marches.

How could a decent human being live amongst such debauchery as what went on in that city? How could she not be as horrified as he and Pinchas had been? And yet, when he remembered her eyes, he couldn't help thinking there was more to her than he wanted to give credit for.

At that moment, Rachav turned from the window in her apartment, sensing that something was wrong. She glanced around the room, counting heads, noticing that some were missing. She ran from room to room, and found Faryel playing with her niece, but couldn't find Hessa anywhere. She cried out, frantically, for her sister, inciting the other adults to do the same.

Papa inquired of the other children about Hessa. It was reported that she had stormed off after an argument with Anwar, saying it was too crowded in the apartment; and declaring her family to be stupid for hoping the god of the Yacovites would save them because they stayed inside. They were also stupid for believing there was anything to be saved from.

Rachav wept openly, and soon Faryel wept with her.

Y'hoshua led the army around the moat, silently, save for the ominous music of the bugles. Today was unique—this was supposed to be their day of rest, yet they were marching longer than they had all week. And the Arown, which was supposed to stay in the place set aside for it inside the Temple, was circling the city prominently in the procession, borne by four priests on poles. Yet all this had been specifically mandated in the orders given Y'hoshua by the awesome Commander of El Elyon's Army.

When the Yacovim came full-circle for the seventh time that day, Y'hoshua called a halt. The dirge-like melody ceased, and the priests blew a long, loud note from their bugles. Turning to face his troops, Y'hoshua commanded, "Shout! Hashem has given the city into our hands!"

The tribal generals under Y'hoshua relayed the order by shouting themselves, and the entire army bellowed a battle cry that echoed off the imposing walls they surrounded.

Y'hoshua felt the vibration of the ground under his feet grow worse. He glanced out toward the plains and saw a huge ripple moving across the land, like someone's leg moving under a blanket. The huge crustal tide swept directly toward them and those who saw it braced as best they could.

The ground heaved them up in the air and most fell sprawling. Then the ripple was beyond them and water splashed up and out from the moat, which lay cracked, broken and churned in the aftermath. The crustal tide advanced toward the formidable walls of Bet-Yariq.

Inside Rachav's apartment, Shondonah fainted when she saw what the crustal tide had done, and that it was heading straight for her. Mother screamed, as did Faryel and Dariv's wives. Shondonah's husband ran for the front door. "We have to get away from the walls!" he exclaimed. "We'll be crushed!" Rachav called after him in protest, but he was gone.

Whatever scoffing jeers the Gibborites atop the walls had ready to hurl at their puny adversaries froze in their throats as the crustal tide heaved up the ground under the moat and continued toward the city wall. The stones of the structure lurched under them, then came apart. In a matter of seconds, the legendary wall was fractured into a million pieces. Chunks of stone and gigantic warriors mixed into an avalanche that hit the ground with a tremendous rumbling crash as the crustal tide swept through the entire city and its wall, razing it to its roots.

All except in one place.

Salmon wasn't aware he was holding his breath, until his lungs stung him enough to realize he needed to suck air. The city was reduced to rubble in a matter of seconds—except for one jagged section of wall. That surviving part of the wall had a window with a red rope hanging out of it. He stared at the scene with a slack jaw until his old general, Kalev, burst on the scene to capture his attention.

"Let's go!" Kalev shouted. "Straight in! Let's take the city!"

The bugles continued blowing "Attack." Salmon faced his fifty, shouting, and motioned with his spear arm for them to follow him.

The entire army broke formation and charged straight in. The moat was no obstacle, since the water had drained into the cracks in the ground. The once-mighty walls were now just a circular pile of ruins that made the slope of the mound higher. The city inside the erstwhile barrier was leveled. Those still alive within it were either wounded or dazed.

The warriors of Yacov tightened the circle as they advanced. Swarming in between piles of rubble, the tribes began to overlap and mix.

Titanic warriors either banded together or faced the Yacovim alone as the noose tightened around the city's surviving resistance.

Othniel and several others surrounded a group of nine Gibborim. The Gibborim were trapped, but the superior reach of their spears prevented the Yacovim from getting in close enough to inflict any damage. They also had the advantage of "high ground" from their vastly superior height, and could thrust their huge spears down behind where the warriors of Yacov normally held their shields. In this way, one of the young Yacovites was speared through the shoulder, and staggered back, bleeding bad.

Othniel wondered how this stand-off could be broken. He decided that the only way to get past the reach of the enemy was speed. If he could dart past their spear tips fast enough...

Just as he was thinking this, a sword-wielding warrior from Gad, who had mixed in with them, charged through the ranks and somersaulted under the legs of one of the giants. As he rolled to his feet behind the enormous spear man, his sickle sword flashed out, hamstringing the giant. But before most in the vicinity had time to register what had just happened, he leaped into the air and thrust his sword into another Gibbor's back. By grabbing onto that one's belt and bracing one foot against his victim's massive thigh, he achieved for himself a springboard, and the leverage to launch himself at a third Gibbor.

As the giants turned inward to deal with the tempest among them, they exposed themselves to attack from the Yacovim cordon.

"Let's go!" Salmon bellowed. "They're ours, now!" And he charged forward, thrusting his spear into the side of a giant, in the space between the breast and back plates.

Like lions hunting large prey, the smaller warriors closed in to engage the trapped giants, who now were stifled, and getting in each other's way. The giant with the slashed hamstring toppled to one side, using his shield to break his fall. With the gigantic spear pointing up at a useless angle, Othniel surged forward, grabbed it, then used it as a lever to crank the giant's wrist around into an unnatural angle. The weapon popped out of his grasp. Othniel stomped on the giant's sprained arm, and thrust his own spear into the giant's neck.

Other warriors of Yacov exploited the situation and scored their first kills. The giants' makeshift defense crumbled, and Othniel's comrades picked them apart.

The Gadim swordsman (Adonijah son of Yaddom, whose name would be famous throughout all the tribes by the end of the day) proved to be instrumental in the dismantling of many a Gibborim unit. His agility, instincts, skill with a sickle sword, and ferocity, made for many a quip about how he might as well be the giant, and the Gibborim be the runts.

Near Othniel's first skirmish, a lone giant charged Yacov's advancing line. Daghai and Achan ran to meet him, splitting up to come at him from two sides. The giant swung his pike in a deadly blur. Achan slipped under the arc of the weapon and stabbed upward with his spear, piercing the giant's stomach under his armor. The giant roared in pain, swinging his pike directly at Achan. Achan dove under the swing, rolling into the giant's ankles. The giant tripped over Achan and fell forward, where Daghai pounced on him, delivering the death thrust into the back of the neck.

Achan and Daghai exchanged a glance and a nod, then resumed the advance with their countrymen.

Most of the sling-bearing men of Yissakhar carried no other weapons as of yet, and so were trained to march behind spear men—usually Y'hudim, whom they pitched tents beside in camp. But after most of the warriors with spear and shield had passed over one neighborhood in the city's ruins, the rubble shifted right in front of a unit of slingers, and dozens of giants shot to their feet from where they were hiding in ambush. The Yissakharim were completely surprised, and their hastily aimed stones bounced harmlessly off Gibborim armor, or missed completely. Eliab retreated with a jump and backward scramble until he could reload his sling with another stone. He slung one, then another, and another, as fast as he could load, wind up, and release.

The giants charged, and the slingers fell back, unable to halt the counterattack. It looked like a breakout was underway.

Y'hoshua stood atop a pile of wreckage, surveying the battle, with his runners, buglers, and guidon bearers standing by. He noticed the ambush and impending breakout

."Yissakhar ran into some trouble," Y'hoshua said, mouth inclining toward his runners, but eyes still fixed on the action. "I want Ruven to push in on the left flank, and Gad on the right. Isolate and eliminate. Then Yissakhar can reorganize quickly and fall in behind Z'vulun."

"Yes Sir!"

The three relevant runners took off toward the respective tribes to relay the orders. Guidon bearers for Ruven, Gad, and Yissakhar ran to raise their tribal banners behind the buglers, who blew the appropriate commands. Y'hoshua signaled with his javelin, for good measure.

The worried slingers were relieved to see hundreds of spear men rushing to their relief on the left, and swordsmen on the right.

One of the swordsmen was Adonijah, who again tumbled forward between the legs of a bare-headed giant and struck upward with his sword, inside the armored kilt of the giant, who screamed and staggered back, falling and busting his huge, oblong head open on a chunk of masonry protruding from the rubble.

Abidan made a war cry as he wound up for a throw, and the cry spread through the ranks as waves of Ruvenim spear men crashed into the giants, driving them back into the swords of the Gadim now behind them. Abidan released his shot, and the smooth stone hit one Gibbor in the eye. The giant went down, clutching his bloody face where its eye had been. Other slingers let fly when they had clear shots, and the giants winced, flinched, and seemingly danced as if a cloud of hornets were stinging them. They were stabbed and sliced up with swords and spears.

While his army mopped up the last pockets of resistance, Y'hoshua again turned to his runners. "Remind all the tribes that nobody is to keep any loot for themselves. No trophies or plunder."

Before the Y'hudim runner departed, though, Y'hoshua pulled him aside, pointing to the jagged section of wall still standing. "Find Salmon and tell him to go fetch the woman who helped him. And her family."

"Yes Sir!" the runner replied, and raced off.

Y'hoshua turned to his buglers and locked eyes with the son of the High Priest while gesturing with his javelin in a beckoning motion.

Pinchas strode over to the old field marshal and asked, "Yes Sir?"

Y'hoshua pointed to the precariously standing portion of wall. "Head over there. When Salmon arrives, join up with him. Bring out Rachav and her family, and escort them back to Stone Circle. You know where to put them?"

Pinchas nodded. "I noticed the extra tents you had pitched in camp, with nobody staying in them."

"Good. When you get them there, have Salmon stay with them until I get back, and have a chance to debrief them."

"Yes Sir." Pinchas hurried off to make it happen.

# Annihilation and Exception

# (Rachivel)

The asteroid chunks continued to fragment as they passed Shabtai and hurtled on toward the orbit of Tzedek.

For those of you who suspect that the storms, tidal waves and quakes were caused by the approach of Ma'adim, you are correct. That is not, however, to say that El Elyon didn't give his people this victory–for it was he who set the red planet in that intersecting path. He adjusted the planetary orbits long before, to achieve his purposes–of which the effects of Ma'adim's gravitational pull that day were only part.

Of course the Yacovim didn't know all this. Having only a rudimentary grasp of astronomy, or any sort of science, they didn't know exactly how this miracle was accomplished. They only knew that they obeyed the seemingly ludicrous plan presented to them through Y'hoshua, and after they had fulfilled their part, the walls of Bet-Yariq came down just as promised.

As some citizens of the city had noted over the years, the mortar which held the cut stones together was of a different color in some sections. In the section Rachav and her family lived inside, a mortar had been used that was strong enough to hold the stonework together when the rest of the wall collapsed. Barely; but barely was enough. That mortar had been mixed in a different way from a different substance. For those who believe it was merely coincidence that Rachav and her family lived in the section built thusly...well, coincidence is a foolish concept.

After the walls came down, the battle in the human dimensions was a walk in the garden. The more important battle took place where the soldiers did not perceive it.

While Al Illah's offspring fell to the much smaller Yacovim, Al Illah himself was confronted by Mikhayel. Their swords flamed to life and they closed with each other in the space over the city. Drawing strength from the new moon and the rivers of blood spilt in the recent child sacrifices, Al Illah swung a decapitating blow. But Mikhayel ducked under it and swiped his own fiery blade up across his opponent's torso. Wincing from the pain, Al Illah nonetheless thrust his sword toward Mikhayel's belly. But the warrior weaved and parried, piercing Al Illah's side with a quick riposte. Al Illah bellowed with pain and retreated.

He fought desperately, but Al Illah ultimately had to withdraw and surrender the city.

The city was utterly destroyed. Of course, outside Rachav's family, the human gene pool had been so corrupted that even some people with no visible Gibborim traits carried the disease. There might have been some genetically uncorrupted children left in Bet-Yariq, had they not been slaughtered in the high places as ritual sacrifices—most of them after molestation by one or more adults in the temple sex rituals. What adults in the city weren't genetically corrupted were morally incorrigible, as they approved of all the abominable practices around them.

Speaking of molestation, all the animals in the city were corrupted as well, and genetic tampering had turned some of them into grotesque monsters.

Y'hoshua burned the city to the ground, and pronounced a curse on anyone who might rebuild it.

Most of the soldiers understood that the city had to be destroyed, but some thought the prohibition against taking plunder was unreasonable. "Spiritually charged" items are part of a concept unfamiliar to many, but they were common in Bet-Yariq. Curses and other spiritual infections could be transferred through inanimate objects. El Elyon wasn't against his followers taking plunder, *per se*–the prohibition against it in Bet-Yariq was for their protection. But even those who didn't understand, or believe that, obeyed simply because they feared angering their god.

Not all of them though, unfortunately.

# A General's Discouragement

Yebdod was one of the few casualties of the battle. A wounded Gibbor had kicked him in the chest, breaking ribs with a massive foot. Soldiers of Yissakhar brought Yebdod back into Stone Circle on a litter, and a small crowd gathered around him. A girl named Shoshanah, Aksah, and his mother tended to him. Though he was in considerable pain, he wasn't coughing up blood, which was a good sign.

With the smoke of Bet-Yariq pluming into the sky beyond Stone Circle as dusk darkened to night, Yebdod's comrades brought him to the cookfire, laid him down gently and tried to make him comfortable.

"Does it hurt?" Zuar asked, sincerely.

"No, Zuar, it feels wonderful," Yebdod replied. "You should go out and have this done as soon as you can."

The others laughed. "Well, he's still got a sense of humor," Othniel observed.

"I wonder if that Gibbor had six toes on each foot," Achan mused, stroking his beard in an exaggerated pose of deep thought. "Take your shirt off Yebdod, so we can look at the imprint."

Everyone laughed, including Yebdod, who grimaced from the pain of laughing.

"I told you not to make him laugh," Abidan said. "With broken ribs, laughing is no better than riding a galloping camel."

"Well, I wish you'd told me that earlier," Achan said, then cupped his hands around his mouth. "Cancel the camel race!"

They laughed some more, then fell silent when Y'hoshua strolled up to their fire, with Kalev, Paltiel and Elizaphan in tow. Everyone but Yebdod stood and saluted.

Y'hoshua scanned the group, gaze coming to rest on Yebdod. "This must be the injured man. How are you doing, soldier?"

"It only hurts when I breathe, Sir," Yebdod replied.

Everyone chuckled at the quip, including Y'hoshua.

"By all means, then," Kalev said, deadpan, "let's put a stop to that right now!"

They laughed again, a bit louder. Y'hoshua squatted beside Yebdod and squeezed his shoulder. "I heard there's no blood in your spit. That's good. Just stay as still as possible until you start to heal. Move around too much and something important might get cut by the broken edges."

"I'm trying not to move, Sir," Yebdod said, serious now.

Y'hoshua rose and addressed Yebdod's friends. "Men, I hope you remember today for the rest of your lives, and tell your children about what El Elyon did here in our sight. No enemy can withstand him. There is no other god like him."

Othniel nodded, and they all verbalized their agreement.

Y'hoshua gave them all a salute, then located Abidan, pulling him aside. "I need a word with you, soldier."

"Of course, Sir," Abidan said, following Y'hoshua to a spot well away from the cookfire.

"I have a mission I'd like you to participate in," the old field marshal told him. "You'll have to pack light, move fast, and do some climbing."

Abidan nodded. "I'm at your service, Sir.'

"Meet me at the command post once you're ready," Y'hoshua said.

Abidan saluted and marched for his tent.

Y'hoshua turned to Kalev and Elizaphan. "I need both of you to give me a man, too. Should be experienced, with an eye for terrain and tactical considerations. Also needs to be somebody who can keep their mouth shut."

After Y'hoshua and his generals left their cookfire, the comrades resumed their seats. Spirits were high. They rehashed experiences from the battle and joked boisterously. Most of them had an anecdote or tidbit of detail about Adonijah the Gadim. Othniel suspected that most of the tales were passed on from someone else, and not observed directly. Already embellished somewhat, too. But he felt too good to dwell on negative things or criticize, even inwardly.

Aksah, Shoshanah, and some other young women brought fruit, bread, and kettles of stew, which they set over the fire. When she had stepped outside the glow radius of the fire, Aksah smiled and waved at Othniel. He waved back, discreetly, trying not to let her smile turn him stupid. But then she gestured with a toss of her head that he should join her.

Othniel rose and left his friends, approaching warily but encouraged by her friendly countenance.

They exchanged perfunctory greetings, then Aksah asked, "Are you well?"

"Yes. Fine. Not a scratch. Why?"

"What was it like? Were you scared?"

Othniel frowned as he thought about it. "Yes. A little bit. Excited, too, to be honest. But off-balance through the whole thing."

"Off-balance? What do you mean?"

He shrugged and took a deep breath. "We've been going out and marching around that place for a week, then coming back to camp. Today started out just the same, and even though the chain-of-command told us today would be different, it was hard not to assume it was just business as usual. Strange business, that is. As usual."

Aksah nodded. "Understandable."

"But we kept marching around. The Gibborim were taunting us from the walls, but we had orders to keep our mouths shut. I tell you, it got harder and harder to obey that order as the time went on."

"I can imagine," she said, touching his arm, briefly.

He liked her touch. But remembering Achan's advice about the fairer sex, he tried not to let on. "Salmon...everyone from Kalev on down...they told us that Hashem was going to give the city to us. And of course I believe in him. But I just didn't know how we were going to get through those walls."

Light from the cookfires made the contours of her face glow. She looked even better to him than normal, but Othniel was reliving the battle now, and focused mostly on that.

"When I felt that big quake coming, and saw the ground heaving up, then I got pretty scared. I was so afraid, it didn't occur to me that this was how Hashem would knock the wall down. But I kept yelling, like we were told. Then, all of the sudden, the walls were down. Before I even had a chance to let that sink in, officers were yelling for us to charge in. So I charged, with all the rest of them. We climbed through the moat, the rubble, and then were inside, fighting the Gibborim who were still alive. I was off-balance. It was the same old thing every day for a week; then everything happened so fast. The whole city was leveled–all except one part of the wall, which somehow remained standing..."

"I've been hearing about some Gadim warrior named Adonijah," she interrupted. "Did you see him?"

Othniel let out a deep breath and nodded. "I didn't know his name at the time, but yes. I saw him attack some Gibborim that we had surrounded. He was fast, and didn't hesitate."

"He sounds very brave," she said.

Othniel nodded, but tried to suppress a frown.

Be strong and bold. He'd heard that phrase probably a thousand times since Moshe's last speech. Y'hoshua had made it his personal mantra. Adonijah wasn't any more courageous than Othniel. He had been about to attack the giants himself, when Adonijah charged in. The Gadim wasn't more courageous–he just acted faster.

"What's the matter?" Aksah asked.

The voice of her father surprised both of them. "I'll tell you what's the matter: the two of you standing so close–and together without a chaperon, nor my permission."

Othniel whirled toward Kalev's voice. The old general stood a few paces away from them, difficult to spot, where the firelight didn't reach him.

Othniel saluted and stammered, "I-I beg your pardon, Sir. She was just inquiring as to news from the battle today."

"Is there some news you can give her that I can't?" Kalev asked, gruffly.

"It's not that, Sir..." Othniel began.

"Then what is it?" Kalev demanded.

"It's just that I knew you are always busy, Papa," Aksah said, approaching her father with eyes cast down, respectfully.

The reply was technically to what his daughter said, but his cold glare was on Othniel as he spoke it. "No matter how busy I may be, don't ever assume I'm not looking out for my daughter."

"No Sir," Othniel said. "Of course not."

"Back to your mother, girl," Kalev commanded, pulling her along with him.

As she was taken from Othniel, she turned back to lock eyes with him one last, brief time.

Othniel would spend many subsequent days trying to interpret what her expression meant in that moment. Was it apologetic? Desperate pleading? Embarrassed?

He needed to consult with his own father. Surely the marriage could be arranged? But he would wait for a while, and allow Kalev's temper to cool down. The old general scared him.

Rachav and her family moved into the tents set aside for them at Stone Circle. While relieved that most of them had survived, Rachav mourned for her brother-in-law and Hessa—both crushed under the rubble when the walls collapsed.

But rather than being grateful that the Invisible God had spared them, Mother blamed him and the Yacovites for Hessa's death. And, though she didn't say it in so many words, Mother's attitude seemed to imply that Rachav and Papa were responsible, too.

Rachav wept for her younger sister for long periods every day. To a lesser extent, she wept for her now-widowed older sister as well. As the men of Bet-Yariq went, she supposed her sister's husband hadn't been too bad, though he had been an occasional customer of hers.

Also several times a day, something caused her to remember that her profession back in the city was a thing of the past. The prudish Yacovites had no prostitutes among them, and very strict rules protecting unmarried women. Though Mother occasionally complained about the loss of family income, Rachav was grateful for the change. Having no affection toward the culture in which she grew up, she was prepared to completely embrace that of this new nation, with the solitary Invisible God—whatever changes that required.

And there was an abundance of changes. Nothing about this new life was familiar—even the atmosphere. After living in the city for years, a tent in Stone Circle was quite a change all by itself. And it was mostly a welcome departure—the air was cleaner and the ambient noise was far less disturbing. Also, there was some intangible quality that gave her a sense of comfort among these strangers.

Nevertheless, the Yacovites didn't exactly welcome her with open arms. The women regarded her with suspicion, and the men avoided her altogether. For the first few days, she began to suspect she would always be an outcast, as long as she lived.

Then one day after having been given time to mourn those lost to them, Pinchas came to visit with a scroll in hand. Rachav was happy to see a friendly face. Pinchas greeted her warmly, and introduced himself properly to her family. Then he had them sit encircling him, and began to teach them about his people and their god.

# A Costly Message

Soldiers and engineers were busy all over the new military headquarters outside Urshalayim, digging trenches, building fortifications, modifying existing buildings and the like. Inside Binaizek's old house—now a royal palace, Adonaizidek went over intelligence reports and military plans with General Puadir and the senior officers of his army. Outside, a messenger arrived in a chariot, jumped down and ran to the door of the palace.

Guards ushered the messenger into the presence of the god-king.

"O king, live forever," the messenger greeted him, bowing low before him. "I have news of the Yacovites."

"Tell me," Adonaizidak said, with a bland, disinterested tone.

"They have crossed the Yarden. Their Invisible God stopped the flow of the river and piled its water up to the sky. They crossed in a single day with no casualties. On dry ground."

The king maintained his bored tone. "I've been hearing these wild rumors for many a day, now. Surely you've got more news than just that?"

The king's officers chuckled at the preposterous nature of the story—and the messenger's seriousness about it.

Sweat dripping off his nose, the messenger continued, "Furthermore, o King, they have conquered Bet-Yariq and laid waste to the entire city. There are no survivors, save for the family of a woman who collaborated with them."

"What!" snapped the king. The messenger flinched at the harsh noise of the word.

"The city is destroyed, o King," said the messenger.

"If this is some sort of jest, it is not a funny one."

"Bet-Yariq is the strongest city in the region," a king's adviser reminded the messenger.

"Impossible!" Adonaizidek cried, the magnitude of the disaster still sinking in. "How could they have breached the walls?"

"The god of the Yacovites knocked the walls down, Sire," the messenger replied.

"Nonsense. It must have been the same earthquake that toppled our walls," the king speculated out loud. 'It hit Bet-Yariq too, evidently."

"It must have been worse over there," another adviser said, thoughtfully, "to knock *those* walls down."

The king rose from his throne and began to pace. 'I'll tell you what it was: It was Nergal. You see how close his wanderer is in the sky. We've heard what he's doing to the tides in the sea. He's shaking the earth, too. The people of Bet-Yariq failed to please him. He thirsts, and they haven't provided enough blood. We need to increase our sacrifices immediately."

"There was no shortage of sacrifice in Bet-Yariq, O King," the messenger said, still bowing. "They had passed every last infant through the fire in hopes of getting help from the gods. I'm telling you, everyone is terrified of the Yacovites and their god. All other gods are powerless before him."

The king stopped pacing and cried, "We'll just see about that. Guards!"

Four guards rushed in from the door, looking to the king for instruction.

Adonaizidek pointed to the messenger. "Secure him."

The Guards grabbed the messenger, who panicked, struggled, and protested his innocence. Adonaizidek extended his arm, palm-up.

"Sword," he said.

A Guard handed the king his sword and Adonaizidek reared back with it.

"Lord of Righteousness," the messenger pleaded, " I've done nothing wrong! I've only faithfully carried out your orders to the letter! Don't punish me for what others have done, or for me reporting truthfully!"

The king swung the sword. It only took two blows to sever the messenger's head from his shoulders. The priest of Hapy winced at the shower of blood.

"Ah, that feels a little better," the king said. "Send messengers to our neighboring courts. I'm calling a council to resolve this Yacovite problem."

The advisers looked at their king, the decapitated Messenger, then each other, and exited in a hurry.

# Trade-Offs of a New Life

Tremors continued to shake the ground at Stone Circle, threatening more quakes to come.

The army didn't train after Bet-Yariq. The soldiers were allowed to rest, though the generals met with Y'hoshua every day.

Rachav was still adjusting to her new life. The customs of their adoptive nation had shaken the whole family up, and even checked Mother's sharp tongue. Men scowled and women reprimanded her when Mother spoke disrespectfully to Papa. During one of his visits, Pinchas explained Hashem's expectations regarding the roles set aside for men and their wives. Mother didn't agree with these new customs, but feared ostracization from their new surrounding neighbors.

Back in Bet-Yariq, Rachav hadn't interacted with women her own age much. In Yacov, both sexes tended to stay apart during daylight hours, and conducted themselves very carefully when they did mix. Older women taught the younger ones during certain times; and females segregated themselves according to age at other times. It was much the same for males. Rachav was not yet completely familiar with how the patterns sorted out, but she sought out the Yacovite women and went out of her way to help with the cooking, sewing, foraging and other chores. It seemed all the women her age were already married, and most were either pregnant or had at least one child already. The more of those babies she saw, the more she longed for one of her own.

A pang of sadness swept through her chest. Mother had obtained a potion from one of the priestesses back in the city, and Rachav never got pregnant by any of her customers. What she wouldn't do now to have her very own baby...

At first, the other women behaved as though Rachav were invisible. Their conversation would dwindle to silence when she joined them. When forced to speak to her by circumstances, they were terse and flat. But they were adjusting to her presence. They continued to converse when she was in earshot, now. One of them—Shoshanah was her name—told her "thank you" when Rachav picked up some fire kindling she dropped.

There was still a long way to go before she was ever fully accepted, and perhaps she never would be. But she already liked this new life better than the old one.

She went out with a foraging party between meals one day, The women talked and joked as they went; Rachav listened at first, but didn't try to participate, feeling she was not welcome to do so, yet. As she gathered fruits, grain and nuts, she became lost in her thoughts and oblivious to the conversation. When she thought to look around and get her bearings, she noticed she had wandered off from the group far enough that she didn't know where they were anymore.

Several women were gathering out in the valley, but far enough away that she couldn't tell which ones were from her group. Then she saw a figure approaching from the direction of the river, and she recognized the walk. It was Salmon.

She knew the army posted lookouts and guards out in the areas surrounding Stone Circle, and with Bet-Yariq destroyed, she need not fear any local marauders. But she would feel safer if she was with somebody she knew. And someone like Salmon was better still. She stood erect and waited for him.

When he drew near enough for facial features to appear in sharp focus, she smiled. He nodded acknowledgment, looking wary.

"Rachav," he greeted. "Looks like you got separated from the others."

"If you're going back to Stone Circle," she asked, "May I walk with you?"

After a slight hesitation he said, "Sure. Come on." He continued on his way without waiting for her.

She took long strides until she caught up, then matched his pace.

"I didn't recognize you with the head covering," he finally said.

She remembered that he had spent most of his time in the city inside her apartment, where she uncovered her hair out of habit. She was beginning to gather that the Yacovites considered this to be shameful, unless it was a woman's husband who saw her hair. And of course that was not the only thing they considered shameful.

They walked wordlessly together for a time.

"Pinchas has been teaching my family about your god," she said, as a way to open conversation.

"Oh? And what do you think, so far?"

"I think he's the One True God," she said. "The Creator God."

He looked askance at her for a moment. "I'll say one thing for you: it didn't take long at all for you to get serious about religion."

"After what he did to the river?" she asked. "And the city walls? While preserving my family through it all, just like we agreed. Of course your people have seen many things just as impressive. Maybe more so."

Salmon shrugged. "My parents and grandparents did."

Now he was looking forward as they walked but she turned slightly to study his face. "It must be wonderful to have grown up knowing that the Most High—The God of Gods—is himself invested in the welfare of your people."

He sighed. "It can be a terrific burden, though. The heathens can indulge in tremendous levels of wickedness without angering their gods. But El Elyon holds us accountable. The punishment he reserves for us is more fearsome than the wrath of a hundred enemy gods."

"If I were born into Yacov," she said, "I'd be so thankful that the father of all the gods had set aside my people as his own."

He forced a smile. "You're right. But you've been accepted into my people, so share in the gratitude."

She looked away, and her smile faded. "Well, I don't exactly feel like I'm accepted, just yet."

"No?" he asked, innocently. Then, after thinking about it, he frowned. "Well, yes, I suppose that makes sense. It will probably take a while, but if you and your family are willing to assimilate, you'll be welcome here."

"Some people will probably never welcome us," she said.

He glanced at her eyes thoughtfully, but said nothing.

"I'm trying to assimilate," she said. "I want to."

"You'll do fine."

They came to an acacia tree, Several colorful jars and pots were drying in the sun, Under the tree's shade sat a young boy, using an old modified chariot wheel as a spinning platform to shape a lump of wet clay into a vase.

Rachav noticeably brightened when she looked it all over. "Oh my. This is wonderful."

The boy looked up from his work. "Thank-you, Gvirti."

She was unfamiliar with the word, and turned to Salmon, confused.

"It's a term of respect," he explained. "Children address adult women that way."

This was a pleasant surprise, after living under the same roof with a disrespectful younger sister for years. "May I look closer at some of your pottery?" she asked the boy.

The boy nodded. She stooped to pick up a spherical pot with a lid, painted with bright, simple designs. "This is so pretty. It's a work of art." She showed it to Salmon. "Look at the colors. And the shape– it's perfectly round."

The young potter beamed, obviously proud of his work and glad someone appreciated it.

Salmon studied the pot for a moment, then said, "It's got a flat spot." He pointed to where he saw the flaw.

Frowning, the young potter stood, wiping hands on his apron. "Really? Where? Show me please, Sir."

He walked over and followed an imaginary line from Salmon's index finger with his eyes. "Oh. You're right." He stretched his hands out for the pot, and Rachav handed it to him.

She noticed his annoyed expression, and said, "It's a very nice pot, really. You did a great job."

"This one was shaped by my sister," the boy said, rubbing his hand over the flat spot as he returned to his seat.

Salmon resumed his trip back to camp and Rachav went with him.

"I probably never would have noticed that, if you hadn't pointed it out," she said.

Salmon shrugged. "Picking out flaws is something I do as part of my job every day."

"You mean your job leading other soldiers?" she asked.

He nodded.

Rachav thought, again, of her situation. She bit her lip, wondering if she should say what was on her mind. Finally she gathered up her courage and just blurted it out. "You're the only Yacovite I know, besides Pinchas."

He raised one eyebrow.

"It's not easy for me, here. If you wouldn't mind, may I accompany you when I have to leave the camp? At least, for as far as is convenient for you?"

He frowned again. She had an idea what he was thinking. These people had very strict mores regarding unmarried men and women fraternizing. On top of that, she was a foreigner to them. And unclean. "You know, the heathen woman," she imagined them saying, behind her back, "the prostitute." He was counting the cost of her association to his reputation—and she didn't blame him.

"Please," she said. "I won't burden you much. It would just be nice to exchange a few friendly words on a regular basis, with somebody I know. Somebody who won't judge me for what I used to be."

He worked his jaw but still wasn't ready to speak, it seemed.

"You may not understand why it's so important to me," she said, not having realized why, herself, until speaking her heart out loud. "But I've just turned my back on everything I've known all my life a few days ago. And I know this life is better, for many reasons. But still, I'm really out of sorts, here, and I desperately need somebody to talk to. Even if it's talk about something not terribly important."

"I'm not a talker," Salmon said. "You know Pinchas. He visits you regularly, already. And he loves to talk."

He spoke the words with dismissive finality, as if that were the end of the matter. She fell back a couple steps and said no more, knowing that if she tried, she might become entirely too emotional.

Y'hoshua prayed at the Temple every morning and evening, as part of his daily routine. On his way to Temple in the morning, Abidan and two others entered camp and intercepted their field marshal.

Y'hoshua saw them and stopped. They were coated with the dust of travel from the knees down. Their hair and beards were matted with sweat, skin a shade darker from exposure to the sun.

Abidan saluted. "Sir, the reconnaissance patrol is back, all accounted for and ready to report."

Y'hoshua returned the salute and clapped Abidan on the shoulder. "Good. Meet me at the Command Post in an hour."

"Yes Sir," the soldier replied.

After morning prayers, Y'hoshua and the men from the patrol sat at the table inside the Command Post tent. Y'hoshua had questioned them about what they had scouted–particularly the towns of Bet-El and Ahyee.

Now Abidan waved toward the other scouts. "I can only echo what the others said, Sir: weak defenses, a small garrison...it shouldn't be difficult at all. The march up the mountain side will probably be more dangerous than the attack on the city. In fact, we should really only send about three thousands to take it. That's more than enough for the job, and the rest of the army can stay here."

A tremor swept along the ground underneath them.

"What about Bet-El?" Y'hoshua asked.

"Not even enough fighting men to be considered an actual garrison," Abidan said.

Y'hoshua studied the map for a moment, then looked up suddenly and flashed a perfunctory smile at his scouts. "All right. Well, thank-you, men. Get something to eat; clean up; get some rest; and report to your units. You're dismissed."

The scouts saluted and exited the tent, leaving Y'hoshua alone to ponder the information they'd brought him.

# A Foothold on High Ground

The order came down through the ranks that a contingent of select warriors would be detached for the next step of the campaign.

With Bet-Yariq's garrison no longer a threat, Y'hoshua could move onto the weak city he had targeted from before the campaign had even begun. Ahyee and Bet-El would be easy to conquer, yet would give him a foothold on high ground roughly halfway between the north and south extremes of Kenaan. Once Y'hoshua took it, he would fortify it, and it would be literally downhill to nearly every other city in the land.

Y'hoshua's orders left plenty of leeway for his generals to work out their own tribe's plan, but he encouraged them to include, in each one's 250 man force, experienced officers with mostly young troops. This would ensure the green soldiers caught up a bit in terms of experience, under capable commanders who would work a little harder to minimize mistakes. This struck all the senior officers as a reasonable guideline, and their tribes followed it.

Of the officers chosen from Y'huda, Salmon was overlooked in favor of more experienced lieutenants, who were placed in command of *ad-hoc* fifties drafted from regular units. Othniel felt honored to be one of the warriors detached. He and Avnur were assigned to a fifty with a mixture of men from other clans,

As the contingent marched out from Stone Circle, Othniel scanned the camp for Aksah, but didn't see her. It would have been nice to get a smile and wave from her as he left. Their last conversation, interrupted by her father, played repeatedly in Othniel's mind.

Kalev's obvious disapproval stung. He saw this special assignment as an opportunity to prove himself to both Aksah and her father.

An excited buzz spread through the three thousands when scuttlebutt revealed that Adonijah the Gadim was among them, promoted to brevet-lieutenant for the operation. With men like that in their number, and with the incredible victory at Bet-Yariq under their belts, how could anything but glory await them today?

They marched into mountainous country, the rugged uphill slopes getting increasingly steep along the way. Morale started out very high, but was blunted by fatigue over time.

Ahyee came into sight after several hours of the grueling march, and the town's crumbled defensive wall might have normally inspired confidence for the impending action. But by this time, hardly any man could think beyond merely wanting the relentless climb to end. The Yacovim were strung out haphazardly all down the winding path from the lowlands. Paltiel, who had been placed in overall command, signaled for his marshals to rally on him.

The officers were gasping for breath when they reached him. "Yes Sir? one asked, leaning forward with hands on knees.

"You need to get the men into some kind of order," Paltiel said, a little irritated. "Has discipline completely broken down?"

"I'll take care of it right away, Sir," Abidan said. He had been brevetted to the rank of marshal for the operation. "It's just that the climb has really tired them out."

"They can rest after you get them into position on the left so they can guard the flank. There's no way our archers should be out in front of the shock troops like this."

Abidan and the other two acting marshals panted out their acknowledgment, turned, and trudged back to their thousands.

Winded officers yelled orders to their units, to form up properly, and for stragglers to catch up. Tired and irritable voices echoed off the mountainsides, while order was ponderously wrought out of chaos.

Avnur leaned on his shield and turned his hanging head toward Othniel. "If only Y'hoshua could see us, now. We've got javelineers in front of us, with archers and slingers up in front of them."

"This is sloppy," Othniel agreed. "I've never seen us so disorganized. And Abidan is normally a very strong officer. I would never have believed he'd let us get so unorganized."

"Maybe, if they let us rest for a bit and drink water, we'll sharpen up for the last push," Avnur said.

"It's a weak objective," Othniel said, gesturing toward Ahyee, "and El Elyon is the mightiest of the gods. But still, something doesn't feel right."

Paltiel had, indeed, intended to let the troops rest before moving up to the attack. But all the yelling and mobbing around had attracted attention and lost them the element of surprise. Warriors from Ahyee and Bet-El, most of whom were busy repairing their flattened city walls, streamed over the rubble to form up in battle lines facing them.

Shouted orders grew shrill and frantic as the enemy appeared ready while the Yacovim were still sorting themselves out.

The enemy's buglers blew the attack signal. Formations of warriors charged down at the exhausted, disorganized Yacovim.

"Here they come!" somebody screamed.

Adonijah looked over the scene, sheathed his sword, and ran toward the enemy. Shield in one hand, he plucked a banner from a guidon bearer with his other and signaled for his countrymen to advance. All the units were still hopelessly mixed, but as long as the spear men marched forward, everyone else could fall in behind them, with the archers and slingers drifting out to the flanks...

Before most of the spear men could reach the front, a swarm of arrows arced through the air and tore into the massed mob. The Yacovim saw at least a dozen of their brothers and cousins fall, pierced through.

Adonijah turned to address his countrymen, now mostly behind him. "Let's go! Spear men to the front! Shields up! Javelins fall in behind! Archers to the right flank! Slingers to the left! Launch at will!"

With his back to the enemy, Adonijah never saw the fatal missiles streaking his way. He winced when arrows struck him in the shoulder and thigh. Then a javelin came through his back and out his stomach. His eyes bulged and he looked down at the horrendous wound, staggering. He opened his mouth, but only blood came out. He fell.

The Yacovim were stunned, and froze in their tracks.

Another wave of arrows brought down a dozen men, and then they noticed the charging enemy about to close with them.

A handful of slingers from Benyamin, still out in front, turned tail and sprinted to escape the charging warriors. As they ran past other archers and javelineers, those men joined them. Other exhausted Yacovim, farther back, saw them running and also turned to flee. Panic spread through their ranks. Like a rockslide of a few pebbles triggering an avalanche, the force of three thousands was routed in a matter of seconds.

Othniel and Avnur were jostled by fleeing Warriors running past. Othniel planted his shield, thinking the army would regroup to fight once the spear men formed a shield wall, But spear men were fleeing, too.

Then Avnur tapped him on the shoulder and pointed. A group of Yacovim were running right at them, chased by enemy warriors screaming a battlecry and striking them down from behind. Avnur bolted.

Othniel's heart melted in fear. He was all alone, now, and would be surrounded in seconds with nobody to help him. He whirled and fled as fast as his feet would carry him.

# The Culprit Revealed

While Rachav foraged, Anwar and Nadir hauled water into camp from a spring at the ruins of Bet-Yariq. Once the lessons with Pinchas were complete for the day, all the cooking, cleaning, and other camp chores were done, Rachav found an isolated spot in the camp to watch the sky darken and Ma'adim glow. Her younger siblings played. The rest of her family congregated around their cooking fire while digesting supper.

Rachav had a lot on her mind, and nobody she felt comfortable discussing all of it with, so she sat by herself and let her thoughts roam.

A man came into her field of vision, walking slow and swiveling his head as if searching for something. When he caught sight of her, he held her gaze and approached.

She had never seen this man before, and had no idea what his business with her could be. Maybe he was somebody assigned to help with her orientation.

"You must be the prostitute," he said.

She didn't know how to respond, so she just watched as he came up to stand over her.

"It is you, true?"

"Why would you greet someone this way?" she asked. "Why would you ask such a question?"

He appeared to be in his 40s, or close to that age. He had a long face, with a droopy mustache that laid on top of his beard instead of merging into it. "Our women have been wearing the same clothes for many years," he said, then grabbed a loose fold of her dress, rubbing it between thumb and forefinger. "It hasn't worn out in all those years, but still: none of it is quite like this."

"I'm not a prostitute," she said.

"Right. Not now, anyway. Such business isn't practiced among my people. It would be frowned upon." He smiled.

Rachav didn't like his smile. It made her feel slimy.

"My people would frown on it...if they learned about it," he continued. "How much did you use to charge for...?"

Her discomfort was increasing by the second. She hoped her father or older brother would leave the cooking fire and come over for some inquiry or request, but nobody stirred. She searched her surroundings, looking for some means of escape.

Salmon strode into her peripheral vision and stepped up beside the man.

"Benyamim, are you not?" Salmon asked.

The man jumped at the sound of the voice and turned. After a quick visual evaluation of the newcomer, a sneer settled over his face. "And you are

Y'hudim. What of it?"

"It looks to me like you're not welcome here," Salmon said, locking eyes with him.

"Again: what of it? She's a foreigner."

"She's a sojourner," Salmon corrected. "Were you not taught how to treat sojourners with dignity and respect?"

The man turned away from Rachav to face Salmon fully, straightening to his full height. "This woman is a..."

"Be polite, now," Salmon interrupted, wagging his finger with one hand while resting the other on the pommel of his sickle sword.

The man looked Salmon up-and-down for a moment, then at Rachav, then back to Salmon. He pursed his lips, then walked away.

Once the man was far enough away to no longer be visible, Rachav breathed a sigh of relief. "Thank-you," she said, softly.

"Has anyone else threatened you?" Salmon asked.

"No." She thought about his question and her own answer for a moment, then said, "To be technical, I suppose I can't claim that he threatened me, either. I merely *felt* threatened."

Salmon nodded. Looking toward the dark horizon, he said, "I'll see about assigning a guard detail for you and your family. We don't tolerate rapists or murderers. But just because we don't have any among us right now doesn't mean somebody might not aspire to be one."

Still a bit disappointed by Salmon in their last encounter, she wasn't sure how to respond...or if she should even try. But she noticed he was squinting at something in the distant dark, south of Stone Circle. She herself peered into the night, searching for the source of his preoccupation.

The beaten, dejected column of soldiers straggled back to Stone Circle well after nightfall. The cooking fires had dwindled down to glowing coals and most people had gone to bed. The night watch (and others still awake) initially met them with enthusiasm, but it soon became apparent that something was wrong.

Paltiel would have rather faced a rabid bear than to give his report to Y'hoshua. The old field marshal had trusted him, and he not only utterly failed, but three dozen men died under his brief command. For most of the march back to camp, Paltiel searched desperately for some excuse to avoid meeting Y'hoshua face-to-face. But short of his own death, there was none.

Y'hoshua was stunned; then furious; then ashen, before he called for his other generals. What the men in the ranks didn't know is that, afterward, Y'hoshua tore his clothes, put dust on his head, and led his tribal generals to the Temple where they lay on their faces, crying out to the god who had deserted them, after the incredible victory at Bet-Yariq.

Othniel wanted to avoid his friends, some of whom were still reclining around the fire, but Avnur trudged right up to them and began sharing the news. Othniel strode straight for his family's tent, hoping everyone was asleep and he could slip in without waking anyone. But before he could duck inside, his father stepped out.

"Othniel! You're back. How did it go, Son?" Before the last word had left his lips, he made out enough of his son's countenance to deduce that the battle had not gone well at all.

"We were routed," Othniel replied, blankly.

Kenaz let this sink in for a moment, then asked, "Were the enemy's numbers more than what we heard?"

Othniel shook his head. "It wasn't that. We were all worn out from the climb; we didn't form up in time; then before we could even join battle, Adonijah was killed right in front of all of us..."

Kenaz's eyebrows furrowed. "Something is wrong. We've fallen out of favor with Hashem. What did we do?"

"We ran from them. Total panic. I ran like a coward, Father."

Kenaz didn't notice these last words, consumed with pondering what might have caused the catastrophe.

Othniel had been rehashing the disaster all the way back from where their panic flight had ended. The mountain climb; the sprint; the fear; and all the other emotions had utterly exhausted him. He fell into bed and dropped unconscious almost immediately.

A night without dreams would have been merciful, but Othniel suffered one after the other in which he demonstrated cowardice.

While the content of his dreams contributed to his restless sleep, there was also much yelling, movement, and loud talk in camp that night. When his father shook him awake, the sun had just risen and he felt just as tired as when he lay down.

After dressing and stumbling out of the tent, Othniel saw that all Yacov was assembling by tribes. If the Radiant Mist weren't still hovering over the Temple, and the tents not still standing, he would have assumed they were relocating again—as they'd been doing all his life. But that wasn't the purpose of this formation.

Y'hoshua and the tribal generals strode up and down the ranks, addressing the people. Kalev, even more stern-looking than normal, paced back and forth in front of Y'huda, lecturing them angrily. The gist of it was that somebody had broken faith with El Elyon and taken loot from Bet-Yariq; and the guilty party would soon be revealed.

"How will he be revealed?" Avnur wondered, aloud.

"It sounds to me like it was just poorly executed tactics," remarked Achan, under his breath, "not any sort of divine rebuke."

Several nearby soldiers studied Achan closely—especially Othniel and Avnur.

"Discipline broke down on the climb," he continued, shrugging. "Unit integrity was scrambled; the enemy formed into battle order before our forces were ready...it's not a curse, or any act of the gods. Just basic military principles in action."

Othniel kept seeing the image of Adonijah pierced through by the javelin. As Achan rightly deduced, they had been caught exhausted and unprepared. But looking back, it was at that moment, when Adonijah fell so suddenly and finally, that Othniel knew El Elyon had handed them over to defeat.

Part of him knew that the debacle wasn't all his fault. But on the other hand, he kept imagining that if he had acted fast enough...done something...he might have changed the outcome.

"When the order comes down," Kalev called, "we're going to pass and review in tribal order."

The order came down. Kalev called a left face, forward march. The marshals, captains and lieutenants echoed the commands, and the formation began to move, in sync with all the tribes.

Eleazar stood with Y'hoshua as the tribes marched by. When the Y'hudim passed, one of the translucent stones on Eleazar's breastplate lit up. Y'hoshua and the priest stared at each other for a moment.

The culprit belonged to the tribe of Kalev, Y'hoshua's oldest friend.

The officers called a halt, and the formations were given a right face. When the Y'hudim saw Y'hoshua and Eleazar approaching them, a nervous buzz swept through the ranks.

"Why are they singling us out?" a young soldier asked.

"Because the guilty party is in our tribe," an older soldier answered, grimly.

Othniel couldn't believe what was happening. Someone from his own tribe was the cause? What had they done?

The field marshal and high priest passed in front of the tribe, then stopped in front of Zerach. They ordered the clan to step forward, then passed in front of it.

Othniel was horrified—he knew people in Zerach's clan. How much worse must Achan feel, knowing the culprit was one of his kinsman?

When Eleazar passed in front of Zabdi, the stone on his breastplate lit up again.

Zabdi's family was called forward. Othniel caught a glimpse of Achan as they stepped forward. He was ashen—obviously mortified.

Y'hoshua and Eleazar passed in front of the family, and the stone lit up when they came before Achan.

*No!*

No, it couldn't be! This was some sort of mistake.

Y'hoshua's piercing gaze settled on Achan. They were close enough that their voices carried to where Othniel stood in the formation.

"Son," Y'hoshua said, "you best give glory to our god."

"All glory belongs to Hashem," Achan said, with a quavering voice. "He is a mighty god. He knows everything. I see that, now."

"He already knows what you did," Y'hoshua said. "Now tell me—the whole truth."

"I...I have transgressed," Achan stammered, his voice sounding choked. "While we were mopping-up in Bet-Yariq, I saw a really nice cloak from Shinar, and a treasure in silver and gold. So I...I took them, and hid them in my tent."

Othniel's heart sank. He just couldn't believe all this.

"Like every soldier in the army," Y'hoshua growled, "you were told that everything in the city was off-limits, and nothing was to be taken for yourself."

"Yes Sir."

"What part of that did you not understand?" Y'hoshua demanded.

"It was...I didn't...I just...I coveted."

Y'hoshua shook his head, glaring at Achan, then motioned to the runners from the Y'hudim camp, and they trotted over.

"You know where Achan's tent is?" Y'hoshua asked.

One of the three nodded.

"Go there," Y'hoshua ordered, pointing. "Find the Shinarim cloak, silver and gold stashed there, and bring it to me here."

"Yes Sir!" they chorused, and took off at a sprint.

"Every soldier in this army was warned several times to take no plunder from Bet-Yariq," Y'hoshua said, walking in a tight circle around Achan, whose face was downcast, "We don't issue these orders to deprive you of something good. We follow the orders of El Elyon. And he isn't trying to deprive you, either. Is he so untrustworthy that you have to violate his commands in order to provide for yourself; to secure your future? He has taken care of us all these years, and promised to keep doing so, but you have to look out for yourself just in case he stops?"

"No Sir," Achan muttered.

"More often than not," Y'hoshua said, "his prohibitions are to protect us. Objects...material...things...they can be spiritually charged–for good or evil. And these cities we are at war with–they are brimming over with evil. You have no idea what curses and diseases you brought into the camp, to infect your family... neighbors..." Y'hoshua continued moving in that tight circle around Achan, first glaring at him, then shaking his head with bitter anguish. "And all for greed, Achan. Your lack of faith has brought evil into our midst, after we've gone through such extremes to keep our nation morally blameless. Your envy caused our defeat yesterday, and killed three dozen of our men. We can't allow this curse to fester or spread. It has to be removed, to restore us to our god. You understand this?"

After a speechless moment, Achan mumbled something Othniel couldn't make out.

The runners returned, carrying a richly colored robe and two heavy purses. Othniel felt a pain like he'd been punched in the stomach. He'd always looked up to Achan, as many others seemed to. He couldn't have even imagined a scenario like this; but if he could have, he would have assumed Achan to be above anything so petty and unethical.

Y'hoshua examined the stolen items, careful not to touch them. Speaking to the runners, he gestured toward Eleazar. "Make sure, once this stuff is gone, you report to the priests for the purification rites."

"Yes Sir," they said.

Y'hoshua had not just the army, but everyone, including Achan and his family, march to a nearby valley.

So angry his voice cracked, Y'hoshua yelled at Achan, loud enough for the entire nation to hear, "Why did you bring this curse upon us?" He waved his arm to indicate all of Yacov. Then he waved back toward where the Radiant Mist hovered over their Temple. "Our god brings a curse down on you, today."

Quickly and clinically, Achan was executed in the valley.

Just like that.

When he returned to Stone Circle, Othniel was too overwhelmed to speak to anyone, or do anything but sit in his tent, staring into space.

# Overwhelming Redemption

The tribal generals all waited around the Command Post tent, discussing recent events, and what the new orders from their field marshal might be. When Y'hoshua returned from the Temple and entered the tent, they all rose to attention.

Eyebrows furrowed and jaw set at stern angles under his gray beard, Y'hoshua sat at the map table and said, "Take your seats."

Leaning forward, Y'hoshua pressed his index finger down against the west-southwest edge of the ink blob that represented Ahyee on the map.

'I'm drafting 2,500 good men from each tribe," he said, meeting the gaze of the generals sitting closest to him. "30,000 of our best troops infiltrate tonight and hide behind the city, here."

"That's ten times the entire original force," Bukki remarked.

"That's right," Y'hoshua said. "Any issues with that?"

Nobody answered.

"Tomorrow I bring up the rest of the army," Y'hoshua continued. "That's every last soldier, in case you're wondering."

The old field marshal went on to outline a plan that took advantage of the enemy's morale, and recent memory. His generals privately thought the plan was overkill, but asked no questions and raised no objections.

Light bouncing off Ma'adim filtered through the overcast sky and painted the hill country in soft crimson relief that night. Thousands of Y'hoshua's finest troops moved into position on a rocky slope west-southwest of Ahyee, directed silently by their officers with hand-arm signals. Once in place, they settled in for the night. One man napped while the next man kept watch, and officers checked, double-checked, and re-inspected their units for readiness.

At daybreak Y'hoshua arrived with the main force on a hilltop north of Ahyee, facing the city. By prearranged instructions, 5,000 archers from Menashe split off and crept due west to take camouflaged positions in a flat, rocky plain called the Arava. From this location they had a good view of both Ahyee and Bet-El.

Sentries in Ahyee saw the army assembling to their north and sounded the alarm. The Garrison was roused, and the king himself ventured out to oversee the battle. Soldiers shook off the weight of sleep and stumbled to their formations, still strapping on their armor.

"Look who's back for more," one of them said, laughing.

"I guess they're ready for another lesson," said another.

"Happy to oblige," replied a third soldier, gleefully brandishing his javelin.

A tremor rumbled along the ground, and the rubble of their city wall shifted. A soldier of Ahyee peered through the clouds toward the huge red planet. "Shouldn't Nergal be pleased at how we defeated the Yacovlites before? Why is he still shaking the ground?"

"It's the god of Yacov shaking the ground," a comrade said, starting to worry. "The one who knocked our city walls down."

"He may have knocked our walls down," an officer said, "but he obviously can't make his followers fight."

A murmur of laughter rippled through the defenders as they formed their battle line.

"There's more of them this time," a soldier observed. "Wow—a lot more."

"Good!" blustered the first soldier. "Maybe they'll die like men this time, instead of running away like frightened little girls."

"The more who stand and fight, the more we kill," added another.

The raucous laughter increased with each successive boast from their ranks.

The king of Ahyee stood facing his battle line and motioned for silence, then knelt, bowing his head in a prayerful pose. His garrison followed suit. "O mighty Nergal," he intoned, "we thank you for coming to strengthen us in this battle. Let each of us cut down a dozen Yacovlites, and the blood will flow in a great feast for you."

When they rose from the prayer, the warriors of Ahyee roared their battlecry and tensed up like vicious dogs straining at the leash, barely able to wait for the command to attack.

A more severe tremor than before grew into a minor quake, as if in reply. Men on the battle lines struggled to maintain balance as the ground shook under them.

Y'hoshua signaled with his javelin, his buglers relayed the command audibly, and his troops advanced.

"Here they come," announced an officer from the other side." Let's give them another warm welcome!"

The king of Ahyee signaled for the attack. His men exploded from the battle line, charging downhill at the Yacovites.

The front ranks of both armies clashed. Like a heavy stone rolling through tall grass, the warriors of Ahyee seemed to be too powerful a force to be hindered. The center of Y'hoshua's main force gave way and began to fall back.

The king of Ahyee watched the Yacovites turning tail just like in the first battle. He turned back toward the city, where some of his garrison remained. "Join the pursuit! Every single man of Ahyee had better get out there and cut down some Yacovites...right now!"

One of his officers approached tentatively, glancing back at the city. "But Sire, shouldn't at least some of us...?"

"Do I stutter?" snapped the king. "I said every last one of you and I meant it!"

The officer bit his tongue, bowed, and turned to relay the order.

Every able-bodied man in Ahyee grabbed a weapon and charged out to join in the victorious rout.

Meanwhile, the garrison of nearby Bet-El, watching the battle develop, could hold fast no longer. Their courage had soared after watching the Yacovites thrown into panic at the first battle. They hadn't shared in the great victory then, but they wouldn't be denied this time.

With a fierce battlecry, they surged over the ruins of their own city wall and toward the fight.

With the garrison of Bet-El charging into their rear, and Ahyee hitting them from the front, Yacov appeared to be caught in a trap. But as the two cities' warriors plowed deeper into the Yacovite center, Yacov's left and right wings lingered and folded in on their flanks. And as this was happening, the 30,000 man detachment hiding behind Ahyee rose and poured into the city, setting fires as they went.

This time, Yacov was not forbidden to plunder, so the detachment looted before burning.

The warriors from Bet-El bore down on the Yacovite rear, but before they made contact, the archers hidden in the Arava rose from cover, nocked, drew, and loosed a volley right into the flank. The hail of arrows landed with devastating effect. The force from Bet-El were stopped cold. The next volley fell on their wounded, disorganized ranks.

While that threat was crushed, an officer of Ahyee happened to take a backward look during the advance, and saw funnels of smoke rising from inside his city.

A man abreast of him noticed his preoccupation and threw back a glance of his own. His step faltered and more soldiers noticed him falling behind, turning to see what the concern was. The realization that they had been duped spread through Ahyee's ranks, and horror followed in quick succession. In a matter of seconds their morale collapsed.

That is when Y'hoshua signaled for the center of his main force to abandon the ruse. They halted their feigned retreat and reversed course again, crashing into the enemy. Simultaneously, the wings pressed against Ahyee's flanks. Predator and prey had just swapped roles. The Yacovites cut down their antagonists by the droves. The city was looted and burned. Ahyee and Bet-El were annihilated in short order.

At sunset, Y'hoshua had the body of the king dumped at Ahyee's city gate, and buried under a heap of rocks.

"Let this be a monument to succeeding generations," Y'hoshua proclaimed, "that no city and no king can stand against El Elyon, and it was only our transgression that caused defeat on the first engagement."

After the area was secured, plunder divided, and the troops fed, Y'hoshua had a simple altar of stones set up in the mountains, and presented offerings to Hashem. Then he read all Moshe's writings aloud, lest his people again forget what was expected of them.

# A Zealot's Insights

The army, save for a detachment to secure the foothold just conquered in the central highlands, marched back into Stone Circle not quite flushed with victory. More like relief and satisfaction. They were reconciled to their god, and there was an unspoken consensus to stay that way...which meant policing each other to make sure that nobody else brought a curse upon the whole nation.

Not exactly celebratory, most of the army stayed up for a while after reaching camp, in mellow conversation amongst themselves or with family. Othniel went straight to his tent. Even though one of the first to lie down, he might have been the last to actually fall asleep

Salmon spent some time with his men, giving praise or correction where due. After all, for most of them this was only their second battle, and it was important that he reinforced the good practices while identifying and eliminating the bad ones. He missed young Othniel while making the rounds. The young warrior had done nothing requiring admonition; Salmon just preferred to check on all his soldiers after a battle, to keep track of how they were handling the stress of war.

He would make a point of talking with Othniel the next day.

After a time, Salmon separated from his men and found a quiet spot to repair his shield strap. Where he sat, he faced the Radiant Mist, glowing so bright that the L'vim camp was well illuminated without fires.

As he worked, a figure walked through that square camp and

turned, heading straight toward him. Even through dark and distance, Salmon recognized the figure by its walk. Pinchas strode right up to him, gave him a greeting, and sat beside him.

"How are you, my fellow spy?" Pinchas asked, with a faint smile.

Salmon flashed back a familiar grin. "I'm holding up fairly well. And you?"

Pinchas yawned and stretched. "Quite an eventful few days we've had. Now that the war has started, it's hard to keep up with all the action."

Salmon shrugged. "I'm not having trouble keeping up with it."

"But you're a soldier. You're out in the thick of it." Pinchas pulled at his priest garments. "We get all the news second or third-hand. First our army is inexperienced and outclassed. Then you're invincible. Then you've been beaten so badly that El Elyon must have abandoned us, and we'll be blotted out forever as a nation. Then you've destroyed a troublesome city in such lopsided fashion that some of our women speculate that you're nothing but a mob of bloodthirsty brutes."

This last statement caused Salmon to raise his eyebrows and give the priest a studious look. "We're not bloodthirsty, Pinchas. We simply follow orders that we've been told come straight down from our god."

Pinchas' easy smile flattened. He locked eyes with the soldier. "You still see El Elyon as a cruel tyrant?"

This surprised Salmon. He had once thought of The God-of-Many-Names that way—when he was a young boy. How did Pinchas know that? He shook the thought away. "No more than any other god."

"Other gods are murderous tyrants," Pinchas said. "Isn't it ironic that *ours* gets accused of what *they* do?"

"Other gods aren't as bent on punishing their own worshipers as ours is," Salmon said.

Pinchas studied him, nodded, then showed a sympathetic smile. "You notice shortcomings more than the average man," the priest said, "including in yourself. That's why your fear of El Elyon goes beyond what he requires of us."

Salmon let that sink in.

"You recognized Achan's vices long before we came to Bet-Yariq," Pinchas continued, brow wrinkled. "You don't think the punishment was too harsh. You think Achan should have been judged much earlier."

Now he was on target. "How do you do that, Pinchas?"

The priest hunched his shoulders. "We're all given different gifts. You have gifts for war and leadership. I am able to perceive things that can't normally be seen or heard."

Salmon nodded, remembering what he'd been told about the son of the high priest. "I saw a pattern with Achan early on. He was charismatic–hard not to like; but there was a lack of integrity, lack of honesty, a cold pragmatism...it showed up in little ways. Nothing that merited bringing him to Moshe...just...like in some things he would say. The way he exaggerated certain details in an anecdote, and omitted others, to make himself look better. Subtle little ways of making others look bad, or making himself out to be the hero...or victim. And there was this assumption that everybody owed him something. He took another man's knife once, but when I caught him he claimed he had mistaken it for his own, and made a big laughing production of it, like it was some embarrassing comedy. Like I said, it was all minor enough at the time that I couldn't bring him before the judges. Later, almost the same exact episode played out with a gold piece that belonged to someone else. Then a baby lamb."

"If a man isn't trustworthy in small matters; he probably can't be trusted with larger affairs," Pinchas said.

"And Achan proved that axiom, didn't he?"

"Achan had to be dealt with harshly," Pinchas said. "We have to purge evil from among us. We can't let a single man's iniquity doom the entire nation. But there's something you don't understand, Salmon: El Elyon is perfect in his justice, yes. But he's also perfect in his mercy. The latter sometimes overrules the former, because of that."

"He didn't show us mercy at the First Battle of Ahyee," Salmon said. "He punished the entire nation–and three dozen men lost their lives–because of what Achan did. Certainly he is a mighty god, who can crush our enemies. But he is equally ready to stomp *us* into the ground, grind us under his heel, the instant we deviate from his instructions.

Pinchas' lips twisted for a moment. Evidently troubled by Salmon's grasp of religion, he took a moment before responding. "I think perhaps that is how your father was with you. That is why you regard El Elyon's discipline as you do."

"You're saying El Elyon hasn't ground men under his heel?" Salmon challenged.

Pinchas took a deep breath. "Yes. El Elyon has unleashed his wrath upon men before—and his wrath is a terrible thing to behold. But honestly, his final judgment only comes after people are given many chances to do right. Hashem can stomp you into the ground— as you say—if he sees your heart is hardened. Of course. But Hashem can also rehabilitate men with moral failings. Look at our forefather, Yacov—hardly a paragon of honesty or integrity when he started out, was he? And yet Hashem made a nation out of him."

Everyone knew the history Pinchas referred to—how Yacov had swindled his brother, for instance—igniting a bitter feud that continued through their offspring to this day.

"But if you lived in Yacov's time and knew him," Pinchas said, "you would have assumed him unworthy of rehabilitation."

"No I wouldn't have," Salmon replied, automatically. "Is that your gift of perception talking, because...?"

"Just observation," interrupted Pinchas. "You don't forgive easily. You don't miss mistakes or forget them. It's part of what makes you a good leader. Your fifty might be the best trained men anywhere, because you train them so well, and correct all the failures so diligently. But it also makes you prejudiced against Rachav."

Salmon flinched, and stared at Pinchas with a confused expression.

"I noticed the energy between you and her when we were on our mission. Not because of a spiritual gift, either. Anyone would have noticed it. But you look down on her, because of how she fed her family while forced to live among those scum."

"She slept with those scum!" Salmon reminded him, defensively.

"Who knows how many? And don't forget, she's one of them to begin with."

"You're talking about the young woman who saved our lives, at risk of her own?"

"Well, granted," Salmon said, softening his tone for a moment. "But still..."

"She could have just as easily turned us over to the Gibborim. That was the safest choice for her at the time. She would have earned praise among her people for delivering us over to torture and death."

"Then she would have died with the rest when we took her city," Salmon said. "Look: all due accolades to her for how she helped us. But you're a priest—you know the law better than any of us. You can't justify the life of debauchery she led."

"But she wasn't under our law then, Salmon. She had never even heard of our law. I'm only just now teaching it to her and her family. How can she be held accountable for what she was never taught?"

"We put Achan down for the curse he brought among us. How much more of a curse is this woman carrying?"

"I would say none at all," Pinchas said. "Is our god not powerful enough to purify her? This is a woman who didn't know our god, yet took a leap of faith for him. And since she's been with us, she's shown total commitment to learning the law and keeping it. She is more devout than most of our own women, I'm sad to say."

Salmon fell silent after that. It was never a good idea to argue with Pinchas, he decided, because the priest was too smart, and never joined in a debate unless he knew the subject at hand quite well.

Most unnerving, perhaps, was that he knew of Salmon's attraction to Rachav. It was a thorn in the side Salmon thought he had adequately hidden, but the priest had seen right through it. Could everyone see through it? Could Rachav herself?

The danger was even worse than he thought. He needed to avoid her altogether, so that this "energy" Pinchas noticed could die out.

Pinchas rose, putting one hand gently on Salmon's shoulder. "You're a good man, my friend. But there is much you still need to learn about our god...and yourself."

Pinchas strolled back to his own tribe's camp. Salmon rose and marched toward the soldiers of his fifty who were still up. He would start the guard assignment for the family of the harlot right away.

# Of Gods and Idols

The visitors rode toward Stone Circle slowly, as if weary from a long journey. The party of six, with a larger armed escort, stopped to marvel at the ruins of Bet-Yariq for a time before riding on. But before they reached Stone Circle, sentries intercepted them.

"Who are you and what's your business here?" challenged the leader of the sentries.

One of the travelers pulled the cloth from covering his nose and mouth, tucking it up into his turban. "I'm an ambassador, on a mission from my king. I'm sent to speak to your king."

"We have no king except Hashem, the creator of the universe," replied a zealous young sentry.

"This doesn't require a speech," reprimanded the sentry leader. He glanced over the party of visitors, noticing how worn out their clothes, sandals, and wineskins were.

"Where do you come from?" asked the sentry leader.

"We hail from a land far south of Mizraim." the ambassador said. "But news has reached even us of your exploits, and your god. More information than that, we prefer to reserve for your leaders."

"Our chief is Y'hoshua son of Nun," the sentry leader said. "I'll take you to him, but your escort will have to stop outside our camp."

A contingent from the army was assigned to watch over the armed escorts, while the ambassador and his aides were brought in to speak with Y'hoshua and the tribal chiefs.

The field marshal and his generals were going over a plan to move the bulk of the army up to Ahyee, and conduct further operations from there, while leaving women, children, and a strong guard force at Stone Circle. When the visitors were announced, the meeting was temporarily postponed.

Othniel bent over the edge of the river and reconsidered his plan to bathe. With the level finally dropping as summer set in, the water was still so muddy that he didn't want to get in it. He stood and straightened. *Oh well.* He had wanted to at least wash his face, but his primary motivation for coming to the river was just to get away from everyone else.

Something—a soldier's burgeoning instincts, perhaps—caused him to glance behind him. A lone figure approached on foot from the direction of Stone Circle. He turned to watch, at first getting his spear ready. But the shape and gait of the figure was distinctly feminine. As it drew close enough to him to identify specific details, he recognized her as Aksah.

Despite his melancholy, the sight of her sped up his heart rate. But while he normally would have been excited by the potential of this encounter, and flattered that she sought him out, today it made his frown deepen. The timing was bad. He knew he was no fun to be around lately, which was one reason why he kept to himself as much as possible.

"I know you weren't thinking about swimming in that filthy water," she said, as she stopped a few paces from where he stood.

He really liked the way she was put together, and he considered her face to be the most exquisite work of art he'd ever beheld. But it was difficult to appreciate even that in his current state of mind.

"It is very muddy," he said, trying his best to sound friendly, but probably just barely managing civility. "No reason at all to choose this water over the springs in Bet-Yariq."

"I haven't seen much of you lately," she said.

He didn't know how to respond. She noticed he'd been acting the hermit. Did that mean she missed him?

To pose that question directly to her might be too overbearing. To say something like, "So?" would be rude. So would just ignoring the question.

"Has somebody asked for me?" he inquired, carefully.

"Well, I was curious where you've been," she said.

That answer cheered him up a little.

"I was going to ask you what happened at Ahyee," she said. "And check to see if you'd been hurt or something."

"That's nice of you," he said. "I wasn't wounded, though."

"You look like you have a lot on your mind," she said.

"I do."

"Would you like to talk about it? I listen well."

He tried to smile, but couldn't get his mouth to move right. He backed away from the river and sat heavily, leaning against the trunk of a tree. She sat down next to him—much closer now than when they were standing. He liked that, too. But now she watched him expectantly and he felt obligated to speak his thoughts.

"All the plunder we took from those two cities in the mountains," he said, shaking his head. "I just keep thinking, if only Achan would have waited. He could have grabbed all the loot he could carry, and not be in violation."

She made a sympathetic noise in her throat, scooted a little closer and put a hand on his arm. "You really admired him, didn't you?"

"Yes," he said. "I still can't believe...everything."

She rubbed her thumb back and forth through the hair of his arm. He found the touch comforting. Perhaps it was more of a maternal gesture than what he preferred, but at least it did indicate that she seemed to care about him.

"I never could have imagined any of that, either," she said.

"Anyway," he sighed, "I wasn't trying to avoid you, specifically."

"I'm glad," she said, lips curling up ever-so-slightly. Lips that he spent far too much time thinking about. She gave his arm a squeeze.

Suddenly, he tensed. "Your father—where is he?"

"Oh, he's in some briefing with Y'hoshua and all the other generals," she said. "We should be safe for a while."

That was good, but Othniel wanted to be able to spend time with her even when her father knew about it. He wanted Kalev's blessing. How could he get to that point?

He kept the dilemma to himself, wanting to enjoy his time with Aksah instead of obsessing over what seemed like an impossible situation.

"What are you looking at?" she asked, trying to follow his gaze.

"It's storming in the mountains again," he replied, nodding toward the Aborim in the distance, under dark clouds, with black diagonal streaks between them and the mountains.

"It seems to rain everywhere but directly on us," she said, now focusing on the storm. "True?"

"Another blessing from El Elyon, I guess," he said, trying to smile.

She sighed and stretched.

"Have you thought much about what life will be like after the campaign?" he asked her.

"All the time," she said. "I daydream constantly about living the rest of my life in one spot; not moving around constantly. And inside a house instead of a tent."

"So you're a daydreamer?" he asked, studying her face.

"Oh yes. Hopeless!" Her laugh had a melodic quality to it. "You've seen how rich the soil is. Anything would grow here."

"With enough water," he agreed, nodding.

"I've already got my garden mapped out," she said, tapping temple with index finger.

Othniel was still thinking about water. On the other side of the river were rich, fertile valleys that were easy to irrigate. This side was so mountainous, they would have to depend on El Elyon to send the rains in season. Avram, the father of Yitzak, who fathered their ancestor, Yacov, had offered his nephew first choice on the lands he wanted. The nephew, of course, chose the lush valleys east of the river, leaving Avram and his offspring the rugged mountain country of Kenaan.

"Are you listening to me?" Aksah asked, looking askance at him. "Did you even hear what I said?"

"Of course," he said, and tapped her temple with his own index finger. "What else do you have mapped out up there?"

With a relieved smile, she said, "Oh, the names of my children, for one thing."

With just a few touches, some conversation, and subdued laughter, she had raised his spirits from the depths, he realized. "You've decided on the names, have you? I suppose your husband won't have an opinion."

"Oh, he'll love the names I've come up with," she replied, smugly, eyes twinkling.

"And El Elyon has revealed to you how many of your children will be sons, and how many daughters?"

She giggled and shook her head. "I have enough names for all contingencies."

He laughed with her.

"Don't you think about children, Othniel?"

It was a forgone conclusion, he assumed, that every man wanted a son to carry on his family line. "What do you mean?"

"Well, how many do you want?"

"I don't have a specific number in mind. Some things take care of themselves." He wiggled his eyebrows at her. "If I marry a good woman who knows how to be a good wife, I might just have hundreds."

She slapped at him playfully. He caught her hand, as if defending himself. After the mock "attack" though, he didn't release it; and she didn't pull it away.

"Have you ever imagined what they might look like?" she asked.

"You're a creative person," he observed. "You exercise your imagination a lot, I see."

"Is there something wrong with that?"

He shook his head. "Not at all. I like that about you."

"Good. But really? You don't think at all about what your children might be like?"

He sighed and changed position so he could lean back against the tree at a more comfortable angle. "Well, I'd like it if my daughters were a lot like you."

She made a strange noise and kissed his cheek, then pulled back slightly to beam at him. She took a better grip on his hand, and reached over with her free hand to clutch at his arm as she leaned her head against his shoulder.

They sat together for a while, staring across the river, imagining a home, a garden, sons and daughters.

For the first time in what seemed like forever, Othniel was able to forget about the First Battle of Ahyee, and about Achan.

Rachav noticed the party of visitors when they arrived—as did everyone in Stone Circle. Even when foraging took her close to where the armed escort waited for the ambassador, she didn't think much of it. Life with the Yacovites was full of strange new experiences, and maybe this was just one more.

She asked the soldier who had been assigned to keep an eye on her family, "Who are these people?"

"It's a delegation from another country," the soldier replied. "Word is, they want to establish a treaty with us."

"Wise," she said. "I'm surprised more nations that have heard of your god haven't rushed to form alliances."

The ambassador didn't return to his escort for many hours. When he did, he and his party were shown to a place outside camp where they could stay the night. The place was not far from the tents assigned to Rachav's family.

It was normal for someone who had traveled a great distance to spend at least a day resting, before turning back. And so that is what the visitors did.

In the morning, Rachav saw the party eating breakfast. She recognized one of the ambassador's assistants.

A former customer.

Curious about him, she nevertheless was more worried that he would recognize her and draw attention to the shameful past she hoped would never be dredged up again. She was careful to keep her back turned as much as possible while going about her routine. She was also careful to keep as far away from the visitors as was possible.

Some priests, and others from the L'vim sat with the visitors all that day. The offer was made early that the visitors were welcome to come outside the outer court of the Temple and worship Hashem.

"Thank-you, but no," the ambassador said, with a nervous laugh. "That won't be necessary."

"I beg your pardon?" a priest asked, brows knitting. "You traveled all this way to make peace with us because you've heard that nothing and no one can stand against our god...yet you don't want to know him?"

The visitors all glanced around their own countrymen, but eventually their collective gaze focused on the ambassador. He wiped sweat from his forehead and said, "True. We don't want him to destroy us, but we'd prefer to serve our own gods."

"You mean your own gods who can't protect you from him?" a priest suggested.

"Well, um...yes," the ambassador said.

The priest pointed at the stone idol resting on a wooden pedestal at the center of the visitors' encampment. "That is the god you prefer to serve?" he asked.

"It is a representation of our god," the ambassador said, uncomfortably. "It is sacred, because it bears his likeness. He dwells within it sometimes. It can receive our worship in his stead, when he chooses not to show us his image directly."

"Let me make sure I understand this," a priest said. "You have an opportunity to know the ultimate god, who created the world; and the wood, the stone, the metals that your so-called "gods" are made out of. And he created man, who formed your 'gods' out of wood, stone, or metals. But you would rather worship lifeless objects?"

"We wouldn't expect you to understand," the ambassador said.

"I think we do understand," an angry-faced priest said. "You want Hashem's mercy; you want his blessings; but you don't want to give him anything in return."

"It's not just a stone idol," one of the ambassador's men stated, hotly. "It has power it is foolish to disrespect."

Now Pinchas rose to his feet. "Let me give you a practical demonstration of religion," he said, strolling toward the idol.

The visitors watched him apprehensively, some twitching as if about to stand.

Pinchas poked the statue with his staff. It toppled off the pedestal and *thump*ed on the ground.

The visitors gasped. Some of the escorts shot to their feet, hands on weapons.

"Why would you disrespect our god this way, Yacovite?" demanded one of the escorts.

Pinchas turned to face the guests, shrugging. "When he puts himself back up on this pedestal, I'll apologize."

An escort began to draw his sword, The ambassador, flushed, held his hand out in a restraining pose.

"If your god can't even protect himself," Pinchas asked, "how is he supposed to protect you?"

A member of the embassy staff cleared his throat. "Tell me something, Yacovite: If someone were to knock down that tent in your camp that serves as your temple, and burn everything in it, would your god stop us?"

"If he chooses to," Pinchas replied, "then most assuredly. But we don't worship the tent, or any of the lifeless objects inside it. The God of Gods is not contained in physical objects. The whole world couldn't contain him—in fact, it's the other way around: he contains the whole world. We are only figments of his imagination."

One visitor pointed to a priest he had debated earlier in the day. "You criticize our god for all the sacrifices he demands." He now waved toward the ruins of Bet-Yariq. "Yet your god commands you to put entire cities to the sword. How is that any better?"

"The Gibborim are an abomination," the priest replied. "They are a perversion of El Elyon's creation, as are the monstrous beasts they breed. Just as a doctor must cut out a cancer before it spreads to corrupt the whole body, so must these abominable species be removed."

"That is heartless," accused the visitor. "It seems you serve a cold, bloodthirsty god."

"Are you in a position of authority over the gods?" asked the priest. "How is it that you can judge the Creator according to your standards? Are you all-knowing? Are you perfection incarnate? On what foundation rests your right to judge the Creator of all things–including you?"

"I'm a living being!" the visitor retorted. "With a heart. And a mind. Who can love. Who can feel."

"Who can lie; and covet; and lust; and steal; and swindle," Pinchas quipped.

"You know nothing about me!" the visitor declared, turning towards Pinchas. "And you're no better than me!"

Pinchas shrugged. "You are right in that. I have the same mortal weaknesses you do. That's why I don't presume the right to judge the Creator of All Life by my own flawed, subjective standards."

"We don't understand everything about El Elyon and what he does," the first priest said. "We are part of his creation, like you. We are not all-knowing. But we don't need to understand everything. What we need to understand is that El Elyon is the ultimate authority. If he does it, or says it, or allows it...then it is right–by the very nature of who he is. There is no higher authority. We may not like or agree with him, but what does that matter? Our emotions and opinions don't qualify us to judge him."

Flustered, the visitor crossed his arms and said, "I may not be perfect, but I know what is right."

"Is that so?" Pinchas replied. "And how do you know that you know what is right? Can you prove this? Would every other living being agree with your standards of what is right and wrong?"

"There are some things that are universally known, yes," the visitor said.

"Like what?" Pinchas asked.

The visitor glared, but had no verbal response.

"If everyone agreed about what is right and wrong," another priest said, "there would be no wars. You wouldn't be here seeking an alliance with us."

"I just know there has to be a better solution than subjugation by this Invisible God of yours," the visitor said, stubbornly.

"Subjugation to this god?" Pinchas suggested, pointing to the idol laying on the ground. "Tell us of his ways, so that we may evaluate his justice."

The visitor offered no response.

"So that we may judge him by your lofty standards," another priest added. "Or our own."

"So our god is not perfect," the visitor admitted. "I haven't found one who is, yet. But we'll follow him until we find one who is."

Pinchas and the other priests shook their heads, sadly.

"Tell us Yacovite," said a young member of the embassy staff. "can the followers of your god be deceived?"

Pinchas noted that several of the young man's fellows shot him a nervous glance.

Another priest answered, "Of course. We are not El Elyon."

"But if he is so powerful," persisted the young man, "couldn't he protect you from deception, too?"

"If he chooses to," the priest replied, patiently. "People do what is wrong all the time, and he usually lets them do it. He wants us to choose to do what is right, and gives us room to do it, or not do it."

The older, wiser heads saw that tempers were flaring and decided to end the debate. The priests bid a polite farewell and left.

Pinchas was thinking about the one visitor's obsession with deception, and the reaction of his colleagues, but noticed a fellow priest watching him from the side as they walked.

"I'm intrigued by something you said, Pinchas."

"Oh?"

"When you said we are but figments of El Elyon's imagination. Did you get that idea from something Moshe taught?"

"No," Pinchas said. "Not exactly. But after listening to Moshe all my life, I've given much thought to how we relate to our Creator. Then one night I had a dream—I think it was a vision..."

At the urging of the other priests, Pinchas did his best to put the vision into words.

He had seen himself, standing among his tribe. The scene expanded, and he saw his tribe standing among the nation of Yacov. His point of view pulled back farther, and he could see Yacov spread out across the land. Farther back, and the shape of the continent was clear, but Yacov and other nations shrunk into patterns of specks, then shrunk smaller still until they disappeared as his perspective pulled back farther to put the continents in context on Kadur Ha'aretz. His perspective pulled back farther and he was able to place Kadur Ha'aretz among the other planets orbiting Hammah—their sun. Farther back, and the solar system was just one of several. Then he could see the entire galaxy. Then several galaxies; then hundreds... Back farther until the entire universe was just a speck in an amazing patchwork of such specks.. Then back even farther, and he passed through some sort of membrane, backwards, and his field of vision was filled with a pool of fire. Farther back. The pool of fire was one iris in a pair of eyes. Farther back, and he beheld an awesome being of dazzling colored lights.

El Elyon.

The entire universe was contained in the god's mind.

Then Pinchas noticed the being sitting at El Elyon's right hand—more solid, with a physical form—at least in the dimensions Pinchas was used to. Both figures were shrouded in the Radiant Mist.

Pinchas did his best to describe all he saw (though his limited vocabulary could scarcely do it justice), and the other priests asked him several specific questions about the second being, beside El Elyon. He answered the questions as best he could, and one of them exclaimed, "That sounds exactly like the being Y'hoshua encountered. The commander of El Elyon's army!"

"Yes," Pinchas agreed. "It does, indeed."

"Hashem," stated an older priest, simply, nodding his head.

As the L'vim departed, the visitors muttered to each other. Some sneered with outrage; some smirked with a gloating twinkle in the eye.

# A Hasty Alliance

Rachav was relieved when the visitors left on the third day. She wanted to forget all about them. But As Pinchas was teaching her family, later, Nadir brought the subject up.

Pinchas informed them all that the visitors had secured an alliance between their kingdom and Yacov.

"I thought The God-of-Many-Names was giving all of Kenaan to Yacov," Anwar said. "Doesn't that mean you have to vanquish all the kingdoms that are already here?"

"Yes," Pinchas said, patiently. "But these men were from a kingdom far away–not one established in Kenaan."

Rachav glanced at him sharply, unsure what, if anything, she should tell him.

Pinchas conducted the day's lesson, then pulled Rachav aside afterwards. "You gave me a look, earlier," he said. "Did you have a question, or something you wanted to say?"

Rachav bit her lip, then asked, "Am I to understand that Yacov can't make a treaty with nations inside Kenaan?"

Pinchas nodded. "No kingdom from inside any of the land promised to us."

She chewed on her lip a bit more. "I, um...recognized one of those men. He was not from a far country."

Pinchas frowned, eyes narrowing. "Who was it?"

"One of the men on the ambassador's staff."

"How do you know where he's from?"

Her face heated as she said, "Many of my former customers were quite loose with their tongues. This man was a Hivite from Giveon."

Pinchas blanched after the words registered. "Are you certain?"

She nodded, still blushing.

Pinchas grew wide-eyed, shot to his feet and bolted.

She stood to watch him run toward the center of the camp.

Though Yacov didn't have cavalry (despite all the opportunities to take horses from defeated armies that did), they kept enough horse stock for messengers and special details. Y'hoshua dispatched a small force to intercept the foreign delegation before it returned to Giveon.

The ambassador dismounted to face Salmon and his pursuit force.

Salmon, who had been put in charge of the pursuit detail, dismounted and confronted the ambassador.

"So you're from a far off country. Is that right?"

The ambassador didn't answer. It seemed to Salmon he was stubbornly making an effort to hold his chin up so he could look down his nose at his accuser.

"I guess lying comes very easy to the Hivim," Salmon said.

Some in the escort, and the delegation, lowered their heads to stare into the dirt. The ambassador maintained his defiant attitude.

"Why the hoax?" Salmon asked.

"Well," the ambassador said, "to put it simply, we don't want to be destroyed like the other nations."

They stood staring at each other, wordlessly, for a few moments.

"I have a message directly from Y'hoshua," Salmon announced. "During your visit with us, you had disputes with our priests about whether our god is just, or all-powerful." Salmon raised his voice so that all those present would hear. "It's only because we didn't consult him that you were able to trick us. It's only because El Elyon is just that Y'hoshua is not going to put all Giveon to the sword. We cut covenant with you. And even though you obviously can't be trusted, we will act honorably and uphold our end of the treaty because we won't have Hashem's reputation profaned."

"We are your grateful servants," the ambassador said.

"Interesting choice of words," Salmon said. "Because that's exactly what you will be from now on. We'll spare you and your people, but you're going to cut our wood and carry our water. Understood?"

"What you say is good," the ambassador said, mechanically.

# War Councils

Kings and generals were gathered at Binaizak's former estates (now an impressive military installation). They sat in council, trying to settle plans for how to defeat the Yacovites. All parties visiting Urshalayim brought priests and representations of their gods, and they kept the blood flowing steadily with a child sacrificed each day.

Adonaizidek took leave from the war council to meet with the priest of Moloch at one of the recently finished high places on the estate. The priest of Enki was there as well, though the Mizraimite priest was not invited.

The priest of Moloch handed the king a pinch of some dark substance. "Chew on this, o king, and swallow the juices."

Adonaizidek did as instructed, while a priestess arrived to hand a small bundle to the priest of Moloch.

A bronze figure of Moloch stood upon the small pyramid, and a fire blazed in the huge brazier at the waist of the statue. The priest and priestess unwrapped the bundle, revealing a tiny infant. Awoken by the sudden exposure, the baby was wide-eyed, noticing its unfamiliar surroundings. Chanting to Moloch, the priest placed the baby on the statue's built-in cradle—the brass arms, hands, and spread fingers of the idol, sticking out flat like a shelf. The baby began to cry. The priest continued to chant, while some unseen servant, down inside the pyramid, began operating the machinery that caused the statue to rotate. Both the priest and priestess chanted loud and steady. The baby screamed and shrieked, waving its little arms as the heat intensified. The statue continued to rotate so that the cradle, and its tiny occupant, passed right over the flames, which licked up in between the brass fingers of Moloch.

Adonaizidek's vision distorted. He was aware of his surroundings and the sacrifice taking place, but that faded from his consciousness as he began to perceive the overlapping scene. The colors were bizarre, the ambient noise was different, the temperature was colder, and there was much more activity than what he had seen with his physical eyes in this scene superimposed over the reality of a moment ago. As the baby died, its little body combusting, energy burst from it in several directions, which was absorbed by a gathering of fantastic beings. He recognized Nergal, resplendent in fantastic armor, sitting on a fiery red horse. He also noticed the moon god, the storm god, and others.

The god with the appearance of a minotaur, after licking up the blood of the sacrifice, smiled, pointing at Adonaizidek while nodding at the satyr. The satyr nodded back, then beckoned a being with the head and talons of an owl, but the body of a man.

The being drew near, and spoke to Adonaizidek. "The time is near, my child. A battle against the Great Tyrant is upon us."

Adonaizidek bowed. "I know what I must do, my Liege. But the others are afraid. They don't want to attack the Yacovites."

"That problem is already taken care of," the owl-god said. "The Hivites have formed an alliance with the Yacovites. Even now, a messenger is approaching with this news."

"What?" Cried Adonaizidek.

The owl-god raised one talon, calming the king with the simple gesture. "Let the messenger break the news in the hearing of the other kings. They will be infuriated. Lead them in an attack on Giveon immediately. The Hivites are formidable warriors, but they don't inspire fear like the Yacovites do."

"Of course, my liege. But the Yacovites..."

"Attack Giveon, and Yacov will come to you."

"Will my allies not desert me when the god of Yacov..."

"Don't concern yourself with the Great Tyrant. And they won't desert you. They'll be flush with victory over the Hivites, and still in a battle rage. Remind them of how the Yacovites suffered defeat at

Ahyee: their god failed them then. He doesn't give them victory in every battle. When they finally took Ahyee, how did they do it?"

"By overwhelming numbers, and a crafty ambush," Adonaizidek replied.

"But you have the overwhelming numbers this time, my child. You can trap and destroy Yacov before their god realizes it."

"Your victory over Yacov will give us victory over the Great Tyrant," the minotaur said. The sphinx nodded its agreement.

The satyr pointed down with one hand, and up with the other, with a confident smile. "As below, so above."

"Not that I am in a position to question you," Adonaizidek said, with a humility he'd never demonstrated among men, "but there are some men who argue that every rebellion against the Great Tyrant has failed, and proven disastrous for the rebels."

"The Rebellion has yet to be executed correctly," the satyr replied, solemnly. "With sufficient resources and proper implementation, we will dethrone him once and for all."

"But for now," the owl-god said, "get your subjects, and the other kings, to fixate on the treacherous Hivites. Don't give them cause to think about the Yacovites or the Great Tyrant, until it is time to fight them."

"Yes, my Liege," the Titan king said.

The fantastic beings, and the strange realm they occupied, faded from the king's perception. All he could see, once again, was the world of men and animals. He was still a bit dazed, but left the high place for his newly-renovated court-away-from-home.

Adonaizidek couldn't miss the opportunity to demonstrate to the other kings, generals, and their staffs, that he had favor with the gods, by prophesying the arrival of the messenger, and his news, in advance. Most of the visitors seemed unsure whether they should believe him or not. Some were visibly skeptical. Those who took the prophecy at face value were angry at the disloyalty of the Hivites, and proposed immediate mobilization for an attack.

While the council was at an impasse for how to proceed, the

messenger arrived at court. Adonaizidek commanded him to speak.

"O King, live forever," the messenger said, bowing low to Adonaizidek. "Your servant has compiled reports and is prepared to give you the most current news."

"Report," his king said.

"The Yacovites redoubled their efforts for a foothold in the central highlands," said the messenger. "At the Second Battle of Ahyee, they captured both that city and Bet-El. They put both kingdoms to the sword, burned the cities to the ground, and buried the respective kings under piles of rock at their city gates."

Kings groaned and cursed at this news. Adonaizidek stroked his beard, betraying no emotion. Word had reached him concerning these developments prior to his encounter with the gods.

"And furthermore, o King," the messenger said, "the king of Giveon has effected a treaty with Yacov."

Profane reactions buzzed through Adonaizidek's court. He was vindicated, but that did nothing to quell the outrage of the visiting kings.

"Well," quipped King Japhia, "now the reason is confirmed why the king of Giveon isn't here."

"He's not late," King Hocham agreed. "He never intended to show up at all."

"The men of Giveon are great warriors," King Piram said. "We really needed them on our side."

"What are the terms of the treaty?" King D'vir asked the messenger.

"Mutual military assistance, when possible," the messenger said, still bowed. "And the Hivites are their servants henceforth."

Adonaizidek would normally slay the messenger where he bowed, but the message proved his favor with the gods—and it would help him stir the other kings to action, based on what the gods told him. Besides, he'd been killing so many messengers in recent months, he was probably close to ensuring that nobody would ever deliver messages for him again. He waved a dismissal before he thought too much about grabbing a sword.

Relieved, the messenger wasted no time exiting the briefing room.

The other kings watched Adonaizidek.

He could read the fear in their eyes. None of them wanted to face Yacov, or his god. But there was a smoldering fury there as well, due to the betrayal by the Hivites.

Fortunately, the solution had already been given to him.

"Mobilize your armies," he said. "We march on Giveon. They will be annihilated for their treachery."

Hocham's nostrils flared, obviously liking the idea. D'vir appeared to feel the same.

Hopefully, all of them would be too furious about the betrayal to remember their fear.

King Piram chewed on his fingernail and said, "But won't Yacov come to their aid once they are under attack?"

Adonaizidek cursed silently. "Not if you act now," he said, confidently. "If we march right away, trap the Hivites quickly in a siege, we shall prevent the message from getting out."

"Yes," King D'vir said, turning to the commanding general of his army. "Let's march at once!"

"Let's not forget," said Adonaizidek, "that the gods are uniting behind us."

Generals and kings nodded, grimly.

A short time later, five massive armies converged, marching on Giveon. The number of troops was like the grains of sand on a beach.

# Call to Battle

Hivim messengers arrived at Stone Circle late in the afternoon with word that a coalition of five armies had invaded their kingdom, like masses of ants swarming over a day-old carcass. Giveon was besieged and they begged Y'hoshua to remember their treaty.

Y'hoshua knew many of the men in his army were resentful about the treaty. He also knew that the five-kingdom coalition had chariots, cavalry, and outnumbered Yacov's lightly-armed militia by overwhelming proportions. Yet he saw the opportunity in it, as well: He could quickly defeat the strongest kingdoms in southern Kenaan in one decisive battle, rather than a piecemeal campaign which would drag on for many years. It would still take time to pacify all the towns and villages; then there was northern Kenaan, with all its Gibborim kingdoms... But here was a chance to shorten the timetable significantly. He might even be able to pacify the South before winter.

What mattered more than any strategic plans on either side, though, was that El Elyon was more than a match for all the gods of Yacov's enemies.

Y'hoshua issued orders to the tribal generals to form up their troops. They would march at sundown, to arrive at Giveon by dawn.

Salmon mustered his men, inspected them quickly, then left them briefly to find Rachav near her family's tent.

When she recognized him, her eyes widened in surprise. "Hello."

"Hello," he said, quietly.

"I thought I wouldn't be seeing you again," she said, with a guarded expression. "What brings you here?"

Salmon hesitated, glanced back toward his fifty, then faced her again. "We're moving out," he said. "I don't have much time. But it's been revealed to me that..."

She searched his face with her intense, dark eyes, obviously confused. Even through her veil, and mostly obscured by the dim of dusk, she was beautiful. It must have been the most natural idea to her heathen mother that Rachav's beauty could be monetized for the family's benefit. It was a savvy business decision in their alien culture, with no social stigma or moral objection to even occur. It was also a cruel decision. Yet Rachav did as she believed her family required, and the lifestyle hadn't erased the decency at the core of her character.

"First of all, Rachav, I thank you on behalf of all my countrymen that you informed us of the Hivim deception."

She shook her head slightly. "Your countrymen are my people now. I consider it to be my duty to look out for the interests of Yacov."

They were silent for a moment. Salmon glanced at her repeatedly, but she looked down, like a dog he might kick any moment.

"I judged you in ignorance," Salmon finally said. "I dealt with you harshly, in words and actions. I regret that."

Another long period of silence ensued, and Salmon worried she might never respond.

"I forgive you," she said, voice cracking.

He was glad she did respond, but still surprised she said nothing more. "So easily?"

She nodded with a sad smile. "I'm learning much about your history, and your god. At first, it was tempting to see him as some merciless despot with a volume of rules no person could hope to follow faithfully. But I'm learning about his love...how patient he is...how he seems to seek excuses to show mercy to even the worst transgressors."

She sighed, and a tear trickled out of one eye. "I've examined myself: a whore and a liar, who has been bowing down to statues since I was a young girl... But, simply because of one little act of faith, he spared me and my family. As if my past doesn't matter. As if he were my father—who loves me like his own child."

She wiped her eyes and looked away. Instinctively, Salmon grasped her hand in his.

"It wasn't a 'little' act of faith, Rachav. It was huge, and took great courage."

She stared at their hands. Realizing that the contact was inappropriate, he let go of her hand and took a half-step back.

"I should have been more sympathetic," he admitted. "It must be very difficult for you with no friends or confidants. When we return...assuming I'm still alive...I'll have a talk with some women I know—women who I don't think will shun you."

Her gaze bounced between both of his eyes for a long moment before she said, "You don't owe me any favors, but thank-you just the same."

Jaw stiffening, he said, "I said I'll do it, and I will."

"Friendship can't be arranged, Salmon."

"Maybe not," he said, "but barriers against it can be taken down."

The bugles sounded. The voices of generals, marshals, captains and lieutenants shouted commands as the troops fell in and formed up according to standard order of march. Salmon's attention was drawn to his tribe. He turned back to her and forced a smile. "I have to go. But I want you to know...I'm glad you were spared. I'm glad you're one of us, now."

Rachav stared at the ground as if afraid to meet his gaze. In a voice barely above a whisper, she said, "May our god bring you back safely, Salmon. And should you decide to visit me again...I would be pleased."

Her eyes flickered up to meet his gaze for a passing instant, before lowering once again.

Not knowing what else to say, Salmon turned and trotted away toward his formation.

The forced march lasted all through the night, and the

mountainous trek was much longer than the journey to Ahyee. Normally, the army would need at least a few hours rest before engaging in battle, after such a march. But El Elyon compelled Y'hoshua to hit the Coalition Forces with the element of surprise fully intact.

The mountains rumbled ominously under their feet. Ma'adim rose that night as large as a chariot wheel. Everyone who looked up at the enormous planet noticed something they'd never seen before: two tiny black moons orbiting the red wanderer in opposite directions. Both were dark—one nearly black.

Priests of other nations speculated that the god Nergal had brought his planet this close in order to hurl the moons at Yacov and destroy their enemy with two mighty blows. The Yacovim avoided such speculation. They knew El Elyon had created both Ma'adim and it's moons, and must have his own purposes for displaying this great wonder. Those who paid careful attention to what Moshe had taught them remembered that visible objects were placed in the heavens to mark seasons, days, years...and for signs to the people who could see them from Kadur Ha'aretz. Ma'adim had been brought this close to commemorate something—possibly the looming battle.

Though the moons of Ma'adim were small, they were still larger than the asteroid chunks that had streaked into the red planet's gravity; so humans could not see the meteor storm curving toward Kadur Ha'aretz.

The Hivim capital of Giveon was fully encircled by the armies of the five kings, but just as the messenger had told Y'hoshua, the largest concentration of coalition forces was in the saddle between two hilltops, a short distance from the besieged city. Y'hoshua passed behind them on a southerly course, then hooked east to cut off any retreat back to Urshalayim.

While Y'hoshua watched the tribes of Yacov deploy on the reverse slope of the eastern hilltop in the ghostly pre-dawn glow, General Paltiel crept up and squatted beside him.

"We've found the main chariot force," Paltiel whispered. "They have tents pitched behind the lines, just like the Hivim reported.

Nobody is stirring yet, besides the sentries."

"It's doubtful they expect any challenge to a force of their size," Y'hoshua replied. "But if they even imagined opposition, they'd assume the relief column would march from the direction of Ahyee."

In fact, Y'hoshua mused, he had intended to transfer the bulk of his army to Ahyee and Bet-El, and conduct operations from there. He would be doing so right then, had the coalition not attacked Giveon first. He sent runners to fetch Shemuel and Hanniel.

When the two generals reported, he pointed up to the peak of the hilltop and told them, "I want your archers on that high ground there, ready to support our shock troops."

They acknowledged his orders and were soon off to oversee the deployment. Meanwhile, runners brought the remaining tribal commanders to Y'hoshua. Kalev and Elizaphan knelt on each side of him, at his beckoning.

"Attack at sunrise," he told Kalev. "Right into the charioteers' bivouac." He craned his neck the other way, to address Elizaphan. "Your primary task is to take the horses when the attack starts. Secondarily, I need you to harass those being pressed by Y'huda. Don't give them opportunity to regroup for a counterattack, or even organize for an orderly retreat."

"Take the horses?" Elizaphan asked.

"And hamstring them, like normal," Y'hoshua said. "We trust in El Elyon, our god. Not in cavalry or chariots."

Elizaphan sighed, disappointed. "Of course, Sir."

"Be strong and bold," Y'hoshua said.

These two generals nodded, and were dismissed to make it happen. Y'hoshua waved to the remaining generals, so they would gather in close.

"Benyamin's slingers will support Naftali and Ruven to attack the ridge line. There's a smaller chariot force there—take them out first. When they break and run, Ruven pursues. Herd them toward Gad's ambush."

"You're assuming they'll break at first contact," Bukki observed, skeptically.

"They'll break," General Pedahel said. "You worry about your own assignment."

Bukki looked about to retort, but bit his lip.

"Split Dan into two forces," Y'hoshua told Bukki. "While Y'huda hits the charioteers, you close in on this concentration of enemy infantry from both flanks. That drives them into Yissakhar's ambush."

"Sir," Bukki said, licking his lips nervously, and glancing toward the massive city of tents which sprawled out from between the hilltops far enough for them to see part of it from their current vantage point, "even if all this goes according to plan, there's just too many of them. A million or more will be able to escape and come back to crush us sooner or later."

"We still win the day," Paltiel said. "The battle is ours and they won't recover quickly."

"Hashem is delivering all of them into our hands," Y'hoshua said. "We can't let any get away."

"We haven't forgotten the plan, Sir," General Ahihud told Y'hoshua, with an annoyed glance toward Bukki.

"Good," Y'hoshua said, with an air of finality. "I suggest you get back to your tribes to make sure everyone is in position before I pass the signal."

"Yes Sir," his generals chorused, and scurried back to their respective commands.

Soldiers maneuvered quietly, in hordes, all across the slopes facing Giveon from the east, and crept into attack positions.

Dark clouds hovered over the land but an opening in the overcast sky was expanding, so that Ma'adim hung threateningly over the main chariot force's camp through that aperture. Light from the moon and the red planet shone down on the sea of tents, where sentries dozed and multitudes of Coalition soldiers slept soundly.

The tremors had stopped hours ago, and now it was unusually still and quiet.

The edge of the sun began to crest the horizon.

"May Hashem show himself mighty through us," Y'hoshua said,

rising to his feet.

He waved his javelin and the buglers blew the attack. Guidon bearers signaled with their banners, and the spear men rose and surged forward.

# War in the Hidden Realm

# (Rachivel)

The asteroid chunks continued to break apart after passing Tzedek, until the smallest of them was the size of a mill stone. They streaked toward Ma'adim, and would have just skimmed through the red planet's stratosphere on a straight trajectory toward Noga, but the gravity of Ma'adim grabbed at them as they passed. Its gravity wasn't strong enough to pull them down into the red planet's surface, or even pull them fully into Ma'adim's atmosphere. But it did alter their course. They hooked around Ma'adim and hurtled toward Kadur Ha'aretz—a swarm of interstellar boulders large enough not to be completely burnt up upon atmospheric entry.

As Adonaizidek had been saying, the gods had indeed joined forces, and were taking a stand against Hashem at the Kenaan Land Bridge.

One god eavesdropped on Y'hoshua's briefing to his generals, and went to divulge it to a priest, who would then report to the five kings. But a strong force of El Elyon's Warriors intercepted him. They subdued him and locked him away in the prison reserved for false gods.

The remaining gods took positions all around Giveon—in the air, on the ground, and inside the ground. They brandished double-edged swords, battleaxes, and warhammers, all pulsing with a cold paranormal glow. They watched the stars, knowing that El Elyon had committed to this war. Indeed: in due time, the Warriors appeared from their stars. Though varying multiples of light years away, their advance was rapid, and they assembled *en route*. Mikhayel stationed himself at the front of their formation.

Mikhayel led them down into their deployment around Giveon, facing the contingent of determined gods opposing them. The Commander appeared from the ether, and gave Mikhayel his orders. Swords flamed to life and the opposing forces closed for battle.

El Elyon's Warriors formed a detachment to intervene in the battle on Yacov's behalf, while the main force was assigned the task of preventing the rebel gods from intervening for the Five Kings' Coalition.

Enki, Nergal, Moloch, Al Illah Dagon, Chemosh, and the others were confidant that the battle of the gods would mirror the results from the battle of men.

# A Preposterous Command

Thousands upon thousands of horses were tethered in an expansive corral next to the camp of the main chariot force. Bored and drowsy sentries walked their posts, oblivious to the movement just a short distance away.

The blast of bugles echoed through the mountains. With a resounding battlecry, Y'hudim shock troops poured into the charioteers' camp. Othniel was one of many who had volunteered for a special assignment. He got his torch burning, kneeling behind the temporary protection of a couple spear men Then he set about lighting tents on fire behind the lead skirmish line advancing through the camp.

Teams from Z'vulun rose from hiding and rushed the sentries posted at the horse pen. Once the sentries were out of commission, their tribesmen broke into the corral and began to hamstring the horses.

This was another practice that many didn't understand. With no chariots or warhorses for their army, it seemed only logical they should take them from the armies they conquered. But they didn't.

Charioteers awoke with a start to find their camp on fire around them. Bugles blew, voices shouted, all contributing to their confusion. They staggered outside their burning tents only to be skewered and trampled by waves of massed spear men. Those who gathered their wits quickly, and were located where they could escape to the horse corral, ran from the spear men right into a killing ground. Javelins brought down the half-dressed soldiers before they could reach the horses. Others, on the edges of their camp, had a chance to flee from the chaotic death from the east...but fled right into a hail of arrows from the hilltop overlooking them.

So far as could be discerned, all the Coalition infantry were Gibborim. When the first bugles blew, Danim formations closed on them from two sides. The surprise was nearly complete, as initially only the sentries could put up a fight and thousands died before they could emerge from their tents. Thousands more awoke to fire, smoke, echoing bugle calls and the shouts of men...and mistakenly turned on each other. But their numbers were so enormous that even with such grievous losses, most of them had time to collect their weapons, come outside, and identify the enemy. What they didn't have time for was to organize into their normal units and form shield walls. As a result, they faced Yacovim phalanxes individually, or in small, ineffective clusters.

At the center of the largest Coalition camp, as yet not penetrated by the attacking Yacovim, the flap of a large, ornate tent was pushed aside and Adonaizidek stepped out, still buckling on his royal armor. His attendants staggered out of their own tents, half-dressed, looking bewildered. The king called to a soldier passing nearby. "What's happening?"

"Lord of Righteousness, the Yacovlites are attacking!" the soldier replied.

Adonaizidek turned one way, then the other, looking for visual confirmation. All he could see were burning tents, smoke, and men running to and fro. His surrounding attendants looked to him with expressions of panic.

"This is good," he announced in a loud, confident tone. "The night guard can delay them while the main force gets ready. I'll send my chariots right into their flank."

Another passing soldier who heard this stopped to address him, with a hasty bow. "O King, live forever...but the night guard has been slain, and the main force is already under attack. The Yacovites are everywhere!"

"Nonsense!" the king declared. "They don't have even a tenth of our numbers."

With sudden fury, a quake shook the ground underneath them. It pitched and swayed with such force that they all lost their feet and tumbled. The ground cracked in several places they could see, opening fissures that swallowed Gibborim by the hundreds.

"The god of Yacov fights against us!" cried a terrified attendant.

Adonaizidek flashed him a scathing look, then turned his attention to Ma'adim above. He rolled into a kneeling, bowed position and lifted his hands. "O Nergal, god of war: strengthen our arms; speed our feet; and we'll kill so many Yacovites you'll get drunk from their blood!"

The Naftalim charged through the encampment along the ridge stretching across Giveon's south walls, burning tents and putting confused giants to the spear. Those further back in the camp, who had time to don armor and come out with weapons, had difficulty forming due to the relentless shower of Ruvenim javelins. Their commanders chose to fall back fast, out of javelin range where they could regroup and counterattack. Unfortunately for them, they fell back right into an ambush. Slingers from Ashear pelted them from a distance, then Gadim swordsmen waded into both flanks and cut them down by the droves.

However, there were just too many enemy troops—the warriors of Yacov couldn't slay them all before the surprise advantage slipped away. Huge pockets of Coalition infantry formed up and stiffened even as the Danim pressed them hard from two flanks. As fast as the Danim could skewer them just wasn't fast enough, and the battle stretched out through the morning hours. Y'hoshua saw Dan getting into trouble despite surprise, superior position, and sound tactics. Thankfully, the lead waves of Y'hudim had swept completely through the main chariot force camp. He sent a runner to Kalev with instructions to march to Dan's relief and hit the enemy infantry from a third angle.

Adonaizidek stood inside a circle of the other kings in his Coalition, and their generals, imploring them to rally their armies and fight. "They have only one god; who will be hard-pressed by many powerful gods."

"If we don't seize the initiative when opportunity presents itself," said King Hocham's general, "we will have to fight them anyway, and likely when the situation can't be adjusted to our advantage"

"True," Adonaizidek said, pouncing on the general's logical point. "Our only options are to fight or surrender. And we've heard what they did to Bet-Yariq, Ahyee and Bet-El once they took those cities. If we don't fight them now, we'll have to fight them anyway, at a time and place of their choosing–and they can attack us one-at-a-time, when we are not standing unified against them. More importantly, our gods are united and behind us...but will be angered if we shrink from this opportunity."

A general's runner apologized for interrupting, but pointed along the ridge where a large mob of Gibborite infantry formed into phalanxes. The nearest Yacovite formations were dwarfed by them. When the Coalition infantry advanced against them, the Yacovites were pushed back.

Adonaizidek pointed at the skirmish. "They had the element of surprise, but we're taking control anyway. Once our chariots are hitched up, they'll regret ever coming out to meet us on the field."

"We have no chariot force," Piram said. "They hit us there first. The charioteers were slaughtered like pigs on a spit, and the survivors were scattered. Besides that, the Yacovites have captured the horses."

Adonaizidek felt cold shivers of panic crawling along his skin, but he recovered quickly after concentrating for a moment on how the battle progressed along the ridge. "Nothing to worry about," he said. "Our infantry is enough to handle nine armies the size of theirs. And their god is no match for our gods."

Plans and unit integrity rarely remained intact after contact with the enemy. Othniel observed this first-hand as the soldiers in his detail became mixed up with the first two waves of shock troops on their way through the charioteers' camp. Still, he was one of the first to fight all the way through and out the other side. Charioteers were not used to fighting on foot, and the contingent were overrun with little difficulty (whereas, if allowed to form up with chariots and horses, they could have devastated the foot soldiers of a normal army).

Othniel and the soldiers with him looked forward to resting for a few moments after clearing their objective, catching their breath while succeeding waves caught up to them. But orders passed down that they were to march to Dan's relief immediately.

Panting officers formed them up, and the gasping spear men moved out.

The Y'hudim formations enjoyed initial success against the enemy infantry as they advanced into them. But resistance stiffened. Fully armored giants poked at them with their own spears, with double the reach of any Yacovim spear man.

The advance faltered.

Othniel dodged a huge spearhead thrusting toward his midsection, and lunged forward, jamming his own spear into a Gibbor's knee. The giant howled and stepped back, pulling the spear, and Othniel, with him. Othniel tried to tug his spear out, but it was lodged solidly. He yanked again, as hard as he could this time, and the spear ripped free. The giant cried out again and his wounded knee buckled. As he stumbled, soldiers on either side of Othniel pierced the Gibborim warrior through gaps in his armor. Before he could strike back or recover, Othniel lunged again, ramming his spear through the giant's neck. This time he yanked hard the first time to dislodge his spearhead. The giant slumped forward, bleeding out.

Like many of Yacov's soldiers, Salmon had found for himself an enemy's sword. It was huge, with a blade wider than his arm and as long as his leg. When confronted by another Giant, who thrust his gigantic spear at Salmon, he grabbed the spear shaft and used it as an anchor for a wild maneuver Like a spinning move in some sort of deadly dance, he uncoiled his body and hacked out backhanded with the sword. He slashed the Giant's stomach, then spun back, released the huge spear, and darted away from the giant's next lunge. He ducked and dodged as the spear thrust repeatedly at him. Gradually the giant slowed, as his stomach wound kept bleeding. During one of the giant's lunges, Salmon swung the sword again. The Gibborim's gigantic fingers were caught between the blade of the sword and haft of his own spear—and chopped off. While the giant watched his fingers hit the ground, in disbelief, Salmon knocked the spear out of the giant's thumb-hold with his shield, side-stepped, and thrust the sword through the skirt straps into the Gibborim's groin. The giant screamed and doubled over, where Salmon cleaved his head from his body.

Othniel looked left and right, seeing that his comrades had dispatched giants in a bloody line extending in both directions. Momentarily, he felt relieved at overcoming the Gibborim line.

Then he saw an enormous wave of giants screaming and charging straight for him. In an instant he could tell that the giants had them outnumbered many times over. There was no possible way they could repel the charge.

"Shield wall!!" screamed the officers.

The Y'hudim responded according to their training, locking shields together high and low, spears cocked, sticking through the narrow gaps. It was a tactic that would, and had, worked against other enemy attacks—sometimes even when the enemy had the numerical advantage. But these were gigantic Gibborim and their numbers were overwhelming.

Othniel, gripped by terror, gritted his teeth, closed his eyes, and prayed to El Elyon that his death be quick but meaningful.

Above the soldiers forming the shield wall was a great zipping noise. They opened their eyes, peered between the shields, and beheld a scene that took their breath away: a storm of hot, glowing rocks shot down from the sky and tore through the charging Gibborim, cutting a huge, fiery swathe through rank after rank on a downward slant until they plowed into the ground, leaving smoking furrows up to where they came to rest.

Gradually the shields came down. Othniel and the others stared, astounded, at the sight before them. One moment an unstoppable tidal wave of weapons and armored flesh was about to crash through and sweep them into oblivion; the next moment the remaining body parts from that living tidal wave were strewn over the smoldering landscape of terrible destruction. The Yacovim soldiers turned to one another, each man wondering if his eyes deceived him.

The voice of Salmon roused them from their dazed wonder.

"Finish them!"

They turned toward Salmon, then followed the line of his gaze and noticed handfuls of Gibborim survivors running from the hellish scene.

Spear and shield at the ready, Salmon ran after the shocked, demoralized enemy. By twos and threes, his comrades joined the pursuit, cutting down the fleeing giants from behind.

Similar scenes played out all over the mountain.

The five kings and their entourage were on their way to the nearby skirmish when the quake surged with renewed fury, sending them all tumbling. The ground cracked and tore open suddenly. Gibborite infantry were swallowed into the fissure by the thousands. Adonaizidek watched with horror, then worried that the ground would swallow him as well. The quake's energy dwindled, and the kings rolled to hands and knees to push themselves up. The ground continued to shake, so it was a struggle to maintain their balance. They noticed Gibborite survivors fleeing from the site where their comrades were devoured by the fault.

"Come back here!" D'vir bellowed. "Stand and fight, you cowards!"

A general's runner blurted out, "They're not cowards, o King. Nobody can stand against the Yacovite god when he rises to shake the world."

Adonaizidek scowled, surveying the carnage all around. "We'll fall back along the Urshalayim Road and regroup."

"Um...Lord of Righteousness," General Puadir said, "that's the direction they're attacking from. They've cut us off from Urshalayim."

A swarm of panicking Gibborites ran past, trampling fellow Coalition soldiers who inadvertently got in their way. King Japhia swung his gaze between the fleeing Gibborites and the trampled bodies...then turned to flee himself.

Adonaizidek bounced his gaze behind him at his fleeing allies, to the enormous mobs of Gibborites (in a panic flight straight at him), then to the trampled bodies...then he himself turned to flee.

Soon after the quake subsided, the Shimonim archers ran out of arrows. But not targets. As the battle raged on, a strong force of enemy infantry hinged in the middle to swing in on them from two sides, like the jaws of a bear. Nearly defenseless, the Shimonim found themselves trapped between a rocky cliff and the closing pincers of angry Gibborim. With very little in the way of close-range weapons to fight with, they would all be slaughtered.

Then a swarm of meteors crashed down. One hit in the midst of the Gibborim formation, and exploded. Less than a second later, another hit and exploded some distance from the first. Then another, and another, in quick succession. The chain of explosions sounded like a close, extended crack of thunder. Each blast sent burning rock fragments in all directions, ripping through Gibborim with savage force.

Many of the archers couldn't bear to watch the carnage, terrified that the next exploding meteor might strike near them,

But none did.

In an instant, the mountain slope below them was littered with thousands of Gibborim bodies, dead or so horribly wounded that few could stand or walk.

General Shemuel ordered his tribe to venture downhill to take the enemy's weapons and finish the ones still breathing. His archers stumbled down, ears ringing from the explosions, and followed his order as if in a trance.

A quiver spread through the ground, by sound and feel. Most of the archers assumed it was another quake getting started, but movement caught their eye and they turned heads toward the source.

Waves of enemy cavalry charged straight toward them at a full gallop. The pounding of all those hooves blended together in a fearsome rumble. Officers yelled orders for their men to take what weapons they could and retreat to the high ground they had occupied moments before. It would probably be their last stand, but they wouldn't go down without a fight.

Y'hoshua had made neutralizing the threat of chariots a priority, and evidently that part of the plan was a success. But somebody, somewhere, had missed this enormous cavalry formation, now bearing down on them. El Elyon had miraculously saved them from death just moments ago, but it appeared he would now let them be cut down and trampled *en masse*.

The horsemen charged on, hurdling the bodies of their allied foot soldiers as they came. The uphill slope seemed to give the horses no trouble, either. Could nothing so much as even slow them down?

The rumbling of the ground grew more intense as the pounding hooves drew closer. Then, as if some contest were taking place to determine who or what could shake the ground more violently, a tremor swept along the mountain, growing into a quake. The ground rolled and pitched with quickly growing intensity. Men and horses lost their balance all across the high country. What remained of city walls collapsed. The ground underfoot cracked, and cliffs thrust up where none had existed before. In other places the ground split into deep fissures. One huge, yawning chasm opened right in front of the charging cavalry. The lead waves disappeared into the crevice without a chance to even slow down. Succeeding ranks slowed, but couldn't stop in time, and down they went. Some horses did manage to stop in time, but were knocked in by others crashing into them from behind, or the ground simply falling out from under them.

The ground reeled to and fro like a drunkard, and then the chasm pinched together. The screams of horses and riders was drowned out by the din of tectonic grinding.

The quake lasted a while, felling trees and starting avalanches. The great battle paused as men sought protection from the quake or simply found objects to grab onto until it subsided.

When the ground settled again, Y'hoshua surveyed the battleground. The meteor storm hadn't harmed his army at all, but the devastation it wrought on the enemy was incalculable. He quickly estimated that the Coalition's once-insurmountable numerical advantage had been slashed down to a sixth of what it was. Every soldier on both sides was stunned by the spectacular destruction on display. Now was the time to exploit that. He signaled his buglers and they blew "Pursuit." Guidon bearers ignored their own terror and signaled to the tribes. Officers found their voices and relayed commands. Yacov renewed its efforts and pressed hard on remaining Coalition Forces.

The enemy, by this time, was too disorganized to do anything but run. It wasn't even a retreat, but a panicked rout. Yacov pursued them west-southwest down toward the lowlands, and Y'hoshua advanced with his army, making constant adjustments to their deployment as he went.

Even as they left the smoking craters behind them, more meteors fell in increasing volume. The strikes up to this point had evidently been merely a precursor to the full force of the cosmic storm, which continued its pattern of falling exclusively on Yacov's enemies.

Y'hoshua prayed as he walked, "You alone are faithful, El Elyon. You've rescued us too many times to count, and given us a great victory we can't possibly take credit for."

He examined the sky. Ma'adim loomed so close that fear of a planetary collision was understandable. But what absorbed his attention most was the sun. The army of Yacov couldn't possibly run down all the fleeing enemy by nightfall. Y'hoshua reckoned it would require another six hours at least. "Your servant needs your counsel, Hashem."

At mid day, another quake shook the mountains. Y'hoshua paused, grabbing onto a bush to steady himself as the ground shuddered underneath him. Even with the bush to anchor him, he lost his balance, but managed to sink to his knees gently, rather than fall hard. He wondered if this was Hashem's way of letting him know he needed more time in prayer.

The quake subsided. Y'hoshua bowed his head to the ground and closed his eyes. His staff waited, politely turning their backs, forming a circle around him. He didn't speak much, but listened without moving for about half an hour.

When the old field marshal rose, his staff and runners were astonished at the first command he issued.

"Hammah, stand still over Giveon," Y'hoshua said, extending his hand toward the sun. "Lebanah, in the valley of Aiyalon."

# A Day Like No Other

Winds blew with hurricane force. Black thunderclouds roiled through the East, spitting lightning. Quakes ravaged the land, and meteors continued to fall, Ma'adim rolled ponderously on its axis while shifting slowly across the sky, but the sun froze in its position.

Yacov pursued the survivors of the Coalition down into the lowlands. Thousands were struck down at Bet-Horon, while tens of thousands fled toward fortified cities like Azakah. The generals ordered their tribes to intercept before sanctuary could be reached, and some battles unfolded right outside city gates.

As Y'hoshua set up a temporary Command Post in the Aiyalon Valley, messengers from Yissakhar found him and reported that the five kings had hidden themselves in caves far to the south, near Makkedah. Y'hoshua sent word back that the caves should be sealed off with boulders and a guard detail left to watch them, while the bulk of the army maintained pursuit. When the messengers were on the way, Y'hoshua had his Command Post struck and packed. He and his staff marched to join the guard detail at Makkedah, where they would establish a temporary headquarters.

Othniel was exhausted, sore, and splattered with blood when he dragged into Makkedah with his fellow Y'hudim. It seemed this day was lasting forever, but he had not yet heard about Y'hoshua's amazing command for the sun to stop its travel across the sky. He could think of little besides slaking his thirst and a little rest in the shade.

The canyon around Makkedah funneled Yacovim troops into a defile guarded on both sides, where rear echelon staff handed out water and food to the weary combat troops. Nearly every man now carried a sword in addition to his specialty weapon. Not a sickle sword like the Gadim, but a big, straight double-edged sword taken from a fallen Gibbor.

General Kalev personally greeted his troops as they straggled in to drink water, eat quickly, and resume pursuit. He called out to his soldiers as they passed, congratulating them on their performance and encouraging them to finish the fight with courage and determination. His gaze fell on Othniel, and he fell silent for a moment before greeting the next soldier.

Othniel's blood boiled. Had he not been on the verge of collapse, he might have let his anger out against Kalev. Instead, he stumbled on. A man from the headquarters staff handed him a gourd of water, and he greedily drained it in great gulps. He was handed another gourd and a plate of food, then stumbled up a rocky incline to sit in the shade.

Somebody squeezed his shoulder from behind. He was too tired to look who it was. Then Salmon sat next to him with his own gourd and plate.

"You fought well today, kinsman," Salmon said. "I'm proud of you."

"Thank-you," Othniel replied, with barely enough energy to chew his food. "But did you see back there? Kalev might as well have slapped my face and spit on me."

Salmon shifted around to find a comfortable position, and said, "I won't pretend to know why our general behaved that way, but I can tell you I'm honored to fight beside men like you."

Daghai, from their clan, shuffled up and took a seat beside them. "You've never said anything like that to me," he said, grunting with relief once the weight was off his feet. "The closest to praise I've ever heard from you is, 'Get in step! Hold your shield like this! Can you possibly move any slower?' You should be flattered, Othniel."

True enough, Salmon was not one to hand out compliments. Under different circumstances the praise would have lifted Othniel's spirits tremendously.

"It would be nice if our general could at least do something besides insult me," Othniel grumbled.

"I could have told you he would be this way, before you set your heart on Aksah," Daghai said.

"I'm hardly the only one to show an interest in her," Othniel said.

"Ahh, but you committed the ultimate crime," Daghai said. "You got her to show an interest back."

Othniel removed his helmet and squeezed his temples. "This is all impossible."

"Nothing is impossible for El Elyon," Daghai said, "as he keeps proving to us."

"That's good for El Elyon," Othniel said, "but how does that help me?"

"Pray to him," Daghai answered, simply. "Ask him to let you know if you should pursue her, or forget her. If he wills that you have Aksah, he'll open a door for you."

"Only for Kalev to slam it shut," Othniel said.

Daghai shrugged. "Our god is more powerful than Kalev, or Y'hoshua, or even Moshe. If Hashem wants it for you, he might even use Kalev to bring it about."

Salmon wiped his mouth and stood. "We need to get going."

"Hey, I just got started," Daghai protested, nearly choking on his food.

"We're not going to have daylight forever," Salmon said. "We've got a mission to finish."

Daghai took one last bite of food, swigged down some water and wiped his hands. "Yes Sir."

Othniel set aside his plate and gourd. "May I catch up with you?"

Salmon raised one eyebrow as he studied Othniel's face.

"I just need a little time to pray," Othniel said.

After his prayer was finished, Othniel marched off in the direction his comrades had gone. Ahead of him was a commotion, and a crowd of soldiers that fairly blocked passage through the canyon. As he drew closer, he saw a handful of richly-garbed giants being escorted out of a cave. From their waists up to their heads were visible beyond the Yacovim soldiers. Othniel crowded in to get a better look, and was surprised to recognize Y'hoshua in the middle of the crowd.

The giants were herded into a line and forced to their knees at spearpoint. Y'hoshua paced in front of them and addressed the Yacovim who were present. "These men here are the kings over the armies we fought today. As you can see, we have rendered our enemies leaderless."

Y'hoshua pressed the point of his javelin into the back of Adonaizidek's neck, and kept the pressure on until the king was prostrate, face in the dirt. Y'hoshua growled at the other kings, who assumed the same position. Then Y'hoshua replaced the javelin point with the sole of his foot. All the captive kings changed colors, beholding this outrageous insult. But there was little they could do with a contingent of Yacovim soldiers surrounding them, ready to carve them up.

"There's no need to fear any of our enemies, or their gods," Y'hoshua proclaimed, loudly. "We have to be strong and bold, and El Elyon will do this to all our enemies, no matter how large their soldiers, or armies. No matter how powerful! Nobody and nothing can stand against our god." He waved upward toward the sun and Ma'adim. "You are all witnesses: even the heavenly bodies obey his commands. Who can thwart the promises of our god?"

As Y'hoshua spoke, the Yacovim soldiers within earshot grunted or shouted their agreement, punctuating his speech.

Othniel was taken aback when Y'hoshua walked right up to him and grabbed his arm.

"These captives are considered god-kings, and even worshiped by the heathens. But they are frauds! The only true god, and the only true king, is the one we serve!"

Soldiers cheered their agreement, Y'hoshua tugged Othniel along by the arm toward the captives.

"Why do people worship dumb statues as if they were gods?" Y'hoshua continued. He pointed at the humiliated captives. "Why do they pledge their souls and lives to creatures like these? These reprobate scum can't even rescue themselves—how can a man trust them to rescue him?"

Y'hoshua positioned Othniel next to where King D'vir bowed, then faced Othniel.

"Othniel, son of Kenaz, you fought well so far, today," Y'hoshua said.

Othniel blushed at the attention he was getting from the crowd because of these words. How did Y'hoshua know he fought well? How could he possibly keep track of a lowly spear man among the families, clans, and tribes of Yacov? How could Y'hoshua even know the name of one soldier among the fifties and hundreds and thousands of his army?

"Put your foot on his neck," Y'hoshua said.

Othniel placed his sandal on the back of the gigantic captive's neck and pressed down.

Y'hoshua gestured toward D'vir, addressing the crowd. "This is a 'god-king' over our enemies. Othniel is just a spear man in the Yacovim Army. But who has his foot on the other's neck?"

"Othniel!" cried a chorus of soldiers.

"Look at the size difference," Y'hoshua said. "This so-called god-king is gigantic...powerful...has authority over cities and peoples and can end the life of man, woman or child on a whim." Y'hoshua gestured towards Othniel. "Our countryman is of normal stature—less than half the size of this 'god-king.' He's a young soldier, on his first campaign; and has nothing near the strength of this giant. I ask you: what is the difference between these two that caused the seeming lessor one to prevail?"

The crowd responded with a murmur of various answers.

Y'hoshua gestured toward Othniel and D'vir, in turn. "The difference is in the god each one serves! No creature can thwart the promises of El Elyon—not soldier or king; man or 'god.' The people who trusted in this 'god-king'—or any god besides El Elyon—are being destroyed today."

Y'hoshua clapped Othniel on the shoulder—a gesture the young soldier took for a dismissal. He took his foot off the giant's neck and slipped back into the crowd.

"How many of my generals are here right now?" Y'hoshua asked.

Kalev, Paltiel and Elizaphan pushed their way to the front.

"El Elyon is giving us extra time," Y'hoshua said, pointing again to the sun. "After a little water and food, we have to complete our victory today. But I want every general in this army to stop here and take the time to step on the neck of these so-called god-kings." With a beckoning gesture, he urged the three generals presently there to start.

Kalev and Elizaphan stepped on each captive's neck, in turn. The crowd cheered when Paltiel jumped from king to king, landing on one's neck with every bound.

"This is what our god is going to do to all the gods of our enemies," Y'hoshua declared. "And all people who follow them."

Othniel watched the proceedings for a moment, then realized he would have to run hard to catch up to Salmon and his fifty. Strangely, though, he now felt he had the energy to do it.

He left Makkedah with his feet slapping the ground in a steady staccato beat.

Before the day was over, all the tribal generals would make their way through Makkedah, and step on the necks of the "god-kings."

But the day was far from over.

# When Wanderers Pass

## (Rachivel)

El Elyon had established the orbits of Ma'adim and Kadur Ha'aretz precisely so the two planets would intersect each other's orbits on a set schedule, and every so often they would experience a near pass. A near pass-by of planets causes an energy transfer through orbital resonance.

The sun did not literally stand still, as the eye witnesses to the event would tell their children and grandchildren. But then, they knew nothing about orbital resonance. What actually happens is the energy transfer causes a polar shift that throws off all the compass points, also affecting orbit and rotation. While all this was happening, the sun appeared to stop and remain fixed in place for a full day, due to relative positions of the sun and the eye witnesses' position on the surface of the planet.

El Elyon worked out the timing of these near passes, knowing how history would unfold and that he could use the effects of the energy transfer to the benefit of his followers...and the confoundment of his enemies.

If you find that level of precision and forward-planning incredible, just consider the accuracy of the meteor storm. Meteors are rocks– inanimate objects. It's ridiculous to suppose they could differentiate between a Yacovim and his enemy, much less alter their own course to strike one and not the other. Yet the meteors fell only on the enemy that day, killing more of them than the soldiers of Yacov were able to kill, at final count. And it is the mother of all understatements to say that the meteor storm was put into motion long before anyone on the battlefield was even born.

Nonetheless, this day marked the closest the two planets would get to each other. From that day on (during the span of everyone alive at the time), Ma'adim shrunk in the sky, and the epidemic of natural disasters would dwindle with its retreat.

The reputation of El Elyon, however, and the fear he inspired, would not dwindle as quickly.

# Aftermath

There were many promotions by the end of that day, as units were split and reorganized to outflank, encircle, or otherwise trap pockets of the enemy. Common soldiers became lieutenants; lieutenants became captains; and captains became marshals.

Salmon was promoted to captain, though the hundred he took command of was barely over the strength of his old fifty.

The battle of Bet-Horon (as it would later be known) degenerated into a chaotic mop-up operation, but on a strategic scale. Disorganized Coalition Forces were isolated and destroyed as quickly as possible, for all Yacov's generals worried that when the sun finally did go down, some of the enemy would certainly escape.

Alas, the sun finally did sink toward the horizon. Y'hoshua had Makkedah put to the sword, and established camp there, surrounding his temporary Command Post. The five "god-kings" were slain, hung from five trees for all Yacov's army to see, but cut down before sunset.

Like nearly everyone else, when Salmon and Othniel dragged themselves into camp, they were thirsty, hungry, utterly exhausted, and every muscle in their bodies sore. Othniel fell asleep by the fire in mid-motion of raising spoon to lips. Salmon passed out halfway through the task of removing his armor.

Makkedah was a convenient campsite for Kalev, because it was inside his tribe's allotment of land. Just a short march to the east was Kireath-Arba, and a shorter march to the south was D'vir—named after the king whose neck Othniel stepped on. Armies of the remaining southern kingdoms had reached the safety of fortified cities like these before the Yacovim could engage them.

Kalev had explored the outskirts of Kireath-Arba long ago, during the infamous reconnaissance mission assigned by Moshe. There were better areas, to be sure: more fertile, or more picturesque. But Kalev fixated on Kireath-Arba, and was overwhelmed with the compulsion to one day make the surrounding land his home.

The trouble was, the city's strong fortifications had survived all the recent quakes, and three of the most powerful Gibborim generals had escaped behind its walls with enough giant warriors to make it an extremely difficult prize to capture. And the longer they could hide behind the walls, the more organized a fighting force they would become.

Kalev marched east the next morning, leading a weary, hungry tribe of warriors.

The elongated day had enabled Y'hoshua to annihilate the Coalition Forces of the five kings, but that had motivated the remaining heathens in the south to consolidate, redeploy, and fortify. Y'hoshua wanted to dislodge them before they could dig in too deeply, but there were just too many pockets of resistance to mop up piecemeal. He gave each of the tribes their own assignments so they could sweep and clear multiple areas simultaneously.

Kalev surrounded Kireath-Arba, cutting off all routes in and out. He sent scouts to the walls by night to see what they could and report back. Reluctantly he decided that (save for a special intervention by Hashem) the wise thing to do was besiege the city, as they would have besieged Bet-Yariq under normal circumstances. He left a few thousands to forage in the captured villages and maintain the siege while the bulk of the tribe returned to Stone Circle. He instituted a rotation plan that would ensure the troops conducting the siege were well-fed and rested.

They would have to wait it out until the three generals either surrendered, or grew too weak to defend the walls.

Other generals used similar strategies to subdue the southern kingdoms.

# Wounds to Flesh and Soul

What soon became tribal reserves returned to Stone Circle in seemingly random stages, were reorganized, then parceled out to relieve besieging forces or pacify other areas with weaker defenses.

Salmon's hundred was in one of the first stages to cycle back to Stone Circle. He and many of his soldiers were in poor shape. Everyone was sore from the marching and fighting, but something was so wrong with his shoulders (especially the right one) that moving his arms caused spikes of pain to shoot up and down his body. The palms of his hands were shredded into raw, bloody pulp from an unending succession of blisters. All that was the result of using his new giant sword in the last several skirmishes. But the jagged wound running from his left armpit down his side had been inflicted by a giant's sword wielded by its original owner. His comrades had bound and bandaged it back at Makkedah, but blood seeped out whenever he moved around too much, and the loss of blood made him weak and dizzy.

Families greeted their husbands, sons, and fathers with tears and warm embraces. Midwives and their pupils tended to the wounded. L'vim came by to pray with the soldiers, and collect their portion of the plunder.

Salmon collected his wounded men and marched them to the hospital area for treatment. He passed out in the heat of the day, waiting for the nurses to make the rounds.

He came to when it was a bit cooler, as he realized somebody was moving his body around. His eyes cracked open and he saw a blurry vision of two soldiers and three women struggling to remove his armor and relocate him from the bench outside one of the tents. His eyes closed again. He was stretched out and laid down on a flat surface with something soft under his head. The comfort was greatly appreciated, though he wasn't lucid enough to put it in words. "Thank you," a soft, feminine voice said. "Just leave him there and I'll tend to him."

He felt a pleasant warmth on his forehead and forced his eyes open again. He blinked and a smooth, oval shape began coming into focus, framed by black silk flaps and a gray dome. He blinked more and saw that the black silk was hair falling out from under a gray scarf, and the oval was the face of a beautiful woman with dark eyes and full, soft lips.

Rachav removed her hand from his forehead, saying, "Thank Hashem there's no fever."

He grimaced and tried to speak her name, but his mouth only moved noiselessly.

"Do you know where you are?" she asked.

He tried harder to force sound out. "Stone Circle. The hospital area?"

She nodded and smiled. What a wonderful smile, he thought. I feel better just looking at it.

She gently cut away his bandages, and the smile faded. She wrinkled her pretty brow in concern. "Oh, Salmon...how long have you been walking around with this?"

He instinctively shrugged as he began to reply, but the resulting stabs of pain froze the words in his throat.

When his nerves calmed down, he forced out, "You should see my opponent."

Her hand touched his cheek this time. "Relax and be still. I'll be back."

When Rachav returned, a midwife came with her. It was obviously the woman teaching her about medicine, judging by how she handed out instructions and explanations while they worked.

Together, the two women raised Salmon up from his bed to drink water. It caused pain and increased bleeding, but the midwife assured Rachav that it was necessary, for what came next, that the patient be well-hydrated.

What came next was stitches. The midwife had Rachav heat the needle in a fire until it glowed, then douse it and the wound with some harsh-smelling liquid. Salmon cried out and Rachav made a sympathetic noise, but the midwife threaded the needle without a comment, and began to sew his flesh back together in a very businesslike manner.

Once finished, the midwife left to tend other wounded, leaving Rachav to bathe the patient with a sponge.

Getting the blood, sweat and grime washed off him felt good, and the tenderness of Rachav's ministrations with the sponge was very soothing. Salmon didn't know how to express his gratitude. His dizzy mind was more intrigued by her than ever. Her former lifestyle just seemed totally incompatible with the sympathy and kindness he saw in her right then. While watching her, he saw a vision of her comforting a little boy–tending to a scraped knee and kissing his forehead to make him feel better.

Then it occurred to him: after all the men she'd been with, shouldn't she...?

"Where are all your children?" he blurted, in a gritty, scratchy, wavering voice.

The sponging stopped in mid-motion. Her eyes widened and her gaze met his, before dropping straight down.

"I have no children," she said, blushing.

"How could that be?"

"My mother gave me a tonic to drink," she replied, quietly. "It prevented me from ever conceiving."

"Oh," he said.

She resumed the sponge bath.

"It's none of my business," he said, after a moment. "I didn't mean to be rude, or bring up matters you're trying to forget."

"I would be curious, too," she said, "if I were someone else, knowing certain things about the heathen prostitute now living nearby."

"Thank-you," he said, "for taking care of me."

She wrung out the sponge one more time, then pulled a blanket up to his waist. "Pull that up to your chin when it cools down tonight," she said. I've got to help with the other wounded. Be as still as you can be and try to get some sleep."

He watched her rise and walk away. He would never guess what kind of life she led back in Bet-Yariq, to look at her now. *A whore with a heart of gold.* The cliche was as old as civilization, and a ridiculous one at that. Except, perhaps, in this one case.

The next morning, Rachav and the midwife helped Salmon rise and walk to his own tent. The midwife explained that he should avoid any sudden moves—and minimize all movement as best he could. But he should also get up and change position now and then, to avoid bed sores. They checked his wound again before leaving him alone with his thoughts.

The next day Rachav returned, without the midwife, to check the wound. She brought him food, water, and an ointment she massaged into his shoulders.

"What is this?" he asked, turning up his nose at the smell of the substance.

"It's something that's good for sore muscles," she said, with determination, as she struggled to knead it into his shoulders. "You're like a bundle of knots. No wonder you scowl all the time."

"I scowl?" he reacted.

"You are the ultimate champion scowler," she said, rubbing more ointment on and digging down into his muscle with fingertips and knuckles.

He moaned.

"What's wrong?" she asked.

"It hurts, Rachav. I'm already in pain, and you're making it worse."

"I'm making it better, she said, still kneading. "Don't be a baby. It may cause some discomfort for a little while, but you'll feel much better once your muscles loosen up."

"What is that you're putting on me?"

"It's a mixture of oils and herbs my grandmother used to make. It's good for cramps, pulled muscles, even torn muscles. It makes you heal faster."

"It smells awful," he complained, his pride maybe just a bit chapped from her rebuke.

She grew still, staring at him with eyebrows raised. Then she deliberately swiped a dab of ointment out of the jar, with her finger, and smeared it across his upper lip.

Salmon's face contorted as the odor went right up his nostrils at full dosage. He reflexively reached up to wipe it away, and winced, groaning from the resulting waves of agony.

She giggled at his disgusted expression. "How do you like that, Mr. Scrunchy-Face?"

He fought through the pain and rubbed the ointment off his face as best he could.

"Agh! It's in my skin now, right under my nose! I can still smell it."

She went back to work on the area between his neck and shoulders, showing him a smug grin. "That should teach you to whine and complain when I'm trying to make you feel better."

She had a point, he realized. And after a some time of her massaging, he did begin to feel better. When she left to make her rounds, he was sad to see her go.

Othniel was looking forward to seeing Aksah when he made it back to Stone Circle. Even better, Kalev had rotated back with the first thousands relieved from siege duty, but had rotated back to Kireath-Arba, now. He wouldn't be around to sour whatever time they could spend with each other.

Aksah didn't live up to his hopes of a warm greeting with a big smile, though. She didn't even come out to greet him when his thousand marched up to camp. He sought her out, and found her attending to chores. She was polite, but her voice was flat and attitude almost indifferent.

He held his arms out to his sides, as if inviting a nurse's inspection. "Healthy from head to toe," he announced, cheerily.

She gave him a perfunctory smile but continued working, saying nothing.

"What's wrong?" he asked.

"Nothing's wrong," she replied. "Why do you ask?"

"I thought you would be happy to see me," he said.

"I'm happy to see you," she said, still concentrating on her work. "I'm glad you made it back safe."

Obviously, something had changed. This was not the same Aksah who had leaned her head on his shoulder and shared her hopes with him. What could have erased all the progress they'd made?

His thoughts naturally went back to the shame from the First Battle of Ahyee. But had he not proved at Bet-Horon that he was not a coward?

To everyone but Kalev, he supposed, remembering the general's shun at Makkedah.

She continued to forage as if he were not there—or didn't matter.

"Aksah," he said.

"Yes?" she still didn't look his way.

"If something is different now, from when we sat together at the river, you need to tell me."

She said nothing; still wouldn't look his way. Just ignored him.

He made a few more attempts to open a conversation, but it was obvious she wasn't interested. It was like they didn't even know each other.

Bewildered and somewhat angry, he left her and trudged back to camp.

Her behavior perplexed him deeply. Had the time they spent together before Bet-Horon meant something to him, but not to her? Maybe she had experiences like that with other men, so it was nothing noteworthy. That was a painful and embarrassing possibility. But he couldn't know for sure if she refused to communicate with him.

He loved her...probably had since they were children...so it hurt.

Then again, maybe it wasn't love. After growing up with her, did he still not truly know her? Perhaps his love...or whatever it was...had blinded him to her true nature. He'd heard many older people (especially his mother and other women) talk about how love could do that.

Othniel saw his father sitting outside his tent, removing his sandals. His mother set a jar of water next to him and dipped a ladle in, holding it to his mouth to drink. After that, she kissed the side of his face and said she would have food ready for him soon. Othniel wished he hadn't seen that right then, because it reminded him of what he had hoped he would one day experience with Aksah.

As he drew close, his father looked up and noticed him. "Hello, Son. Mother should have the meal ready soon. Want some water?"

Othniel nodded and sat on the other side of the water jar. "Thank-you. Have you got a moment to talk, Father?"

Kenaz massaged one of his feet as he turned to study his son. "Of course. What troubles you?"

"Did you ever speak to Kalev about Aksah for me?"

Kenaz frowned. "I did. I'm afraid I have no confidence that the match will ever be made."

Othniel looked away, shaking his head, slowly.

Kenaz chewed on his lower lip while watching his son, then said, "She's his only daughter, Othniel. And a child of his old age."

"Yes, I know. And I look too young. Or whatever reason Kalev despises me."

"Othniel, I know you have an emotional connection to Aksah. And at your age now, probably a strong desire for her."

Othniel didn't respond to that, but it certainly was true.

"That's not always a consideration when arranging a marriage," Kenaz continued. "It's been this way for thousands of years. Since before Yacov was even a nation, in fact. Parents have many considerations when trying to secure a match, and feelings aren't the most important one."

Othniel knew this. He'd certainly heard it enough times. But his heart was in the habit of trying to overrule his brain.

"Of course, it's nice when the match is made with somebody you already care for. But wise parents, who love their children, will try to find a match that will compliment their child. These emotions you feel...they can fade. In fact I'm sure they will, in time. What is left once they do, if the match is not otherwise a good fit?"

"I know," Othniel said, dipping some water out of the jar. "I know. I listen to you and mother, and you've told me many times."

"Well, on the other side of that," Kenaz said, "is another one of Hashem's rewards: you and your wife can grow to love each other deeply, even if you didn't have all those feelings at first, like what you feel for Aksah now. And that love lasts longer, and endures more than those giddy emotions ever will."

"Because love is more than an emotion," Othniel recited, then took a drink.

Kenaz reached over to gently squeeze the back of his son's neck. "I know how strong those feelings can be, Son. I know it's hard to accept what I'm telling you, when you're drunk with them. Just believe me when I tell you that, should you never have Aksah as a wife, it doesn't mean that you'll never be happy. That contradicts everything you're probably feeling right now, but I promise it's true."

They were quiet for a time, Othniel just staring over the camp, toward Aksah's family's tent. "Did you hear how Kalev treated me at Makkedah?" he finally asked.

Kenaz nodded. "It angers me too, Son. He had no cause to shun you that way. You're a good soldier, and proven yourself in battle repeatedly."

"But maybe he still considers me a coward because of Ahyee."

Kenaz shook his head. "Why just you, and not everybody else who went there the first time?"

"Father...do you think I'm a coward? I mean, even though I fought there the second time, and around Bet-Horon...maybe in my soul, secretly, I'm still a coward."

Forgetting he was now barefoot, Kenaz stood, pulling his son up to stand facing him. "Look at me."

251

Othniel met his father's hard gaze.

"You are no coward, Son. You've never been one. I pity any man who accuses you so. I won't allow that from any other soldier; from Kalev; or even Y'hoshua himself. And not from you, either. Understood?"

"Yes Father."

The two of them sat again.

"I've wanted Aksah for a long time," Othniel finally said. "Since her father hates me, for whatever reason...I don't want to waste more years hoping for something I'll never have. Maybe I should get used to the idea that whoever my wife will be, it won't be her."

Kenaz showed him a smile that seemed almost sad. But then, everything was sad to Othniel right then.

"I've been meaning to talk to Shimson," Kenaz said. Your mother and I will invite he and his wife over tomorrow night, to talk."

Shimson had a daughter named Shoshanah who was not spoken for. Othniel hadn't thought much about her before. He hadn't thought much about any girl but Aksah. "I don't mean to rush you, Father. We'll be returning to the siege soon, anyway, true?"

"Oh, there is no rush," Kenaz said. "And I'm sure nothing will be agreed before we march. Betrothals take some time, anyway. But it's never too soon to begin determining if there is a good match."

Othniel nodded, glumly.

"I wish I could have prevented you from fixating on one girl at a young age," Kenaz said. "Only Hashem knows what wife the future has for you, and a young man is likely to pick the wrong one on his own. You shouldn't have set your heart on Aksah, and you shouldn't set your heart on Shoshanah. Let your mother and I find out who is best for you."

Othniel nodded, already trying to put his heart in subjection to his brain, but not having much luck.

The house of Shimson supped with the house of Kenaz later that week. Afterwards, the news spread rapidly throughout the camp. Most people had known about Othniel's crush on Aksah for many years, and most assumed they would be matched, eventually. A possible match between Othniel and Shoshanah was gossip that every woman who knew them considered worthy of discussion and speculation. Some of the men, too.

The next night, Othniel sat alone by the dying fire after everyone but the sentries had gone to bed. He'd done this every night since returning to Stone Circle. It might turn out to be a regular practice, since he had a lot on his mind that kept him awake, lately.

Aksah appeared out of the dark and approached him, tentatively. His heart leapt, at first, but joy quickly transformed to dread as he considered the reality of the situation and her coldness toward him.

"What are you doing here?" he asked, not bothering to stand.

She sat across the fire from him. "I heard about you and Shoshanah," she said.

"We're not betrothed. Our parents are just talking." He immediately regretted betraying his concern over her opinion on the matter. "Why do you care?"

He half-expected her to snap some equally hostile retort. She didn't. Her voice sounded strange, almost choked, as she said, "I'm sorry I didn't answer you before. You deserve to know why...why I'm acting different toward you."

She wiped at her eyes, but he didn't consider why she might be doing that, until later.

"My father spoke to me before he left," she said. She paused for a moment so long, he wondered temporarily if that was the extent of her revelation. But then she wiped her eyes again and said, "He told me that he wouldn't keep me in his house forever, that I have entered my child-bearing years and it is time for marriage."

"Foolish me," Othniel said, "but I assumed that's what you wanted. And that it was me you would prefer for a husband."

She ignored his remark. "Furthermore, my father said he would soon determine who to match me with. And that it would be someone he knows to be worthy."

"So of course that couldn't possibly be me," Othniel said, bitterly.

"Knowing how my father speaks to you...and *about* you," she replied, quietly, "I don't think there is any chance you and I will ever be married." She sniffled and stood, abruptly. "I just want you to know...I have to abide by his decision, no matter how I feel about it."

She left the way she had come, disappearing from the dull firelight.

Rachav visited at least once a day to inspect Salmon's wound, and his spirit was lifted each time he saw her. She encouraged him to move around a little bit more every day, and in time escorted him for walks outside the camp after checking his stitches.

An abscess developed in the wound, and part of the stitching had to be opened up to treat it.

Some physicians were known to put maggots in open wounds to eat away the infected flesh. Salmon was thankful such was not done to him. The midwife taught Rachav to change the bandage every day, after pouring some stinging liquid into the abscess, then letting it air out for a while.

On one of their first walks, they passed by the tree where the young potter liked to work. Again, Rachav marveled at his craftsmanship, and the artistic flair of his painted designs.

The potter shocked her by lifting an exquisitely crafted vase and dashing it against an exposed tree root, angrily. She sucked in a breath, making a little gasping sound that drew the attention of both Salmon and the potter.

"Why did you do that?" she asked.

"It was worthless," the potter replied.

"Worthless? It was perfect. You obviously invested time and effort to shape it. Why would you destroy it?"

The boy grabbed a shard from the shattered vase and held it up to her. "It was perfect, when I made it," he grumbled. "But insects got into it while the clay was still wet."

She took the fragment and examined it. There were what looked like tunnels burrowed through the clay on the inside, and a dead insect half-buried in the now dried clay.

"Oh, that's awful," she said. "But you couldn't even tell from the outside. It looked perfect, before you broke it."

"But it wasn't perfect," the boy said, irritated. "I made it a certain way, and it wasn't that way anymore. It was ruined. If I wanted vermin inside it, I would have put them there myself."

Rachav sighed. Salmon took her arm and steered her away. As they resumed their walk, she said, "Maybe it wasn't perfect anymore, but it was wonderfully made. And it would have served just fine, to hold flowers and water."

Salmon would have shrugged, but pain had trained him to avoid that gesture. "He's the one who formed it out of the clay. He has the right to do whatever he wants with his own creation, doesn't he?"

"Such a waste," she said.

"I've seen him go through this before," Salmon said. "If the clay hadn't already hardened, he would have repaired it. He'll start over and make a new one."

She fell silent, looking sad.

They spent a lot of time together, and Salmon came to treasure it. He took an interest in stories from her childhood, the things she liked, and her insights into the nature of people. What he liked best was how her hopes for the future were so far removed from the sort of life she used to live. She accepted all his people's ways without protest, which must have been difficult; and with Pinchas' teachings, she was learning more about his religion than what he knew.

Salmon corrected that by inviting Pinchas to his tent, regularly, to share his knowledge. And Salmon kept his word about finding some friends for Rachav. He talked to his sisters, cousins and aunts, encouraging them to include her in their social circle.

The next time she took him for a walk, the subject came up. She surprised him by saying, "I'm certainly grateful. But I've already found someone whose company has brought me much joy."

"Oh?" he replied, feeling a pang of jealousy. "Who might that be?"

She stared at him crossly for a moment, then blew a puff of air out the side of her mouth at a strand of raven-black hair which had fallen down to her cheek. In frustration at his ignorance, she sighed, "You."

"Of course," he said, after a moment. "Of course."

Later, when alone and missing her company, he decided that he should have responded differently.. She'd been nothing but kind to him, and let her guard down with him since leaving Bet-Yariq. As a warrior, he took vulnerability as an invitation to attack—a good reflex in combat, but not necessarily a noble habit when interacting with the more delicate sex. Revealing her vulnerabilities to him was a major sign of trust, but the way he reacted possibly struck her as a violation of trust.

If a child wanted to make a pet of a kitten, they had to treat it gently, and prove repeatedly that they would not try to hurt it if it allowed them to get close. They had to earn its trust. Some friendships could be like that.

Rachav was letting Salmon get close, and he should be at least flattered. He should prove she was safe with him emotionally, instead of constantly condemning her in his heart for her former life, reminding her of it, or shunning her as if she were still a whore.

During their next walk, she was a lot more guarded than she had been. She didn't seem interested in small talk, nor in giving more than one-word answers to his inquiries about her family, her studies, and how she was adapting to living among the Yacovim. His frown deepened as he realized his worries about scaring her away had proven valid.

"Rachav," he said, "I want you to know something."

Despite her silent aloofness that evening, this got her attention. She inclined her head toward him as if to say, "I'm listening."

"My opinion of you has changed since I first met you," he said.

She stopped and turned to face him. He stopped, too.

"You've been very patient with me..." he started, then chewed on his lip for a moment. "Or, what I should say is, I've been very brusque with you. And I shouldn't have been."

"Is this an apology?" she asked.

He shrugged and nodded.

"I have to ask you," she said, "because you never actually say you're sorry."

"Not to make excuses," he said, "but I'm around men...my soldiers and superiors...all the time. Men talk a certain way to each other, and that's what I'm used to. I've never been around women very much. Not enough to learn how to talk like a woman, anyway."

"Talk like a woman?" she repeated, still speaking soft and quiet, her gaze lowered.

"Well, that's not exactly what I meant." He licked his lips. "I understand that I can't talk to a woman the same way I talk to my soldiers. Nor can I expect you to perform like my soldiers...not that I was trying to train you or anything..."

Her face was a mask right then. He was sure hundreds of thoughts and emotions were bouncing around in her mind, but couldn't confirm it by her inscrutable expression.

He scratched his neck and sighed. "I worry that I've probably hurt your feelings. More than once. I'm not used to considering feelings when I speak or act. Anyway...I'm sorry."

"I understand," she said, eyes still downcast. "Your parents died when you were very young. You probably didn't see them together for long enough to learn what children normally learn, just by watching."

"Um...how do you know about my parents?"

"I asked Pinchas," she replied, so quiet he almost didn't hear her. "And others who know you."

"A lot of children were orphaned at a young age in Yacov," he said, defensively. "I was well taken-care-of. Members of my clan looked after me."

She said nothing, but did sneak a quick glance up at him.

"Since you already know about my parents," he said, "then you know that they can't arrange a marriage for me."

Now she looked up deliberately, and he could read anxiety all over her features. "B-before you go any farther, Salmon. It's only fair that I tell you..."

"What?" he asked, confused.

Tears streamed down her face as sudden as a flash flood. He

stepped forward to grasp her hands, but she backed away, holding up her right hand so her palm faced him. He stopped and lowered his hands.

"I'm barren," she said. "That tonic my mother used to give me...it seems to have closed my womb forever."

He wasn't sure what to say or think, so he just stared at her.

"It wasn't my...smartest decision ever," she continued, haltingly, "but I stopped taking it, secretly. Foolish and disobedient, yes. But I really wanted..." She took a deep breath and choked back a sob. "There was a man that used to come to me. He wasn't like the others. He was kind, but very lonely. I wasn't revolted by the thought of being with him, as I was with so many others. Anyway, I hoped...I really wanted a child, even if...but...but it didn't happen. All that time poisoning myself with that tonic, I lost forever any chance of..."

She was seized by convulsive sobs, spun, and ran away into the dusk outside of camp. He heard her anguished cries slowly fade as the distance between them grew.

# A Siege Cut Short

Inside Kireath-Arba, the defenders kept their strength and sanity longer than most men would have. After sacrificing the children within the walls to Moloch, they ate them, drinking their blood to slake their thirst. The women among them were next.

The siege dragged on for months. Kalev was beyond impatient to take the city, but holding discipline about it so as not to needlessly amass casualties in his tribe when they did assault the walls. He felt a mixture of relief and apprehension when Y'hoshua forced his hand.

Kalev's old friend, and commanding officer, needed everything in the south wrapped up before winter, so they could launch the northern campaign in the spring. That meant Y'huda's allotted land had to be completely pacified within a couple months; which, in turn, meant he had to conquer Kireath-Arba immediately, then move on the remaining strongholds.

Kalev brought the entire tribe back from Stone Circle—save for a couple thousands to help guard the camp.

In the middle of the night, a detachment from Yissakhar, temporarily assigned to Kalev's command, slung volleys of burning rags knotted around small stones over the walls. Before all the defenders were roused out of sleep, the city inside was in flames.

A battering ram was brought to the gate under a shield wall, while slingers harassed what few Gibborim could be spared from fighting the fire to drop objects or throw javelins at the ram force. When the gate was breached, teams went forward all around the city walls with ladders, ropes and grappling hooks, or siege towers.

The defenders might have been able to stop two or three threats simultaneously, when wide awake, but Yacovim warriors were flooding into the city from every direction, while the fire raged all around them.

With the surprise and confusion, it wasn't hard to isolate individual giants and wipe out the garrison piecemeal.

Salmon was mostly healed, but hadn't been sent to participate in the assault.

Othniel fought like a lion. He was relentless. His anger and frustration gave him seemingly endless reserves of energy. Officers noticed, too. With Salmon temporarily out of action, one of Salmon's lieutenants was brevetted to take his place. Now they needed to promote someone to take the lieutenant's place. Othniel's name came up in after-action discussions.

The Gibborim Generals Talmai, Sheshai, and Ahiman, escaped through a secret tunnel under the wall, when it was obvious the city was lost. Kalev sent a detachment, with some of his best scout/trackers, to hunt them down.

When the last resistance had been mopped up in the city, no structure remained standing except the walls. Mass graves were dug; idols were burnt or otherwise destroyed, and the plunder (that which wasn't forbidden) was taxed. Kalev declared that new houses and barns would be built as soon as the war was over, and that he had Y'hoshua's blessing to cut out an estate for himself on the fertile slope outside the walls.

But, speaking of Y'hoshua, his urgent timetable meant the Y'hudim had to march forth immediately to finish pacifying the region. That meant Kalev had to split the tribe further in order to march on all the enemy strongholds simultaneously.

# The Impossible Prize

Enemy morale was low, and the Kenaanim put up little resistance. One distinct exception was Kireath-Sepher. It was a mountain fortress, with steep cliffs on three sides. The only approach was straight at the front, where the defenders' had all the advantages–high ground; cover; concealment; shade... Great reserves of water and rations had been brought inside the repaired wall, so they could withstand a siege well into the winter–past Y'hoshua's deadline for pacifying south Kenaan. They had also stockpiled arrows, javelins and boulders to hurl down upon an attacking force. Scuttlebutt spread that Talmai had entered the fort and taken command of the garrison. Some rumors went further–speculating that all three Gibborim generals were inside the walls.

Kalev was directing a sweep through the villages near Kireath-Arba, but a messenger found him and gave a report on the situation at Kireath-Sepher.

"A frontal attack would be suicide," the messenger said. "The terrain funnels all possible avenues directly into their heavy defenses. There is no other approach possible, so all they have to defend is that front wall. We were crammed together on the mountain path marching toward the walls, and a hail of arrows caught us with nowhere to run or hide–except behind the bodies of our comrades. Some of the lightly wounded men rushed forward from there, with arrows sticking out of legs and shoulders, only to be pierced through by javelins. Later, an assault team was sent forward with a battering ram under a shield wall. Ladder teams couldn't fit through the defile with them, and were driven away by arrows as they waited for their turn to squeeze through. Anyway, as soon as the ramming team drew near to the gate, the giants simply dropped boulders on top of them. The boulders smashed the men right through their shields."

Kalev questioned the messenger at length, and came to the conclusion that a siege was the only way to take the fort. The defenders could be starved out if cut off for long enough, but aside from that, only direct intervention by El Elyon could overcome such formidable defenses.

Kalev spent the night praying for just that. But the next messenger who arrived didn't bring news of another miracle—he brought a weather report on winter closing in, and Y'hoshua's demand for an update.

Kalev summoned all the messengers from around Kireath-Arba, plus his own tribal runners. On the soil of a pomegranate grove he paced back and forth before them. "I want this message sent throughout the tribe—and throughout the nation, if that fails to bring results: the man who is able to take the fortress of Kireath-Sepher...as a reward, he will receive the hand of my daughter, Aksah, in marriage."

Kalev didn't want to give his daughter up to any but a worthy man. A man who would volunteer for such an assignment...and succeed...was probably the closest to a perfect match he would ever find.

Inwardly, Kalev believed the city wouldn't be taken without a siege—disappointing his old friend and commanding officer Y'hoshua. But nobody could say he didn't offer the most powerful incentive he had

When the word came down and reached Othniel, he grunted in disgust. So this was how Kalev planned to find a "worthy" match for Aksah. Only officers would even be allowed to try, since only an officer would have enough men to attempt an assault.

Most officers already had wives; but there was a young one: Haliel son of Burshai, who was still unmarried, and infatuated with Aksah from afar. He led a hundred on an attack against Kireath-Sepher, and few survivors made it back from the slaughter.

Othniel had done his best to forget about Aksah, but Kalev's offer caused him to ponder the whole situation anew, every waking hour. Shoshanah seemed like a pleasant enough girl, from what he knew about her, but Aksah was still the wife he truly wanted. This was an opportunity that would never arise again, he realized. And a chance to prove to Kalev (and himself) that he was no coward–that he was worthy of Aksah.

If only he was an officer.

The third time his marshal visited the various hundreds and fifties under his command, to repeat Kalev's incentive, Othniel pushed to the front rank and proclaimed, "Give me a command of my own, Sir, and I'll take the city."

"Who are you, soldier?" the marshal asked.

"Othniel, son of Kenaz, Sir."

The marshal sought out the captain of Othniel's hundred, who conferred with him in subdued tones.

"What do you know about this soldier?" the marshal asked.

"He's brave, and fights with great valor, Sir," the captain replied.

"Does he have leadership potential?" the marshal asked. "He looks too young to even be in the army."

"I think men would fight for him," the captain said. "Othniel inspired many in his clan by his actions at Kireath-Arba. He's under consideration for promotion, since a lieutenant has been moved up and there's currently nobody leading his fifty."

"Very well," said the marshal. "I approve, effective immediately, his promotion to lieutenant, on the condition that his first assignment be the conquest of Kireath-Sepher."

And just like that, Othniel had a chance to either win Aksah or die trying.

The opportunity filled him with hope; but also with fear. Failure didn't just mean his own death, but also that of the men in his fifty.

Othniel asked for a full day to plan his attack. The marshal, feeling the pressure from both his superiors and the approaching winter deadline, reluctantly agreed.

Othniel stretched prostrate and prayed, before doing anything else. Then he developed a concept for the operation and worked out a plan to execute it.

News of the Second Battle of Ahyee had spread throughout Kenaan, and it was unlikely the defenders could be drawn down from their ramparts into an ambush by a feigned retreat. The only chance he had, Othniel decided, was a stealthy infiltration by night to surprise the sentries–like the original plans had called for at Bet-Yariq. Only there were no apartments in the wall, and no collaborator inside to lower a rope from a window.

Othniel had his men tie cloth around some grappling hooks while he spent the late morning requisitioning black garments for his fifty to wear over their armor.

In mid-afternoon a violent storm rolled in from the north. Most everyone sought shelter from the deluge, except the Gibborim sentries on the wall, who were soaked through. Peals of thunder echoed through the mountain as lightning flashed from all angles. Save for that sporadic illumination, darkness closed over the region long before sundown.

As Othniel adjusted his plans, he couldn't decide if the weather was the enemy storm god foiling his plan, or El Elyon providing cover. He hoped for the latter.

Othniel had his men try to get some sleep before the operation. He himself tried, but couldn't.

The lightning abated and the rain settled down to a drizzle before stopping completely. Just as Othniel began rousing his men, an icy wind flared up. The thick black clouds blocked any light that might have reflected off the moon or Ma'adim, so the visibility was very low.

He formed up his men and checked their weapons and equipment. He ordered them to jog or bounce in place. Those who made too much noise were told to rearrange their gear or tie it down better. Othniel's heart raced the entire time, but outwardly he did his best to emulate Salmon's demeanor before battle: calm, confident, and with high expectations of his soldiers.

Othniel's fifty marched up the path to the fort, but halted just before they came to the narrowest part of the defile. He peered toward the wall but couldn't locate the sentries. It was so dark, he could scarcely distinguish the wall itself from the surrounding blackness. Leaving his men behind, he crept forward. He shivered from the bitter cold, and from the fear of an arrow or javelin pinning him to the ground at any second.

Othniel felt, more than saw, the nearness of the wall before he ran into it. Slow and quiet, he removed his sword and haversack, and set them gently on the ground. Out of the haversack he extracted a hefty coil of rope tied, on one end, to a padded grappling hook.

His racing heart beat even faster, knowing the noise of the hook could easily give him away. And the more throws he attempted, the more noise he would make.

Othniel used his hands to check the padding tied around the parts of the grappling hook. He positioned the coil of rope, and measured some out so that a length of it, with the hook on the end, dangled from his hand. He wound up as if preparing to loose the sling of a giant—the grapple spinning in a circle, causing a rushing sound as it cut through the cold, wet air. He timed his underhand throw to maximize the momentum, and released. As the coils of rope raised from the ground and straightened, pulled by the heavy object, he cringed. If he had released too soon, it would fall short, hitting the outside of the wall and bouncing back toward him. If he had released too late it would fly straight up, then come crashing down upon him...or fall somewhere to his rear. He strained to hear a sound, or discern some other clue as to where it might have landed.

He heard nothing but the drip of water from the wall and cliffs. But the rope extended out and up into the darkness. He pulled on it, and it went semi-taut. He pulled some more. Hand-over-hand he drew back the slack until he could give it a deft yank but it wouldn't budge.

The sentries of Kireath-Sepher got a tremendous soaking when the rain came down in sheets. They intended to keep their posts, but when the subsequent wind blasted into them, it felt like blades of ice slicing right through clothes, armor, flesh and bone. After a few minutes of trying to endure that, the commander of the watch left his youngest soldier to guard the wall while he and the rest retreated into the city to change into dry clothes and return. That young Gibborim endured the cold wind for a little longer, but finally sank down to seek what shelter he could behind the rampart.

He assumed the faint, muffled *thump* he heard had been caused by his own violent shivering, since he repeatedly bumped some part of his body against the stone structure he hid behind. He was sure he would be sick after this exposure, and might very well die from a fever. He thought he heard more sounds—a sliding noise followed by a muffled *clink*. He willed his shivering under control and strained to listen more intently, unable to make out anything but a thousand persistent drips.

Yet, the second noise he heard (assuming his ears hadn't played a trick on him) was a metallic sound. He wanted desperately to just huddle behind the wind break until relieved, then get out of his wet clothes, dry off and warm up. But what if the noise was from the watch commander's armor or something, as he climbed back up to the ramparts and caught him loafing? Worse yet: what if it was those accursed little Yacovites trying to sneak up on him?

He summoned all his willpower, and with a groan, stood up into the freezing wind.

Bracing himself with hands against the cold, wet rock, he peeked over the wall.

He saw nothing. All was so dark, he couldn't even gauge how far below the ground was. He sensed no movement other than what the wind blew. There was no unit of Yacovites bringing up a ram or ladders—of that he was certain.

The higher Othniel pulled himself up the wall, the more his muscles ached. He forced his mouth wide open to quiet his breathing as it got heavier. The haversack and sword strapped to his back made the endeavor all the more difficult. A dozen times he thought his strength would give out and he'd fall to his death. Finally, his quivering arms hoisted him onto the ledge of the wall's rampart. Thankfully the furious wind was at his back, rather than trying to sweep him off the ledge.

Just getting this far was quite an achievement. No soldier had even touched the wall—much less the top of it. But now wasn't the time to celebrate. Fighting to keep the wind from pushing him over, he slid inward and eased himself down over the inside of the rampart. His feet touched solid stone and his legs absorbed the impact of the drop. The rampart came about chest-high to a Gibborim; to a Yacovim like Othniel the top edge was out of his reach even standing tiptoe with arms extended upward.

Taking huge gulps of breath as quietly as he could, and sore arms protesting, he reached behind to draw the giant sword as he stole forward slowly. Only able to see a short distance in any direction, he picked his way along the wall by feel, astounded to find no sentries. When the wall ended, up against the mountain cliff, he doubled back, slow and cautious.

Just past where the grappling hook hung on the inside edge of the rampart above him, Othniel halted when he sensed movement ahead of him—movement involving considerable mass. A huge figure leaned against the wind, hands braced on the stone ledge, looking down the outside of the wall, before turning and squatting with its back to the wall, shield held overhead for relief from the water being blown over by the wind. It was a Gibbor, who would surely detect his presence any moment.

Othniel lunged forward, thrusting the huge sword into the unprotected area under the giant's shield arm. The giant cried out in surprise and pain, lashing out with the shield. Othniel was already stepping back in case of a riposte, but was still within the giant's reach. The swatting motion caught Othniel in the head, knocking him backwards and down. The giant lumbered to its feet, bleeding heavily and enraged. Othniel blinked to clear his foggy vision and scrambled to rise, still reeling from the blow.

The giant thrust his spear toward his human adversary. Othniel dodged and charged forward, past the heavy spearhead and inside his opponent's guard. With the captured giant's sword from Bet-Horon, he swung with the strength of terror. The heavy blade cut into the Gibbor's wrist, snapping the bone. In the process of staggering forward, one of the Gibbor's feet was in the air, moving forward. Othniel rolled under it, then sprang up, pushing against the bottom of the gigantic foot before diving away behind the enemy.

Already off-balance, the giant went tumbling. Despite a last-minute grope at the edge of the wall, he fell off. Othniel heard a tremendous crash from the darkness below.

Giving himself little time for his fear to build further, Othniel searched along the wall past where the Gibbor had been. He encountered no more sentries. Curious, but now was not the time to ponder that, either. He muttered a prayer of thanks and found the staircase leading down.

The steps were huge, but he bounded down two-at-a-time. The staircase turned. Halfway down that flight, he saw an orange-yellow glow of flickering light. Sheltered from the weather, a lit torch illuminated an area between the staircase and the city gate. Two enormous armored bodies lay tangled and lifeless on the ground. Evidently, the sentry he tripped off the wall had fallen directly on top of a comrade guarding the gate, killing him instantly.

But the second dead Gibbor wasn't the only gate guard. His partner saw Othniel descending into the soft pool of light and charged with spear cocked. Othniel saw him coming but didn't know how he could defend himself against the gigantic warrior. All he could think of was that he should stop, and remain where the stairs gave him "high ground" above the level of the huge sentry.

The giant moved into striking distance and thrust with his spear. Othniel weaved sideways at the last instant, avoiding the strike. The Gibborim's spear was enormous—easily thicker than the largest part of a normal man's forearm—but Othniel swung the giant sword into the shaft, hard. The heavy blade bit into the wood, deep. The sword was nearly ripped out of his grasp as the Gibbor yanked back on the spear. While Othniel regained his balance, the sentry thrust again— higher this time. Othniel ducked underneath. The spearhead hit the stone wall, and sparks careened off into the cold air. There was a cracking noise, and when the guard pulled his spear back, a section of it fell down to hang from the stump where Othniel had hacked at it.

The Gibbor stared at his broken spear, disbelievingly Inspired, Othniel leapt forward to the edge of the step, grabbed the dangling piece, and swung the sword, severing it from the shaft the giant held. The giant stepped back, lifting his weapon to stare at the broken end, his shield hand pushing the helmet back on his oblong head, then scratching his brow in perplexity.

Othniel quickly exchanged weapons from one hand to the other, so that now he held the spear section in his right. He shuffled back, planted his feet, then hurled the partial shaft with the heavy iron head on the end. He aimed for the neck, but the missile sailed high. Just as the thought formed that he had missed, the spearhead pierced the long forehead of the Gibborim, just under the edge of his bronze helmet.

Othniel couldn't see any blood in the poor light, but the Gibborim fell back like a great tree chopped through at the base, hitting the ground like an enormous sack of melons.

Othniel glanced right, left, forward, and back. He saw no more immediate threats. He gulped for breath and bounded down the remaining steps, racing for the gate, his breath leaving puffs of steam briefly in the chilly air. He reached the gate and pushed up at the crossbar. It was massive, and didn't budge. If it wasn't so high up, he would squat, put his back under it and heave up with his legs.

There were three dead giants nearby. He turned to retrieve one of the spears that was still intact, and saw several lit torches bobbing in the distance. He froze for a moment, watching. Gibborim soldiers were approaching from different parts of the city. The light was too limited for them to see him or know what was happening, or they would be moving at a run, but they would be there in just a minute or so.

His heart pounded harder and faster. He leapt forward, plucked a spear off the ground and ran back to the gate. He jabbed the spearhead into the wood of the crossbar from underneath, squatted, gripped the spear shaft as tight as he could, and put his leg muscles to work. He growled and roared from the exertion as he struggled to stand. The crossbar tipped up, up, up...and finally cleared the brackets. With one last effort, he pushed the crossbar, with the spear, away from the gate and let go.

The elevated end of the huge beam dropped, hitting the ground with a loud *thunk*. Already fatigued from his recent efforts, Othniel knew he had to swing the gate open or all was for naught. He set his shoulder against one door of the gate, dug his feet into the wet ground and strained with his legs. With an echoing creak, the gate swung out.

Once he got it in motion, he was able to keep it swinging until it was wide open. He tried to shout to his fifty waiting in the defile, but he was out of breath, and could barely manage a gasp.

He turned again, and now saw that the torch-bearers were running toward him. He staggered back to the inside, reached up on tiptoe to dislodge to torch, and returned to the open gate, waving the torch and trying again to shout.

He heard the cacophony of running feet from two directions, then the bugle call for "Wall Breach" echoing through the mountains outside the fortress city.

He turned wearily back and wielded his sword. The torch-bearing giants were close now, shouting and cursing in load, guttural voices. He didn't have the strength left to fight any one of them, much less all of them.

Then his men rushed through the gate with a battlecry of their own. They formed a semicircular shield wall, blocking access to the gate from the inside.

Othniel leaned back against the gate door he hadn't yet opened, hands on knees, wheezing for breath. The bugle continued to sound. If only his men could hold off the Gibborim for long enough...

Before he had completely caught his breath, Othniel heaved against the remaining gate door. Just as he swung it fully open, the vanguard of Y'hudim warriors funneled down the defile and poured through the gate.

Now from inside the wall came the crash of arms. Othniel took deep breaths while following slowly. His work was not finished, but he needed time to catch his wind.

So far as Gibborim infantry was concerned, there weren't many tactics in their repertoire. In fighting humans, sophistication had seldom been required—just hack the puny soldiers down with sword, axe, and spear, as if swatting grasshoppers. Armies throughout Kenaan only introduced archers, cavalry and chariots because they sometimes went to war with other Gibborim kingdoms.

By the time of the Battle of Kireath-Sepher, the soldiers of Yacov had reduced fighting Gibborim down to a science. To make the quickest work of it, the trick was to isolate a giant from his fellows whenever possible, then come at him from at least three directions. When unable to break up the enemy's unit integrity, a strong force of shock troops would form a shield wall and harass them with the spear, while archers, slingers, or javelineers tore into them at a distance, from behind the last rank of spear men, and skirmishers with sword and shield would attempt to fold around the flank. The Yacovim were seasoned veterans by now, and settled into whatever drill fit the situation with minimal direction from their officers.

By the time the troops directly in front of Othniel had encircled a unit of Gibborim thusly, he had regained some of his wind. His job now, as he saw it, was to find and destroy the enemy garrison's leadership. He slipped through the battle and found his own fifty. Once they were able to break contact, he pulled them back to regroup, then led them on the search.

During the fight, the cloud cover began to break up, and the fortress city was bathed in dull light from Ma'adim and Lebanah. They found the palace, with unit guidons festooned around it. His men systematically cut down the guard force posted there, securing the building room-by-room.

Othniel found the enemy general in the inner patio garden, part of the courtyard surrounded by the segments of the palace which had ceilings. The clothing and flesh of the general, along with the ground surrounding his body, had been scorched black by the lightning bolt that seared through his chest and melted the heart on its way through his enormous torso.

At daybreak, Othniel hoisted the guidon of his clan over the captured fortress. His captain and marshal sought him out, congratulated him, and remarked that his promotion had been no mistake.

Two days later, all the tribe formed up in front of General Kalev and Field Marshal Y'hoshua at Kireath-Arba. Kalev announced that their entire tribal allotment of land was now pacified, and the cheering from Y'huda took a while to subside. Then Y'hoshua praised the tribe for its accomplishments so far, inspiring more cheers with the news that the army would now be resting for the winter.

Then the old field marshal turned to face his long-time friend. Still addressing the tribe as a whole, he said, "Not many of you were alive yet, when Moshe sent me, Kalev and ten others to reconnoiter the land. But I knew then, just as well as I know now, that this soldier was the finest our nation had to offer. Sometimes I've wondered why I was chosen to replace Moshe, instead of your general."

Kalev flashed a perfunctory grin, but otherwise kept his composure. Some of his officers and men, however, chuckled at this.

I told myself back then," Y'hoshua continued, "that if I had 10,000 soldiers like Kalev, I could conquer Kenaan in a month!"

The Y'hudim boisterously grunted affirmation of the prowess and stout heart of their tribal commander.

"But right now," Y'hoshua continued, "it's the proper time to acknowledge a brave young soldier who is following in Kalev's footsteps."

The entire tribe shifted its attention to one of its clans. That clan turned inward toward one specific family. That family turned inward to Othniel, with smiles and back slaps.

Y'hoshua called Othniel forward. The entire tribe leaned or stretched to get a good look at the soldier being honored, as he ran to present himself. Salutes were exchanged, then Y'hoshua had Othniel face the tribe.

"And as I understand it," Y'hoshua called out, "a reward has already been promised for this soldier's valor!"

The tribe roared. Every man had heard about the incentive Kalev had offered for taking Kireath-Sepher, yet thousands of them announced this bit of common knowledge as if it were news.

Y'hoshua gestured to Kalev, then took a step back and to the side. Sober-faced, Kalev stationed himself beside Othniel. Looking to the side, he said, "For exemplary leadership and exceptional courage in the conquest of Kireath-Sepher," Kalev said, "I hereby offer Lieutenant Othniel...the hand of my daughter, Aksah, in marriage."

Horns blew, tambourines jangled, and voices lifted in song. Othniel turned to seek the source of the noise. A large party of women and musicians emerged from behind the barn on the property Kalev had claimed as his own. They turned a corner and proceeded on a course directly toward Kalev and Othniel.

The young soldier's chest tightened and stomach fluttered, while his gaze remained locked on the procession. As they drew near, he recognized several of the singing women. Some were from his own family, and the rest from Kalev's. A priest was with them.

They reached Othniel, finished their song, and opened ranks. There in their midst, hidden from sight until now, was Aksah. She wore an elegant dress and head covering, as well as perfume with a fragrance like wildflowers.

Othniel hadn't spoken to her since that night back at Stone Circle. At times, doubt nagged him as to whether she was a willing bride or not. There were times, in the past, when it seemed his affection for her was mutual. Yet there were also times when he would have sworn she was nearly indifferent to him. After their conversation by the fire, he had pictured her married to some other man, and bearing that man's children. He assumed they would grow apart from there, rapidly, eventually forgetting one another and perhaps never seeing each other again. in fact, he was still quite dazed by the turnaround of circumstances.

He wondered if she had also settled in her mind that she would marry another, and would be disappointed by this sudden change.

The marriage would take place now, regardless. The priest and her father were present to conduct the betrothal ceremony; his own mother was in the party...and here came his father from the ranks of soldiers to join them. Kalev had given his blessing (reluctantly, Othniel was sure), and Aksah would do as her father commanded.

But Othniel feared she would do it out of obligation, with a heavy heart because she would prefer some other fate.

Maybe this was all a bad idea. Maybe he shouldn't force Kalev to make good on his promise to the man who captured Kireath-Sepher. If Aksah would be unhappy with him, then he would be miserable, too. Better to not have her, and eventually be able to forget her.

Aksah stepped toward him, her eyes downcast. Then, as the priest took his place and began speaking, her gaze swept up to meet Othniel's. Her moist eyes glowed. Her tentative smile conveyed a jumble of emotions: nervousness; contrition; relief; hope; maybe desire; maybe love. But Othniel didn't see disappointment or a burden of obligation.

She took hold of his hands and leaned into him for a moment, the side of her face against his chest, and took a deep breath. Othniel pulled one hand free and slid his arm around her back, pulling her tighter against him.

Kalev was stone-faced. The priest cleared his throat. "Remember, this is just the betrothal–not your wedding night."

The people nearby chuckled nervously as Aksah stepped back from Othniel, beaming.

But she kept hold of his hand.

# Fidelity at Scale

It was a short winter. Troops from each tribe were rotated out to occupy the conquered territory in the south, while the bulk of the army camped back at Stone Circle.

Though they had destroyed several armies with cavalry and chariots, Yacov still had none of its own. Nearly every soldier now had a sword, however, as well as other captured weapons. The Gadim trained the other tribes in the use of the sword, though it was only a secondary weapon for most of them.

Fully healed by the spring, Salmon regained command of his hundred and led them out for the northern campaign. He was as demanding as ever on his men, but they were crack troops, now, and consistently made him proud.

Each tribe was becoming more self-sufficient, and occasionally acted independently.

Y'hoshua swept northward methodically, city by city. After taking each objective, he strengthened his position, resting his army while ensuring they could not be thrown back by a counteroffensive. Then he pushed forward again, to capture more ground. Some kingdoms put up stiffer resistance than others, but they all succumbed. Some battles were so one-sided, and the sense of inevitability was so strong for everyone following the progress of the war, one might assume it was Yacov with all the giants in the ranks.

The old field marshal, despite his strategic success, began to show signs of failing health. He delegated more and more of the tasks he used to handle himself, and preferred to direct battles via messages borne by his runners, rather than standing amidst his formations, signaling with his javelin to the buglers and flagmen. He also relaxed his tight control, allowing his generals more initiative than was his habit. Some generals thrived as a result, while some slipped, and he was no longer vigilant enough to keep on top of it all.

More young men reached fighting age as the war ground on, at a rate that more than replaced battlefield losses. The roster of Yacov's army swelled, and promotions abounded in the lower and middle ranks. Salmon was moved up to marshal, while Othniel made captain, and a new lieutenant took his place.

Morale climbed drastically as the war reached its conclusion. Wild celebrations broke out immediately after cities were captured, and more time was spent allotting houses and farms than was spent studying maps, hashing out tactics or drilling the troops.

Othniel and Aksah spent more time together than ever before, but still hadn't yet consummated the marriage. A condition of the betrothal was that the bride and groom would remain with their parents until the war was over. Then Othniel would receive his land allotment, and prepare a place for them.

Salmon led his thousand back to Stone Circle one last time after the Battle of Hazor. The veteran marshal now had a scar down his torso to match the one down his face, and he was an expert with the gigantic Gibborim sword. His men, weary but jubilant, were smart, tough, disciplined warriors who considered themselves the best in Yacov's army. He agreed with them, though there was always room for improvement.

Once he'd performed a head count, relayed orders through his captains, and dismissed the thousand, he strolled over to one of the springs at the ruins of Bet-Yariq to bathe. Still weary after his bath, but refreshed, he dressed and took a different route back to camp.

Along the way, he smiled when he noticed the young potter working under the same tree he'd seen him at so many times before. Only he wasn't quite as young anymore. Zuar was there, talking with the potter and a girl. Both boys' voices had changed, and they appeared to be close to military age, now. Salmon adjusted his path so that he'd pass right by the tree.

"What?" the girl asked the potter. "What's wrong with it?"

The potter, seated as usual, held a large jar up at eye-level, peering inside it. "They certainly worked fast, this time," he said.

"What did?" the girl asked.

"Mud daubers. Come look."

Contorting her lips and noisily sighing, the girl stepped over close to examine it. She stamped her foot and cried out in despair.

"Does that mean you're going to destroy it?" Zuar asked, though he seemed to be much more interested in the girl than in the fate of the jar.

The potter felt the wall of the pottery between thumb and forefinger, frowning. "It's still a little wet. Not completely hardened..."

He picked up a tool and used it to scrape along the inside of the jar. He extracted the tool and flung a glop of wet clay, mud, and insect off of it and out away from his work area. "Put it back on the wheel, quickly," he told the girl. "You might still be able to smooth it out."

"Yes, brother," the girl sing-songed, taking the jar, and carrying it to the wheel.

"Let me help you with that," Zuar said.

Salmon glanced along the ground, noting all the pottery fragments accumulated over the last few years, from work the potter had destroyed for one imperfection or another. Then he scrutinized the jar on his way past. Vermin had infiltrated what was otherwise a marvelous work of art, and begun to corrupt it from the inside. Only this time, the vessel's creator determined that it could be repaired.

Well after he passed the tree and the scene was behind him, he pondered this exception. Why hadn't the potter smashed it and started over, as he so often had? Because the clay was still malleable enough for the infestation to be eradicated.

And because the creator recognized the potential in the vessel, deciding its value was high enough to merit the extra work necessary to restore it.

Salmon dreamed about the jar that night.

After northern Kenaan was vanquished, Y'hoshua brought the nation together one last time under the Radiant Mist. He spoke at length to the tribes of Yacov.

"I won't be with you for much longer," Y'hoshua said. "The war is over; the promise is fulfilled; and my journey has come to its end. Soon, I will lay down in the ground and rest with my forebears. I leave you with a clean conscience that I led you with honor. You now have houses you didn't build; wells you didn't dig; crops you didn't plant. After today, I will release you to your allotted homes. May you enjoy the peace that follows."

The people cheered.

"But don't ever forget where we came from, nor the road we traveled to get here," Y'hoshua said.

They were sobered from their jubilant mood when he reminded them of how easily their parents and grandparents rebelled against Hashem; how they refused to trust in he who had never failed them, while proving themselves untrustworthy time and again.

While listening to the historical summary of his people, Salmon was struck by how unworthy his nation was to have a god like Hashem.

The moment Moshe had turned his back, after leading them out of slavery in Mizraim, the people made an idol, accredited their deliverance to *it*, and worshiped it. They grumbled about being in a desert with no food or water. El Elyon fed them with the frost bread, and gave them water from solid rock, but they complained about that, too. Some staged a rebellion against Moshe. At one point they brought foreign women into the camp, fornicating with them in detestable pagan rituals—even inside the Temple. Time and again they scorned their deliverer. Time and again, they demonstrated that they would rather be slaves again, than to be faithful to their protector. Time and again El Elyon punished them, but healed and restored them after they cried out to him for forgiveness. And then, when it was time to march in and occupy the land he'd promised them, their courage failed. They accused El Elyon of leading them out of Mizraim only so they could die in the desert. And their words became a self-fulfilling curse. Every whining, ungrateful coward of that generation died in the desert, until only Y'hoshua and Kalev were left. Then El Elyon presented the next generation with the same opportunity.

Salmon remembered something Pinchas taught one time: that a marriage was a crude model of Yacov's relationship with their god. Every time the Yacovim trusted in something more than they trusted in Hashem, or lived as if anything else was more important than him...they were like a wife who refused to remain faithful to her husband.

Yacov, Salmon realized, was a whoring adulteress. It grieved him to admit it to himself...but how much more it must have grieved the god who had done so much for his stiff-necked people. How could Hashem continue to love them in the face of infidelity after infidelity?

And yet, he had.

His love had healed Yacov. Under Y'hoshua, with the exception of Achan's disobedience, they had enjoyed a golden age of victory and intimacy with their god. Hashem gave them those victories, but nations throughout the known world now revered Yacov as a result.

The unfaithful whore had been restored to a position of honor. Yacov was sanctified.

Y'hoshua finished his final address to them by saying, "Choose today which god you're going to serve." His hard, piercing gaze swept over all the assembled tribes. Some flinched when his stare raked through them. "If you still won't trust in the god who has brought us here, then serve the gods he judged in Mizraim." The people murmured their protest. He pointed eastward. "Or if you choose the worthless statues our ancestors worshiped across the river, then serve them."

"No!" cried thousands of voices.

Y'hoshua gestured toward the ground they stood on. "If you want the gods of Kenaan and the Gibborim, who our god defeated, then choose them."

The nation roared, "No!" with one voice.

"As for me," Y'hoshua declared, "and everyone who is under my direct authority henceforth...we will serve El Elyon."

"We will serve El Elyon!" Yacov vowed, as one.

Now Y'hoshua pointed into their midst. "Good. You are witnesses against yourselves, then. You have confirmed that El Elyon is your god; and you will serve him. Remember that, in years to come."

Rachav had listened to the farewell address with her family, wedged in between the tribes of Ruven and Shimon. When the assembly broke up, each person wandering back to their own tent for the night, her family was noticeably quiet compared to the boisterous Yacovites on every side. Rachav exchanged waves and smiles from a couple women she had come to know, but couldn't help noting that she was still an outsider.

When the family arrived back in their area, Salmon was waiting at the tent of her father, with Othniel on one side of him and Pinchas on the other.

"Peace to you," Salmon greeted.

"And also to you," Papa replied, according to the Yacovite custom. "Good to find that you've survived the war, Salmon. What brings you to our home?"

Salmon fixed his gaze on Rachav as he said, "I've come to ask for your daughter's hand in marriage."

Rachav's temperature ran hot and cold, and dizziness came on her suddenly. She stumbled a bit as she approached the man whose image and words had just stunned her nearly speechless.

"I ask personally," Salmon said, "because my parents are not alive to make the arrangements."

Rachav put a hand on his arm. "Salmon, please don't make this decision hastily."

"Woman, I've been anything but hasty," he said, now turning to Papa. "As surely as Hashem lives, I've given this more thought than I've given nearly anything."

Papa grinned as if a gold coin had just fallen into his hand.

Rachav didn't want to admit it in public, or trigger the flood of regrets she would suffer silently by bringing the matter to remembrance, but this was all happening so abruptly... "Salmon, I'm barren!" she blurted.

Mother blanched. Faryel gasped. Anwar and Nadir scowled.

Salmon untied a purse from his belt and held it out to Papa. "I believe you'll find this meets or exceeds your bride price."

Papa took the purse, opened it, peered inside...and his grin widened. "Done!" he said.

Salmon waved left and right, indicating his friends. "Good. These men bear witness that you agree to the bride price and give your consent to the marriage."

Nodding vigorously, Papa said, "And my blessing, as well!"

Rachav took deep breaths and squeezed Salmon's arm. "Are you certain about this?"

Salmon turned back to her and focused an intense gaze straight into her eyes. "I am. But if you are not pleased by this match, I won't force it on you. So tell me now, in the hearing of these witnesses, if you find a marriage covenant with me undesirable."

For a brief moment, Rachav felt trapped. But she closed her eyes and concentrated for a moment, remembering her prayers of the last few years. She remembered her feelings for Salmon, and realized he must finally have strong feelings for her, too—or he wouldn't be here, doing this.

She opened her eyes.

"Salmon, don't you want children?" she asked.

He nodded. "Yes. And El Elyon can open your womb, if he so chooses. He's done it for other women, before you. But even if, for reasons of his own, he doesn't, I still want you for a wife."

She glanced at Papa, Mother, and her siblings in turn as she said, "That is what I want, as well."

Her family cheered to rival the celebrating Yacovites in every camp that night.

"I have a present for you," Salmon told her, motioning toward Othniel. The young soldier handed him a beautifully painted jar, and Salmon presented it to Rachav. She took it, examined it, then stared curiously at Salmon.

He smiled. "Perhaps soon I'll tell you the story of that pottery."

# Epilogue

Othniel and his sons disembarked the ferry after the ferryman secured it to the post on the river bank. It took some time to have the ox pull the cart up the bank onto level ground without cargo falling off and into the water.

As they worked at it, young Habuk said, "But I don't understand, Papa. If El Elyon changed his name from Yacov to Yisrael, why did we still call ourselves by the old name in your day?"

Othniel thought about this for a moment, while keeping the rope taut and using simple words to coax the ox toward him.

"Well, I don't have a good answer, Son. If our god changes something, we should use the new name and quit using the old one. But it's hard to break a habit once it's formed. That's why I'm always telling you and your brother to form good habits instead of bad ones."

"Why does he change names in the first place, though?" asked Yaghaz, steadying the cart as it rolled slowly uphill, pitching and rocking on the uneven ground.

"Yacov meant 'deceiver' or 'heel grabber'," Othniel explained. "Not a good name."

The boys chuckled in agreement.

"Not a name suitable for a nation set aside by El Elyon, either," Othniel added. Trapping the rope between his arm and side for a moment, he mimed grappling with a huge opponent. "But Yisrael–'He Wrestles With God'–we fight to keep hold of our god.

We know blessing comes from him; and not from what we can get from other people by deception. It's like, by changing our name, El Elyon let us divorce from our past, and start fresh."

The boys nodded, apparently accepting his rationale.

As the cart ascended the bank, one wheel dropped into a hole hidden by grass, and the cart was jolted. Cargo shifted, threatening to fall, and Yaghaz moved his hands from the cart rails to stabilize it.

"Careful with the white silk," Othniel warned him. "It gets dirty easily."

"Yes, Father," Yaghaz replied, wrapping a cloth around his dirty hand, so he could stabilize the bolt of white silk, resting atop the expensive blue one.

The cart crested the bank and leveled off on flat ground. They all sighed with relief. Even the ox snorted, as if to share their sentiment.

Without falling cargo to worry about now, the scenery triggered memories in Othniel's mind. He had spent so much time in this area so many years ago, waves of nostalgia assailed him.

"Why are you giving Salmon something so expensive?" asked Habuk, pointing to the blue silk (not yet tall enough to reach it).

Jarred from his reminiscing, Othniel said, "Salmon is a good friend. He and I went through...it's hard to explain, Son."

"You don't buy our other friends gifts like this," Yaghaz noted.

"It's a miraculous occasion," Othniel explained. "Rachav was barren. El Elyon opened her womb, and she has borne a son to Salmon. It's something to be celebrated, and commemorated."

"Mother said the baby's name is Boaz," Habuk announced, proud of himself for having this information to relay—as if his father and brother hadn't heard the news already.

"There's going to be a big feast," Othniel said. "Many of us who served under Salmon during the war will be there. Some of them I haven't seen much since the war. Even Pinchas, our High Priest, is visiting."

For a short time, there was no sound but the steps of the ox and the creaking of the cart wheels. But conversation never ceased for long with these boys.

Taking in the scenery all around him, Yaghaz said, "The other side of the river is beautiful; but this is very pretty, too. It sure is nicer than the Negeb, anyway."

"The Negeb is not so bad," Othniel replied. "Especially with the springs your grandfather gave us."

"Well, the oases are nice," Yaghaz admitted. "But here, there's green grass as far as you can see. And trees."

Othniel brought the ox to a halt by the old circular pile of rocks. He sighed, looking over the old camp site.

"What's this for?" Habuk asked, staring at the stack of stones.

Othniel smiled, leaning back against the cart. "I'm glad you asked, Son. I'm going to tell you about some things that happened right where we're standing. And one day, you've got to remember and tell your own children what I'm about to tell you. Those rocks were taken from the bed of the Yarden."

Yaghaz looked back at the swift, muddy river. "How?"

"It was springtime," Othniel said. "The river was at flood stage. Moshe had just died, and Y'hoshua had been appointed to lead us into the land that was promised to us..."

The boys listened to their father with rapt attention. He conjured up scenes in their young imaginations, but also pointed to things they could see with their eyes from where they sat. He pointed to the monument before them—the namesake of Stone Circle; to the river; to the ruins of Bet-Yariq; to the mountains in the west, where Ahyee and Bet-El were located. He pointed to the tree where he and their mother talked, the time the quake threw her to the ground; and the spot where they sat together daydreaming of a home and family.

The man and his sons assumed nobody else was present. And as far as their eyes could see, that was true. But they weren't alone. Someone watched them.

I don't just mean myself...Rachivel. On the plains of Bet-Yariq, at the very spot where he had met Y'hoshua with a drawn sword years before, Hashem hovered beside Mikhayel, looking on. The enormous Warrior and his Commander observed Othniel passing down the story of the events during Y'hoshua's tenure as judge and field marshal.

When Othniel got to the point in the story in which Y'hoshua warned Yisrael that the war between the gods, and their proxies, was far from over, Hashem and Mikhayel pulled their attention from the humans to glance at each other briefly; then focused their perception across the Yarden.

In the secret planes which overlapped the world of the humans, a line of angry, vengeful gods faced them, glaring.

Waiting.

# The End

# Afterword/Acknowledgments

I saw *The Ten Commandments* (the 1956 movie with Charlton Heston) on TV several times as a child. As I got older, I watched other biblical epics about Samson, David, Solomon, and Ruth. But I never found a full-length feature based on the book of Joshua, which, for many years, was my favorite book in the Bible.

Sure, Joshua was portrayed as a supporting character in films about Moses, but it flabbergasted me that the conquest of the Holy Land was never depicted in a Hollywood movie. Or if it was, I never found so much as a clue that one existed, except for a snippet here and there in dramatizations based on the Bible as a whole.

In 2014, I decided it was time to write a screenplay for just such a movie. While undertaking that project, one reason became clear why nobody had done it before: though there is no lack of action in Joshua to use in what could essentially be a Bronze Age war film, it is a daunting task to arrange the biblical account into a three-act-structure that would satisfy the expectations of average moviegoers. Not that any film maker in Hollywood seems even remotely interested in historical accuracy in general, or biblical accuracy in particular, but a faithful adaptation of Joshua would probably be dismissed from consideration for any number of reasons. After Jericho (the very first battle of the campaign under Joshua's tenure) what follows might seem anticlimactic, by conventional narrative standards. Moreover, the casual reader of English translations misses the underlying supernatural war against the *Nephilim*[1] in the

---

[1] The *Nephilim* are first mentioned in Genesis 6. The context implies that they were a hybrid offspring of heavenly beings and "the daughters of men." The word "*Nephilim*" is

Bible, so the entire Holy Land campaign seems a ruthless bloodbath, and the God of Israel comes off (as a famous atheist once accused) like a "genocidal maniac." Even the capital punishment of Israel's own criminals strikes the modern reader as heartless tyranny. It's not just unbelievers who are horrified, but also those taught a watered-down Gospel on Sundays.

The easy route would have been to simply abuse "creative license" and rearrange the Joshua narrative to conform to modern storytelling conventions, changing details as I saw fit to make it more politically correct as well. In recent memory, a Hollywood feature film was produced based on pagan perversions of the Flood account in Genesis; and simply by giving it the title "*Noah*," the film makers lured prominent apologists from inside organized religion to vouch for its merit. Who knows–by inserting the obligatory Womyn Warrior Tropes, a sympathetic homosexual character, and/or some not-so-subtle neo-Marxist message, my Joshua movie might have even won mainstream Hollywood backing, a multimillion dollar budget, and critical acclaim.

But to paraphrase a pretty wise, important thinker: what profits would be worth me selling my soul to win the adulation of this world?

So I wrote the screenplay with a revolutionary concept in mind: stay true to the source material (which is not to say, true to the typical Sunday School version of the source material). I finished a draft which did not contradict the biblical account, yet was

---

often translated "fallen ones." In the Septuagint, the Greek word is *Gigantes*, which means "Earth-Born." It was historically translated as "giants." (The hybrid beings in question did happen to be gigantic; but that wasn't the meaning of the word.)

This is how the passage was understood in the days of Jesus, right up until somebody decided that the Creator of the universe needed their help revising His account for believability.

Centuries ago, church officials decided Genesis 6 meant only that the male descendants of Seth mated with the female descendants of Cain, and that is the default interpretation in most churches to this day. In other words: what the Bible actually says has been explained away, and replaced with assumptions unsupported by anything else in Scripture.

The Hebrew term translated "sons of God" used in this passage always refers to celestial beings in the *Tanach* (Old Testament). Furthermore, the phrase "daughters of men" is literally "daughters of Adam;" so to believe this "godly line of Seth" revisionism is to assume that Cain was the son of Adam, but Seth was not.

structured and styled such that I believed it could satisfy a modern audience.

Lo and behold, I couldn't get any potential producers to look at it. (Partly because I don't know any potential producers.) Couldn't get any Christians connected with the entertainment industry to look at it. Couldn't even get one of the people who helped motivate this project to look at it.

Was the screenplay any good? Can't say, objectively, because I'm the only one who ever read it.

It had been many years since film school and I had lost touch with the old network. (Short of miraculous intervention, it's impossible to make a movie without a network...even when the movie is animated, which is how I envisioned this one). But, alas, I did have access to the resources to novelize the book of Joshua; so in 2016, that's what I began doing.

The bulk of my gratitude is reserved for the Author of the 66 books that comprise the Holy Bible, and the 40-some-odd human stenographers He used to put it in written form. The thousands of tireless scholars who have toiled over translating the original text for centuries are not to be overlooked, either.

Next on my list is Dr. Chuck Missler. By compiling his own insights with the work of many others and presenting it in a cohesive form, he made a huge impact on my life–and this book. Just to name a few, I've drawn on his "briefing packages" concerning how the Planet Mars played a major part in the long day of Joshua; how the layout of the Israelite camp was one of the "called shots" that pointed to the Ultimate Sacrifice; how the Israelite tribal ensigns correlate to the four aspects of the Cherubim/Seraphim –just to name a few. (That last one was just part of Missler's revelation. What I couldn't include in this Old Testament story was how those four aspects correlate to the four Gospels.)

Though I only discovered his work much later, I also owe heap big thanks to Dr. Michael S. Heiser, who has delved into the original Hebrew of the Old Testament to shed light on "the Divine Council," among other fascinating allusions in the Bible, which are ignored or denied by most preachers and teachers in mainstream Churchianity[2].

I've drawn on the research and work of so many different students of the Bible, I doubt I can remember them all. But I discovered some of them by listening to the podcasts of Derek and Sharon Gilbert. Their "A View From The Bunker;" "Gilbert House Fellowship;"and (now discontinued, I think) "P.I.D. Radio" are podcasts I highly recommend for anyone interested in learning about biblical topics never explored in the average modern church. Gilbert House Fellowship, especially, is well worth the time spent listening to it. As the Gilberts go through the Bible verse-by-verse (in revised chronological order), they synthesize the research of a plethora of other Bible students, illuminating a depth to the content of Scripture you probably haven't found anywhere else. This is not to say I agree with all the opinions expressed or conclusions reached on their programs. But as Derek says at the beginning of each GHF episode, the purpose of the program is to assist "...believers seeking to better understand the Word of God," and that is absolutely what it does.

The majority of the *Apocrypha* strikes me as uninspired drivel at best, yet there are certain apocryphal texts I have found helpful achieving a deeper understanding of the Bible. In particular: the books of Jasher, Jubilees, and a small excerpt from the Book of Enoch. On the one hand, I understand why these books weren't included in the Canon. Yet the three sources I mentioned

---

[2] "Churchianity" is a fitting name for the pseudo-Christianity so widespread today. Jesus, Paul the Apostle, and others warned us about a great apostasy, and it would appear to be upon us now. Gradually, the Church that Jesus commissioned has been subverted. Instead of transforming the world around it, this church has *conformed to the world*.

Churchians come in different flavors. For instance: some teach a "prosperity gospel" while others teach that money (not the *love* of money) is the root of all evil. Some make an idol out of one particular flawed translation of the Bible, while others reject the Bible altogether. Some deny the supernatural and explain away biblical references to it, while others are so desperate to experience the supernatural that they fake spiritual gifts. There is a pacifist gospel; a "social justice" gospel; a feminist gospel (which probably every American church has adopted to one degree or another); a homosexual-friendly gospel; and even an atheist gospel. Whatever snare or deception will work best on you, there's a chapter of Churchianity that caters to it–and the Adversary will use whichever one will best steer you onto that wide, popular path Jesus warned about.

corroborate, provide context, and "fill in the blanks" in some of the historical books of the Old Testament (just as Josephus does for the New Testament) without contradicting the inspired message.

Too much of what is taught from behind the pulpit today is based on tradition, and not the Bible. A sense of propriety prevents certain biblical text from being taught, while emotional reasoning censors other Scripture. As if we human beings, with our lofty morals and wisdom, are correcting the Creator's mistake of including information He shouldn't have. With the same arrogance, we add our own theology to the Word, assuming the Holy Spirit must have forgotten to include something important. This is why, for the modern churchgoer, a story like the one told in this book might seem heretical or even occultic. To the non-believer it likely seems no more Judeo-Christian than the Arthurian legends. (By-the-way, the whole sword-in-the-stone subplot from those tales was most likely "borrowed" from the account of Moses' sapphire staff in the book of Jasher.) So I fully expect a story told this way will not win many fans behind the pulpit. In fact, if it does, that probably signifies a failure on my part.

And speaking of failure: any mistakes, oversights. or inaccuracies are not the fault of anyone I've acknowledged, but mine alone (despite an honest effort). If I become aware of such, they will be corrected in subsequent editions.

There's a famous road paved with good intentions. One good intention of theologians in centuries past was to eliminate or explain away any passage in the Bible which could be construed as supporting polytheism. The Bible clearly portrays Yahweh (El Elyon/El Shaddai/"The God of Many Names"/etc.) as the One True God; but it also documents that *He judged the gods of Egypt (Exodus 12:12).* In the Commandments we are warned not to put *other gods* before Him (Deuteronomy 5:7). The Adversary, called "the devil" and "Satan" in English, is referred to as "*the god of this world*" or "*the god of this age*" (2 Corinthians 4:4) depending on translation (or "prince," which is also how the messenger[3] in Daniel

---

[3]    The word *angel* means "messenger," but, in our lexicon, has come to refer exclusively to created celestial beings. Certainly the word often refers to those; but

12:1 referred to the Archangel Michael). Acknowledging that the ancient pagans were worshiping living entities, and not just the idols formed to represent them, is not polytheistic. It is simply biblical.

Those of us who learned the Bible from an English translation (or worse yet, from "preacher talk") have inherited many assumptions about our Creator. For instance, we assume that "God" is His name. One of the Commandments forbids us to misuse His name (Deuteronomy 5:11). Well, what exactly is His name? Most Gentiles have no idea, except for the cryptic statement given to Moses via the burning bush (Exodus 3:14). But where our English translations call him simply "THE LORD," the original text used one of His names[4]. How many times have we seen references to His name in our English translations, without actually seeing His name in the text? Those translations also use the word "God" as if it is a name (hence we assume "God" is his name), but the word "el" that is translated "god" was a more generic term in Hebrew for a supernatural being that is not necessarily the Creator God. Many of us were taught that the word *Elohim*, which includes the word for "god" with a Hebrew plural suffix, is a reference to the Trinity—one God in three persons. But some Hebrew scholars insist it refers to a pantheon, the Divine Council, or Heavenly Assembly[5]. (Not that they deny the Trinity, as there is textual evidence of that concept elsewhere in Scripture.)

Another assumption we make is that the four dimensions (height, width, depth, and time) we perceive, and are limited to, are the extent of reality. Actually, what we (usually) can't see, hear, or touch

---

sometimes a human being can be an "angel," and sometimes the Messiah Himself plays the role of a messenger, or "angel."

[4] That is, the "Tetragrammaton." This has been pronounced "Yaweh" or "Jehovah," historically, though exact pronunciation is not certain because there were no vowels in the original Hebrew. It's like an acronym formed from the Hebrew phrase the Creator used to answer Moses: "I am that I am." I chose to limit the number of names used for Him, to avoid confusion. I've also substituted "El Elyon" or "Hashem" for the Tetragrammaton when using biblical quotes herein, purposefully, due partly to the uncertain pronunciation.

[5] Psalm 82:1 "God has taken his place in the Divine Council; in the midst of the gods he holds judgment." Deuteronomy 32:8-9 "When the Most High gave the nations their inheritance, when he divided up humankind, he set the boundaries of the peoples, according to the number of the Heavenly Assembly." Job 1:6 and 1 Kings 22 also give us a fleeting glimpse of this Heavenly Assembly.

is *more real* than what we can. Imagine time-traveling back to the Dark Ages, and trying to convince people that things like radiation, magnetism, molecules, atoms, pulsars, quasars, etc., exist. At that time, they didn't have tools sophisticated enough to detect such things. Likewise, we don't presently have the tools to prove the existence of such things as love, souls, spirits, God, or other celestial beings. It takes divine access to perceive what happens in the secret places (Numbers 22:22-34; 2 Kings 6:14-17), because our "reality" was created from dimensions we can't perceive, by a God we can't see or touch. Yet our faith in Him has substance in those Hidden Realms (Hebrews11:1, 3).

In public school, while teaching the class about Greco-Roman mythology, a teacher of mine once claimed that many of the myths sound familiar because the Bible plagiarized from them.

Uh, no.

The oldest book in the Bible is believed to be Job; and Moses wrote the Torah (or Pentateuch) a few centuries later. No doubt some pagan myths precede those times, but God's history was passed down orally (and perhaps via other media, before the Flood) from the very dawn of the human race until the Holy Spirit inspired men to begin writing it down. Any accusation that the Bible "borrows" myths from the pagans is bogus.

It is tempting to dismiss mythology as the work of wild imaginations in superstitious ancient cultures—and that is what most of us do. But if you don't deny the supernatural episodes in the Bible, a lot of anecdotes from mythology bear uncanny similarities. The narratives have been tweaked, obviously, and often in a way to flip the roles of who is "good" and who is "evil." What if some of the myths, shared by the Babylonians; Assyrians; Persians; Greeks; Romans; Teutons and others are really just revisionist history of events which actually happened, corrupted and (in large part) rendered silly by embellishments over the millennia? The Bible acknowledges the existence of other "gods" in forbidding the worship of them, though it goes into very little detail identifying them for the most part. Jude 6 and 2 Peter 2:4 mention angels who sinned, left their "first estate" (KJV), "proper dwelling" (ESV), or "abandoned their posts" (as Rachivel puts it) who were chained and imprisoned in Hell as a result. What sin did they commit to deserve such a judgment? Possibly the corruption of the human genome alluded to in Genesis 6; and/or presenting themselves as gods to the human race, and leading people to worship creatures (namely themselves) rather than the Creator.

Does this not sound a lot like what the Dragon, the Beast, and the False Prophet will compel humanity to do, yet future? In the same book of Revelation warning us about that Unholy Trinity, note that the fourth horseman, on the pale horse, is identified as Death (Revelation 6:8). Could this not be the "angel of death" unleashed on Egypt during the first Passover (and/or the pagan god of death, called Thanatos by the Greeks, Mors by the Romans, Anubis by the Egyptians, etc.)? Even more intriguing is the rider who follows, identified as Hades. "Hades" was the Greek name for the god of the underworld—called "Pluto" by the Romans. Both Death and Hades run roughshod over the Earth before being thrown in the Lake of Fire (Revelation 20:14). And considering this identification of at least one pagan god, does the second horseman (Revelation 6:4) not sound like a dead ringer for the god of war, called Mars by the Romans, Ares, by the Greeks, Baal and Nergal by older civilizations? There are more connections to be made, but these are a couple reasons I don't assume that the ancient pagan myths are strictly the product of primitive man's overactive imagination.

In short, we should challenge our assumptions. We should at least determine whether our beliefs originate in the Word of God, or in some other source.


If you liked this book, please consider posting your thoughts in a review at whatever online bookstore you shop at. Your honest opinion could help me to improve on this work in the future.

Thanks for reading.


Michael Kayser

# Other Books by This Author:

### *The Curly Wolf*

The sleepy-eyed youngster known only as Arizona lives by a simple creed: He finishes the job he's hired for; he doesn't like to lie, be lied to, or lied about; he'll only tolerate so many insults; and he won't shoot anyone unarmed or with his back turned. Aside from that, give him a badge and he'll kill anyone he's paid to.

Now deputized to bulldoze "squatters" off their claims in the Redbud Valley, suddenly he's reluctant to pull the trigger. Who would have guessed simple acts of kindness by the Redbud homesteaders could turn this amoral killer soft? Or maybe it's the affections of *Senorita* Theresa Gutierrez driving him loco. Whatever caused his uncharacteristic attack of conscience, the time is fast approaching when Arizona must either betray his employer or turn his guns loose on the only people to ever offer him friendship.

## *Fast Cars and Rock & Roll*

Deke Jones finally has a car ready to compete in the Conquistador —a short but grueling campaign covering racetracks all over the Southwest United States. He can't wait to challenge the rich boys with their expensive toys, but complications begin stacking up on him before the first flag drops.

First, he is invited to join Stormin' Norman's new rock band for a whirlwind tour. It's a once-in-a-lifetime opportunity to play with a musical genius and he can't let it pass...but it's scheduled for the very week he needs for last minute tuning and modifications for his car to be ready for the Conquistador's tech inspection.

Next, he gets tangled up with beautiful bad girl Lena Castillo, just when he was patching things up with a local débutante he lost touch with after high school. Lena has a deadly superpower: the ability to turn any man stupid—and Deke Jones is no exception.

Jones also crosses paths with five-time Conquistador champ Bob Tilford, and there's bad blood between them from the starting gun. It was going to be challenging enough racing against Tilford with his big-time sponsors, high-dollar mechanic and world-class GT car, but Tilford also has tremendous influence over race officials he doesn't hesitate to use in his grudge against Deke Jones. To keep it all interesting, Deke's co-driver bails on him at the last minute, with no time to scrounge up a replacement.

Get your motor runnin'. Deke Jones is gonna close this summer out with a bang, one way or another.

### Shadow Hand Blues

In 1954 a woman's body is discovered outside a small town in North Carolina. In record time, budding blues virtuoso Waymon "Tornado" Fuller is tried, convicted, and executed for the murder.

In 1994 nomadic hot-rodder, moonlighting private investigator and Tornado Fuller aficionado Deke Jones stumbles upon his hero's guitar, triggering a mudslide of buried truths. Fuller's innocence is one revelation. Another is *Shadow Hand Blues*--the last song he recorded, which Jones has never heard of.

Vintage Fender Telecaster in one hand, steering wheel of his tire-melting Cyclone Spoiler II in the other, Deke Jones launches a one-man crusade to exonerate the infamous musician and find the obscure recording. The blood trails are 40 years cold, but neither corrupt good ol' boy cops, sex industry sadists nor fanatical pyramid-schemers can throw Jones off this case. Unfortunately, this mystery-solving pilgrimage propels Jones right into the bloodstained fingers of a clandestine power elite Tornado Fuller called the Shadow Hand.

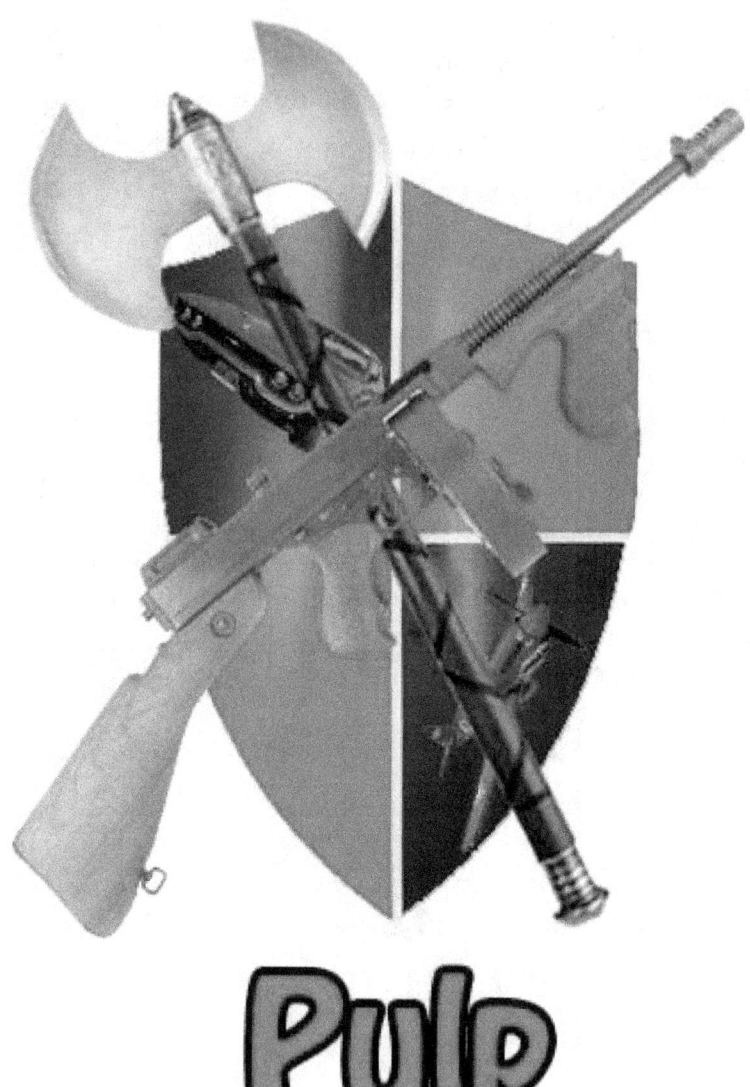